ANGELS IN LOVE

The "mission" was growing very tiresome. It was a wonder that Julian hadn't gone completely ballistic seven times over since he'd set foot on Earthly soil. But having Eponine was such a balm to him. When she wasn't trailing after that insipid boy. But a mission was a mission, and who was he to argue?

And he realized that she was becoming "Eponine" to him. Not "Joy," not her true name, but "Eponine." Because Eponine lived in this apartment with him. Eponine had her head against his chest. Eponine made him breakfast and made him laugh. Joy was to be shared with all of Creation, but Eponine was his and his alone.

I never thought, never in a thousand lifetimes . . . that I could love you, Julian said to himself.

A YEAR AND A DAY

A YEAR AND A DAY

SARA M. HARVEY

LONG MEADOW ROMANCE

A Year and a Day by Sara M. Harvey

© 2006 Sara M. Harvey
Published by Long Meadow Romance

For information on Long Meadow Romance, call 615/514-0172.

ISBN 1-933725-13-3

Design by Armour&Armour
armour-armour.com

First Edition 2006
1 2 3 4 5 6 7 8 9 10

PROLOGUE

VERISIMILITUDE

FROM HIGH ABOVE NEW York City, the clouds looked like a great quilted down comforter that was occasionally pierced by a black and glittering spire of some tall building.

She had nothing in her possession save a *Zagat Survey* guide and an apartment key that had an address neatly written on a slip of paper attached to it. But she wouldn't need anything else until she got into the city. After she got there, well, then she would see what was needed.

She'd done a considerable bit of research, as it had been years and years since she'd last set foot on the firm, warm soil of the Earth. Her companion, however, had never walked upon the ground in a mortal body, and what he knew was death, torture, and blood.

Occasionally, through a small breach in the cloudy blanket, individual pinpoints of light could be glimpsed like a shipwreck's treasure at the bottom of a murky sea. And each of those gem-like sparkles was a life, a life with a story, with a history all unto itself. Each distinct little light was an entire world.

Everything was set; everything was ready. The arrangements already had been made for a place to live for the year. A nice apartment, she had been assured, in a quaint old building. Excitement about the assignment bubbled up inside her once again. She fingered the apartment key; it felt heavy and cool.

Marvelous! She smiled, and it seemed that the stars shone brighter. *What a lovely adventure this shall be!*

Beside her, the shadows stirred. There was a low growl of discontent.

She handed her companion the guide with an airy laugh. *We'll be there soon. Why don't you find us something to do tomorrow?*

No answer came. He did, however, take the book from her.

She looked down through the clouds now swirling up into soft peaks like cotton candy tinted ghostly blue by the pre-dawn sky. She wondered if it was raining there in that city that never slept.

New York City never sleeps, but it dreams.

Silence.

She glanced up at the gathering day drawing a vivid line of

brilliant white across the eastern horizon. The lights below her dimmed only slightly. She smiled. She was already in love with the city, that island fortress of lights and dreams. Her gaze came to rest on the quiet, dark swath that ran through the very heart of town. It was unlike the frantic electric flickering of light nearby, where a multitude of brightly lit roads converged. Times Square pulsed like a beating heart, but it was only an illusion; the dark and shadowed place was the *true* heart of the city. There the trees shivered and sighed as the biting autumn wind danced through the last of the golden leaves. Although it seemed genuine, Central Park had in fact been carefully arranged to best achieve the look of nature. There, in the midst of all the artifice and ornamentation, an ancient spring bubbled up from the bedrock and made its merry way through The Ramble, the only truly wild part of the park. She watched as a sunbeam struck the glittering surface of the water, and she knew it was time to leave.

She gave a beckoning nod to the shadow at her left—a shadow that slept, but did not dream.

Mind you, bring the book, okay?

She did not wait for a reply.

It was time to go. The city was waiting, and she burned to experience it. Somehow the year ahead seemed interminably long, yet far too short.

Time and tide waited for no one. Not even for a creature such as she.

She hoped he wouldn't forget to bring the book with him.

EARTH

THE MORNING LIGHT SLICED down through the sparse trees, making it difficult to bring the world around him into focus. It seemed ethereal and unreal somehow, but he impacted reality with a stunning force as his feet slid out from under him and he landed roughly beside the slick rocks that enclosed the burbling spring. The *Zagat Survey* tumbled out of his grip and landed several feet away. The pain was extraordinary. He pushed himself onto his elbow and took stock of his situation.

Everything seemed to be in order; already the throbbing in his shoulder was fading.

Good, he thought to himself, *humans aren't quite as fragile as I had been told.*

He sat up and brushed himself off, taking a few moments to investigate the thick and sluggish body that he now inhabited. He was pleased to see that his basic physical form was the same as it always had been: two arms, two legs, ten fingers, ten toes, and a head of long, luxuriant, dark curls. He ran his long fingers through it and smiled vainly. He'd had a very short list of non-negotiable demands that accompanied his taking this assignment. Getting to keep his hair was one of them. By nature, the Angel of Vengeance was not a creature of vanity, but he adored his hair and thought it his best feature. He was often heard to lament that no painter since daVinci had ever truly captured its luster. His hair he would be allowed to keep as a human, along with a few basic abilities; they were only to live among humankind for a year and a day, so there was no need to go back to the drawing board. But the wings were right out. He still felt them, though, a shadowy, haunting presence that was sure to gnaw on his nerves.

Slowly, a maddening itch was making its way down both of his legs beneath the heavy blue pants he wore. He rolled up the cuff to find it was not the pants that were irritating him as much as the abundance of hair on his legs. He recoiled and quickly rolled the pants legs back down. He saw the same unfortunate hair on his arms as he pushed up the sleeves of the heavy sweater and coat he wore.

This was not *in my contract!* He plucked one of the wiry hairs from his forearm and yelped at the sharp, stinging pain. He tried to multiply that pain by the number of hairs on his arms, and again on his legs. It wasn't worth it. Not yet, anyway. He decided not to rule out the eventuality of divesting himself of such an unsightly nuisance in the future. He realized there were some rather gaping holes in his knowledge of humanity. He knew they were much the same as the angels, but it was about the little differences that he was ... misinformed. Or at least underinformed.

The light shifted quite suddenly, and he glanced up to see his companion emerge out of the dazzling beam and into the water. It was like Botticelli's *Birth of Venus* in reverse. She actually stepped right into the frigid water barefoot, trailing her blue patchwork skirt into the stream. Luckily, she held her boots in her hand so they would not get wet. She reached out her hand for his assistance; obviously her measly human eyes also were dazed by the strange earthly light. But he made no move to help her. She smiled optimistically at him, then proceeded to stumble far worse than he had and landed face-first in the damp layer of decayed leaves. She rolled over and smiled at him. She had twigs and bits of leaf in her hair, but her grin was irrepressible. She sat up and began to pick at the pieces caught in the soft fabric of her skirt.

Great, she *gets something comfortable to wear!*

"Wow," she laughed to herself as she caught sight of her feet. "Would you look at that? My toes are blue ... how pretty."

He buried his face in his hands and groaned. *She's happy about hypothermia?* He thought of the affliction as a part of his arsenal of revenge, but to her, it was just another blissful discovery. *Of course she is. She's the Angel of Joy. She's happy about* everything. *And I agreed to be her roommate. What was I thinking?*

"I don't remember feeling this clumsy the last time I was here, but it's been an awfully long time," she told him as she crammed on her boots and stood up, "It's okay; I'm not hurt. I mean it did hurt, but I think it will pass."

He gave no indication that he'd heard her.

"Because I am sure you were worried, Vengeance. Weren't you?"

"We're going to need names here, aren't we?"

"I suppose so. I mean, if I remember correctly, *Joy* is a pretty rational name for humans ... but we'll have to find something to call you."

"Hey, if I have to take a dreary Earthly name, so do you!"

"Fine, fine. We'll talk about it on the way." She fetched the book and opened it to the pull-out map at the back. She studied the address written on the key and compared it carefully with the little map. "Okay, it's this way!"

Without waiting to see if he followed, the human incarnation of the Angel of Joy dashed away down the path heading toward a park exit. Out on the streets surrounding the park, they found a warren of police partitions and a sea of humanity pressing against them. Helicopters hovered overhead, and the faint strains of several marching bands could be heard over the din of the crowd and crackle of police radios.

Over the treetops they could make out a few large and colorful shapes.

"It must be a parade!" The joy was clear in her voice.

"Come on, there must be a way around this mess." He studied the book. "See? We don't even need to be on this side. We need the east side. Let's go." A faint twitch of a smile flickered across his lips to see her face fall so completely.

"But . . . it's a parade. It looks like fun. Let's go look!"

"No. We are going to find our apartment before we do anything else!"

"But. . . ." His stern gaze crumpled her resolve and she followed him away from the noise and color on the west side of the park.

IT LOOKED LIKE A very short distance on the very tiny *Zagat* map. They had been walking for almost two hours before he snatched the map back from her.

"How far did you say this was?"

"Just that far," she pointed to the middle of the park and dragged her finger across a few inches to where the streets were numbered in the teens and lower. She held up her thumb and forefinger about three inches apart to further illustrate her point.

"This map is a lot smaller than the real streets, Joy."

"I *know* that."

"Okay. So does the word *scale* mean anything to you at all?"

"Scale? Yes, it's a thing that weighs things. Justice has one!"

He raked his fingers angrily through his long hair. "Um, *no.* Okay, what block are we on?"

"Mmmm," she searched for a sign at the corner. "Looks like we are at Twenty-First Street and Third Avenue."

"We might as well keep going; we're almost there now, from the looks of it." He crammed his cold hands into his pockets and grudgingly forged ahead toward the East Village. At long last the street numbers got small enough to be within range of the address written on the card attached to the key.

"I think we've made it! Now we just have to find the house number." Joy clapped her hands, her eyes shining in anticipation of the next adventure. The tree-lined street stretched out in both directions. Vengeance knew they were still hopelessly lost and told her so.

"Then why don't we ask someone?" She eagerly looked around for a passerby to question.

"Not a chance. We're on the right street. My feet *hurt* and I don't want to waste any more time!" Vengeance turned roughly on his heel and headed east. Joy had to jog to catch up.

THE RED BRICK APARTMENT building nearly glowed with the rich light of impending sunset.

"*Finally*! That is the very last time I trust *you* with directions!" Vengeance double-checked the address on the key and shoved it back into his pocket.

Joy's vibrancy was wilted, and she followed him silently into the lobby. The doorman was reading a newspaper behind a desk. He raised his head when he heard them approach.

"Can I help you?"

She shrugged and shook her head. Two girls came in behind them, each laden with several crinkly plastic bags full of groceries. They nodded to the doorman without breaking stride and headed for the two sets of silver doors in the lobby. The taller girl hit the button in the wall with her elbow, and the doors slid open. They stepped inside. Vengeance followed them and pushed the same button. The other set of doors opened with a soft creak and he ducked inside. Joy scurried across the lobby and slipped into the elevator behind him. The doorman shouted after them, but the small room was already propelling them upward.

It came to a slow halt on the third floor and Vengeance stormed into the hall. He quickly found apartment 3-D and strode right in, leaving Joy to catch the heavy door as it nearly swung closed on her.

He circled the main room, giving the basic furnishings a cursory glance, then ducked into one of the bedrooms. It was small, and it contained a plastic box identical to one that sat in the main room. Curious, he wondered what it did and why there would be two of them in the apartment.

At the press of a button, the glass panel lit up with sight and sound. It drowned out the excited chatter his new roommate was making out in the main room. He liked this thing.

Joy was thoroughly impressed with the charming apartment. She found a comfy over-stuffed couch and easy chair in the largest room. There was also a desk with a computer and a large bookshelf.

"Oh, they thought of *everything*," she squealed and took down a copy of *Les Misérables*. "I remember this book! I love this book!" She began to thumb through the pages, eager to connect with something familiar. She jumped when she heard the woman's voice in the front hall.

"Thank God, you got in safe, I was so worried! I've been asking Jesus all day where the two of you were! The doorman just called to tell me you'd arrived!" She swept in and left the door to slam shut behind her. Her long skirt brushed the tops of her stylish black boots, and she had a hand-knit shawl wrapped tightly around her. Silver bells jingled softly on her wrists as she came toward Joy. "The letter said you'd be in this morning, and of course I had no number to reach you! I'll never set up something like that again, a year's rent in advance or not! I must get a contact number next time! Oh, excuse me, I'm rambling." She ducked her head sheepishly, sending her short, braided pigtails swaying beneath her crumpled velvet hat. She put out her hand. "My name is Hannah, I'm your landlady!"

"Oh! It's wonderful to meet you! My name is. . . ." She glanced down at the book, then stuck her finger in to hold her place. "My name's Eponine."

"*Really?* That's such a beautiful name! A beautiful name for a beautiful girl."

"Thank you," Eponine said, knowing that Hannah was just being polite. She had made sure that she'd chosen her features to be nothing short of plain. "Let me introduce you to . . . my roommate."

"Oh, yes! I'd love to meet her, too!"

"*Him*."

"I see." Hannah clucked her tongue maternally, and Eponine could not tell whether or not she was disapproving.

Eponine knocked on the closed bedroom door. "Come on out here. There is someone you need to meet."

"Who could you *possibly* want me to—" The words died

beneath his deepening scowl as he saw the two women in the doorway.

"This is our landlady, Hannah."

"Landlady. Right."

"Hello!" Hannah grinned at him and extended her hand. He only looked blankly at her. "And what's *your* name?"

"My name?"

"Yes, unless you think that's getting a little personal," Hannah laughed and winked at him.

He glanced back over his shoulder at the television. From the sound of it, some program was just finishing. "No, I can tell you my name. It's . . . uhh . . . Julian. My name's Julian."

"Julian. Julian and Eponine." Her grin was infectious, and Julian had to bite his lip to keep from smiling in return at her. She reminded him of Joy, and he was not terribly pleased by that.

"Have you two had dinner?"

"What does that have to do with anything?" Julian snarled.

Nonplussed, Hannah widened her smile. "It's Thanksgiving, sillies! I want to make sure you get fed. I have plenty to share if you'd like—"

"No, we ate already. That's why we were so late."

"Well, okay, then I'll leave you two to get settled in. But if you get hungry . . . my mother's stuffing recipe won the blue ribbon nine years running at the Davidson County Fair!"

"We'll be fine," Julian reiterated.

Eponine squeezed Hannah's hands. "It was so wonderful to meet you! I am so glad to be living here in your building! And thank you so much for your kind invitation!"

"I have pumpkin pie, too," Hannah said, enticingly.

"We're not sharing a room," Julian chimed in.

Both women looked at him, confused.

"Excuse me?"

"We have our own rooms. I just wanted to make that perfectly clear."

"It's your apartment," Hannah told him with a conspiratorial wink over her seemingly serious tone of voice. "And that's in God's hands, not mine. Good night, you two!"

She let herself out, but not before waving enthusiastically from the doorway and reminding them that she lived on the sixth floor and promising real whipped cream for the pie.

"I put a dash of amaretto in it; you'll love it! Oh, and the phone company will be here tomorrow morning."

The door clicked shut and Eponine rounded on Julian. "Why couldn't we go for dinner?"

"I don't want to go anywhere with her."

"Why not?"

"That woman is *touched*."

"She certainly is," Eponine said with awe.

"I mean touched *in the head*. She is not all there." He ambled back toward the hypnotic flicker of the television. "I am going to bed. Between you and that dingbat of a landlady, I'm exhausted."

"I think she's wonderful!"

"You would."

"I think she's perfectly adorable!"

"I never should have agreed to this. This is going to be a damn long year." He shut his door and Eponine watched it a long moment.

"I am so afraid it won't be nearly long enough. . . ."

HEAVEN

THE SKY WAS DEEP autumn blue, and Julian found it quite fascinating to be looking *up* into it with eyes that were now as ordinary and human as they come. It didn't seem possible that the vast reaches of harsh, airless space were just beyond that layer of safe, secure blue. And it seemed all the more improbable how much lay right outside the crest of human comprehension, somehow beyond and *between* that serene Earthly sky and the emptiness of the eternal night of space: *home*. He suddenly understood how people thought of "heaven" as a place, real and actual, that could be *found*. He knew better. And he was free of it, at long last.

Finally, he thought, breathing the harshly dry winter air, which tasted like bus fumes. Traffic clamored all around him in surprisingly ordered chaos, as people surged from their islands of sidewalks and flooded crosswalks or darted through breaks in the never-ending onslaught of cars. *Darted* wasn't quite the right word. These soft and susceptible humans didn't *dart* like a frightened thing; they walked briskly and purposefully, as if they would somehow be impervious to the steel and chrome of those vehicles should one *dare* to hit them. They were *fearless*, these New Yorkers. He liked them immediately.

Eponine, whom he had almost managed to entirely ignore, shivered almost violently. Her coat hung open and her scarf was askew from her rush to leave the apartment. He hadn't been especially patient with her that morning, but honestly, how long could it possibly take a human female to get ready? He'd told her a dozen times that he wanted to be out of the house by nine-thirty! Plus, she'd gone out on Friday to do some grocery shopping. Hadn't she gotten enough practice dressing herself then?

I do not understand how it could take an hour to figure out which shoes to put on! I am going to have a serious chat with whoever was in charge of her wardrobe. That girl cannot be given that many choices! Although his closet was just as full, he found that pairing slacks with a decent shirt didn't take up too much of his mental capacity.

And although Eponine trembled and her gloveless fingers were turning eerily pale, she was far too captivated with the world around her to think about it. Her brown eyes were stretched as wide as her suitably plain face would allow, taking in every flash of color and every line of texture. He could see her nostrils flaring with the strange new odors of this place: exhaust, greasy fries from McDonald's, pretzels, and occasionally the scent of a person brushing past on the sidewalk. Those smells varied the most: from expensive cologne and perfume to days-old sweat. But ugly or lovely, he could see it didn't matter to her; she was in love with the experience.

She's going to be in love with pneumonia if she isn't careful. He elbowed her roughly, sending her tumbling out of her reverie. "Look, there's a cab!"

"Hey! Knock it off!" She looked quite overwhelmed and more than a little hurt. She rubbed her arm. "That really hurt! You know, you wouldn't be getting away with this at home!"

"No, but we're not home, are we?" He growled, menacingly.

She sighed and was beginning to wish, again, that she hadn't been so eager for this assignment. It was hard to imagine an entire year of this, day in and day out.

So many more important things are at stake here than my feelings, she chastised herself. *And I should be happy that he is even bothering to take some initiative here. That should give me hope that this plan might actually work! If it doesn't . . . I don't know what will happen to him . . . or to the world. . . .*

"So, what magic have you got planned for us today, mister?" She reached for the *Zagat Survey* guide, but he held it back.

"I know where we're going," he said testily. "And what the hell did you say your name was?"

"Eponine," she sighed, exasperated. "*Eh-poh-neen.*"

"Riiiiiight. From that *thing* you're reading."

"*Les Misérables*. The book. It's one of my favorites."

"That's not a book, that's a cube. I don't think books should be thicker than they are long or wide."

"What would you know about books, anyway? You've never even read one, *ever,*" she replied hotly. "You named yourself after the man in that *awful* television program that you watched Thursday, *Julian.*"

He rolled his shoulders back and gave her a wicked smile, "Julian is a *fine* name, thankyouverymuch. And you couldn't be bothered to be interested in what I was watching on TV, so quit breathing down my neck about this whole book thing, missy! *And* you just made us miss the cab!"

"There'll be another. There are dozens."

"Then hail one." He gave her a slightly more playful shove toward the curb, and she kicked him.

No way to behave for either *of us.* Eponine signaled for a cab.

Cars jammed Sixth Avenue, the "Avenue of the Americas" as it was called, but neither of them had any idea why it deserved such a fancy name. It was just like any other avenue in Manhattan, in fact less interesting than some, like Fifth or Seventh avenues.

"So when are you going to tell me where we're going?" She finally thought to tie the plush scarf that was falling off her neck and wrap the thick wool coat tighter around her body. *Heavens, but it's cold here!*

"I have everything under control; don't worry."

"You know, when you say 'don't worry,' that's when I worry."

An egg-yolk yellow cab slowed and stopped right before them. She paused expectantly beside the door and wondered if chivalry would kick in. It didn't.

Sighing, she opened the door herself and slid across the well-worn black backseat. He hopped in next to her and reached through the Plexiglas divider to hand the driver a slip of paper.

"We need to get here." There was only the slightest hint of

uncertainty in his voice; he was still wary of interacting with mortals.

The driver's eyes flicked over the paper, and then he nodded and grunted, pulling out into traffic.

"Well, then," Julian settled back into the seat with a smug grin. "He seems to know how to get there."

"Duh, he's a cabbie," Eponine said distractedly as she pawed through her bag for her book. She found that her gloves were sitting there atop her novel and looked at them perplexed for a moment before stuffing them into her pocket and opening her book.

"You and all your books! This ride isn't going to be that long. Do you really think you're even going to get a *chapter* read?"

She glowered at him. "Don't start this again. Your television isn't any better. I don't understand those shows about the soap."

"They aren't *about* the soap. The soap companies just used to advertise on them; that's why they started calling them 'soap operas.'"

"They are still contrived, I mean, honestly! Who would believe that stuff? It's so *trite.*"

"Trite? Lust, passion, revenge? Please! Soap operas tap directly into the darkest natures of humanity!" He opened her bag and pulled out a few books. "Anne Rice, *Gone with the Wind*, what's this? A *romance novel*? And you're calling *me* trite?"

Eponine shrugged and blushed. "Well, they were on the bookshelf, and besides, there are plenty of dark human passions in all of these, I swear! You might even like them if you'd only be willing to try!" She showed him *We Have Always Lived in the Castle* and laughed. "There's an Uncle Julian in this one, and in the *Mayfair Witches* series, too. Talk about dark! Maybe you didn't do so badly naming yourself, after all. You want to see?" She held the page open and invited him to read over her shoulder with a very becoming tilt of her head.

Julian scoffed. "I'd rather watch *The Bachelor.*"

Eponine opened her mouth, but thought better of answering him. He raised an eyebrow at her, daring her to let loose what was on her mind, but she didn't take his bait.

The cab was slowly moving toward a crowded curb.

Julian sat up. "We're here!"

"And are you finally going to tell me where 'here' is, mister?" Eponine reorganized her books.

"I thought we'd explore the center of divinity of New York City."

"The center of divinity? But we aren't anywhere near Central Park."

"Well, you see, Eponine, dear," he told her slowly, as if he were very patient and she was very stupid, "it's only the center of divinity once a year for *one weekend. This* weekend."

She gave him a quizzical look. "*What* are you talking about?"

"Trust me," he told her and patted the *Zagat Survey*, but she looked far from convinced. "Let's go."

"*Hey!*" The cabbie yelled.

"It's your turn to pay, Julian." She strolled away from the curb with a wide, self-satisfied smile.

He leaned over into the window of the passenger side. Seeing the pack of cigarettes on the dash, he picked them up, studied them, and handed them to the cabbie.

"Don't you worry about that lung cancer," Julian said with a wink.

The cab pulled away, the driver slightly dazed.

"Big tip," Eponine said, drily.

He shrugged and wrapped his black polar fleece scarf around his neck, pulling his curly, dark ponytail out of the way. He settled himself and pulled two tickets out of his coat pocket. Eponine looked around. She had no idea where they were.

"Ready?" His cheeks were flushed with excitement, and he grinned like a schoolboy. A very wicked schoolboy.

Eponine sighed, and had to admit to herself that it was good to see him with a smile on his face for once. She smiled sportingly in return, "For the center of divinity of New York City? Always."

"Good. Come on!"

They melded in with the large crowd on the sidewalk, all queuing up in front of an ornate, art-deco style building. Julian pointed to the brightly colored banner hanging above the door.

New York City Annual Chocolatiers Convention.

"You've *got* to be kidding me."

He shook his head and took a few silver-wrapped Hershey's Kisses out of his pocket. They were slightly deformed from the warmth of his body.

"Chocolate. The natives of South America believed it was a gift from the gods, Eponine. And I tend to agree. It *is* divine! And this, *this*, is an entire convention hall jam-packed with some of this world's best chocolate!" He shivered, but he was smiling. "It's heaven on earth."

HELL

IT WAS BRUTAL REVENGE, and Julian would have been far less upset about it if he'd been the one to think of it. In exchange for allowing him to drag her uptown without a word about where they were going or what they'd be doing, Eponine had asked him for a small favor, just a tiny one, really. Julian couldn't have thought of anything that wouldn't be worth the price of a day filled with chocolate, even if it was followed by a night filled with stomach aches. But there was no preparing him for what she asked for.

Eponine wanted to go Christmas shopping.

Julian had no idea why she'd want to subject herself to such a thing; he knew *he* was not planning on celebrating Christmas. But he'd been the one to coerce her into watching television, and she'd seen all the ads and the news stories and now, *of course*, she wanted to join in.

"Is this part of our mission?" he'd snarled.

"That's top secret! I could tell you, but then, well, you know. . . ." She winked. "Basically at this early point in our stay here, the aim is to blend in. People go to the mall to go Christmas shopping this time of year. And we should, too! You know, for the blending!"

Luckily, however, they had missed the busiest shopping day of the year. Eponine expected that fact to make him feel better, but it did not give him much comfort.

"And just what do you intend to *buy*?"

She shrugged. "I don't know. Maybe nothing. I just want to see what it's like, don't you?"

"No."

"What if I decide I want to buy something for you?" She wandered into the kitchen.

"Like what? Like chocolate?"

"We don't have enough already?" Eponine opened a cabinet and pointed at the rows of shiny wrappers.

Julian grinned, "Nah, you can never have too much chocolate!"

"The chocolate fair was two days ago. I am not buying you any more chocolate!" She rummaged in the refrigerator then turned on the stove.

"Then, how about a satellite dish? Can you imagine six hundred channels? Wow, I'd never leave the house!"

"Julian!"

"Well, what else could you think of buying for me?"

Eponine smiled shyly and carefully reeled him in. "I don't know ... but we have this DVD player and nothing to watch on it. ... And I hear they are selling the entire first season of *Survivor*, the most vengeful, vindictive show ever to air on prime time."

"This sounds like a bribe. ..."

"No, *this* is a bribe." She held the cup of Italian hot cocoa near his hand.

"You are evil."

She smiled sweetly up at him; then she dropped a small square of Belgian bittersweet chocolate into his cup. It began to melt at once, leaving a spiral of dark where it descended through the creamy froth. A soft gasp of anticipated pleasure escaped Julian's lips, and Eponine smiled and gave the mug over to his eager hands.

"The 162 leaves from the Port Authority bus terminal and goes straight to the Garden State Plaza in Paramus, New Jersey."

He looked at her over the mug. He had almost polished off his drink. "You're crazy."

"More cocoa, darling?"

Julian sighed, utterly defeated. "All right, fine! We'll go ... *Christmas shopping*."

"Wonderful! I'll fix your cocoa in a travel mug. The next bus leaves in forty-five minutes."

"I'll go get my shoes on."

THE GARDEN STATE PLAZA was enormous—enormous and packed to the rafters with sweaty, pushy, rude people. Shoppers laden with armloads of paper bags and plastic sacks and winter coats created a prickly hot flood of humanity in a very small space. They very nearly drowned out the droll, piped-in holiday music ... *nearly*.

Julian was breaking out in a sweat and he didn't like it. He was beginning to feel claustrophobic. The old, familiar darkness rose in his being, and he stared angrily at the herds of oblivious people that surrounded him from beneath heavily drawn brows.

Eponine, however, was gaily fluttering through the stores, brightly colored shopping bags in both hands. The one from the big, loud video store contained not only the promised *Survivor* DVD, but *Northern Exposure* and *Firefly* as well.

"So, our favorite shows will always be on," she'd told him.

"*Our* favorite shows? Eponine, you don't have any favorite shows!"

"Well, maybe I'll start."

"With two series that have been cancelled for years?"

She smiled patronizingly and Julian had the unshakable sensation that he'd just lost a fight. He was becoming angry, and that was *never* good.

The place was jammed. "Angry" was beginning to escalate to "furious."

Julian was getting fully tired of dealing with Eponine in this crazed environment. He literally had to drag her away from the small Venetian Carousel near one of the entrances. She had ridden it four times in a row, leaving her purchases in a forgotten pile at his feet. He was resorting to timing her exploits in each store. They'd spent almost an hour in the first one, and he gave her a new limit of twenty minutes. That was quickly revised to ten.

He'd thought at first that this assignment might not be so tough, but now it was obvious that Eponine on Earth was still her irritatingly jovial self. He had hoped her unusually calm demeanor over the first few days would be the norm, but, evidently, she was just getting warmed up.

"This is the most fun I have had in ages! I love this shopping! Look at the happy children! Oh, look, let's go see Santa Claus!" She clapped her hands and dashed away before he could grab her.

Happy children? Like kids who aren't *screaming? Where? Where do you see this, Eponine?* Julian rubbed his temples. "Can we get some food first?"

She pulled up short at the sound of the clear annoyance in his voice.

"But Santa. . . ." For an instant, he thought she was going to cry as she gazed longingly at the fat, white-bearded man in the tacky red velvet suit sitting in the gaudy faux-gilt chair. She sighed and came back toward him. "You're right. We should eat. Sorry if I am getting a little carried away."

"*A little?*" He snatched the Borders Books and Music bag from her hands and made his deliberate way to the escalator. He knew she'd follow him anywhere as long as he had her precious books. He didn't even need to look back to know she was there; he could sense her, like the scent of a cloyingly sweet perfume that would not leave his nose.

Downstairs in the food court, the lines and noise were nearly unbearable. But Julian saw what she meant about the children. Wherever Eponine went, they fell quiet and looked up at her with wonder and awe. People of all ages smiled at her, genuinely and from the heart. They were polite to her; some were even kind.

I guess it's harder for her to hide her true nature from the world, Julian mused, and fumed to find himself smiling at her as well.

They got bourbon chicken with white rice and managed to find seats at a cramped table for two.

Eponine smiled. "Ready to go after we eat?"

Julian contemplated a cutting remark. "Yes, yes I am," he said finally, too tired for anything else. "Do you feel as wasted as I do?"

She yawned, "Mmm-hmmmm, it does seem to take a toll, doesn't it?"

He nodded and wolfed down the rest of his meal as well as the remainder of hers. He did not relish the thought of pushing through the ravening horde to get back to the bus stop.

Where do they keep coming from? And why must they keep getting in my way?

But as they made their way across the food court, through the mob, toward the escalator, yes, the escalator and the blessed, *blessed* exit, Eponine got distracted.

Damn it, girl, I can't take you anywhere!

She was looking at a table of hard-core Christian evangelists. They had teased hair and bad toupees, clickety fake nails and cheap ties.

Eponine was enthralled.

Julian groaned.

A small weasely fellow nearly jumped on her.

"Have you accepted Jesus Christ as your personal Savior?"

He was oily, and he was *touching* her. Julian felt the hairs rise on the back of his neck. He wished for a weapon.

"What?" Eponine, although still smiling, was genuinely confused. "I don't understand."

The man chuckled in what appeared to be a good-natured, if a tad self-righteous, manner and went from having his hand on her shoulder to grabbing her sleeve. "I mean Christ, little lady! Christ! Surely, you've heard of him? You must believe in the Lord Jesus or you shall *burn in Hell!*"

Eponine laughed. The man blanched, and let his narrow jaw fall open. Julian didn't think that rodent-like evangelist had ever had anyone laugh to his face before. He was getting quite upset, but, Eponine being Eponine, she didn't see it.

"Don't you *believe* in Hell, girl?"

"Hell?" she giggled. "People are still preaching *Hell* out here? Why, no, I don't believe in it! There is no Hell."

The man's eyes widened and his sharp Adam's apple bobbed atop the collar of his cheap polyester shirt. "*Of course* there is a Hell! Haven't you ever seen a volcano?"

"A volcano?" Julian broke his sour silence. "What does that have to do with Hell?"

"It's *proof!* Proof of the fiery depths of Hades!"

"Hades isn't hot, it's cold." Eponine said, still laughing, at the same time that Julian said, "You're *cracked!*"

"Hades isn't even a place, really," she continued, charmingly oblivious, "but a person. He's the Greek god of the Underworld. And the Underworld isn't really a *bad* place, I mean, everyone went there when they died. Unless they were some tragic heroes and then they went to the Elysian Fields, which is more like the Norse idea of Valhalla.... See, sir, you really ought to get your facts straight. You'll never convert anyone this way!"

And she bubbled over again with giggles, imagining a line of people signing up for his religion out of a fear of volcanoes and misplaced names.

"This is no laughing matter! *How dare* you laugh at me!"

Eponine lightly waved him off. She was quite wrapped up in her own world, patiently explaining to the man what she thought he should know. "I mean, really, the very *concept* of Hell, the very *word* comes from the Norse goddess of death and the under-world. Her name was Hel—"

She continued, smiling all the while, happy to be sharing the depth and breadth of her knowledge. People were beginning to stop and listen to her.

"... now the brimstone thing happens to be biblical, talking about Gehenna, which I am given to understand was some sort of refuse heap outside the city where trash and often unclaimed or unknown bodies were burned using brimstone, but scholars disagree on that little detail. But it seems the concept of Hell as many Christians see it today was codified by the Puritans in the late 1500s."

"Stop it!" The man cried out. With every word she spoke he was becoming more agitated, and the folks sitting back at the church's table were watching in anxious silence. The crowd that had gathered around them was beginning to edge away, feeling the situation becoming volatile. His hands spasmed from clenched fists to splayed claws. "Shut . . . your . . . mouth, you filthy heathen!"

He reached out for her and Eponine recoiled, a cry of alarm caught in her throat and a look of terror flashing in her eyes.

But Julian had him by the wrist in half a heartbeat.

"Do not touch her again." The man's wrist creaked in Julian's iron grip.

"*Vengeance!*" Eponine hissed below her breath. She stepped forward, trying to gaze defiantly between the two of them. "Stop it, both of you! I won't have it!"

"Don't mock me, you wicked pagan, you Whore of Babylon, you siren with your lovely face and charming lies! Don't you *dare* speak false witness against a man of Christ!"

Whatever well-wrought words of reproof she had at the ready died on her lips. Tears gathered in the corners of her hazelnut-brown eyes. "What did you call me?"

"You heard me, you Jezebel, you wicked harlot taking pleasure in the sins of others! Laugh now while you can, you little witch, but I'll be dancing on your grave come Judgment Day!" He drew back, whether to spit or to slap her, Julian couldn't tell.

"*Don't touch her!*" Julian roared and ratcheted the man's arm back until his shoulder popped audibly.

"No! Stop!" Eponine sprang between them, piercing the dark and threatening aura that had gathered around Julian. "Are you crazy, Julian? Don't do this!"

"Leave me alone! Let me do my job!" He pushed her away and seemed intent on ripping the man's arm from its socket and beating him with it.

"You don't remember, do you? You don't remember why you had to come here with me. . . ."

"What? What are you talking about?" He let the man's arm drop but did not release his grip.

Eponine boldly put herself into Julian's direct line of sight.

"It's not important right now. I thought you wanted to go home, hmm?" she said to him with feigned courage. She showed him the video store bag and her face softened into a smile, "Let it be, let it be now."

She pulled him away, having to unclamp his steely fingers from the man's arm. Security guards were beginning to drift toward them, walkie-talkies in hand.

"It is my duty to save you, save you from yourselves! Witches, heathens, hellcats, both of you, I swear!" The man visibly shook; droplets of spit clung to his pale lips.

Julian snatched up all the bags and stormed off, leaving Eponine behind. Rage came off him like steam, and people cleared a path for him out of pure fear.

Not out of adoration, like they had for her. Ahhh, well.

Eponine stood rooted to the spot, her eyes darting from Julian's retreating form to the man shouting biblical curses in a most apoplectic manner. Her eyes watered and her chin began to tremble.

"Julian," she whispered, "don't leave me. . . ."

The woman at the table glared fiercely at Eponine. "You are going to Hell, you godless little brat. And I will look on you from Heaven, and it will be *my* turn to laugh."

Eponine backed away from the table. "But you don't understand . . . I am an . . . and I wasn't trying to . . . I didn't mean to . . . last time I checked, Christianity was about *love*, not Hell. I mean, *volcanoes*?"

Eponine turned and ran after Julian. The oily man continued to shout, his voice becoming garbled and unintelligible. But he was being detained by security and could not follow.

She caught up with Julian just outside the doors of Ruby Tuesday. Inside, the place was crowded with exhausted shoppers having a drink and a bite to eat.

"Wait up," she gasped.

Julian slowed his tsunami-like pace, though he did not turn around. The bus was just pulling up as they arrived. The doors opened with a petrol-scented hiss, and Julian helped Eponine up the steps. He guided her to a window seat and got her settled. He dropped himself into the aisle beside her and let out a pent-up sigh. She laid her head upon his shoulder, and he saw that she was crying.

"Geez, don't cry. Come on, please?" Anger momentarily

evaporated and Julian awkwardly put his arm around her. "Oh, 'Nine, it's okay, really. That guy was a hack. He didn't know what he was talking about. I mean, volcanoes equaling Hell? I don't know where some humans get their information."

"It's not that," she looked up and swiped the tears away with the back of her hand. "What's *wrong* with some people? Christians aren't supposed to be like that! They were so ... *awful.*" She hiccuped.

"You shouldn't let it get to you."

"But Julian, don't you remember when religion didn't equal hate?"

He moved to speak, the rage and the darkness still coursing through him, body and mind. He saw Christmas lights on the houses they passed and a few menorahs out for Hanukkah, too. His mind brushed a memory, but drew back suddenly as if touching something scalding hot. And then there was nothing but a blot of senseless black where the memory had been. He sighed.

"No, 'Nine. I'm sorry, but I don't. I don't remember. . . ."

PURGATORY

JULIAN ROLLED OVER AND felt something crinkle beneath his cheek. He cracked an eye open and wiped his mouth. A droplet of drool smeared the bottom of the note lying on his pillow.

Ewww. . . . He sat up and rubbed his eyes. A piece of Eponine's stationery had been carefully laid beside his head. He looked at it, uncomprehendingly, then realized she'd written it in English.

> *Julian—*
> *Have gone to the Met. Left some fruit and cottage cheese in the refrigerator for you. I expect to be back sometime after five p.m.*
>
> *Ever yours, Eponine*

It was so ... domestic, the note.

He shuffled over to the kitchen and poured himself a cup of yesterday's cold coffee and rustled around the cabinets until he found the box of Cap'n Crunch. He flicked on the television and watched the weatherman talk about the snow for a full minute before he realized that he meant the snow in New York City. He looked out the window and found that the world was slowly being covered in glittering white.

On a whim, he tossed on some clothes and bundled himself up. He left the television on and ran out the door.

EPONINE WATCHED THE SNOW fall over the Temple of Dendur. The glass ceiling diverted the swirling flakes, making it look as if some magical field protected the place. The museum was magnificent, and she adored being in such proximity to the awed and hushed masses of people. The scent of snow-damp wool and central heating mingled with the dusty-sweet odor of antiquities. This was a magical place. A temple to history and culture. And, of course, it resided within the sacred confines of the park.

This is my new favorite place, she mused as she wandered down to the café, passing out of Egypt and into France via the medieval churches of Europe. She sat among white marble statues and drank cappuccino. Out in Central Park, the world was becoming obscured by a hazy curtain of early snow. Something beyond the gleaming rows of tall windows caught her eye. The cappuccino sat forgotten on the marble-topped table.

Outside, Cleopatra's Needle was standing in stark stone contrast to the feathery, tumbling snowflakes. Eponine reached out and touched it, feeling the icy cold rock beneath her hands, rock that had once baked in the scorching Egyptian sun. The images raced behind her eyes of sweat-glistening faces looking with reverence upon the great monument. She saw the sharp shadow cut across the fertile ground of the flood-plain. She even heard the melodic rise and fall of deep voices as men sang out their chants as they worked the soil. She blinked and cleared her mind. The tall black stone stood alone now in a corner of Central Park. The snow clung wetly in places that were once dampened by the mists of the Nile and the rains of the flood seasons.

"You're in a different world, aren't you? You seem to have managed all right. It sure gives me hope that I can survive here." She smiled up at the obelisk, its shadow falling across her face. She patted the dark rock. "It's all going to be all right, isn't it?"

The stone said nothing, but in that silent stillness was the answer Eponine sought. It *would* be all right, everything was going to work out, even though her situation was as ill-matched as an Egyptian obelisk in the snow.

Glancing around, Eponine spotted a path leading away into a copse of trees whose dark canopies seemed to be holding up the thick clouds. Her curiosity was piqued, and she bid farewell to the towering relic and headed off down the path. The museum and her coffee were completely forgotten.

BELVEDERE CASTLE WAS PERCHED upon an outcropping over-looking the Great Meadow. Its stone turrets and balustrades were dusted with snow. The glittering flurries danced all about it, lending it a fairy-tale aura.

Eponine paused on the path to gaze up it for a few long moments. "I wonder if I shall find a prince inside?"

There was, in fact, a lone figure on the promenade, dressed in black. He looked like a sentry, just pacing back and forth, occa-sionally pausing to stare out over the broad field of snow that stretched out from the pond at the foot of the castle to the line of trees acres away that bordered the Great Meadow. Even more curious now, Eponine investigated.

JULIAN WATCHED THE SNOW fall over the Great Meadow. All the sports equipment had been removed and the acreage looked just like any open field anywhere. He imagined himself lord of such a castle, looking out over his kingdom. Had he done that before, sometime, somewhere?

His memories were sketchy, the recollections dim and trou-bling. He remembered with perfect clarity the moment of receiving this assignment. He had been called to accompany her; he had been told she could not go alone. *Vengeance* was sent to watch over *Joy*.

I'm a damn babysitter.

He could not fathom why he was sent, rather than any other angel in heaven.

Must've been my sterling reputation that sold 'em.

But he could not remember much past then. The meeting, the assignment, coming to the City . . . but before that, everything was a dark and painful blur. Dark, painful . . . and bloody.

He took a deep breath of cold air and felt the icy particles of snow sting his nostrils. He relished the sensation, the feeling of life and energy. Walking among the people of Earth was a new experience for him. For so long, Vengeance had rained judgment down upon them, the people, the very people he walked among. He could look them in the eye now, man to man. And in those eyes he could see how much they *loved him*. Not Julian, no, no one cared about him more than they cared about any other trench-coat-wearing, brooding young man in New York City. It was *Vengeance* they adored, and he could sense it everywhere. On the television he watched endless video clips of wars and bombs and gruesome acts of revenge that were broadcast twenty-four hours a day. He would often stay up watching the television in his room until his dark eyes watered and ached for sleep. And even then, he would leave one of those cable news stations on while he slept. Sometimes, in his dreams, he remembered. It was clear, so perfectly clear, and he swore he would have it still when he awakened. But in the morning light, his memories were only shadows again. Shadows that smelled like blood.

Julian pounded his fist against the balustrade. He felt trapped between two places, two states of being. It bothered him that he was now so comfortable in this human flesh, that he could recall every damn little detail since his arrival: the spring, Eponine's toes, the batty landlady who admittedly was a fabulous cook, the mountain of leftovers on their doorstep that next morning, the chocolate, the shopping ... but before that, there was nothing. Only vacant, aching darkness.

This must be what purgatory feels like. No suffering, no delight ... just waiting. A waiting to which you can see no end.

The back of Julian's neck prickled and he realized that someone was upon the battlement with him. Energy surged though his limbs and his spine straightened. He thought for a moment that he could produce the fiery sword in his hands right then.

Poor unsuspecting little human ... what would you do if you walked into that?

He pivoted on his heel in one smooth motion and came face to face. . . .

EPONINE SMILED AS JULIAN whirled around to face her.

"Well, I suppose there is a prince in this castle after all." She curtsied.

Julian stood blinking at her.

Eponine gave him a wry smile, "Well, I guess I am not much

of a princess, though." She wandered past him and leaned on the wall's edge. "There is quite a view from up here."

He sighed, his mind still clouded with half-remembered dreams. "How did you find me here?"

She glanced back over her shoulder. "I wasn't looking."

"And I didn't want to be found."

"Julian," she touched his wrist and he jerked his hand away from her. He turned away, furtively stroking the stripe of bare skin between his sleeve and glove that her fingers had brushed.

"What are we doing here?" he growled.

Eponine smiled and leaned against the wall beside him. "We're enjoying snow, silly."

"Damn it!" He gripped her by the shoulders. "Tell me, *why* are we here?"

"Julian, please."

"No! Don't give me that sugar-coated everything's-gonna-be-okay crap! I agreed to this assignment sight unseen and all I want to know is what the hell is going on here?" He was frustrated, and molten anger was quickly bubbling up through him. He could not abide *not knowing*. Not knowing meant not acting . . . and that made Julian's nerves itch. "I have been patient with you *all week*. I have played along with this 'let's be human' game. Because as far as I can see it is *just a game*! And it's *pissing me off*! But before this goes any farther, I *need to know*: What are *we* doing here? What are we supposed to be doing here?"

Eponine only smiled with bright sincerity. She gently took his hands from her shoulders and leaned against his body, wrapping his arms about her. Shocked, Julian tried to pull back, but her soft grip was surprisingly strong. She cradled her head against his shoulder, and he felt the wet crispness of the snow-crusted top of her woolen cap against his neck between his collar and his scarf. He inhaled her scent: fresh snow, sweet coffee, and that indescribable feminine *something* that he had begun to notice on human women. Eponine was warm against him, and Julian closed his eyes. It was comforting to feel her there, her body and her presence. Almost of their own accord, Julian's arms tightened around her. His temper was lulled, and he thought of smiling. Even on Earth, she was still the Angel of Joy. Julian surrendered to her, although he knew she was taking advantage of him.

He opened his eyes and the snow was still falling. The first snow of the season. Not a single footprint marred the gleaming mantle. He was sure she'd want to go make snow angels. After all, it was only appropriate. The frightening void in his memory was far from his thoughts as he gazed out over the pure white fields below.

"I told you what we're doing here, Julian," Eponine said softly. "We're enjoying the snow."

BREAKFAST

THE SUN WAS UP and shining brightly in the chill and cloudless sky. The snow flurries had moved on to frost someone else's town. Julian rolled over and groggily looked at the clock. It was just past noon.

He sat up, confused. His mouth tasted metallic and bitter, like blood. He knew he'd been having nightmares again, and as usual was a little relieved that he could never remember them. The frustration and resentment that had boiled over in him yesterday still lingered, and he had that familiar tingle in his belly that made him itch for a fight.

Usually Eponine woke him long before this. Her favorite method was to open his door and start cooking breakfast. If the noise didn't wake him, the scent would.

But not today. He wondered why. For a moment, he wondered if she had been upset after his angry outburst at the park, but regret was something Vengeance never tolerated, so the thought vanished half-formed. Regardless of the reason Eponine was not making breakfast, it did not change that fact that there was no breakfast.

He braved the cold, cold hardwood floor and wandered barefoot into the kitchen. It was dim and empty. In the adjoining living room, the television was still off and the window seat over the radiator also had not been touched. The bathroom was still ice-cold and without a trace of steam. He stood in the center of the apartment, confused.

Where could she be? Unless . . . no way. She couldn't . . . could she?

Eponine's door was still closed. He opened it slowly and peeked inside.

She was curled up in a mass of blankets, a fluffy lump in the middle of the bed with a long ponytail streaming across the pillows. Her room was clean but quite cluttered, with books and clothes all over her bed.

He was always a little surprised by her bedroom. They had been in the city for about a week and Eponine had already decorated her room. She had a few pictures of beautifully photographed landscapes and gorgeously drawn faeries. A prism dangled on a clear cord from her window, and a blue dreamcatcher hung over her bed. Julian had only a TV and did not feel the need for more.

Her bedclothes were dark blue with a celestial pattern and made of the softest fabric she could find.

"It reminds me of home, somehow," she'd told him at the store when she bought them.

She had mountains of comforters and super-puff pillows. It was a wonder she ever found any space to sleep. But she did, snug in the center as if she were sleeping in a cloud.

Julian cleared away a spot and sat down. He pulled the blankets back a bit from her face.

She was a plain girl. Brown eyes, brown hair, freckles. Average height, average weight. Nothing extraordinary about her. She had been very specific about that fact.

But still, she turned heads wherever she went.

Julian sighed and found himself smiling. He swept a strand of hair back from her face, then paused, his hand hovering over her head. Slowly, he brought his hand toward himself and looked at it.

His hand. It was much the same as it ever had been, yet so very different. His hands were smaller now, and broader; they seemed crude somehow. He remembered the myth about humans' being formed from clay and shuddered. There were little wiry hairs poking up on the backs of his fingers, and his cuticles were dry and often cracked. His nails looked dull, and he could not read the patterns swirled on his palms and fingertips. Eponine had laughed the other night when he'd come to her with it.

"Perhaps on Earth, a person's life story isn't written on their hands. Or maybe it is, and we just don't know how to read it."

He sat still and looked at his hands, at the random swirls and whorls and lines and lines and lines and lines. But it told him nothing. Even if the patterns told him he would be doomed to be an outsider forever, like they did back home, it would at least be *something*.

His hands told him nothing.

But his fingertips still tingled from the brush against her cheek. She had tiny soft hairs all over her face. It felt like velvet to his touch. The hair on his face grew bristly and dark. It was a strange thing, this body hair. It clung like ivy to his arms and legs, even growing in a patch in the center of his chest . . . and elsewhere. He didn't think Eponine had any, and it angered him that she still looked so much like her smooth-skinned heavenly self while he was disgustingly covered with dark, coarse hair.

He wanted to touch her face again, but did not.

Instead he rocked the bed. "Hey, Eponine! 'Nine! Nini!"

She grimaced and pulled the covers up over her head.

With geniality dripping in his voice he leaned over her. "Come on, *darling*, it's time to get up now, yes it is! Time to get up and at 'em! Wakey-wakey!"

She opened her eyes. "You frighten me."

He stood up. "What are we doing today?"

She yawned and stretched and rolled over onto her back. She shrugged.

"Eponine, it's past noon already!"

"So?" She yawned again. "Can't I be the lazy one once in a while, mister?"

"What time did you go to bed last night?"

"Three-thirty . . . I think."

"What were you doing?"

"The Internet. I talked to a girl in Orlando, Florida, and a guy in Nashville, Tennessee, and there were all sorts of games: word games, matching games, and *so much to read*! I found a website where people post their stories for each other to critique. It was so much fun I totally lost track of time! You should see it! I'll go start up the computer and show you!"

"But I'm hungry."

"So make some breakfast."

Julian looked over toward the kitchen in despair. Eponine stretched out one pajama-clad leg and gave him a little push with her foot.

"Go on! I am dying to try something you cook!"

He sighed and shuffled out.

"This isn't going to be pretty," he said, and shut the door behind him.

* * * * *

RIBBONS OF SMOKE WAFTED through the kitchen.

The toaster was in the living room, the bathroom, the hallway, and Julian's room.

The Pop-Tarts box was in the living room, the bathroom, the hallway, and Julian's room.

A plate of broken and partially charred Pop-Tarts sat on the table.

Eponine sighed and tried to be a good sport about eating them. Julian looked across the table at her but couldn't bring himself to watch her take a bite.

"No, don't. Let's go out." He pulled the plate toward him.

She gave him an amazingly steady look. "Do I even want to know what happened here?"

"*It bit me!*"

"What did?"

"The toaster!"

She giggled and glanced at the bits of broken toaster all over the floor. "Well, it'll never do *that* again!"

A pink welty burn was starting to come up across the knuckle of his right index finger. He sucked on it and muttered under his breath.

"Come on," she said, "let's go down to Dojo's. And then we can walk over to Kmart and get a new toaster."

"I am never going near another toaster again!"

"Well you're not supposed to stick your finger in it, silly!"

"I couldn't get the Pop-Tarts out! They were burning!"

"What happened to the little lever?"

"What little lever?"

"The little thing on the side of the toaster that you slide down to start it toasting and that makes the toast pop up when its done?"

"*I don't know!* I stuck the stupid things in there and told it to get hot and toast them and it did but I couldn't get them back out again. And then it bit me!"

Eponine nodded sagely, then began to giggle.

"And now, proud warrior, you have defeated that toaster! All hail the great slayer of bread-heaters! Huzzah!"

Julian roughly pushed his chair away and glowered down at her.

"I do not like to be mocked."

"My goodness, Mister Moody!"

Something popped behind his eyes and a white-hot streak of light shattered his vision as his temper escaped his ever-tenuous hold. He wanted to throttle Eponine, but instead he swept the plate off the table and watched it crash upon the floor, sending glass and pastries across the kitchen. He turned away, knocking the chair over, and walked barefoot back to his room. He slammed the door hard enough to shake the windows.

JULIAN DIDN'T TURN WHEN the door opened. He just lay on his bed and stared at the small television in the corner. Some trashy talk show was on. It was almost two p.m.

Eponine glided in and turned off the set. She stood quietly at the foot of his bed.

"I shouldn't have made fun. I'm sorry."

"I guess we both have things to learn, don't we?"

She nodded. "I suppose you're right. It doesn't seem so bad, but I guess being happy about the wrong thing at the wrong time can be hurtful. But I just didn't want you to feel bad for breaking the toaster."

He propped himself up on his elbow and looked past her to the kitchen. It was clean.

"Thank you for picking up the mess," he muttered.

"How are your feet?"

"Just a little scratched up. Don't worry," he gave her a ghost of a smile. "I put socks on."

Eponine nodded and sat down on his bed. She gently rubbed his feet and idly played with his toes.

"I am glad you aren't hurt, then, at least not here." She looked up at him with tears beginning to form in her eyes.

"'Nine! What's wrong?"

"I guess . . . it's that I have never seen you angry with *me*."

Julian sat up. Eponine wiped her eyes hastily and stood.

"Anyway," she nervously straightened her skirt. "I am sorry I upset you. I am going out for a little bit, get some air, give you some more time to cool off. I don't think I am very good at this roommate thing yet. I don't know where to draw the line when you're upset."

"I have just been having a bad day. Seems like everything's been getting under my skin today." He thought back to the conversation on the castle battlement, how irritated he was over the assignment and his lack of understanding about his role in it. He also remembered how easily she brought him under her thumb, and he felt anger threatening again.

"Well, maybe you need a nap. I heard your TV on 'til way late last night. I should know, I was up 'til almost four a.m." There was just a sliver of humor in her voice, but the light in her eyes was dim toward him. She paused as if waiting for something, then left his room, closing the door quietly behind her.

EPONINE PUT ON HER trenchcoat and wrapped up in her scarf and hat. She tucked her fur-lined gloves into her pockets and headed for the door.

Julian was waiting for her there.

He glanced up at her, realizing he was afraid to see the shadows in her eyes, the shadows he had put there. It was a stupid fight, but it had grieved her nonetheless. She was not looking at him. He reached out and touched the back of her hand.

"I wasn't really mad at you, 'Nine. I just lost my temper, that's all."

"Well, like you said, we both have things we need to learn," she told him. "Let's just not do that again." She rose up on her toes and kissed his cheek. "Do you want to come out with me? Maybe we'll get a toaster oven ... it just has a door you open and stick the stuff inside. No confusing levers." She winked at him. "And maybe we can find some food. Maybe start this day over."

"You know," he said, giving her a hopeful smile. "You know, Dojo's serves breakfast all day."

O Tannenbaum

THE TREE LIGHTING IN Rockefeller Square was held a few weeks before Christmas, when the looming holiday was already the only thing on most people's minds. There was a tangible excitement in the air as the decorations went up around the square all afternoon.

Even Julian seemed reasonably happy to go see it. He'd suggested they head out early and try out one of the Ukrainian cafés down the street. Oddly enough, there were two of them within a block of each other.

"How many twenty-four-hour Ukrainian diners does a city need?"

Eponine shrugged. "Two, evidently. So I suppose we flip a coin then?" She pulled a stunningly bright coin from her pocket.

"Where did you get that?" Julian's eyes widened in shock.

"From home, where else?" There was a glint in her eye. Julian could have sworn it was ... *mischief?* "Don't worry, Prosperity gave it to me, for luck, you know, and just in case."

"That explains the shopping trip."

She stuck her tongue out. "Oh, like you didn't go a little spend-crazy at that chocolate fair."

Julian opened his mouth and shut it again. He pursed his lips and gave her a sideways glance. "So that's why there was cash in my pocket every time I reached into it?"

"I thought you'd find it sooner, didn't expect you to ... *magic* ... the cabbie."

"Hey, go with what you know." He reached out and took the coin from her. It was slightly larger than the golden dollar coins he'd seen, but appeared much weightier. And it gleamed like no metal on Earth. It, of course, was made from no metal on Earth. "So, what's the exchange rate on this thing?"

"Enough to wreck the U.S. economy," Eponine plucked it from his fingers and flipped in a shining arc, only to catch it again in her gloved hand. "Ah, Veselka then!" She slipped the coin back into her pocket and crossed Second Avenue to the tinted glass doors. "So, let's keep it limited."

"How limited?"

"Well, late lunch/early dinner to start. Two for non-smoking, please." The slim blonde hostess lead them to a small table near the colorful mural that covered the back wall, and Eponine glanced sweetly back over her shoulder. "And no seconds on dessert," she said, tapping her pocket, "we're on a budget."

WARMED BY THE VERY best in strong Ukrainian coffee, Eponine and Julian gathered with a multitude of both New Yorkers and tourists in the small lane between white stone buildings that led into the heart of Rockefeller Square and the famous skating rink. It was slowly growing dark, the shadows lengthening along the narrow streets around them. A charity organization was handing out free hot chocolate and slim tapers pushed through Dixie cups. The crowd was jovial and rosy-cheeked, decked out in festive holiday sweaters with light-up pins on the collars of their winter coats. News cameras jostled into the throng of spectators, interviewing folks left and right, mostly families with small children. The crowd was massive. Julian bristled and reminded himself to breathe as the familiar dark currents threatened. But unlike at the mall, these people were united toward a common, joyful goal. Not to mention they were being plied with free chocolate.

Across the plaza, on a raised dais, were several organized groups, many of which had signs. One of them was a beautifully drawn tree with the words "Light up the darkness!" above it. Small lights had been punched through the board, which made the tree sparkle and blink with a hundred tiny little stars. Below the tree the sign read, "Season's Greetings from the Pagan Club of NYU!" The girl holding the sign saw Eponine looking at her and gave her a broad grin, making her large and very blue eyes positively sparkle with delight. Eponine waved. But the girl was distracted by someone next to her. They exchanged smiling words and the girl nodded. She handed the sign to one of her companions and took a photo of a group of women holding a sign that said, "Jesus is the Reason for the Season." They laughed together and passed along candles, hot chocolate, and introductions. One of the many news cameras spotted them and suddenly the two groups were the center of attention.

Eponine smiled to herself and tapped Julian. She pointed up at the two groups. Whatever doubts she'd had about religious tolerance from her experience at the mall were dissolved in this joyous moment.

A sudden hush fell across the mass of people. They all stood close by one another, both for lack of space and for warmth, realizing that the master of ceremonies was making some light banter on a stage at the foot of the enormous tree. Things would be happening soon and the excitement became palpable.

"... and a balmy *nineteen degrees*," the emcee was saying.

The crowd cheered valiantly through chattering teeth. Eponine huddled deeper into her coat and rubbed her gloved hands together.

"You okay?" Julian asked her.

She nodded. "Just a little cold. A balmy nineteen degrees, after all."

He laughed and stood a little closer to her. She leaned against his chest, fiddling with his coat buttons and managing to get them open.

"Hey! What are you doing?"

She pulled his coat as much around them both as she could. "I thought maybe your front was a little cold."

He frowned, but the shock of the cold air dissipated and was replaced with a heartier warmth. He chuckled and stuffed his hands in his pockets, letting them rest on her hips.

"Well, I guess it was," he murmured.

"If I can have your attention, ladies and gentlemen!" They all turned their eyes to the emcee. The area had been darkened and a spotlight was fixed upon him. He was someone famous, but Julian couldn't remember his name, and Eponine didn't know him at all. "Now you all should have gotten candles as you came in tonight. Those are going to be very important in a few short minutes, so hold on to them!"

Julian took his candle out of his pocket.

The emcee introduced the children's choir from Grace Cathedral, and they filed onto the stage. They were joined by the New York City Children's Chorus and the Jewish-American Youth Singers. All told, there were nearly three hundred children on the stage. They wore plain gowns of white satin with silver trim.

They began to sing.

They chose "O Tannenbaum" and sang it in German, an ode to the evergreen, a symbol of life in the winter. And as they sang, their sweet, young voices gaining confidence with each word, someone from behind began to light the candles. People from the back touched the flame of their candles to the empty wicks of those in front of them. The spark swept through the crowd like the tide. Suddenly the dim expanse was filled with a multitude of flickering candle flames. The flood of shimmering brightness rushed right up to the foot of the tree and, in a breath-taking moment, the tree itself burst into light. The wave of radiance traveled from its broad bottom branches to the top little boughs until it seemed to break upon the very tip and illuminated a huge crystalline star.

No one moved, no one spoke. The children's choir held their last note and let it fade.

The silence settled. Even the cameramen and newsfolk were still.

Julian felt Eponine sharply draw in a breath of delight.

Silent night, holy night, he heard her say. Had she spoken, or was it his imagination?

The choir took a breath as one and launched into "Deck the

Halls," really playing up the *fa-la-la-la*. The gathering of people cheered. Flashbulbs popped all around them, and candles were blown out or put aside. Photographers scurried here and there. Hot chocolate spilled on the ground, and somewhere a baby began to cry, giving a cue to at least ten more.

It was suddenly chaotic as people tried to push their way out of the crowds to get home to see themselves on TV. The children's choirs broke up into separate groups and took turns singing their own holiday songs.

Eponine sang along. During "Hark, the Herald Angels Sing," she sang only the "angel's" part. Julian laughed.

Their grand finale was to all come together again and sing "The Carol of the Bells."

"I had no idea there were words to this song," Julian mused.

A cheer went up when they'd finished, and the majority of the crowd now moved to leave. The Pagan Club held its blinking sign up high and seemed to make a parade out of filing off of the dais. They waved to the "Jesus" ladies, and the two groups went off in their own directions.

Julian and Eponine stayed until nearly everyone had gone. She was swaying, singing Christmas carols to herself, her eyes transfixed on the glittering tree. Julian found himself humming along and watching the reflections of the Square in the large round ornaments. Finally Eponine pulled herself free of his coat and rebuttoned it.

He frowned.

"What? You were unhappy I got into it, and now you are unhappy I got out," she teased.

He made a grandiose pouting face and looked down the front of his coat. "It's so lonely in here now!"

"Cry-baby." She tickled him, and he instinctively hit her hands away.

She backed off.

He colored.

Eponine gazed at him and hooked her arm through his. She didn't say a word, only smiled up at him until he smiled back. They strolled out of the square and made for the long line of cabs waiting to take the cold and tired people back to their warm homes.

Eponine began to sing "God Rest Ye, Merry Gentlemen."

"Peace on earth and mercy mild! God and sinners reconciled!

Joyful all ye nations rise, join the chorus of the skies! With angelic hosts proclaim . . . Merry Christmas to all and to all a good night!"

"Uh, 'Nine, that's not how the song goes."

She laughed and shrugged. "Hey! You're not proclaiming!"

She slipped her hand under his arm and tickled him again. He convulsed and made a choking noise.

"Proclaim!" She tickled him more, holding tight to his arm.

Julian gasped out between fits of laughter. "Merry . . . Christmas to all. . . and . . . to . . . ah! . . . all . . . a . . . a . . . g-g-good . . . a . . . good . . . *fight!*"

He wrenched his arm free and went for her waist. She howled with laughter, making the mounted police edge their horses closer to investigate. They noticed the scrutiny and ran for a cab, still bubbling over with giggles.

Eponine rolled down the window and waved to the cops as the cab pulled away, "Ooohhh, tidings of comfort and joy, comfort and joy!"

Julian joined her. "Ooohh, tidings of comfort and joy!"

HOLIDAZED

EPONINE BROUGHT HOME A little plastic menorah, some candles, and a booklet of Jewish prayers that she had gotten for free from some guy in a slogan-covered van on West Eighth Street.

They lit the birthday cake candles and sang the prayers for eight nights, following the directions in the pamphlet.

"It feels crazy to do this, Eponine; I mean the Jewish people take their stuff pretty seriously."

She watched the lit flames glimmer in the dim apartment and sighed. "Well, it's supposed to be a learning experience, to understand the culture. I mean have you ever noticed how many winter holidays have light as their central theme? Hanukkah is the 'Festival of Lights,' after all. Fascinating."

He sighed. There was no turning her mind from some things. So they sang songs and ate chocolates wrapped up to look like little coins and "gambled" with them at the toss of the little top. The candles flickered, and Eponine had a special treat for him each night: cookies and fudge and truffles and Turkish coffee. It really was eight nights of magic, but Julian wasn't about to admit to that.

At the end of the week of candles and prayers, Eponine put the plastic menorah and dreidels in a box in the closet.

"I have suffered through worse holidays," Julian said. "So, that's it, right?"

"Silly, it's *December*. It is the most holidayed month of the whole year!"

Julian blanched, "How many more are there?"

"Well, we don't have to celebrate any more. . . ."

He chewed the corner of his mouth, "Okay, but only if they involve treats."

"Do you *always* think with your stomach?" But she was laughing now, and planning. Julian caught a glimpse of the gears turning in her merry mind. She said, "Don't worry, Julian, winter holidays have treats *galore*!"

COFFEE. COFFEE UNDERLACED WITH baking bread. He rolled over, dragging the covers over his head. It wasn't even dawn. He wasn't about to investigate, no matter how good it smelled.

Then his door opened and light flooded his room.

"'Now the light is carried forth, proud upon its crown,'" Eponine's voice sang out beautifully, and she strode forward with a wreath of candles on her head and a plate of steaming rolls and coffee in her hands, "'in every house, in every home, this song shall ring!'"

She stood in a long white gown tied with a red sash; the wreath on her head made of holly and aglow with white candles. She set the plate down on the bed and grinned. "I am sure it rhymes in Swedish."

"What's going on?"

"Happy Saint Lucia's Day, Julian!"

He stared uncomprehendingly at the plate of breads and the candles on her head. "How are you not getting wax in your hair?"

"Holiday magic," she said mischievously. "Now eat up before the food gets cold!"

"What's all this about, 'Nine?"

"December thirteenth. The feast day of Saint Lucia. When this martyred Sicilian saint appeared off the coast of Sweden bringing much-needed food and supplies to the villagers. They say she stood at the prow of a great ship wearing white with a crown of candles on her head. She beckoned them to come and eat. The bread was still warm and they took as much as they wanted. And when they looked back, the ship was gone, vanished into the mist!"

He raised an eyebrow but bit into the roll. It was delicious. "Did you make all this?"

"Oh, yes. Were you wondering why I needed saffron and currants at the store yesterday?"

"Actually, no." He sipped the coffee.

"Well, is it good?"

He smiled, "Yes. Thank you."

"I promised treats for you, didn't I?"

"You did." He could feel the strength of the coffee starting to creep into his body. There would be no going back to sleep now. Resigned, he slung his feet over the side of the bed. "Let's finish breakfast in the kitchen, okay? That way we can both eat and you can blow out your hat."

Her smile broadened, and Julian would swear the candles glowed brighter.

IN THE DULL AND overcast morning a week later, Eponine was singing and bustling about. She left Julian's door open while she noisily made breakfast with the radio on. He stumbled out of bed and into the glare of the kitchen.

"Is this a hint?" he asked her, his mouth feeling woolly and dry. He yawned, and she put a glass of juice in his hand. "What, no nightgown and candles this time?"

She laughed, "Get ready! I want to go out and get a tree and some lights and some more candles."

"Again with the candles."

"I told you, this time of year is all about light!" Her eyes were sparkling. She was all about light. "Tonight is the Solstice!"

"Solstice involves eating, right?"

"Oh, you and food! Yes, we are supposed to eat until dawn. You know, to look at you, one wouldn't think you liked food so much, you're so thin!"

He shrugged, guzzled the orange juice, and put the glass in the dishwasher. "I call first shower."

An hour later, they were wrapped against the winter and heading down to Astor Place. All along the Astor and Broadway areas trees were being sold in long narrow lots on the sidewalk. They were exorbitantly priced.

Eponine poked and prodded in among them searching for the perfect one.

Julian dragged her away to Barnes and Noble, an easy task. That way she could look at books while he had some coffee. They split a gigantic cinnamon roll that dripped with frosting and decided to go across to Kmart and pick up tree lights and maybe some decorations.

"What is supposed to go on a Solstice tree that's different from a Christmas tree?"

"Not much," Eponine took a bite too large and dribbled cinnamon-speckled frosting down her chin. "And we need a wreath. And candles."

"Yes, yes, of course, the candles."

"I keep telling you, it's a prevalent theme all over the world! All these religions, they are really about the same things!"

Julian thought of their disastrous encounter with the Christian fundamentalists at the mall and was glad Eponine had forgotten it. Eponine always forgot the things that hurt her. Sometimes he found it irritating, but today, he was glad there was no shadow on her happiness.

JULIAN MADE A DISCOVERY. He hated Kmart. The heat was up way too high, along with the music. Hideous dancing Santa Clauses shook things they shouldn't have to the tinny and grating tune of "Jingle Bell Rock," made all the more obnoxious with the batteries going dead.

Parents made no attempt to curb their children, who ran screeching through the isles.

It was worse than the mall.

Luckily, however, most of the seasonal section was in the front of the store, right beside the checkstands. There Eponine was able to find her tree lights and a box of silver and gold balls.

Unfortunately, the wreaths and candles were downstairs. Next to the toys.

"Noooooooooo," Julian wailed melodramatically.

Eponine regarded him with a cocked eyebrow and showed him no mercy. They went downstairs.

The basement level was in shambles. A war-torn country had less carnage than what Julian saw there. Boxes pulled over and picked through cluttering up the floor, broken things strewn everywhere. Gangs of children roamed the aisles like packs of jackals, sniffing at the fallen packages of GI Joe and Barbie lying helplessly crushed underfoot. They slipped vagrant Hot Wheels into their pockets and chewed on cardboard puzzle pieces.

Eponine picked her way through the mess and took down a slightly rumpled artificial evergreen wreath from the hooks on the wall.

"Maybe we should get a real one."

"Does that mean we can *leave*?"

She turned to chastise him and saw the shadow creeping into his eyes. She hastily grabbed two cut-glass candle holders and a box of ivory tapers.

"Yes, let's go pay and get out of here."

Outside, Julian took a long breath. He was calm, anger receding and frustration fading. If only that damned bell would stop ringing! He nearly pummeled the Salvation Army Santa.

Eponine put a quarter in the red bucket and pulled Julian away before he could do any harm. They returned to the tree lot in front of Barnes and Noble, and Eponine made a quick decision about the tree and a wreath. In ten minutes they were hefting them and the bags full of decorations back to the apartment.

The place smelled heavenly when they got in, and Julian noticed broth in the crockpot bubbling away. He took a deep breath and tasted sage and bay.

"Stew for dinner?"

Eponine hadn't even taken off her coat before she had begun undoing the ties binding the little tree.

"I thought it would be appropriate, don't you?"

"I can't think of anything better."

Eponine began her preparations.

Julian hovered in the doorway. "So, how long is this going to take?"

She paused in her chopping and looked at him over the neat piles of onions, potatoes, parsnips, and beef. "Julian, it's stew. It has to, you know, *stew*."

"So, is this going to be longer than an hour, or shorter than an hour?"

"Try two hours."

He crossed his arms. "Two hours? What are we going to do until then?"

She slid the meat and veggies into the simmering broth and

clamped on the lid. She wiped her hands on the towel and gave Julian her most winning smile.

"We decorate the tree, silly!"

Before long, the apartment was filled with the rich scent of stew and the sparkling lights of the tree. They even wrapped a shorter string of lights around the wreath.

They settled themselves in for the Solstice Vigil with steaming bowls of stew and homemade biscuits. Eponine lit the candles at sunset. They sat on the floor around the coffee table and ate, chatting about this and that. Eponine replaced the candles when they began to burn low, taking the flame of the old to the new.

"This is the longest night of the year," she told Julian. "After this, winter really begins. Funny thing that winter is considered to be the dark time of the year, but really it's when the days begin to grow longer."

Julian nodded. "Yes, that is strange, isn't it, that the hope of spring begins at the beginning of winter." For a moment, he verged on the edge of profundity, but it passed.

The night went by slowly, and the two of them lapsed into companionable quiet. Julian sat in his favorite chair and watched Eponine watch the candles. She was cross-legged on the couch, alternating between staring intently at the flames and sitting back and looking out the window. Occasionally, she glanced over to him and smiled, but her gaze never lingered anywhere for too long.

He thought of the Pagan Club's sign at the tree lighting, "Light up the darkness." He smiled. In a world of shadows, Eponine was such a light.

Dawn was turning the world strangely white at 6:42 AM. Eponine's eyes were reddened and her face pale. Julian had moved to the couch to stretch out. He was determined to see the sunrise. Something pressed on his shoulder, but he couldn't see it, couldn't dislodge it. He jolted awake and found Eponine leaning against him. Sunlight streamed in from her bedroom. It was just seven.

"'Nine, wake up. It's dawn."

"I wasn't asleep," she slurred, shifting her shoulders and nestling her head against his chest. Her eyes never opened.

Julian laughed and let her sleep. He laid his head back on the arm of the couch and let himself doze off as well.

ON CHRISTMAS EVE, EPONINE had gotten a little Nativity set

and put it up next to the tree. She also set up the kitchen to make a roast for Christmas Day dinner. Julian found a channel on the television that was showing nothing but a hearth with a blazing fire and Christmas music playing in the background from six p.m. Christmas Eve until midnight Christmas Day.

So with the Yule log blazing on the TV, they found themselves on the couch again, this time with brandied eggnog in their hands.

"So, this is supposed to be the birthday of Christ?" Julian asked.

Eponine nodded and sipped her drink. "But scholars say he was actually born in March. December twenty-fifth was only decided upon after Emperor Constantine had a deathbed conversion to Christianity. He gave up the feast day of his patron deity, Mithros, god of the sun. Because as we well know, this is the time that the longest night of the year passes and the sun begins to return."

"So, it's all connected, the pagans and the Christians."

"Inexorably."

"I'll bet they both hate that."

She shrugged, then grinned. "Shall we exchange gifts? Or wait until morning?"

"Well, it's going to be anticlimactic either way. I only have one thing for you, and it's not even wrapped."

Eponine laughed. "I didn't wrap yours either."

She ran to her room and came back with a small red Macy's shopping bag. Julian reached under the couch and brought up a slick yellow and orange bag from Ricky's.

They handed one another their bags and began to rummage in them.

Julian took out a cashmere scarf. It was deep burgundy and the very softest thing he had ever touched.

He put it around his neck and smiled. "Wow, it's warm."

"The salesgirl said if you didn't like it you could bring it back."

He closed his eyes and felt the smooth silky fuzziness next to his skin, warm and soft. He smiled. "No, I think I like it just fine. Now open yours."

Eponine looked into the bag and giggled. She had a deep pink pillar candle in a tall glass jar. The sticker on the jar showed a drawing of faeries frolicking in a field and had the word "JOY" written on it. It smelled like roses. She also found a little jar of iridescent body glitter that smelled like strawberries. She threw her arms around Julian and hugged him tight.

"Thank you! It's all perfect!"

She dabbed glitter on her eyelids and cheeks and made faces at herself in the mirror.

They drank eggnog until late into the night, amusing themselves with watching the occasional disembodied arms come in to stoke the fire on TV.

DAWN FOUND THEM AGAIN on the couch, asleep. It was a near perfect repeat of a few nights previous with Julian's back against the right corner of the couch, his head lolled back onto the arm and Eponine curled up against him. But this time two small packages wrapped in glossy red paper and tied with golden ribbon were waiting on the coffee table for them.

"Merry Christmas, Eponine" and "Merry Christmas, Julian" was written on the appropriate tag in precise handwriting.

Santa Claus had come.

ONE RING

EPONINE YAWNED AND STRETCHED. She had a cramp in her neck and felt a little embarrassed at having fallen asleep on Julian again. She sat up and rubbed her shoulders. The fire still crackled away on the television, playing the tune "Have Yourself a Merry Little Christmas." Julian snored a little. She carefully extricated herself from the tangle of legs and went into the kitchen to put a roast in and start some coffee. She had some vanilla hazelnut that she had been saving for Christmas Day; they had drunk the Irish Crème on Solstice morning.

"Eponine!"

"What?" She brought in a tray of frosted sugar cookies shaped like trees and bells.

"What's all this? You said you only had one thing for me." Julian was sitting up on the couch, looking bleary and rumpled.

"I did."

"Then what is this?" He showed her the two little gifts on the table.

"I don't know."

"Why don't I believe you?"

She took the gifts and looked them over. "There is one for me and one for you. Strange, there is no sender."

"Where did they come from?"

She smiled, her eyes suddenly bright. "Santa!"

"Get real, 'Nine. Santa?"

"Who else knows we're here? Who else can get into a locked apartment on the third floor past a doorman?"

Julian shrugged. He felt more than a little trepidation. "So what do we do?"

"We open them, silly! Move over!" She plopped down on the couch and handed the little square box with his name on it to Julian.

Eponine carefully untied the gold ribbon and ripped one end of the paper, pulling out the box inside and leaving a little box-shaped wrapping-paper shell. She opened the box.

There was a locket inside. A silver heart-shaped locket on a fine chain glimmered on a bed of red velvet in a hinged jewelry box. With trembling hands, she lifted it out of the box and held it up. It slowly twisted, the morning light playing off the raised swirls and flowers on the front. She opened it. Inside, "Joy" was engraved.

"Look, Julian! Oh, isn't it exquisite? Julian?"

He was sitting stock-still. Tatters of red paper littered his lap, and he was staring into his own open jewelry box. He wasn't even breathing.

"Julian," she asked slowly. "Julian, are you all right?"

Carefully, Eponine reached out and turned the box so she could see what was inside.

There was a ring, a simple silver band with the words *"To thine own self be true"* written on it.

"It's lovely," she breathed.

The doorbell rang, and Julian seemed to come back to himself.

"I wonder who that could be?" Eponine dashed to the door. "Oh, it's Hannah!"

The voices of the two women in the entry hall seemed miles away. There were discussions of cookies, fudge, and fruitcake. He heard plates being exchanged along with holiday pleasantries. He took the ring out of its box and stared at it. His face was blank, but his eyes burned. Then he resolutely put the ring on the middle finger of his right hand and continued to stare at it.

"Julian? Are you all right?" He slowly raised his eyes to her.

They were sad, deeply sad, and confused. "Hannah brought us goodies, look!"

He said nothing, only continued to stare right through her.

"What's wrong?"

He shook his head, slowly at first, then vigorously.

"Julian. . . ." Eponine set down the plate of cookies and fudge beside her dish of frosted sugar cookies and put her hand on his wrist. She could feel his pulse beating a chaotic staccato. She slipped her fingers around his hand; his palm was slick with sweat. She was beginning to feel afraid. "Julian, say something!"

He jerked his hand back and stood up. He was shaking.

"Julian!" Eponine stood and faced him in the small space between the couch and the coffee table. "What in the world is wrong with you?"

His pulse thundered in his ears, and he felt like the floor was going to disintegrate beneath his feet.

What does this mean? The ring, Christmas morning . . . what are we doing here? He needed to get free of the music and the sweets and the scents and all the trappings of this holiday that now had a fierce new meaning to him. But Eponine was still speaking, and he could not follow her words. It was like birdsong to him, unintelligible and grating to his ears. No, he had to get free, be alone; he had to think. He stepped toward her, intending to push past her and retreat to his room. Solitude and quiet. Already the blood-drenched memories were beginning to slither into the light of his waking mind. *"To thine own self be true," my self, the self I can only remember in brief and brutal moments. What can that possibly mean?*

Eponine put her hands on her hips, standing between the couch and the coffee table, barring his way to his room. "You are not going anywhere until you tell me what this is all about!"

Unblinking and unseeing, Julian roughly shoved Eponine aside. She impacted the couch with enough force to knock the breath out of her.

"Julian! Stop!"

He kicked the table over and the plates of cookies went flying across the floor. Julian's bedroom door slammed and reopened a moment later. He stalked back across the room, trampling broken glass and chocolate into the hardwood floor. He left the scarf Eponine had given him sitting on the floor next to the ruined cookies as he left the apartment.

Eponine cautiously rubbed her side where she'd collided with the sofa. Satisfied that nothing was broken, although she was sure she'd have a nasty bruise, she wondered what to do next. Tears gathered behind her eyes, but she made herself think things through before she let herself get hysterical.

What's gotten into him? She shakily stood and began cleaning up the living room. She picked up the little written card from Julian's gift.

The ring! "To thine own self be true."... *He couldn't think that it means....*

"Oh, no, Julian!" She ran to the door, but the hallway was empty. She ran to the window that looked out over the street and opened it. Cold, damp air assailed her, stinging her face. She leaned as far out as she could but there was no sign of him.

"Julian! Julian!" She was sobbing now. "JULIAN!"

There was nothing to be done but wait for him to return. Shaking, she closed the window and finished cleaning the apartment.

To thine own self be true. But he can't remember himself, and he doesn't know the truth....

Eponine dropped to her knees and clasped her hands together.

"Oh, World, be good today," she whispered in a prayer. "Vengeance stalks the streets of New York City."

THE LONG ROAD

THE DAY WAS OVERCAST, but the sun's glare was overpowering.

Julian found himself at one of those sidewalk tables selling sunglasses along Union Square Park. He snatched up a pair and all but snarled at the proprietor, a small Asian man. "For you," the man said, bowing obligingly, "for you, Merry Christmas! Merry Christmas!"

Julian was stunned for a moment by the man's fearless generosity. Perhaps he was afraid for his life. He turned and stalked away from the wobbly table without even a nod of thanks. He put the sunglasses on and felt horrible.

Julian's thoughts were a tempest within his mind, whirling over one another and occasionally skimming the surface of that dangerous abyss. He feared looking into it, feared to know what he would find there in his own soul. But the tempest roiled on, and it felt as if it would rend his head in two.

He kept walking, crossing over to Fifth Avenue, which lay mostly deserted this early on a holiday. The wide road stretched out ahead, vanishing with an amazingly crisp line between two buildings, blocks and blocks away. Julian walked on, his feet moving automatically, his eyes seeing what they needed to see and nothing more. It seemed as if the blocks slid past him in a hazy blur, as if they moved and he was still.

The silver band glimmered on his hand, which was turning red and feeling tight in the icy wind. The ring felt disturbingly cold against his already chilled flesh, and he stared at it without seeing it.

To thine own self be true.

Six simple words.

Some sort of divine mandate to be true to himself.

Emotions, memories surged and he stumbled a step. Mothers screamed for their children with no reply but the heartwrenching echoes of their own sobs. Children cried for their parents, calling for them over and over; each time hope faded yet still they called. He heard fire crackle in his ears and gunfire like the beat of a drum. He heard his name sung in the hearts of the people, his true name chanted like a prayer of thanksgiving. This blood, they offered up to him. With this revenge they exalted him. It filled him with exhilaration and dread.

Since time immemorial, he had been a creature of violence. He was summoned to exact the punishment decided upon by Justice or Honor. It was nearly always upholding the weak against the strong, defending honor, and bringing some solace to those without peace, but it was violent.

It was always violent. It always ended in blood and tears.

In the past, the score had been settled, the scales balanced, but not anymore. Each death, each drop of blood spilled, each tear shed for the loss of life was now heaped upon his altar. Vengeance was no longer simply an agent of God, he *was* God. In the minds and hearts of those who slew in his name, he was the Almighty. In his hands were blades, guns, and bombs, but his worshipers believed that the forces of nature also lay in his control. They poured libations for him after catastrophes he had nothing to do with. They saluted him after earthquakes, cheered for him in the wake of devastating storms, blessed his name as volcanoes ravaged the mountains, and wept tears of joy when great tsunamis destroyed a sea shore.

That is the truth in myself.

The sunglasses could not shield him from the bonfires, the great flames of celebration that were often lit with the bodies of those killed in his name. He gagged as his lungs felt full of putrid smoke, and he knocked his shin against a fire hydrant.

Fireworks of pain obliterated his ghastly vision, and the terror momentarily slunk back into the deepest shadows of his tattered memory. Rubbing his leg, he was jolted back into his new reality, living in a placid human body, devoid of most of his ethereal powers in order to play protector to one of his fellows.

And had he been sent to stand beside Justice and Honor in the battlefield?

Was he accompanying his beloved sister, Death, on her awe-inspiring rounds?

Had he been sent out on an investigation with that irritating little killjoy, Mercy?

No.

He was a babysitter to *Joy*. He thought being saddled with Mercy was the worst of it, but he had been wrong. Even Mercy with her big, watery eyes, her plaintive voice that so often moved people to tears, was easier to deal with than Joy. Mercy, he understood. All the things he was not, she was. It was easy enough. He hated her, but he understood her. Joy, on the other hand....

Joy was capricious, emotional, and had no sense of danger whatsoever. Her moods were fickle, sure. Most of the time she was happy; it was her job, but it also meant she was quick to descend into despair. He was not sure what set her off. The maddening hordes of the mall left no trace, but the exchange with the obviously mental Evangelical left her crushed and heartbroken. She took his destruction of the toaster with aplomb but his show of temper had driven her to tears. What was wrong with that girl? She floated, then she plummeted. She honestly believed that Santa Claus was real and had brought them gifts on Christmas morning. She almost never failed to find delight in anything, no matter how repulsive, no matter how depressing, no matter how much it made the rest of the angels think her mad. And she was mad, as mad as she was beautiful. Julian's breath hitched as he thought of her with crystalline eyes and kaleidoscope wings.

Her smile was just as radiant wrapped in flesh with freckles and dimples. He wanted to touch her, to hold her, to apologize for being such a brute. . . .

He'd pushed her so hard. She was so light.

Julian shook his head and kept walking, eyes down.

It was his nature to be harsh, to lash out. He was just doing what he was told, was he not? Being true to himself.

Eponine's voice rang softly in his ears. As he left the building, he thought he had heard her crying. No, it was more than crying, she was desperately screaming his name through choking sobs.

His chest clenched painfully, and he was drawn up short. He could not breathe.

All he could hear was Eponine crying out, calling his name. Fear was so apparent in her voice, fear and pain. And it was not fear *of* him, it was fear *for* him. She was worried; she was afraid; she wanted to protect him. *Joy* was heartsick with concern over *Vengeance*. He snorted a laugh, but it did not dispel the echo of her voice. He clamped his hands over his ears, but she was still there. Of all the things he so often forgot, why could he not escape the memory of her?

A sensation like something molten rising up through his body gripped him. It began deep in the pit of his stomach and wrapped around his ribs, squeezing the very air out of his lungs. It bent him double and crept up his throat, burning every inch.

He gasped a rough and ragged breath, bringing forth a guttural sound. His eyes ached, feeling as if they would bulge completely from their sockets. He stumbled along blindly, falling against a metal trash can on the street corner. He could recall every sensation as he pushed her aside. Why had he pushed her? Something had come back to him, some dark and bleeding memory. Escape, he had thought only of escape. Running to the safety of his room and hiding there until it passed. But she had blocked his path, wanting him to speak to her, wanting to know what was in his heart. Noble, yes, but terribly misguided. He could not unleash the poison in his soul upon her. Her precious heart would shatter under the weight of his confessions, and her delightful laugh would be drowned in the sea of blood he kept locked up in his memory. Why wouldn't she let him pass? Why did she have to choose that moment to become so stubborn?

Someone grabbed her roughly, but by the arms, not the throat. So easily it could have been by the throat, that slender, cheerful throat. There was glass breaking and a great clatter, and Eponine was out of the way. At last, he could get out! Visions surged like a tidal wave behind him, threatening to envelop him if he could not outrun them. Out of the corner of his eye, he saw her. He watched her body slam into the couch, lying perilously still for a moment, but he would not go back; he could not go back. She would have to understand—it would be his end if he faced that rising tide of blood.

I cannot be true to myself; I do not have the strength. Why have you asked this of me?

His eyes would not let go of the image of her body flung haphazardly upon the sofa.

His ears would not stop hearing her cries.

Someone had deeply wounded that sweet, beautiful creature he was sworn to protect!

Someone had hurt Eponine!

It was me.

Julian shuddered from head to foot.

Tears finally broke free and rolled down his cheeks, and his body hitched and hiccuped as he tried to inhale.

He pressed his hands to his face but could not stop them. Glancing up over his sunglasses, he saw that he was at the southern end of Central Park. The late afternoon light suffused it with a warm, golden glow. He ran toward it, collapsing at the foot of a beech tree just inside the gate. Sunbeams slanted around him, drawing delicate filigrees on the ground through the tree branches.

He immediately thought of how marvelous Eponine would say it was.

And then he cried.

Not the racking, painful sobs of a moment before, but a seemingly never-ending gush of tears and a trembling of the belly that made him feel horribly weak. He wrapped his arms around the tree, pressing his face to the rough bark and finding solace in the pain it caused him.

He dug his nails into the trunk. *Damn it, damn it! The Angel of Vengeance doesn't cry!*

The more he thought about it, the worse he felt.

Now, not only had he caused Eponine the greatest pain of her eternal existence, he had also debased himself.

He looked at his ring and it mocked him.

The sun had set. The world had gone dark. He drank it in, lying in the deepest shadows, drowning in sorrow. He melded with the dimness, becoming part of it. He felt insubstantial. Not only bodiless, but soulless as well. It was as if the night had come and stolen him away, leaving only his dark eyes and silver ring glinting fiercely in the gloom.

To what, now, could he be true?

LITTLE BITS OF LIGHT

THE APARTMENT WAS QUIET.

It was a deep and pervasive quiet, not unlike the silence of a tomb. Wan early-morning sun rays gave the rooms an even, silvery light that did nothing to dispel the feeling of a sepulchre. It echoed the pang of loneliness in Julian's soul. He wanted nothing more than to get lost in her streaming light. He never thought he would admit it to himself, but at this moment, he needed her. Vengeance the loner; Vengeance who needed no one. He wanted her comfort, her light, her joy.

The place was empty, utterly so.

Julian searched for a note, something, anything to mark that she had been there recently. He was desperate to find her, to feel her presence, her comfort.

But there was nothing. The kitchen was pristine, and her bedroom was neat as a pin, which was strange because Eponine was so fond of what she called her "friendly clutter."

He leaned against the doorjamb to her bedroom and sighed. Her scent surrounded him, the sweet floral cloud of her perfume and the soft, almost powdery smell that was hers alone.

He didn't know what he was to find, what he expected to find. He wished only that she had been there, waiting. Everything would have been put to rights if she had been there waiting for him. But the apartment was almost entirely devoid of her presence. He wondered, suddenly, if she was gone for good, abandoning him and the assignment. He found that hard to believe. Joy was a hopeful creature.

Julian ached from head to foot, and was covered in dirt and bits of brush. The sunrise had found him slumped in sleep at the bottom of the beech tree, luckily before the NYPD did.

Trembling with exhaustion and, although he'd never admit it, emotion, he retreated to his bed. He fell straight to sleep, dressed and on top of the covers.

NIGHT HAD COME. IT was an awareness Julian felt deep in his bones. He did not open his eyes; he did not want to see the dark and deserted apartment. Strange dreams still danced behind his eyelids. Bruised dreams that tasted like the coppery tang of blood mixed with the bitter, gritty soil of the park. Although he knew it was past dark, the room seemed filled with light. He was lying in softness and warmth, and he felt suspended, weightless, free. He heard songs, songs strange to him but sung in the language of home. Nostalgia stunned him, like a fist clenched in his gut. How could he yearn so fiercely for a place he hated so much?

Perhaps he had been called back. He felt at once relieved and deeply disappointed.

To be home, home where he knew what was expected of him, where he knew his place and his duty with divine surety, no matter how much it pained him, no matter how much he chafed at the bit. It was a thought that tempted a grim smile from his lips. Yet to be gone from this humble little place: The very idea chased that smile away with an icy shiver. Never again to watch Eponine share a pretzel with the squirrels in Washington Square Park or to lose himself in the contrived but addictive dramas he watched during the day on the television. Breath, life, hunger, sensation had all become rather dear to him. He sighed. Eponine had become rather dear to him. *Damn it! It can't be like this!*

Her voice was just a gossamer thread floating on the verge of his hearing. She was singing softly.

He knew that song.

It didn't come from home.

It was being sung in English.

He didn't know the name but it was Eponine's song, from the *Les Misérables* musical.

He opened his eyes.

She was lighting the room.

Light suffused her entire form, lending an ethereal glow to

the bedroom. She was sitting on a kitchen chair she'd brought in with her, singing softly to herself and rocking back and forth. She wasn't serene like most of the other angels; she was ecstatic. Light radiated in fierce waves from her body, forming itself into two arching forms behind her and spilling over into the room. It illuminated her face, her hair, leaving shimmering traces in the wake of her movements.

She stopped singing and smiled at him.

"Hi." She shifted on the chair, wincing slightly as she flexed her ribs. "I am so glad you are home. I was so worried."

"You were worried? About *me*?" Julian lay still, and it occurred to him that he was *in* bed and somewhat undressed. His hands and face were clean, and he noticed his fingers were bandaged.

Eponine simply grinned at him, turning the white light rosy.

Julian pulled the covers up over his head. "Just let me be, 'Ponine. I am not ready to talk to you yet."

"You know where to find me when you do."

She flinched minutely as she got up and picked up the chair. She was trying not to let it show, but he could see that he had hurt her badly. Tears burned him again, and he pushed his face into the pillows.

She told him something, then. She came quite close to the side of the bed, and Julian could feel the delicious warmth of her breath, but all he heard was the muffled silk of her voice. She reached down to stroke his head, but he shied away at her touch. She said something else, then all was silent again. He peeked out of the blankets.

His door was shut and he was alone in the room. Eponine was gone; the light was gone; only cold, empty shadows remained.

He wanted to run and take her in his arms. Apologies would flow from his lips and he would bathe her in his tears and it would all wash her pain away.

He stayed in his bed.

And found that his tears did nothing to soothe his own pain.

AULD LANG SYNE

DECEMBER THIRTY-FIRST. THE WHOLE world had its eyes on New York City.

Eponine was thrilled.

"We *have* to go, Julian!"

He looked up from the television and sipped his coffee. It was only the second morning that he'd come out to be social since the day after Christmas. Eponine had said nothing of that night, but she seemed to regard him with an extra measure of patience. Julian was grateful for it, but still couldn't bring himself to voice anything like an apology.

On the morning talk show, one of the hosts was especially bubbly about her plans to commentate on the evening's festivities in Times Square. Julian felt a little trapped between engulfing waves of perkiness.

"Absolutely not," he said, with a tone that made it clear he was in no mood to argue the point.

"But Julian.... It's the only time we'll be here on New Year's Eve. New Year's Eve in New York City, Julian ... people wait their whole lives to be part of this! We already missed the Thanksgiving Day Parade. I am not going without this."

"Well, you are not going without me and I am not going."

"Julian!"

"What? It's dangerous. Do you know how many people will be down there tonight?"

"It happens *every* year, Julian. If it was really *that* dangerous they would have put a stop to it by now."

She just doesn't get it. There was no way he was going to subject himself to thousands of people crammed into Times Square, drunk and blowing incessantly on noisemakers. There was just no way. He sighed and changed the channel. "You are very naïve, Eponine."

"And you're ...you're pissing me off, Julian!"

He rose and faced her. "I am not going to put myself in that situation, okay? I am not going to be crammed into a small space with a hundred thousand idiots! Someone's gonna step on my toes or yours, and all hell is gonna break loose! I don't do well in crowds like that, understand? Oh, help me, if some pickpocket or pervert tries anything in that throng and *snap goes the Julian*! *Then* they'd cancel your precious little New Year's Eve party!" He stopped for a breath, realizing he was trembling and brandishing the remote control like a weapon. "Besides, they are showing the whole thing live on television." He took his coffee and sipped it slowly.

She nodded. "Okay, that's fair. You're right, you shouldn't go."

He was surprised that she was acquiescing so easily. He settled back into the couch and watched a woman on TV pour glitter on cardboard tiaras for her own New Year's Eve party.

"Well then, I suppose I *should* go to the store; there is nothing for dinner. Do you want anything special?" Eponine was getting her coat out of the hall closet.

"Ohhh, yeah, one of those layered Mexican dip party trays and the stuff you call 'creamy goodness.'"

Eponine giggled. "It's spinach dip."

"Well, it would be good for tonight. And some good bread for dipping." He was making himself hungry; he hoped she wouldn't be long.

She bundled up and got her purse. "Okay, Julian, be good while I'm gone."

He nodded and waved over his head, entranced by the TV showing tall frosted cupcakes with real lighted sparklers on them.

"Oohhhh, if only we could have *those*! Sweet *and* on fire!"

HE SHOULD HAVE KNOWN better. But Eponine had never lied before.

Well, she hadn't *really* lied now, just tricked him.

"Be good while I'm gone" didn't specify how long she would be gone. But she *had* told him she was going to the store.

No, he corrected himself, *she said she* should *go to the store.*

He paced. It was almost ten, and she'd been gone for nearly twelve hours. She wasn't coming back until after that blasted ball dropped.

Julian wondered what to do. The news was reporting that they'd already reached critical mass and sealed off the area; no one else was being admitted into Times Square.

"That doesn't mean me," he growled at the screen.

Decisively, he threw on his coat and hat. His gloves were in his pocket. He had cash and a Metrocard. He headed for the door. Wait, no scarf. He dashed into his room and saw the burgundy cashmere scarf Eponine had given him, crumpled on the floor. He grabbed it and tucked it beneath his collar, against his neck. He closed his eyes a moment, savoring how soft it was and thinking of her. He hadn't touched it since Christmas Eve. He jolted away from the painful memories that followed and ran out the door.

NYPD WAS DIRECTING EVERYONE out of the Forty-Third Street and Eighth Avenue subway exit that popped up across the street from the Majestic Theatre where *The Phantom of the Opera* played. People were swarming everywhere, and it was looking bleak. All the streets were blocked to Eighth Avenue, barricaded with blue police sawhorses and watched by the sternest cops on the force. Mounted police wandered in and out of the crowds. That was proven to be the most effective means of crowd control, because if they didn't respect the police, they at least feared the horses.

It wasn't long before Julian saw his opportunity. There on the corner of Forty-Third and Eighth a woman was arguing with a cop. A small crowd had gathered, as crowds always do at times like these. She was trying to talk her way behind the barricade, and he wasn't being swayed. He might have been if she hadn't kept changing her story about who she had "lost" on the other side: her niece, her daughter, her friend's kid. Julian slipped into the group, just another guy in a dark winter coat. He threaded his way toward the woman carefully. He noticed that people were coming and going on the block. It was just after eleven, and the theaters were letting out.

Perfect.

The cop was just about done with the petulant woman and turned to his comrade for some advice. Julian saw his opportunity to act and slammed his shoulder into the center of her back, sending her sprawling into the officer and nearly knocking her over the sawhorse. Suddenly there was chaos.

The cop grabbed the woman by the shoulders and started to yell. The crowd pushed forward, on the verge of a mini-riot. Julian easily slipped between the barricade and the theater and was instantly mingling with the people on the other side.

There were barricades set up at Seventh Avenue, too, but they were unguarded. He turned left and headed up to the Square.

It was a place transformed. An enormous stage was set up right in the middle of the huge intersection. Thousands of people pulsed to the rhythm of the band playing, as it was too close and crowded to dance. Behind the stage, atop the old *New York Times* building, from whence the Square got its name, was the Cup O' Noodles sign that really steamed, and above that was a long slender silver pole crowned by a smallish sphere of lights. Atop it was this really little ball. Julian was unimpressed.

He ducked into the breezeway of the Marriott Millennium

Hotel and looked for Eponine. It was madness to think he'd actually be able to find her here.

What if she really hadn't come at all?

No, of course she was here. Where else would she be?

She would have gotten here early and staked out a good spot,
somewhere near the front, but where she could still get a good
view of the ball. He pondered a search plan.

Then he saw her.

Not among the vast sea of people in front of him, but up on
the jumbo-vision screens that lined the edges of the Square.

Of course, she'd be near the cameras!

She grinned on the screen, seeming to look right at him.

"And you, are you having a good time?" someone off camera
asked her.

"Oh yes, the best!"

"And where are you coming from tonight?"

"Just downtown, off Astor Place."

"Ah, a local. Any special messages you want to get out there?"

"Oh, yes, thank you! Julian, I'm sorry you couldn't be here
to see this. The TV just can't do it justice. I hope you're not too
mad."

"Did you leave your boyfriend at home?" the interviewer
chided and came onto the screen. Julian realized it was the
woman from the talk show. He couldn't remember her name.

Eponine only giggled. "It's not like that. We're just friends."

The woman flashed a glittering smile for the cameras and put
her arm around Eponine. "Well, regardless, it means that there are
now at least two beautiful women out here with no one to kiss
when it strikes midnight! Hear that, fellas? What's your name?"

"Eponine."

"Wow, what a beautiful name. Okay, me and Eponine, we're
going to hang out here for a while and see if we can find someone
for our New Year's kiss."

Eponine blushed, and the hostess gave her another squeeze.

"Julian, if you're out there, you had better come find your
friend." She winked and passed the live feed back to the studio.

He was floored. Not only was Eponine here, she was just inter-
viewed on national television and got hugged by a nationally
known talk show host. And now that woman was telling him to
come find them!

He dove into the mass of humanity and tried to navigate

toward the camera area. It was slow going, and he found that the front half of the area had been barricaded off as well.

It was only fifteen minutes until midnight!

"Listen," he said to the first cop. "I have got to get in there."

"Sorry, this area has been closed since ten. But you can see the ball drop real well from over there by the McDonald's," the cop said with a smile.

Julian growled. Then regretted it as the man's smile faded.

"I'm really sorry," the cop told him more sternly. "But I can't let you through."

"But I'm Julian!"

"Yeah, well, you're the fifth one."

He let out a long breath. The screens shimmered into life again, showing faces instead of ads. The camera panned the cheering crowd at they began giving time updates to the magic hour of midnight. Eponine was still standing with the TV personalities.

"Well," the hostess said, "I found my husband. Still waiting for the man of mystery, Julian, though."

"I'm here!" He yelled up at the screen.

"It's okay, really, ma'am. I am having a great time."

She turned to the crowd. "Do we want to see Eponine get a kiss at midnight?"

The crowd cried, "Yeah!"

Eponine blushed, but she was laughing. Her face was radiant with all the attention and adoration. Guys were volunteering left and right to be her New Year's kiss. Julian felt hot turmoil in his gut. Like the tears, but hotter, more prickly. His face turned red, and he ground his teeth.

He did not want to see this. He *did not* want to see some filthy and drunk mortal putting his *mouth* on her! It occurred to him that had he stayed at home, he would have been helplessly forced to watch it on TV. At least here he had a chance to stop it, but that time was quickly slipping away!

He dug his nails into the barricade. He would be finding flecks of blue paint under them for days afterwards.

"I'm trying to get to you, 'Nine, I really am," he muttered.

The barricade moved under his hands and he tottered. He met the eyes of the police officer standing there. He was smiling.

"Get in there, Julian," he jerked his thumb over his shoulder and gave Julian a wink. "You only have ten minutes to find her."

He stood, staring at the officer, his mouth agape.

"Go on! You're wasting time! The TV platform is over there."

He nodded. "Thank you."

The crowd was thicker here. No one wanted to let him pass. He felt his temper rise a hundred times, but he had to let it go if he was to get to Eponine in time. It irked him. He pushed through clots of people, often finding himself pressed against barricades on the edge of the crowd with the TV platform nowhere in site. He lost his bearings more than once.

A huge LCD clock blinked on, showing it was three and a half minutes until midnight. It was rapidly counting down. He began to push indiscriminately through the crowd. There were, of course, guards at the foot of the red carpeted dais where the hosts were stationed.

He waved his arms and jumped up and down.

"Eponine!"

She was chattering happily with everyone there. One would think they were all old friends. She smiled with grace and poise for the scores of photographers and TV camera people.

"Fuckin' amazing," he shook his head. "Eponine!"

She didn't hear him. He was getting frantic, now. There were only minutes left and he was *right there*.

"Eponine!" His voice raked through his throat, feeling as if it would draw blood. "'Nine!"

She looked down, seeming like a queen on a throne, gracing her loyal subjects with her glowing countenance.

"Julian!"

Then she became a child, giddy and forgetting the dozens of cameras on her, running to the end of the platform. She fell to her knees and reached out to him.

"Have we found him?" The entire crew rose to their feet and looked over Eponine to try to see Julian.

The announcer called out that there were thirty seconds left.

"Julian! What are you doing here?"

"I have been trying to get to you for hours!"

"You came out here looking for me? You found me in the midst of all these people?"

"'Nine, you've been on the Jumbotron. It wasn't that hard."

She blushed and looked aside. "Oh, yeah, that."

"Somebody get him on stage," came the order from behind them somewhere.

Rough hands grabbed at him, but he spun away.

... Ten ...
... Nine ...
... Eight ...

"Julian, I can't reach you down there!" She was too high to jump and giggling too hard to try and climb down.

... Seven ...
... Six ...

He grabbed the supports of the platform and pulled himself off the ground. His biceps strained, but it was only a few feet; he could make it.

... Five ...
... Four ...
... Three ...
... Two ...

Eponine leaned as far over the edge as she could.

... One ...
... HAPPY NEW YEAR! ...

Their lips met and time froze.

Her mouth was soft and sweet, tasting like honey. And warm! The warmth traveled through his body, a minute shudder of a tickling tingle. He thought he'd let go of the bars and fall, but his arms held firm.

He'd once felt the silken press of rose petals against his mouth as he had leaned in to smell a bouquet. He had been surprised at the thrill of quiet pleasure that had run through him, and Eponine had laughed. If that rose had been vibrant and alive, it still would have paled in comparison to Eponine's kiss.

Beyond the sweet sensation of the physical touch of her, Julian was filled with delight. Her essence spread through him, and he felt joy in his heart and soul. Blissful tears sparkled in the corners of his closed eyes. Her gift. It filled him with pure light and happiness.

The world flickered around them, and he came to realize it was flashbulbs. People were taking pictures of them.

He heard "Auld Lang Syne" being sung in the background.

He came back to his body, his muscles finally beginning to protest as his strength was starting to flag.

The sensations so full and bursting with emotion remained, but seemed to grow hollow as he parted from her. His arms began to uncoil of their own accord, and he slowly sank into the crowd. The flashes still lit his world like lightning, casting bizarre shadows across Eponine's face. She remained kneeling at the edge of the platform, a smile on her lips that reached from the depths of her heart to his. She touched his face just as he slid beyond her grasp.

The crowd swallowed him and he lost sight of her.

All around him, drunken people stomped and pushed, trying to get home. The magic of the moment was gone, and he hadn't even seen the ball drop. It sat on top of the Cup O' Noodles, blinking on and off along with the year written in lights below it. He was jostled away from the dais. All around him was kissing, drinking, fighting, pushing, laughing... he felt weak. His lips tingled furiously and his knees were rubbery. His arms were uselessly numb.

The chaos closed in around him like unrelenting ocean waves. Someone clutched at his arm, and he was powerless to stop it.

"I am so glad you came!" whispered a breathless voice near his ear.

Eponine was beside him. She put her arms around him and held him tight.

"Are we friends again?"

He had no words for her. He trembled, deep inside. It felt as if his very organs were shaking. He couldn't speak. He only gave her a stricken look.

Eponine met his gaze silently, her mouth a slim, straight line. He looked away. She caught his chin and gently turned his head back toward her. He had never seen her so calm, so filled with unearthly quiet. Then she smiled. Not her usual loopy grin, but a smile that bespoke a serenity he had never thought possible for her.

"Thank you." She took his hand and squeezed it, then brought it to her lips and kissed it.

She led him out of the crowd. They parted easily for them, the celebrities of the night. Cheers and pats on the back followed them all the way.

She took him to the back of the TV platform where a worn-out intern handed them both clipboards.

"What's this?" he managed to ask.

"Releases, to use our images and stuff." Eponine was her usual bubbly self again.

"But we aren't supposed to...."

"Don't worry," she winked. "Fifteen minutes of fame. They won't remember us tomorrow."

She signed with a flourish. *Eponine Allegresse*.

Julian sighed and made up a last name for himself. *Julian d'Sanguise*.

AMONG EPONINE'S MOST CHERISHED possessions was a videotape of that New Year's Eve sent to her by the production company. There was a framed photograph of their kiss on the wall in the living room for as long as they lived there. It may still be there. The city rejoiced with them for about a week, but the memory faded with the New Year's resolutions as everyone went on with their lives.

JULIAN THREW HIS RING across the room and wanted to tear out his hair.

After New Year's Eve, he knew nothing of who or what he was, only that it was obvious that Eponine loved him. He wanted to be mistaken about what he saw in her eyes that night as the city counted down and he felt as if he'd moved the Earth to reach her kiss. But there it was in the tape that he watched sometimes at night, with the sound turned down low and all the lights out, and there in the image on the wall. He could see that she was in love with him.

After so long, languishing in loneliness, he thought such a thing would bring him peace, but instead it kept him awake most nights. His mind reeled through lists of why and how, but it made no sense to him. He was not a creature made for love, no matter what all those books about angels said. Maybe the rest of his kind, but not him. His divine soul had been forged for a different reason, a stern, harsh reason. His was the very heart of ruthlessness; he was the incarnation of settling the score; he took the eye for an eye and the tooth for a tooth. He was Vengeance, and there was little room for such things as love in his heart. But her kiss had shone a light into dark places, dispelled the shadows for a moment, and now they had returned darker than ever, and he longed for that light again. He ached every moment for her touch and yearned for those sweet brown eyes of hers to look at him with such utter adoration again. But yet, she could not, she should not want to touch him, to love him. She was a creature of innocence and light, and he was made for bloodshed and destruction. For Joy to lay her head upon Vengeance's shoulder was too much for him to comprehend.

In all the millennia I have wrecked horrendous revenge upon the wretched world, I never thought the cruelest vengeance of all would be to fall in love. And I have done it to myself. . . .

AFTER SCHOOL SPECIAL

EPONINE HAD THE HABIT of going down to the corner grocery every morning, even if it was only to buy some fresh fruit or a bouquet of flowers. Twice a week, she passed by a class of students from the Ukrainian School. They were on their way to the Children's Art League, farther down Seventh Street. They were in the second grade, and their teacher was a young woman named Ms. Branch. Eponine looked forward to Tuesdays and Thursdays when she would see them in their two lines, clad in gray uniforms, eagerly heading toward their beloved art class with Ms. Branch in the lead and their teacher's aide, Mrs. Devareaux, in the rear.

This particular Tuesday, it was especially warm for late January, and they had their coats half off and were running wild. Ms. Branch was alone and wore the look of a mother whose love was still strong but whose patience was wearing thin.

"Oh, Eponine, thank heaven!"

Eponine smiled. "Where is Mrs. Devareaux?"

"Had her baby on Friday morning!"

"Oh, my, that was early! Is everything all right?"

The children, by this time, were swarming their favorite friend, tugging on her coat and cooing "Poninny" over and over. For some, their grasp of English was rudimentary at best.

"Yes, everything is fine; he was just in a hurry." Ms. Branch was trying to collect the students back into their lines. "But I am short-handed now until Easter Break at least!"

"Well, let me help you walk them over to the Art League." Eponine gave the children a wink and a smile. "Would you like that?"

They cheered and surrounded her, now tugging her along.

"I want to show you my picture!"

"I made a vase!"

"Last week I got finger-paint in my hair!"

They chattered all over one another, trying to get close to Eponine. Little hands grasped each of her fingers and pulled.

She carefully extricated herself, wincing each time her knuckles cracked. But she was smiling.

"JULIAN, GUESS WHAT?"

He came out of his room. "Where have you been? You left before breakfast, and it's almost dark!"

"Oh, yes, yes, I am getting to that!" She tossed her coat across one of the kitchen chairs and spun around, her laughter filling the small apartment.

"What happened to you?"

Her skirt swirled around her legs, getting tangled as she ran toward him. Julian loved that dress of hers, the one tie-dyed in pale blue and white. It looked like the sky. She caught his hands and swung him around, giggling madly.

"It's the most wonderful thing! I am going to have children!" she said.

"Would you mind explaining that, please?"

She nearly cackled and drew him close, wrinkling her nose and pressing her forehead against his. "And what do you think I've been up to? Immaculate conception?"

"No," he chuckled, "not exactly."

"Do you think I mean to *eat* them, then?" She was still close to him, still clutching his hands, holing them against her belly.

He laughed again. "No, that's not at all what I meant. So what's this news about children?"

"I am going to be a teacher's aide over at the Ukrainian School!"

"Uhhh, okay. . . . Whatever possessed you to do that?"

"Well, the usual aide is out on maternity leave."

"Oh, I see, *she* had the immaculate conception," Julian snickered.

Eponine ignored him. "So I will go help out a few hours a day during the week."

She let go and danced around the kitchen, opening cabinets and fixing a snack of strawberry jam and graham crackers.

Julian stared. "And what am I supposed to do, then?"

"You?" She stopped, her skirts swirling up again so he could see her matching sky-blue silk leggings. "What do you mean?"

Julian shrugged. "You'll be gone all day?"

"Only on Tuesdays and Thursdays, and even then it probably won't be all day." She sidled over to him. "Having some separation anxiety?" She laughed, and it sounded wicked. He glared. "You can come with me for show and tell. I'll bet they'd love that!"

Julian rolled his eyes. "You'd probably introduce me as some sort of beast, I'll bet. When do you start?"

"Where do you think I have been all day today? And I go back again on Thursday!" She poured herself a glass of milk to have with her treat and took it with her to the front room.

"Are they paying you?"

"I asked them not to. It's not like we need money. And they need it more than we ever would."

"How noble of you."

She gazed at him, her head tilted over. It never occurred to her that, just because she was happy about something, it did not automatically make him happy about it.

"Never mind. I think it will be good for you to get out and do . . . stuff. Just don't get too attached to them. You won't be here long." Julian sighed. He knew better than to deter Eponine from something she'd set her mind to.

THE LANGUAGE BARRIER WAS no problem. The children all were supposed to be speaking English in the classroom. But during recess, they were allowed to use their native tongues, which ranged from Ukrainian to various dialects of Spanish. Eponine amazed them by her ability to communicate with all of them simultaneously, understanding and responding to them as well. She spoke to them in every language at once, a variation of the Tower dialect of the most ancient Babylonian. And soon she found herself going to the school every day of the week, even if only for a few hours.

The children gathered around her skirts every afternoon at one o'clock. She read to them each day. She read them *Harry Potter*, Shakespeare, *Alice in Wonderland*, Shel Silverstein, and the Brothers Grimm.

She fed them with laughter and smiles, and they drank in every drop, growing radiant and articulate.

She chattered endlessly about them at home. Julian stayed in his room more and more.

ON A RAINY MONDAY, the kind of day that could dampen the brightest spirits, Eponine sat with her brood clustered around the radiator. She was teaching them a song in Gaelic about a girl who was transformed into a swan when her sister tried to drown her. Tabitha climbed into her lap and laid her head on her chest. Her tiny hands curled around the lose strands of Eponine's hair. She then began to fiddle with the locket at Eponine's throat.

"What's this?" she whispered when the song was done.

"It's a secret. Would you like me to share it with you?"

"Yes! Yes!" They leapt to their feet and shouted.

Eponine waited, counting slowly in her head. "Are secrets about yelling?"

"No." The children quieted.

"Are secrets about jumping?"

"No." They sat back down.

"Now I am going to tell you a story, and then I will reveal the secret."

They began to whine. "Awww!"

"Are secrets worth patience?"

"Yes."

"Very good." She settled in and spun the thoughts through her mind before speaking. "Well, I shall begin at the beginning. Once upon a time . . ."

. . . THERE LIVED A PRINCE in a cold, gray castle. The world he knew was a cold, gray world, and he thought himself utterly alone. His eyes were black as night and his hair as dark as a raven's wing. But he was beautiful, beautiful as an angel.

He lived all alone, cloistered in his fortress of stone and will.

He did not know he was a prince.

He did not think of himself as an angel.

And since he had no one to love him, he thought, of course, that he could not be loved.

One day, on one of those rare occasions when he ventured forth into the light of the sun, he was walking in the woods. And in a simple glen, near the mouth of a spring, he came face to face with a girl. He had never seen such a creature before and was understandably confused.

She smiled at him and followed him home. She lived in the castle with him, bringing in wildflowers and berries and filling the shadowy walls with light and life and color.

She gave him a mirror, so that when he smiled, someone was always there to share in his joy. But he never needed it; she became his joy and his life.

As such things often are, life could not stay unchanging forever. Time moves forward, and life moves ever onward.

She crept into his room one night and cut a lock of hair from his head. She closed it inside the little locket she always wore, so she could always keep him close to her heart.

In exchange, she kissed him.

It was, as such things are, a kiss of magical means. It opened his eyes from sleep and opened his heart from its despairing dreams. He smiled at her.

"Do you love me?" he asked her.

"You are always in my heart."

Then the sun rose, and she melted away like the dew.

The dream faded. But now the castle was filled with memories of warmth and laughter.

THE STUDENTS LEANED FORWARD as one, their collective breaths held.

Eponine glanced about her conspiratorially. "Are you ready for the secret?"

"Yes," they whispered in return, barely daring to move a muscle, any of them.

Eponine opened her locket.

Inside was a single curl of very dark hair.

They gasped, their eyes wide.

The final bell rang, and they jumped like nervous cats.

Eponine laughed and clapped her hands. "Get your things! It's time to go home."

She followed Ms. Branch and walked them to the door and looked out at the icy rain. They scurried to their parents and guardians and the school bus. Eponine wished she had brought her umbrella.

Out of the steel mist came a shadowy form. Someone in dark clothes was holding a celestial-patterned umbrella. The girls began to chitter quietly, watching the glow that came into Eponine's eyes. Julian came to the steps and stopped. He looked blankly at the clutch of children, who unabashedly returned his stare. He glanced up to Eponine and gave her a half-hearted lopsided grin.

"You forgot your umbrella, 'Nine."

"Thank you, Julian. Are you here to walk me home, too?"

"Yeah, I thought, uhhh, I thought I'd come see where you worked."

Eponine was thrilled. Somewhere behind, a girl whispered a bit too loudly to her friend, "Do you see his hair?"

"It's the same," replied her friend.

Julian raised an eyebrow, but chose to ignore the comment.

"Yeah," he continued, trying to sound light, "thought I'd leave the castle for a bit."

The gasps and giggles that went up all around shocked him. He looked a little helplessly at Eponine. "What'd I say?"

"I'll tell you later," she whispered. She waved to her class and Ms. Branch. "I'll see you tomorrow!"

They walked home together, huddled under the umbrella, Julian walking with a stiff stride and Eponine gliding along beside him. Within a block, they had fallen into step with one another.

"Ms. Branch, do you think Eponine is *really* magic?" Tabitha asked, sounding mostly as if she wanted to make sure Ms. Branch agreed with her.

For her part, Ms. Branch considered a dozen answers, but only said, "Yes, I do. I really do."

SUNSET AND CANDLELIGHT

SUNLIGHT STREAMED IN THROUGH the tall, narrow windows. The bedside clock was blank.

Julian rolled over and groaned. He felt groggy, like he'd overslept.

He pushed a few buttons on the clock, but nothing happened. He picked up the remote and tried to turn on his television. Again, nothing.

Grumbling, he shuffled out into the kitchen. The microwave was dead and the fridge was dark and disturbingly tepid. He tried the front room television, just to be sure.

"Yep," he muttered, "the power is out."

He pushed open Eponine's door.

"Hey, 'Nine, we got no—" His voice died in his throat. The morning sun had not made its way into her room yet. The place was cloaked in soft, gray shadows and still held onto the chill of night. She was lying in the center of her bed, an array of pillows and blankets surrounding her like dark blue jersey-knit clouds. Her hair had come loose from the band she usually wore to bed and was draped across her pillow like a tawny shawl. The reddish-gold highlights couldn't be seen at all. It was only the second time he had ever seen her asleep, he realized. Usually, they parted ways at bedtime and didn't see one another until sometime the next day, whenever Julian decided to get out of bed or when Eponine came home from the school.

There was something alluring about her lying there. Something fragile and helpless and trusting. She shifted and stretched, snuggling back into the covers. Her eyes flickered open, looking quite dark in the low light. She looked at him, without moving. There was no moment of confusion or panic; she just smiled at him. Julian looked away, feeling heat rise into his face. He forgot why he had come into her room.

"Good morning," she said in a voice husky and low from sleep. "This is a rare treat, you waking me up."

"The power is out," he blurted.

Eponine sat up. "It is?" She scowled and looked at her clock. The second hand was dutifully marching around the brass-trimmed face. The minute hand clicked toward ten-thirty, and the alarm rang. She silenced it, and only the soft *tick-tock* remained.

That thing would drive me nuts, ticking like that all night, Julian thought.

Eponine tugged the pull-cord of her bedside lamp, but nothing happened.

"Goodness, I wonder how long it's been out."

Julian shrugged. "Dunno, but the fridge is in bad shape. It's getting warmish in there. I wouldn't trust the milk."

Eponine climbed out from beneath her soft mountain of bedding. She rolled her shoulders back and forth and tottered into the front hall. Julian followed her to the closed-circuit building phone near the door.

"Hello, this is Eponine in apartment 3-D . . . we seem to have no power. Can you please tell me what's wrong?"

Julian listened but couldn't understand the doorman's garbled responses.

"Yes. Yes. Oh, really, three a.m.? Well, I think it's a little late for my refrigerator. Uh-huh. Oh, well that would be awfully kind of the building manager. When do you think it will be back? Oh. Oh. That long? Oh, really? Oh, that is so sweet of Hannah. Yes, we will. What? They have to cut that, too? I see. No, it is better to be safe, I suppose. You don't think it's dangerous, do you? That we'll freeze to death in here? Uh-huh. Okay. Yes. I understand. Well, there isn't much we can do. Yes, I will keep my receipts. Oh, she will? Oh, she's wonderful! I will ask my roommate, then. Yes. Right. Okay. Thank you." She hung up the phone.

"That didn't sound like it went well."

Eponine leaned against the wall and crossed her arms. The apartment was growing quite cold, and Julian fiddled with the thermostat to no avail.

"Don't bother," Eponine told him. "It seems that there was a problem in the wiring last night. The doorman isn't sure what happened, but something about the old wiring in this building and the fact that everyone's got computers now and it's taxing the system." She glanced over at their computer and shrugged. "But the point is that something in the wiring blew last night about three a.m. Shorted out the big fuse box in the basement . . . you know the one that is so cleverly located next to the boiler and the furnace?"

"Oh, don't tell me. . . ."

"So the heat and hot water are off too. At least until they can get someone in here to fix it, which is proving difficult on a Sunday morning."

"No wonder it's so cold in here. So what are we supposed to do?"

"Well, the doorman said the building manager would reimburse all the tenants for any loss of food in the refrigerators as well as the hotel fees if anyone can't sleep here tonight. They are not sure how cold it's going to get."

Julian nodded. "That's damn decent of him. So, what do we do?"

"I guess we'll see how it goes. Let's take the things out of the kitchen that are going to spoil and go out for the day. No sense staying here."

"I could really have used a nice, hot shower."

"Just think of how wonderful it will feel tomorrow." She stretched mightily, her flannel pajama top rising up and showing off her dimple of a bellybutton. The pajamas were printed with clouds, and her pale tummy looked like a strip of sunlight breaking through an overcast sky. Julian laughed and Eponine blushed. "Go get dressed!"

IT WAS A CRISP, late January day and the city was awake and going about the day-to-day grind of a Sunday. The Jewish shopkeepers were getting their storefronts ready for the week and many Christians' places were closed while they took their own day of rest. As usual for a Sunday, the cafés were crowded to bursting. They wandered down Astor Place to West Eighth street and ended up going for a late breakfast/early lunch at Johnny Rocket's. They sat at the private booth facing Greene Street. Eponine pulled nickel after nickel from her coat pockets and kept the jukebox busy. She decided her favorite songs were Three Dog Night's "Joy to the World" and Save Ferris's rendition of "Come on Eileen." She ate an entire Smokehouse cheeseburger and half a side of fries. Julian was impressed. He ordered a number twelve and took the lion's share of the side of fries.

They sat and watched people come and go along the sidewalk, sipping their chocolate Cokes and singing along with the music. The waiter kept refusing to bring their check, saying they were far too entertaining and couldn't leave yet!

Finally, after two hours, even Eponine was bored and wanted to move on. She smiled up at the waiter and he finally gave in. She mulled over the figures, not bad all in all, less than twenty dollars, and hummed "I'm A Believer."

"So, Wade," she read off his nametag. "Valentine's Day is coming up. What kind of plans do you have?"

He blushed. "None. There is a girl though. . . . But I shouldn't be telling you this."

"Oh, no, really," she touched his hand and grinned up at him. "Does she like you?"

He nodded and said quickly, "Yeah, but we are both kinda shy. . . . She gave me her number and I'll bet she's just waiting for me to call . . . but I can't find it."

Eponine folded the bill into fourths and rose to leave. Julian slid out behind her and took their coats. She handed the bill to Wade and gave him a kiss on the cheek. He unfolded the paper as the door shut behind Julian and Eponine. Instead of the bill, all that was written there was a phone number.

The cash drawer balanced perfectly that night at closing, and Wade married Samantha two years later.

THE AFTERNOON WAS SPENT window shopping along West Eighth Street. It was an enjoyable stroll through some of Eponine's favorite stores, like India Imports and Uncle Sam's

Military Surplus. She knew all the owners and never left without being given some little bauble. They finally ate a light dinner of hot dogs and tropical smoothies at Grey's Papaya and watched the sun set over Washington Square Park.

Eponine sat on the edge of what once was the fountain and sighed. The street performers were packing up for the night, and the weekend crowds of students and picnickers were rapidly dissipating. The golden light cast long shadows of the trees upon the deep red façade of the New York University Library and made the building glow.

"There are times when I wish I could freeze a moment and put it in my pocket to take out and enjoy whenever I pleased."

"It's getting cold enough out here to freeze anything!" Julian's nose was quite red, and he could easily see his breath and hers. He dreaded the loss of sunlight, for then the temperatures would further plunge. He was not looking forward to sleeping in their cold apartment.

Eponine turned to him and gave him a cockeyed grin. Her face was pale, and her cheeks shone with livid pink spots from the cold. The flesh at the base of her neck was splotched where the cold silver of the locket rested. It seemed she had forgotten her scarf. He slid over to her and untied the lush cashmere from his neck and wrapped it around hers. He watched her revel in his body heat before trying to remove it and hand it back.

"I am not cold," she said, firmly.

"You lie."

"I don't!" She showed him her gloveless hands, which were looking red and raw in the chilly air.

"Eponine, you're cracked, girl! You are going to catch pneumonia!"

She smiled dreamily, "I wonder what that would be like?"

He stared at her, open-mouthed. "You *cannot* be serious!"

"No, I am not. Not really."

"Then where are your gloves and your scarf?"

"I guess I forgot them. My gloves are usually in my pocket, and I couldn't find my scarf this morning." She shrugged and folded her hands on her lap. Julian swore he saw her fingertips turning blue.

"Let's go home."

"And you expect it to be warmer there?"

"We'll have *blankets* there!"

She turned away from him, closing her eyes and letting the

last rays of the sun dance across her eyelids. She took a double handful of frigid air and held it to her chest. Then she reached over and took Julian's hand. Her fingers felt as cold as death, and he shuddered.

"We're going home right now!"

She exhaled a steamy breath, and he could see that she trembled.

"This will never come again, this time right now. With the light just-so, and you beside me and the wind exactly like this in my hair." She squeezed him and he felt her fingers creak. "Some day this will all pass away. And so will we."

"Yeah, you . . . tonight . . . if we don't go home!" He pulled her to her feet and she let him.

She shivered against him as he pulled her along through the park. It was cold, the temperature taking a dive in moments after the sun had gone. She stumbled, and he tried to get her to button up her coat and keep his scarf on.

"Eponine!"

She gave herself a shake and him a shy smile. "Sorry, I was getting a little carried away. But do you ever stop to think about it? How illusory this world is?"

"Yes, yes, all the time."

"Oh, you don't." She ground in her heels at Broadway.

He was nearly carrying her now.

"I'm sorry, Julian."

"You're just cold, 'Nine. Let's get home, okay? You can philosophize all you want once we get back to the apartment, okay?" She always chose the very worst times to be dreamy! "And don't go about forgetting your winter clothes anymore!"

They got to the dim doorway of their building and greeted the bundled-up doorman, who was sitting over a battery-powered light trying to read. Julian looked at the pitch-black stairwell and sighed heavily.

"Oh! Now I remember why my gloves weren't in my pockets!"

Julian was almost afraid to hear it. "Why?"

She held up a squat taper and a matchbook. "I brought a few, just in case."

She lit the candle and headed up the stairs, leaving Julian to chase after her.

He caught her on the landing, still able to see his breath even inside the building.

"Eponine...."

"Yes?" She gave him a charming look, seeming more like herself than she had out in the park.

"You worry me, you know that, right?"

She danced out onto their floor and took out her keys. She skipped over to the apartment and opened the door with a flourish. Her lilting laughter filled the hallway.

"As well I should, Julian, my dearest, as well I should!"

The apartment felt like a refrigerator. A few degrees colder and they would have been able to see their breath inside.

Eponine calmed considerably as she went about the house and lit the rest of her candles.

I guess she is more concerned with the illusory nature of electricity right now.

She disappeared into her room, taking her light with her. Julian waited on the couch but she didn't reappear.

He cautiously peeked into her room. She was wearing her blue silk long johns under her flannel pajamas and was nearly buried in her bedding. She was huddled near the votive on her bedside with an open book in her hand. She looked up and cocked an eyebrow.

"Don't you want to change?"

"Change?"

"You aren't going to sleep in all your clothes, are you?"

Julian shrugged. "I hadn't thought about it. Are you going to bed?"

"I was thinking about it. So you should go get changed!"

"What does your going to bed have to do with what I am wearing?"

She rolled her eyes and crawled over to the corner of the bed. She leaned over and untied his shoes, then pulled him down on top of her. He landed badly, one shoe flinging off and skidding into the hall. She extricated herself and shut the bedroom door, leaving it open a crack for ventilation, as the scent from her candles was already nearly overpowering. The whole room smelled like vanilla and roses.

Julian continued to lie on top of her pile of blankets. He realized he was shivering and that his foot was cold. Eponine knelt beside him and pulled off his other shoe. She dropped a pair of sweat pants onto his lap.

"These will be softer than your jeans."

She waited. He waited.

It was freezing cold in the apartment, but her bedroom was gradually beginning to warm. The candleglow filled the room nearly to the corners with softly flickering golden light. And it imparted that familiar divine shimmer to Eponine's face.

Without taking his eyes off her, he slid out of his black jeans and into the sweats. She smiled and tugged him to a sitting position.

"Now what?"

She shrugged and a shiver rippled through her. "I'm cold."

She dove under the covers.

"Aren't you cold?" came the muffled question.

He sighed and picked up his end of the blankets and looked in. She was only a deeper shadow in a realm of dark. Something glimmered in the dimness, and Julian reached out to touch it. It was small and cool, metal and heart-shaped. He felt Eponine's breath on his forehead. He was holding her locket. She lay down and he had no choice but to follow. For some reason, he did not want to let go of her necklace.

The bed was icy, and he wished for warmth.

Julian rolled onto his side and drew up his knees, one arm close to his chest and the other lying across the short distance between them. He could see nothing, but he could feel her there. Her body heat, her breathing, her heartbeat. His hand was still closed upon the locket. The backs of his fingers gingerly touched the smooth flesh of her chest.

One arm slipped over his shoulder and another beneath his head. He allowed her to hold him. She relaxed and fell asleep almost immediately with a contented smile on her face. It would be hours before Julian could allow himself to do the same. There was too much to comprehend: the sensation of the soft bedding enclosing his body in comfort and warmth, the scent of the candles and of Eponine's perfume and of her body, the gentle weight of her arm draped across his shoulder, the rhythmic sound of her sleepy breathing, and the knowledge that he was sharing her bed. It was nearly too much for Julian to bear. He knew there would be no sleep for him, but he realized that he did not mind it in the slightest. The sensory flood filled him entirely, and he found that he was pleased by it. In the candlelight, Julian smiled.

He opened his empty hand and took a sample of the air. Then, as gently as he could, he drew the locket close. He pressed his hands to his chest.

"This will never come again, this time right now," he whispered. "Yes, I wish I could just put it in my pocket, forever. Some day, this will all pass away. And so shall we."

ANOTHER NEW YEAR

"WELL, WELL, FANCY MEETING all of you here."

The schoolchildren stopped, their two lines dissolving into a mass that divided down the center to let Eponine pass.

She was as surprised as any of them to see Julian leaning on the railing in front of the Children's Art League.

"Julian, what are you doing here?"

He laughed and leaned onto his tall, black umbrella as if it were a cane.

"Do you know what day it is?" he asked her, giving the overcast sky a quick glance.

"Why, yes, Julian, it's Tuesday. Obviously you know that, too, since you've met us here."

"Ha! That is where you are wrong, 'Nine. I mean, yes, it *is* Tuesday, but it's not just *any* Tuesday."

She gave him a humoring smile and wanted very badly to kick him. Ms. Branch was now standing between the two of them and her students looking a little nervous.

"Listen," Julian whispered.

In the distance, over the sound of early morning traffic, was the occasional *pop!* and cheer.

"What is it?" asked a few of the more inquisitive children.

Julian leaned over them, bending over the top of his umbrella. "*That*, little ones, is the magic place we are going to today!"

They gasped as one and began to chatter amongst themselves, their voices rising in pitch and fervor.

Ms. Branch fixed Julian with an icy stare. "*Excuse me?*"

"We're taking a field trip," he told her definitively. "It's Chinese New Year today."

He then made a grandiose bow and turned on his heel, heading back toward the school. He beckoned to the children over his shoulder.

"Come on, little ones! We're off for an adventure!"

They were torn, looking between Julian with longing eyes and their teacher and Eponine with worried glances. Eponine ran to catch up with him and the children gladly followed, skipping and pushing but never getting ahead of them. Ms. Branch had no choice but to go along. And she had to admit, had she known it was Chinese New Year, she would have made a similar plan.

They flowed into the subway station at Astor Place, just slipping through the turnstiles. Ms. Branch tried to swipe her card, but the screen kept telling her she was paid in full. She closed her eyes and walked through. They were already cramming into a subway car.

Eponine was singing "All the Pretty Little Horses" with the children happily joining her in the choruses, "Black and bay, dapple and gray, with a coach and four, my little baby!"

THEY EMERGED INTO A dull glare of a cloudy Manhattan morning, but it was soon forgotten in the shimmer of a thousand red and gold decorations that covered all the buildings on Canal Street. The Chinatown streets were closed to cars and instead were full of people of all ages and races dressed in everything from jeans to traditional Chinese garments. The air crackled with fireworks and throbbed with drums.

They wandered west to the corner of Canal and Broadway where men were selling lucky cakes under the awning of Pearl River Trading Company. The children watched with interest as the cook poured rich yellow batter into a cast-iron pan that had twelve indentations in it. After only a moment over the grill, he flipped it over and gave it a firm smack on the cutting board. Twelve little golden cakes tumbled out to his waiting assistant, who deftly scooped the steaming hot treats into a white paper bag. They were a dollar a bag, and somehow every child ended up with his or her own dozen. They tasted like warm, spongy fortune cookies and made their insides feel toasty in the chilly air. Ms. Branch sighed and felt overwhelmed. Eponine handed her a bag of her own fortune cakes and gave her a hug.

"Don't worry," she whispered.

The poor teacher could only nod.

Julian led the class down into Chinatown itself, finding a good spot on Elizabeth Street to watch the parade.

The children watched in awe at rituals that they had never before seen, or even heard of, in most cases. The dragon dancers swirled by them, the great beast's grotesque and shimmering mouth opening and snapping shut. It was at least twenty feet long, with a leonine head that nodded and long-lashed bulbous eyes that could blink. Dancers huddled under the yards and yards of red and green silk, their legs showing underneath like a centipede's. The dragon moved in a serpentine motion, the head bobbing up and down and occasionally held straight up over the lead dancer's head. It didn't seem to bother anyone that the handlers of the great puppet could be seen. Young boys ran around it playing drums, and slender young ladies wandered among the crowds passing out fortune cookies and jade trinkets. The pounding echoed in their chests and they all rocked in unison, lulled by it, only to jolt at the fierce staccato of the firecrackers.

"Gotcha!" Julian laughed at the surprised and stunned faces. Eponine smiled warmly at him; he was that wicked schoolboy again.

"You see," he told them, "the dragon is very lucky, and it makes a stop at the doors of all the shop keepers who bring out treats for it. That way they will have good luck and good business through the coming year. The firecrackers keep bad spirits away. And look, people are bringing their kids to be blessed by the dragon."

They looked back toward the street just as the dragon turned away from a family group and headed straight for them. Some of them shied, but a few stuck out brave hands to try and pet the colorful beast. The dragon wagged its head and blinked its eyes, swaying over the children's heads. They cheered, as even the most recalcitrant of them grinned broadly and welcomed the dragon's blessing with open arms.

The parade passed along, and the children craned their necks until they could see no more of the colorful costumes or hear the richly pounding rhythms. Julian then ushered them into a small alleyway between two stores that lead to a tiny shopping center with a small restaurant.

They crowded into the minuscule establishment and were awed into silence by the process of cooking that went on there. The restaurant served only soup and rice bowls that were cooked in ancient-looking ceramic crockery right in an open fire. The cooks pulled the covered pots out of the hearth with a huge wrought-iron hook and dropped them right onto the dented and heat-marked stone tabletops. The children burned their fingers trying to get the pots open to look inside. The sweet-faced wait-resses brought them training chopsticks held together at the top by a rubber band. They also brought porcelain, ladle-shaped spoons that no one could fit into their mouths, not even the adults.

Ms. Branch was wary of what she was eating, but the children did not seem to care that it was glazed duck and roast pork together with snow peas and whatever that black slimy bit over there was . . . some kind of mushroom, it seemed.

Finally, the satiated horde wandered back out of the alley and into the festivities. The dripping early afternoon wasn't dampening anyone's spirits. With the parade now over, dragon dancers cavorted throughout the streets at random, much to the delight of all the truant children.

On the way back, Julian took them by the Happy Buddha Ice Cream factory for free New Year's Day samples. They tried each flavor including green tea, which they hated, and lychee, which they loved.

WITH HEAVY FEET, MS. Branch's second graders finally trudged back up the stairs into the school to collect their things and go home. On their way out, Julian was waiting at the door with bright red envelopes embossed with gold. They were traditional New Year's gifts, supposed to contain money. Each student found inside only a subway token.

"It's worth more than cash." Julian gave them all a conspiratorial wink. "Some day, it will take you exactly where you need to go. Happy New Year!"

Ms. Branch sighed and propped herself up against the doorway.

"That was quite an excursion," she said with an exhausted smile.

"I hope it was all right. Julian can be rather, uhh, forceful."

"No, it was great. I just wish I had thought of it. Now they'll be begging for both of you!"

Julian wandered back to them after giving out the last of his envelopes. "Ready to go, 'Nine?"

"See you on Thursday, Christine," she said to Ms. Branch. "And this time we will actually go to the Art League."

Ms. Branch waved and ducked back into the school, leaving Eponine and Julian on the steps. The children had gone and the air was finally still and quiet, with only the whispering hiss of the rain. Eponine's head spun and her ears rang, but she was smiling. She threw her arms around Julian's neck, then gave him a playful shove.

"You never cease to surprise me! Just when I think I have got you figured out, you do something that just amazes me!"

He hooked his arm in hers and popped the umbrella open over them both. He was grinning from ear to ear.

"Sometimes, my dear Eponine, that's the greatest revenge of all."

SAINT VALENTINE

SHE WALKED AROUND THE block four times, or was it five? She had lost count. Her heart was shuddering in her chest, and she did not want to go home. She had left school early, feigning a bad headache.

Jeremy, the school's music teacher, had run after her and pushed the bouquet of roses into her arms. She had blushed so fiercely that she thought she would faint. And then she had fled, clutching the thornless roses to her chest.

Now she walked in seemingly endless circles around her building, occasionally inhaling the rich and fresh fragrance of the roses. It would be dark soon, and she didn't know what she should do. It seemed that any decision would lead her down a road she did not wish to take. She did not wish to bring the flowers home. Julian would have a thousand questions, and she didn't think he would like her answers. She did not wish to throw the flowers away. Jeremy was a sweet young man who deserved better treatment than that. So she walked.

It had begun so innocently. Eponine had been correcting papers at her little table at the back of the classroom. The children had been given assignments about Candlemas and the feast day of Saint Brigid. It was mostly a lot of coloring and a few questions to answer. She sang Brigid's cauldron song to herself as she drew smiley-faces in the margins of her students' artwork.

"So, you're the one who taught them that song!"

Her heart leapt into her throat, and she dropped her pen. "Goodness, you scared me!"

"I'm sorry," he stepped into the classroom. He was a tall,

slender man with sturdy shoulders and blond hair that trailed into his eyes. It was cut close along the bottom and rather long on the top, giving him a very youthful look. "I didn't mean to startle you. I don't think we've been formally introduced. My name is Jeremy Peyton. I teach music here once a week."

She rose. "Oh, it's a pleasure, Mr. Peyton, I'm...."

"You're Eponine, I know exactly who you are." He blushed slightly. "The kids can't stop talking about you. Ms. Branch's class or the others. And please, call me Jeremy."

He came toward her and extended his hand. She shook it. His eyes lost focus for an instant as he touched her, then he blinked several times, seeming to clear his head. His eyes were the steely blue of the Atlantic and were fringed in the longest gilded eyelashes she had ever seen. He stepped away from her, dropping her hand and rubbing his suddenly sweaty palm as discreetly against his pant leg as possible.

"I'm sorry, I had no idea, you'd be so ... so ... beautiful." He was quite embarrassed now and looking away. "Excuse me, that was horribly unprofessional of me. Uhh, I'll be going now, sorry to bother you."

She looked at him with her head tilted to one side, trying not to laugh at his very real discomfort. She found him strangely disarming and gave him a warm smile.

"It was no bother, Jeremy, really. Actually, I would love to sit in on your class some time. Will you have my children next week?"

He digested her words and managed not to laugh. "Yes, your students are in my early class next week."

"Good, I will see you then!" Eponine gave him a dazzling smile, for she really was excited at the prospect of sitting in on his class.

"Yes," Jeremy laughed nervously and backed toward the door. "Say, are you going down to the cafeteria for lunch?"

Eponine nodded. "Yes, I am."

"Would you mind some company?"

"Mind? No, no. I would be ... delighted."

She fell into step with him and began to ask him all sorts of questions about his past, his education, his life in the city. She was surprised to find him waiting for her downstairs again the following day. He made some excuse of forgetting something he needed in his classroom and deciding to stay to eat lunch with the rest of the staff. He forgot something every day that week.

He was a very intriguing individual. He knew a handful of Irish drinking songs in Gaelic that he had picked up in the Dublin pubs one summer he'd spent there trying to learn the Celtic harp. He took black and white photographs all around the city in his spare time, when he wasn't teaching or studying for his master's degree in music at the New School.

ON THE MORNING OF February fourteenth, Eponine was sitting in the front of the room telling stories while the children worked on little mailboxes to house the Valentines that would be distributed later in the day during the party.

"Now in Rome, at the time Claudius was emperor, I believe, it was a crime to be a Christian. A crime punishable by torture and usually death," she told them gravely. "Many of the early saints are martyrs from this time period, Christians who would rather die then give up their faith.

"Now, at this time, there was an upright Christian man by name of Valentinus who was in the Roman prison awaiting execution for his beliefs. All the family he had in the world was his daughter, Julia, who was blind. His jailer was a kind man. Remember, not all Roman citizens agreed with the Emperor's decrees, but to violate them was to incur death upon themselves. This jailer, he was not a martyr. He had a large family that subsisted solely from his income, and he could not risk his life in such a manner. But he did what he could for Valentinus. He allowed Julia to come visit him every day and stay many hours there. He even promised to look after her upon Valentinus's death. The jailer was really a good man at heart.

"But the day came for Valentinus to be executed. Julia held her father and wept. He said to her, 'Daughter, I go now to a better place, to the loving arms of God. If you have faith as I do, you will know this is true. But I promise to send you a sign that I made it to my soul's home safely.'

"The jailer sat with Julia while the executioner took Valentinus away. He turned to her and said, 'Your father gave this to me to give to you upon the hour of his death. He told me I was not to read it to you.'

"He handed Julia a folded piece of parchment. She heard the axe fall and the crowd cheer. But her father did not cry out. Tears filled her eyes, and she said a prayer for his soul. She imagined a light all around him as his pure soul ascended into Heaven.

She closed her eyes, for the light seemed so very real. When she opened them, she found it was the sun that was so blinding.

"In her hand, she saw the parchment. Upon it was written the words, 'My Daughter, Believe in love and all is possible. I love you.' It was signed, 'Your Valentine.'

"Valentinus was killed on the fourteenth of February. And we commemorate his bravery, his faith, and his love every year on this day as we sign our sweet messages to one another, 'from your Valentine.'"

Most of the children had ceased their project making and were rapt with attention. Someone slowly applauded from across the room. Eponine was pleasantly surprised to see Jeremy there.

"I liked your story." He gave the children a mock-stern glance, which set them back to working on their Valentine mailboxes, and led Eponine out into the hallway. There sitting on a table was a bouquet of one dozen long-stemmed red roses.

"Goodness!" She bubbled over with giggles and gathered them up in her arms. "They are lovely!"

Jeremy blushed, "No lovelier than she who holds them. And I mean that, 'Ponine. I know you don't think of yourself as pretty. Well, I guess you aren't pretty; you're beautiful."

"Oh, you are quite silly, Mr. Peyton." She looked away, pretending to be absorbed in the inspection of the roses.

Impulsively, he took her hand and kissed it. "My dear 'Ponine, by God above," he sang, changing the words to "A Little Fall of Rain" to suit his present needs. "If I could win your heart with words of love!"

Something dawned on Eponine. She looked from Jeremy to the roses and back again. She dropped the flowers and ran into the classroom. Ms. Branch turned with a jolt from the chalkboard.

"Eponine? Are you all right?"

"No," she said. "I don't feel well at all. I think, I think I should get home."

"What's wrong?" The children began to murmur worriedly.

"I have quite a headache," she lied. "It's nothing serious, I am sure. But I best go home. I wouldn't want to get anyone else sick."

She smiled bravely and collected her bag. As soon as she was back in the hallway, she began to run.

Jeremy was waiting on the steps, slightly out of breath from having rushed to beat her there.

"I'm sorry," he stammered. "It was forward of me to give you those roses, but Eponine, I just can't get you out of my mind. Please, don't be angry with me!"

Eponine's chest ached dully to see him look at her with such pained affection.

"I am not angry with you." She smiled in spite of herself. "You have a beautiful voice."

He put the flowers into her arms and closed her hands over them.

"Take them," he whispered, urgently. "'Believe in love and all is possible.'"

Eponine feared she would faint. She turned and sprinted away from the school. She ran the few blocks home, but could not bring herself to go upstairs. She walked around the block to think.

Her feet had control over themselves as they took her round and round. Her mind reeled.

Jeremy was in love with her!

She had no idea what it could mean, only that it was doomed to fail. There was no way she could ever love him in return! And even if she could, she would break his heart when she left New York, when she left the world. And what about Julian?

What would Julian think? The icy dread stopped her nervous wandering. She shivered to think of his reaction. Would it be cold fury? Or burning rage? Would he threaten Jeremy?

Perhaps she could sneak the roses into the house and keep them in her room. She did not have the heart to throw them away; how could she do that to Jeremy? She feared that hurting him would still the music in his heart, and that thought tormented her as she made her way around the block again. But she could think of no other resolution than that, unless she left the school and let him forget her.

Yes, she could make him forget her. She knew a way that would work. A way that would gently remove her from his mind and heart. But something about that prospect saddened her. Thinking about his cool blue eyes turning away from her deepened her sorrow. Thinking about those eyes looking with love and longing upon another drove a spike into her heart.

He would sing to her, no doubt, bring her roses and take her photograph in black and white among the trees in the park. Eponine growled at these thoughts and imagined a perfect, cherubic, blonde waif.

She stumbled and realized it had grown dark out. While the sun had not yet set, it had slipped behind the tall buildings, throwing the street below into near-twilight shadow.

With her head hanging, Eponine forced herself to go into her building.

JULIAN WAS JUST SETTING a steamy pizza box down on the kitchen table. The ivory tapers in the cut-glass holders from Solstice were brightly flickering.

"You're just in time!" He was smiling. "We're having a Valentine's Day feast! Tah-da!"

He showed her the pizza, half pepperoni, which was his favorite, and half Blanca, which was hers.

"Look, they did a great job keeping the sauce off your half. I gave the guy a big tip. Ooh, pretty flowers . . . got an admirer at school?" He gave her a wink and a playful nudge, then went to set the table. He was taking it rather well, she thought.

Eponine slumped down at the table, the weary-looking roses lying across her lap. She had tears in her eyes.

"Yes," she croaked through a tight throat. "He is the music teacher."

"Music, hmmm? Can he sing or does he just play?"

"Both, I guess. He went to Ireland to study the harp a couple of summers ago."

"Ahhhh, Ireland. I like Ireland. They've got great pubs over there. Couldn't get used to the warm beer, though." He poured her a glass of ice water from the filtered pitcher and sat down across from her. "You going to put those in water, or just stare dreamily at them all night?"

She looked up miserably at him. "Jeremy, the music teacher, gave me a dozen red roses for Valentine's Day, Julian."

He looked perplexed. "Did he hurt you? Was he untoward?"

"No, he was actually very sweet to me. I think he's quite smitten."

Julian laughed. "Poor little mortal. I'd hate to be in his shoes. Ahhh, well." He bit into his pizza. Eponine could only stare.

"And you don't care?"

"Should I? It's not like he's harming you. What's wrong with a paltry little human having a crush on you? He hasn't tried to kiss you, has he?"

"No, not on the lips. He kissed my hand, though."

He raised an eyebrow at the image, but laughed it off. "Poor fellow, he has no idea what he's in for." Julian set his dripping slice down and stood up. "Oh, I almost forgot!"

He dashed back to his room and came back with a red paper shopping bag. It was tied at the handles by a white satin ribbon. Eponine was swamped with bitter confusion. Where was the jealousy? Where was the anger? Julian was acting as if he couldn't be bothered to care. He was acting as if he wasn't in love with her.

"It's no bouquet of red roses, but it's your Valentine from me."

She pulled the ribbon and peered into the bag. Inside was a medium-sized brown teddy bear. Around his neck was a red velvet ribbon upon which was strung a cardboard heart. Julian had written "Your Valentine" upon it.

"The store clerk said you'd like it. Well, at first she suggested lingerie, but I convinced her you really wouldn't appreciate that."

Eponine was speechless. She had nothing for him but a card she had not yet written.

"Thank you, Julian," she said, dazed, and took the crumpled roses and plush teddy bear to her room.

"Where are you going?"

"I am going to bed. I have had enough of today!" There were tears in her voice as she slammed her door.

Julian watched her go. He was beyond confused. He waited to see if she would return. It didn't look as if she were going to. He looked upon his nice dinner and sighed, his heart sinking. He pulled out his dog-eared copy of the February issue of *Cosmopolitan* and flipped through it.

He had done everything right. He'd even kept his cool about that horrendous mortal who was sniffing about his territory! He angrily tossed the magazine aside and went back out to finish his pizza.

"I hope she'll explain it to me in the morning." He flicked on the television. "Hey, *The Princess Bride* is on!"

With spirits lifted, he took his pizza and a can of Coke and sat down on the couch.

He was annoyed that Eponine's beau hadn't gifted her with chocolates instead.

VANITY

SHE CAME HOME WITH a long, thin rectangular box from

National Wholesale Liquidators over on Broadway. She disappeared into her room with it.

When dinnertime had come and gone with no sign of her, Julian went to her door and knocked.

Eponine didn't answer.

Quietly, he opened the door. She was sitting on a small, wobbly bench in front of a dressing table with a glass top, tubular silvertone legs, and an oval mirror attached to it.

Eponine was leaning forward on the bench, gazing into the mirror. It was the only one in the house besides the medicine cabinet in the bathroom.

She was crying.

Julian was taken aback. He wavered in the doorway, "'Nine? Are you okay?"

She didn't turn, only nodded, very slowly.

"Uh, no. I don't think you are." He came in and sat down on the corner of her bed. He looked at the reflection of her face, seeing himself there behind her. But they seemed miles away from one another.

He smiled and waved. Her focus wavered, and she made eye contact with his image.

"What do you want, Julian?" Her voice was hardly a whisper.

He shrugged. "Dinner. With you. Can you tear yourself away for an hour? Or are you too entranced with your own looks?"

She closed her eyes, and her forehead fell against the glass. "Go away."

He growled, straining to keep his patience. He had never seen her act this way. His concern ran deep; Eponine had experienced quite a bit in the past few days. He tried to speak gently to her. "What's going on?"

But when she turned to him, her eyes were as fierce and menacing as any divine creature's could be. "I said get out!"

He was speechless. He licked his suddenly parched lips and let out a long breath.

"Joy. . . ?" he said, gently.

She made no reply, just turned back to the mirror and pointedly ignored him until he left the room, closing the door behind him. Julian's hand lingered on the doorknob, and he debated with himself about going back and confronting her.

I'll give her a little time. Maybe she'll be willing to tell me what's wrong later.

IT WAS LIKE A circle of light that contained her whole soul. In it, Eponine could inspect every last bit of her face. If she turned right she could see her ears, the nape of her neck, the pale line of her part as it divided the mousy brown waves of her hair.

She tilted and twisted her head until she thought she had looked at every piece.

Then she started over.

But she could not find it. She could not find that spark of loveliness that she saw reflected in Jeremy's eyes and the eyes of many of the men she saw around her.

Her face was nondescript. Her skin was nothing like shimmering alabaster nor rich ivory, but instead looked more like plain and pale eggshells. Freckles dotted both of her cheeks and crept across her nose. Her nose was a little too straight, in her opinion, and from one angle a little too long and from another much too short. Her eyes, she thought, were a muddy brown, not clear and onyx-shaded like the women in Chinatown or bright and amber-colored like the ladies in the Irish pub she'd visited with Jeremy. Her lashes were as long as they needed to be, but nothing fancy. On the whole, she looked every inch as plain as she'd asked to be. She had wanted to blend in, to be anonymous. Looking down upon the Earth from on high, she had thought it would be better that way, easier to go unnoticed. But now, living in the body of a human, it tore at her soul to be just a face in the crowd. She had forgotten about the current of emotions in which it was so easy to drown, that being human meant shifting moods, uncertainty, jealousy, and a hundred other petty things.

Oh, why didn't I ask to be beautiful?

She laid her head upon her folded arms. Her brows arched like streaks of dirt across that blank slate of white.

Why does Jeremy look at me so, if I am not lovely? Is that why Julian is being so calm in all of this and letting me go so easily? Is he glad to be free of my attentions?

She shivered. Her flesh seemed to her to be molded of dough, dull and opaque. She trembled with the impotent anger and frustration that has plagued nearly every young woman since the dawn of time. Was she beautiful? Was she worthy? Tears began to gather again in the corners of her eyes, making them red and swollen. It turned her stomach to see herself in such a state.

As an angel, Eponine was majestic, flawless, peerless, incomparably lovely.

As a human, she was an ordinary girl and rife with the flaws that fill all human faces. Even wrapped in the dust of human flesh and sinking into the treacherous swamp of human doubt, she was still an angel within. She never took into account her joyful spirit, her warm smile, her innocent and loving nature. Instead, she sighed and wiped her tears with the back of her hand, not comprehending that even enveloped in that seemingly dull and ugly flesh, she still shone like a star.

I wish I had chosen to be beautiful.

ENVY

THE GIRL WAS HER worst nightmare made flesh.

Her name was Ursula, but Eponine despisingly called her "Cosette," after the sappy heroine in her favorite book, *Les Misérables*. This girl was in Jeremy's music theory class at the New School, and he talked about her regularly. She was a gilded soprano. She played three instruments. She spoke four languages. She was also a photographer in her spare time.

Jeremy had talked her into taking the class pictures at the Ukrainian School for practice.

Eponine was formally introduced to her at lunch. It was a perfectly awful way to end what already had been a rather dismal week for Eponine's self-esteem.

"Ursula, *this* is Eponine," Jeremy said, with a smile as bright as a summer day. He stepped back as they shook hands, his face showing his naïve belief that they would become fast friends.

Eponine smiled politely and attempted to ignore the gaze of those gorgeous seawater-green eyes as they traveled over her face. Ursula could not hide the smug grin that tugged at the corners of her mouth. She laughed brightly and gave Jeremy a playful pinch on the arm when she released Eponine's hand.

"Oh, silly! You had me worried. From the way you've been talking about her, I thought you were bringing me to see an *angel*. Why, she's just as plain as any girl!" She gave Eponine a conspiring wink. "I thought I'd have to eliminate you for the good of the rest of us women on the planet. You'd think he had looked upon Aphrodite herself to hear him go on about you!"

Jeremy blushed. "Well, maybe I exaggerate a little, but

you can see why, can't you? Don't you think she's wonderful, Ursula?"

Both Eponine and Ursula gave him an incredulous glare. He had *no* idea how to introduce two attractive women to one another. He put his arm around Eponine's shoulders and hugged her close. She hadn't managed to utter a word and still had no idea what to say. She smiled good-naturedly and gave Ursula the self-deprecating roll of the eyes that she had seen so many young woman do on television.

"She's just a peach, Jeremy, really." Ursula wasted a last glance on Eponine and then focused her attentions upon him. "Now did I hear you right, there is a dark room at this school?"

"Well," he looked a little embarrassed. "It's homemade. I put it together down in the cellar. Would you like to see it?"

"Oh, would I ever!" Her voice trilled like a flute, and he smiled to see her so interested in something he'd created. "Would you like to see it too, 'Ponine?"

She shook her head. She didn't even know about the darkroom in the cellar. He'd never uttered a word of it to *her* before. But he was giving *Cosette* the entire rundown of its supplies and capabilities without really waiting for her to reply.

"I have papers to grade," Eponine muttered in a voice that sounded like wind moaning in a hollowed-out log on a cold winter night.

"Okay, then I will see you after school," Jeremy told her with a distracted smile.

Ursula was pestering him with a hundred questions.

Did you even like *photography before you met him, Cosette?* Eponine wondered if her face betrayed her venomous thoughts.

"Oh," Ursula's radiant face fell. She gave a fabulous impersonation of distress as she realized Eponine was not coming along. "I guess if you have work to do. We'll miss you, though. It was nice to meet you."

"The pleasure was all mine." With a dignified air, Eponine turned and walked purposefully back to her classroom.

She sat and stared at the papers until the words swam, and still she couldn't concentrate. All she could see was Ursula's eyes like the sea and flesh like the snow and voice like the lark. She wondered if Jeremy would ever look upon her again.

For some reason she couldn't fathom, that thought made her cry.

AVARICE

IT WAS A TRICKY matter, money.

Not too much should just be *produced* out of their pockets, but not everything could be paid for by ... other means. Eponine and Julian had to keep a close eye on what they did so as not to draw attention to themselves.

Eponine was never much for fashion or flashy things, but somehow she was beginning to find that the accumulation of objects made her feel better.

She went out into Manhattan to shop that Saturday, alone. She bypassed her usual haunts on West Eighth Street and instead went uptown to the boutiques. She searched for hours to find the perfect sweater or skirt, a blouse to bring out the color of her eyes or her hair. But her success was very limited.

Frustrated, she went out to New Jersey's Garden State Plaza Mall the next day. Again, she went alone, slipping out before Julian was awake. It was much quieter and nearly tranquil in late February in comparison to holiday time.

But again, she found that nothing whatsoever brought out the hidden beauty lurking within her somewhere. Then she saw the beauty salon....

"So what would you like, honey? Blonde? Black?" the beautician asked. He was smartly dressed, all in black, and had a quick smile and an easy-going manner.

Eponine thought about it. She couldn't go blonde; that would look too much like that little tart, Cosette. It came to her in a spark of brilliance. "Make it red."

He chattered and trimmed and painted the thick dye through her hair. She loved the sensation of having her hair washed for her, then cleverly brushed and styled. By the end of it, she knew all about his mother, his boyfriend, and some worry about a blood test result. It was an easy thing to peek into the future and assuage his fears. He was so happy, he forgot to ask her for money.

She felt better once she was back in the mall, tossing her flame-red hair and thinking quite highly of herself for the first time in a week. The shop a few doors down from the salon sold glasses, but also advertised colored contact lenses. Eponine was intrigued.

"I don't need glasses, but could I still get colored contacts?"

"Of course," the violet-eyed optician laughed. "I don't need glasses either. I just have always wanted violet eyes. So *alluring*, don't you think? What color eyes have *you* always wanted?"

"What goes best with red hair?"

"I think green eyes look prettiest on a redhead."

"Then make mine emerald," Eponine told her.

The contacts felt funny at first and drove Eponine to distraction. But after a few times of taking them out and putting them back in again, they started to feel more comfortable. She got a box of five pairs of vibrant green contacts for forty dollars, materializing two crisp twenties from her pocket with a smile.

Next, she walked straight into Nordstom with her head held high. She let the two salesgirls dress her in whatever they saw fit and even agreed to let them take her downstairs to the MAC counter for a complete makeover. She cheerfully opened a Nordstom account and got fifteen percent off her entire purchase.

Eponine came away with her indigo cotton batik skirt and ruffled linen peasant blouse in a shopping bag; she wore instead a short skirt of sage green wool with a matching jacket and an embroidered silk shirt. She brought home a slim, tailored dress of black crepe and a pantsuit of mustard gold with a green chiffon blouse. Her feet were crammed into tight leather pumps with a fashionably thin heel and pointed toe. Two more pairs of similar shoes were in the shopping bag along with a thick wool winter coat with a real mink collar.

She bought shiny rings for her fingers and had her nails painted. She selected a slender gold watch and pearl drop earrings.

She was stunning.

The more people stared, the more Eponine smiled.

She saw them look at her clothes and her jewelry. She saw them admire her fiery hair and captivating eyes. But they never *saw* her, they only *looked* at her. Children didn't run up to her. Adults didn't smile and move out of her path. She was pushed and crowded and ignored in the evening rush hour. Just like everyone else.

She went to school Monday morning and Ms. Branch was shocked. But she smiled blandly and asked if Eponine had a job interview or some other special event. Eponine just demurred and gave her what she thought was a dazzling smile.

The children were not as eager to see her as they usually were. Eponine didn't notice that some of them were even afraid of the new her.

At lunch, she overheard Ursula grumbling catty remarks about her beneath her breath.

Eponine grinned, smug and satisfied.

Jeremy came to her table and, after what seemed like a moment of thought, he sat down across from her. He seemed nervous and simply stared at her for a long time. Eponine curled a lock of coppery hair around her fingers and gave him a coquettish smile that she had practiced for hours the night before.

"Wow, 'Ponine. Were they giving free make-overs or something?"

"You don't like it?" She gave him a pretty pout with her ruby-painted lips and blushed-up cheeks.

"No, no, it looks . . . gorgeous. It's just so different. You look like the cover of a magazine."

She sat up straighter, her eyes shining. "Do you mean it?"

"Yeah."

She preened. "Why, thank you."

"Yeah," he said, again, distractedly. "Hey listen, I have to go. I am, uhh, doing some color timing tests downstairs, and I, uhh, I had better make sure it's all done properly or our yearbook is going to look mighty strange." He laughed uneasily and glanced around the room with nervous eyes. He gave her a self-conscious smile and scooped up his tray, most of his lunch remaining untouched. "See you tomorrow, maybe."

Jeremy beat a hasty retreat from the cafeteria and Ursula nearly pounced on him, but he brushed her aside. She shot a black look toward Eponine.

Eponine grinned and flashed her emerald eyes at the sulky cherub. Ursula left the cafeteria in a huff.

Eponine gloated for the rest of the day.

SLOTH

THE SUN STREAKED IN through the windows. Julian basked in it. It was Sunday, which meant Eponine would not be getting up early to go anywhere. He stretched. He wondered what he should have for breakfast. But dozing was a much better option. It was well before nine in the morning, and he thought perhaps that he might climb out of bed about eleven, maybe noon.

He rolled over, wrapping the blankets up around him. The flannel sheets felt so soft and velvety, so warm against his scruffy cheeks.

He heard Eponine shut the bathroom door.

Damn, girl, don't you ever sleep in?

She had been acting funny lately. Ever since she'd brought home that vanity set she'd been moody and depressed. It wasn't at all like her. She'd been behaving strangely since Valentine's Day, come to think of it. He sighed and pondered getting out of bed and confronting her.

He listened for her in the next room. He heard the drawers open and shut, and the mirrored cabinet squeaking a little on its hinges. Then the shrill noise of the water turning on; it shifted to a staticky sound as it was diverted to the showerhead. The glass door quietly rumbled shut and the even staccato of the water was interrupted. She was in the shower now. It would be a good twenty minutes at least before she'd be done and he could to talk to her.

The hiss and splash was very melodic, he realized. He could hear the water rushing through the pipes in the wall beside his bed. It was . . . hypnotic. The sound drew him in, like a song he could barely hear that was always changing.

Julian closed his eyes. He followed the noise with his ears. It was like trying to catch a butterfly dancing on an errant wind. The water, along with the radiator's quiet ping, sounded like a stream chattering along over the rocks, leaves occasionally falling into it, dew drops sparkling in a glittering morning sunbeam, trembling, then falling like diamonds into the water.

He was sitting there, in a patch of silky green grass, the delicate kind that seems to sprout up only in the wake of rainstorms. The sun was dancing through the branches of stately trees in little swirls along the ground. He sighed and stretched out, dipping one bare foot into the stream. With one arm curled behind his head, he took a deep breath and dozed happily in the warm light and gentle breeze. A shadow fell across his face and he cracked one eye open. Eponine was there.

She seemed so tall and luminous with the prismatic corona of sunlight behind her. She was smiling, with the entire delight of the world flowing through her. She titled her head and laughed.

"Hey there, lazybones. What are you doing?"

"Waiting for you," he said with his usual rakish grin. He patted the ground beside him, and she dropped down to her knees. He rolled over onto his side and looked up into her eyes.

"Well, I'm here. Now what?"

"This." He breathed deeply and scooted down the bank a little and put his other foot in the stream. His eyes drifted shut, then slowly opened again. "Nice, isn't it?"

She laughed again, a sweet, shivering sound like birdsong, and produced a small, carved wooden comb out of thin air. She gathered his head into her lap, stretching her legs out beneath his neck. She combed his thick dark hair over her thigh. Julian lay there, toes being tickled by the stream, sunbeams slanting across his face, Eponine combing his hair and singing. Nothing could be nicer.

He dozed off, comfortable as a cat.

HE TWITCHED AND WOKE. His mouth felt sticky and his head ached.

The light was dim and he was in his own bed.

He sat up and felt queasy.

His bedside clock read 3:56 PM.

"Oh, not even...!"

He shambled into the kitchen. The microwave agreed and so did the VCR in the living room. The house was quiet. Eponine was gone. He stood dumbly in the middle of the kitchen, trying to remember what it was he wanted to ask her about. His head felt like it was full of cotton. Whatever it was, he could ask her when she got back. She was probably at the museum, or the Farmer's Market, or out for a walk in the park. She'd be home soon and he'd remember what it was he needed to tell her by dinnertime.

He got a Coke out of the fridge and went back to his room. There was a hockey game on TV. Although he didn't care much for the Red Wings, he did want to see them beat the Mighty Ducks.

But he had fallen back asleep by the second intermission.

GLUTTONY

IT WAS SHORTLY AFTER one a.m. when Julian woke up.

He was quite awake.

He was bouncing off the walls awake.

And he was hungry.

Out in the kitchen, he made a stunning discovery.

Eponine was not at home. Nor did it look as if she'd been home at all that day. It was the middle of the night on a Sunday, now Monday. She should have been in bed hours ago.

The door to her room was half open and dark and full of shopping bags. She'd been home, at least, but she was gone now. It was not like her to stay out so late on a school night. He searched the kitchen for a note but found none. Nothing in the front room either, nor in his room, or even the bathroom. This wasn't at all like her, and his dreadful concern came crashing back down upon him. Her mood swings and strange behavior, and now this . . . it didn't make sense.

He felt his stomach sink.

Where could she be?

He began to pace. He could feel that he had too much energy and that it was not a positive kind. He bundled up. Outside, the night wind seared his face with cold. It sank deep into his body. He felt like his very blood would freeze beneath all the layers of wool he wore.

Yet, when he wandered into the newsstand/deli, he went straight for the ice cream.

Moments later, he was strolling the bleak night eating a pint of Ben and Jerry's Half-Baked using a milk chocolate Lindt bar as a spoon.

He was surprised to find how much better it made him feel. It didn't staunch his stomach's cry for something solid, however. He found himself sitting at the counter at Veselka with a cup of its famous coffee in his hands. Veselka was one of the pair of twenty-four-hour Ukrainian cafés in his neighborhood, and it still didn't cease to amaze him that there were *two*, and that both Veselka and Kiev each pulled in enough of their own business to stay afloat. He did find it somewhat disturbing that when the traffic was light he could see one restaurant from the other.

Julian ate a full dish of spinach and cheese pierogi with a side of kashi and half a loaf of challah bread. He eyeballed the three-bean chili but decided against it. As he paid at the front counter, he noticed they sold Lindt bars, too. And they had the chocolate cream-filled kind, his favorite. He bought two and went back out into the night, regretting the three refills of coffee.

By the time he felt worn out enough to go home, it was past four a.m. He had eaten both chocolate bars and was feeling sick. Eponine would know what to do. He hoped she'd be there.

Her door was shut. Julian breathed a sigh of relief that she was home at last and carefully crept into her room.

He bit his tongue not to cry out.

Her hair was *bright red*.

He backed out of the room, his nausea suddenly doubled. Julian's stomach surged and he ran for the bathroom, tripping on a black high-heeled shoe.

He stumbled to his knees on the cold tiled floor and slid forcefully up to the toilet. He was momentarily distracted from the tide of vomit rising in his throat by several bottles of make-up, nail polish, and perfume.

"What the...?" His abdominal muscles seized, and his words were drowned out by the surge of sticky, half-digested chocolate and gobs of kashi. He draped himself over the bowl and retched repeatedly. His hair worked loose from his ponytail and fell directly into the whole mess.

He wanted to cry.

He lay there panting on the frigid floor. He needed a shower. He wanted to wake Eponine and get lost in the tenderness of her sympathy. But he lay where he fell, gasping for breath and gagging on the bitter residue left in his mouth. He was reasonably certain it would be some time before he'd be able to even *look* at chocolate again, much less eat it.

"This has to be the dumbest thing I have ever done to myself."

WRATH

AFTER A SHOWER WITH some of Eponine's very tranquil scented Vert de Bamboo shampoo, Julian felt like a new man.

It was only just after five o'clock on Monday morning, so Eponine would be awake soon. He wanted to speak to her. Especially now, after he'd seen her hair and all the shopping bags from the mall. He went into the kitchen to put on some coffee. He noticed her black trenchcoat tossed carelessly over the back of one of the chairs. It wasn't like her not to hang her coat on the hook by the front door. He took it to the front hall and hung it beside a coat he had never seen before, black and plush with a

fur collar. It was brand new. Why in the world had she bought a
new coat? She had her trenchcoat that she loved to wear, as well
as the gray Navy coat she'd gotten at the military surplus over on
West Eighth.

There is really something wrong with that girl.

He noticed that a small pile of papers lay strewn on the
kitchen floor. They must have fallen from the pocket when he'd
picked up her coat. It was a handful of receipts and a few notes
written in the scrawling script she used when she was in a hurry.
Each one was folded in a tight little square, some weird habit that
she had acquired since coming to New York. One was bulkier
than the rest, and was folded in a much neater fashion. Written
carefully across one side was one thing: "Jeremy."

Julian felt nausea rise again, but it was quickly replaced by ice
in his veins. A deep cold fury washed through him and settled into
a heavy lump in his belly. Without thinking, he unfolded the paper.

It was written on the stationery from Kiev and had the current
date on it, along with the time: 1:15 AM. While he had been
gorging himself at Veselka, she had been not even three blocks
away at Kiev. If he had walked directly home, he would have
seen her there, no doubt with a plate of boiled cheese pierogi. He
sighed; Eponine liked Kiev's pierogi better than Veselka's.

His eyes unwillingly returned to the note.

"My Dearest Jeremy. . . ."

Julian looked away. The coffee maker gurgled, and he stared at
the dark liquid slowly dribbling into the decanter as steam coated
the underside of the cabinet. He shouldn't read the letter; it wasn't
addressed to him.

"I think of you often, more often that I care to admit to
anyone, including myself."

Damn it! This is none of your business.

"There is no way we could ever have a relationship, you and I.
But sometimes I cannot help but dream."

His blood froze. The lump of ice in his stomach grew and
began to creep down his legs.

"I dare say I shall never show you this letter, but I write
it anyway, thinking it will perhaps clear my heart of these
wandering images of you. But these feelings you must have for
me . . . I wonder what shape they would take, were you given free
rein to express them.

"The other night, I had such a wonderful time with you at

the pub. Black 47 is an amazing band, and I am ever-grateful to you for introducing me to their music. And I much admire your restraint when you found me both tipsy and ticklish!"

Julian's cheeks burned, slowly melting his frozen insides and setting them to boil.

So, that's where she's been! He had known she was planning to meet with some of the teachers for drinks after school last week, but it hadn't occurred to him that she and Jeremy might have gone off somewhere together afterwards.

"I could see in your eyes you wanted more from me, but I was happy that the gentleman prevailed and you settled for a kiss."

He crushed the paper in his shaking fist.

The other bits of paper were on the table, and he went through them like a madman until he found it: Jeremy's contact information—phone number, address, e-mail—all written in a boxy, compact script.

He was dressed in a flash and stuffed his hair into a dark blue knit watchcap. He crammed the note and the address into his pocket with his gloves and was gone before he could think about what he was doing.

THE SIX TRAIN HE caught made every single stop between Astor Place and the Upper East Side.

Julian paced the car, almost snarling with impatience. Sometimes he sat for a stop or two, then got up and began moving again. One of the few other people up and about that early was watching him. She had dark hair and eyes and regarded him over the top of a book. She was reading *Les Misérables*. She reminded him of Eponine.

"Can I ask you a question?" he said, finally turning to meet her gaze.

"Is it about directions? People *always* ask me for directions," she laughed. "Must be a gypsy thing."

His brow furrowed. He noticed the glossy braid that was draped over her shoulder and the hem of a tattered silk patchwork skirt that peeked out from under her black overcoat. "Well, actually, yeah ... do you know if this train stops near Seventy-Sixth Street?"

"Has a stop at Seventy-Seventh. Where are you trying to go?"

"East Side. All the way east," he said, trying not to grind his teeth.

She was nonplussed. "Sure, walk a block down and take the cross-town bus. I can show you where. I'm heading to the Met Museum, and Seventy-Seventh is as good a stop as Eighty-Sixth for me."

She gave him a sincere smile. He softened for a moment and sat beside her.

"Don't get too comfy. Here's our stop." She hopped up and deftly slipped her bookmark in place, put the book in her little blue backpack with a blonde cartoon girl on it, and slipped it over her shoulder. She crossed the train's threshold just as the doors opened. Her timing was impeccable. Julian had to jog a few steps to catch her as she dashed up the stairs. She did not stop to check and see if he was following.

It's sink or swim with this girl!

As if she could hear his thoughts, she glanced back and, with a sly smile told him, "If you can't keep up, *gadjo*, don't bother getting on the wagon."

She did pause for him to catch up at Lexington Avenue. The light was red. Julian was pretty sure if it had been green he'd have fallen far behind. It irritated him how winded he was already! The girl turned south and led him cheerfully to the next block and the bus stop.

"Here we are . . . coming on six o'clock, bus should be here any minute. Your Metrocard should let you transfer for free."

"It's awful early to be going to a museum, isn't it?" He thought about Eponine's frequent visits and couldn't remember her ever leaving before nine in the morning.

"I have an internship that starts at seven, and the employee cafeteria opens at six. We're doing an installation. Thankfully it's almost done."

Julian nodded grumpily and leaned on the bus stop pole. He was trying to return his breathing to a normal rhythm. "Still damn early to be up and perky."

Her eyes narrowed a moment. "I prefer the term '*frightfully energetic*' to '*perky*,' thankyouverymuch!" She gave him a wink. "Besides, it's only 'damn early to be up' if you've gone to bed!"

"I see. Well, thanks for your help."

"You look awful. You need a blessing," she said with the same imperturbable grin. Impulsively, she pulled off a glove and took his bare hand in hers. "May joy be yours all the days of your life."

Julian felt a wave of *something* rush through him. Or was it just the shock of feeling this stranger's warm fingers touching his skin? Before he could recover, the girl was trotting off, tossing her multi-colored chenille scarf over her shoulder and giving him a wave before disappearing around the corner.

AT A QUARTER TO seven, Jeremy was skipping down the stairs of his shoebox of a rent-controlled studio. It was small but cheap, and it was in a lovely old stone building overlooking a small park and the East River. He was quite surprised to find someone on the front stairs waiting for him.

Julian wished he had a cigarette in his hand; somehow it would have made the mood just perfect. He locked eyes with the pretty-boy blond as soon as he stepped out into the crisp morning air, and smiled. Jeremy was taken aback, but returned the smile and made for the opposite side of the steps, away from Julian. Julian cut him off. He was grinning now.

"Hi," Jeremy said, cautiously. "Do I know you?"

"Nope."

"Then, uhhh, what do you want?"

Julian sighed and whistled through his teeth. "Something I don't think I am going to get. But that's not important."

Jeremy took a step back and unconsciously pulled his book bag across his chest in a defensive posture.

Julian laughed darkly. "Smart boy."

"What do you want? If it's money, I've got forty bucks and a Metrocard on me. Just take it, okay?"

"I don't want your money, idiot. Don't you think I would have hit you over the head or shot you by now if I did?" Julian advanced a step, watching Jeremy struggle to retain his position. "I want to know something."

"What?"

"What are your intentions with Eponine?"

"Eponine?" Jeremy couldn't hide his surprise; he almost laughed. "Who are *you*, her brother?"

"Just call me a concerned third party," Julian folded his arms.

"Boy, are you a lousy liar." Jeremy shook his head. "You must be Julian. She's told me about you. And honestly, I have been wondering when you'd come breathing down my neck. Platonic, ha! I've never believed a word of it."

Julian's face flushed hot, and he began to quake. He advanced the few steps between them, put both hands around Jeremy's throat, and pinioned him against the wall.

"What do you want with her? Answer me, now." He closed his fingers over the windpipe, feeling the delicate bones there. Jeremy's Adam's Apple bobbed helplessly, fluttering like a trapped insect in his iron grip. The color began to rise into Jeremy's face and then faded.

He made a strangled sound and Julian gave him a good shake, pelting his skull against the masonry façade.

"What was that? Were you saying something? I can't hear you."

Jeremy nodded, and tried to swallow. Julian slowly released him, and the other man collapsed. He rubbed his throat and glared daggers up at Julian.

"I should call the police," he rasped.

"I know where you live."

"That's a threat."

"No, I call that a promise. Now talk. Eponine...."

"Do you really want to know?" He struggled to pull himself up by the railing. He leaned heavily onto it for a moment, catching his breath. "I'll tell you. The truth is, I don't know what I want from her. I have never met anyone like her. And something tells me I never will again."

Julian rolled his eyes.

"She makes me feel like no one else." Jeremy's gaze wandered across the street, over the bare treetops. "You know how a woman looks at you sometimes? And you can see how she wants you? In her eyes, you can see how she sees you?" He paused, expectantly.

"No," Julian said, humorlessly. "But, please, go on."

"Some girls look at you like you're dinner, like you're prey. Some girls look at you and you know that they are undressing you in their minds. Some size you up for wealth. You can see their eyes on your clothes, your shoes, your hair, everything, taking it all in, trying to guess how much money you have. But Eponine.... When she looks at you, all you can see in her eyes is love. It's like she is looking right through you, clear into the center of your soul. Like she sees all your faults and forgives them. She can see who you really are, and she can still love you."

He turned toward Julian with a glazed expression.

"Don't tell me you've never seen it. You live with her. You see her morning and night. You *must* have seen it." Jeremy's eyes grew shadowed. "I see it when she talks about you. And when she looks at me, I can see the *possibility* of that love, and I crave it. I want her like nothing else."

Julian recoiled as if he'd been slapped. His shadowed and bloodshot eyes narrowed. Something glinted there like quicksilver: a moment there, then gone.

"You had better take care, Jeremy." His voice had gone stone cold, and he appeared even more menacing. "She won't love you the way you want her to. She can't."

People began to meander out into the streets, walking dogs, jogging, heading out for work. It was a cold and bright late winter Monday in Manhattan, just like any other.

"You don't know that. You can't presume to tell me who Eponine can love and who she can't," Jeremy said defiantly.

Julian laughed. *Dear heavens, this ass is arrogant.*

"Give it up, little boy. Eponine isn't for you. Go find yourself someone more suited to your level. Someone daft, someone blonde." *Someone mortal.*

Julian squared his shoulders and walked away. He was enveloped by the shadows that still clung between the walls of the narrow street as he vanished from Jeremy's sight.

LUST

EPONINE RETURNED HOME IN mixed spirits on Monday afternoon. Jeremy seemed to find her lovely, yet he also seemed afraid of her. He was nervous after school, and for the second time that day, pushed *Cosette* aside. That made her smile, yet his behavior seemed distant from her as well. And now that she thought about it, the children weren't their usual selves, either.

What's wrong, I wonder? I'm beautiful now, aren't I?

Her delicate brow was creased with thought and worry when she entered the apartment. She was muttering to herself as she stumbled into the hallway, dragging the front door closed behind her. She drew a breath to call a greeting to Julian. But the only sound that came was from her backpack hitting the floor. Color rushed to her face.

Julian was sitting in his favorite chair reading the letter she had written in secret to Jeremy. A letter she had never intended anyone's eyes to see but her own. Julian's face blanched and he slowly turned, avoiding looking directly at her like a child who has been caught in the act of something he knew better than to do.

His gaze finally traveled up to meet her own, and by the time his eyes settled on hers, he was open-mouthed and nearly trembling. He rose, letting the letter flutter to the floor, forgotten.

"Eponine.... What happened to you...?"

"What do you think you're doing?" she cried, running to catch hold of the letter and tripping over her own high heels. In a near-panic, she kicked them off and stuffed the letter into her pocket. Her eyes burned with tears and it made the contact lenses hurt, but she refused to let Julian see her cry. She wanted to fall through the floor and disappear.

Julian stood rooted to the spot and watched her. Her movements were jerky and quick, almost desperate. He nearly dizzied himself looking from her eyes to her clothes to her hair. He thought he was going to be sick again.

"Eponine..." he began again, but could not find the words to finish.

"*What?*" she hissed at him, hastily swiping at her eyes and smearing her make-up.

Julian bristled. "What do you think you're doing? You look like a . . . well, like something I don't think you want to be compared with."

She gasped, insult flaring hot in her cheeks. "It's none of your business!" Her control shattered, and the tears fell.

"Like *hell* it's not my business, I am your guardian, remember? Supposed to be looking out for you! And look at you . . . you dyed your hair! You have something in your eyes to make them green! And those clothes...!" He felt tears stinging his own eyes. "And because of what? That *Jeremy*? That stupid, useless, disgusting *mortal*?"

His steely fingers had her roughly by the arm before she could react, and his other hand jammed deep into her pocket. He deftly slid away from her with the letter in his hand. He methodically tore it into tiny pieces. His eyes seemed as if they would burn right through her. Then, without losing that piercing eye contact, he backed into the kitchen, lit a burner on the stove, and dropped the bits into the gas flame.

"I could so easily do the very same to him. And I would like to. I would like it very much."

Eponine's body shook, whether from sorrow or fury, Julian couldn't tell. He watched the small muscles at the edge of her jaw quiver and guessed she was angry.

His temper ebbed for only a moment, replaced by plain shock. He had never seen Eponine *angry*.

She forced a calm note into her voice. "So, are you telling me that you are *jealous*?"

His eyes narrowed. "Of a skinny, ugly little human? Please, spare me!"

A darkly triumphant smile tugged up just one corner of Eponine's painted mouth. "How do you know he's skinny and ugly? Or stupid, useless, and disgusting, for that matter? How do you know anything about him at all?"

Julian returned the smile with a wry and bitter twist. "I followed him, of course. Had to make sure he wasn't some mad rapist or something. I won't have *my* ass raked over the coals back home because you go running off to have your jollies in a back alley with some stranger."

He enjoyed seeing the minuscule flinch of the skin around her eyes and mouth as he spat the words at her.

"Not only is he ugly," Julian sneered, upping the ante, "but he's a coward. I mean honestly, Eponine, if you are going to go falling for some paltry human, at least make him a respectable specimen!"

Eponine rolled her eyes. "I am finished with this discussion. In fact, until further notice, I am finished with *you*."

"Excuse me?" Julian recoiled as if she'd slapped him, then advanced on her, his hands clenching and unclenching at his sides. "What does *that* mean?"

She paused with her hand on her bedroom door and spun on her heel. "What, have you lost what little brains you have left in your head? You've crossed the line, Julian. I don't need you or your drama. I am done speaking to you. Completely. Until further notice. Is that understood, or shall I explain again but with smaller words this time?"

He threw her against the door, knocking her head into the wood. He leaned hard against her shoulders. "This is bullshit and you know it."

She tried to kick him, but her stockinged feet slid on the hardwood floor. Julian held her very painfully by the shoulders, his fingers digging into her flesh, to keep her from sliding down. It probably would have hurt her less to just let her fall. He wavered between feeling righteous in his revenge and guilty for harming her.

She fought helplessly in his grip and tried to keep from whimpering.

"You're a bastard, Vengeance, and I hate you! I hate you!" She flung the words at him like a weapon, meeting his eye with a fierce gaze that let him know in no uncertain terms she had meant every word.

He let go and she landed flat on her bottom with a stifled yelp.

"But you love *him*. The *mortal*. That's disgusting." He loomed over her and pulled her hair until she cried out. "And what is this? What possessed you to *do that*?"

"Leave me alone!"

"No," he said, crouching down beside her. His voice was measured and calm and utterly terrifying. "Not until you explain some things to me. Obviously, when I let you out of my sight, you get yourself into trouble ... dyeing your hair, sticking things in your eyes, falling for humans!"

"You get away from me and get away from me now!"

He felt deeply sick at heart to see her scrambling to get free of him, to see Joy so filled with raw, ugly emotion. But his cruel nature prevailed, and he showed her a serpent's smile.

Julian pulled her chin up so he could look directly into her overly bright green eyes. "Or else what? You're going to ... what? Hurt me? Leave me? Go home? Run to Jeremy?" He mocked her openly. His anger and jealousy flowed through him, turning his blood to ice.

She collapsed into tears. Her shoulders caved in, and she fell forward, pressing her forehead against her knees. And then she continued to melt, sliding out of his grasp until she lay supine on the floor. Her spine was twisted uncomfortably, but she made no motion to right it. One cheek was pressed against the woodgrain and one arm was splayed out before her, the other pinned beneath her. Julian watched the tiny rivers of tears flow silently from her eyes and puddle on the floor.

He sat back on his heels. He had no idea what to say. He had never been so angry with one of his own kind before. Words tumbled over one another without much thought.

"Sometimes, I want to take you in my arms and destroy you, Eponine," he whispered, hoarsely. "Do it quickly and gently, before this world can kill you slowly. You are too good for it, too pure, too beautiful. Look what it's done to you already."

He lifted a lock of her hair and let it sift through his fingers. It fell into Eponine's eyes, but she did nothing about it. Her gaze was distant, dead. He had no idea if she was even listening to him.

"This world is despair and darkness," he continued. "Joy cannot live here without being crushed."

"This world needs me." Hers was the voice of a breath of wind. "Needs me sometimes to touch the face of this Earth with a body made from dust."

"Does it need your heart?" Julian surprised himself by finding his voice choked and his words faltering. "Does it need you to love one of them?" At last, he voiced the sharp sliver of jealousy that had been paining him so deeply.

She stirred and pulled herself up onto her elbow with a groan. "Why do you think I love him?"

"Well, for starters, your letter. . . ."

"That wasn't addressed to you. That, no one was supposed to read. Not even Jeremy," she sighed. "Especially not Jeremy."

"Do you love him?"

"I don't know. I won't lie to you and say no. But I cannot say yes, either." She blew the hair out of her face. "To tell you honestly, Julian, I feel things I can't explain. Hurt and misery for no reason, followed by ecstasy. When I close my eyes to dream at night, I see his face, and yours." She began to cry again, but she wasn't aware of it. "When he kissed me, it was just the once, at the pub up by the Port Authority . . . when he kissed me . . . they were your lips. It was New Year's Eve all over again. It was your kiss."

She was in anguish, and it was pristine and perfect, like a martyr. She was fragile and small, yet at once she seemed to possess strength without measure and calm without end, like an angel.

"Your light, it's dimmed." His voice was tender and sad. He reached out and touched her eyelashes, running his finger along the edge of her eyelid. "Let me see your eyes. . . ."

She stared at him in wonder. He touched the edge of the green sphere in her eye. It stuck immediately to his dry fingertip and pulled away as easily as the petal of a flower. He flicked it aside. Eponine drew back when he moved for the other eye. She stared at his fingertip as it neared her pupil, then turned her gaze to his eyes. They were so much darker than they had been before. They were blacker than black, his own pupils widened so far they nearly touched the ring of dark that circled his sable-colored irises.

She blinked suddenly, her eyes feeling fresh and free without the bothersome lenses. She felt alive and light, so very light, as if she would rise straight off the floor.

His eyes closed and he tilted his head forward, his forehead pressing against her cheek. She felt the faint sheen of cool sweat there on his skin and breathed in a scent of spice.

Julian looked up and found himself smiling. There was Eponine. The world was right again. The make-up was washed away by her tears. And her eyes, yes, Eponine's eyes, sweet and placid eyes, light hazelnut brown eyes with that hint of golden shimmer. He'd seen a street vendor selling a stone the very color of her eyes on the way to Chinatown. He ought to buy one to keep in his pocket, so when he wanted to see her, he could look into the little replica of her eyes.

Now those eyes were here, and true again, no longer flat and brilliantly green, but dark and dazzling. He could see the light gathering behind them again.

She looked at him with such an open expression of trust and curiosity that it made his breath catch.

He hesitantly reached up to stroke her hair, to tame that one loose strand that had gotten caught in the corner of her soft trembling lips and slip it behind her ear.

They gazed at one another for a long moment, unable to move, unable to speak, unable even to breathe. Eponine's breath hitched and she let out a shuddering sigh.

"It was your kiss."

As her words caressed his ears, he brought his lips to hers. Gently, they met, just a brush in passing, feather-soft.

Her spine straightened and she pressed forward into him, crushing his lips against his teeth and throwing her arms around him. He tottered back and caught her in his lap.

The room spun into a blur of illumination as a fierce corona enveloped them both.

Her mouth was ravenous against his, and he drank her in. He heard music and laughter. They were filled to bursting with one another's light. Their thoughts sparkled like jewels upon a cloud in that infinitesimal yet eternal realm in the space between their lips. Within this kiss, they could look unashamed upon the soul of the other. It was a moment stolen from time, when the passions of two creatures of divine essence collided in a tiny apartment in the heart of New York City.

The first star of evening shone out of the shadowing sky, bright and nearly terrible to behold for an instant. In that instant, a wish was made.

And granted.

When his shoulder struck the floor, the reverie shattered.

Eponine turned away. Julian lay on his side, panting. He gingerly touched her shoulder, and she jumped as if he'd burned her. From the look in her wide and wild eyes, he thought he might have.

"'Nine," he whispered. "Joy. . . ."

Her face showed both rapture and terror. "What have we done?"

Julian looked about him. The city was silent. Not a hint of traffic, sirens, dogs . . . not a sound. Then the last rays of a blood-red sunset slipped away and the hush faded with it. A car rolled by beneath the window. For a moment, U2 soulfully sang "Angel of Harlem" to them.

They caught their breath and struggled to their feet. Eponine glanced all around, agitated. Julian leaned onto the kitchen counter. He reached up into the cabinet for a glass, filled it with water, downed it, filled it again, and handed it to Eponine. She was dim and distracted, but took the glass and drank it dry.

"What's wrong?" Julian whispered, afraid that he would somehow injure her with his voice.

"I don't know," she answered, still looking helpless. She nuzzled her face against his. "But I do know we shouldn't be. . . ."

"Shouldn't be . . . what? Shouldn't be doing this? Why not?" Without realizing, he had put his arms protectively around her.

She shrugged. "I don't know, but I'm afraid."

His embrace tightened, and he laid his cheek atop her head. His thoughts turned to the question of what would become of her if her purity were to be compromised. He wondered if it would make any difference at all if it were to be his doing, as opposed to some mortal. And if it was a mutual desire, if it really was love. . . .

He banished such thoughts from his mind. He couldn't bear to think of Eponine in such a manner, not right then, with her there in his arms.

She looked up at him. Her face was both radiant and mournful.

"I think I need to go lie down."

He nodded. "Of course."

He released her but she clung to him. "No," she cried into his chest.

"What's wrong, Joy?"

"I couldn't bear to be away from your side at this instant."

"And the next?"

"No, I couldn't bear that, either."

"All right." He led her to her room and laid her down on her bed. He lit two candles on her bedside and watched the light dance on the waves of her flame-colored hair. It was like the night of the power outage, when she had invited him to her bed. It had been all innocence, yet his thoughts had wandered. His thoughts always seemed to wander when he lingered next to her for too long. Again, he pushed aside memories. He was so adept at it now, shoving aside images and ideas, memories and thoughts. Down they tumbled into the darkness of his mind, taking refuge there with his darker side; perhaps these thoughts would do one another good.

He was relieved to see that Eponine was smiling.

"Yes?" He sat beside her prone form on the bed, feigning a smile of his own.

"I think I'm beautiful. . . ." She let out a long sigh. "I have been very stupid this week . . . this month . . . this whole time. I hope you can forgive me."

He laughed. "I know you're beautiful. I have always known."

"I don't hate you, Vengeance. I'm so sorry I said that," she said, her voice faltering. She was drifting. "You're nothing like the rest of us."

"I understand, Joy," he whispered, although he really did not. He drew her comforter up and around her.

"Stay with me, please." She reached out for his hand.

"Right by your side, for as long as you'd like." He was suddenly struck by the gypsy girl's words that morning: *May joy be yours all the days of your life.*

She sighed and curled up on her side, taking his hand with hers.

He sat up and watched her for a long time, long enough for the candles to begin to gutter. Long enough for his mind to begin to wander again. And wander it did, right down that primrose path.

He finally lay down beside her, carefully cradling his body around hers. When she felt him there, Eponine shifted in her sleep, drawing him close against her. She made a soft, contented noise and was still again.

He sighed.

Is lust with an angel still a deadly sin?

ABSOLUTION

THE RAIN WHISPERED AND tapped on the window, and the room was bathed in a soft, shifting light. Julian rolled over and was surprised to find an acre of bed before him. He came fully awake and made the startling realization that he was lying amid a sea of soft blue sheets and pillows in Eponine's room. He lay still and drank in the softness of her surroundings and the comfort of her scent. It took him a long moment to realize that she was gone. Not just from the bed, but from the apartment. Her little brass clock read roughly nine thirty-five.

He groaned. "It's Tuesday."

Eponine was at school. His heart went cold. At school. With Jeremy.

He was surprised at how disappointed he was that she was not there beside him. He had very much looked forward to opening his eyes to a new day and seeing her lying there, just within arm's reach.

Julian sighed and dragged himself from the loving tangle of her blankets. His clothes were rumpled and twisted, and the scent of her bed was on them. He noticed it and smiled without thinking.

In the kitchen, the coffee was made and there was a Post-It on the oven door.

Julian—
I have left you fresh bagels. They are keeping warm in the oven. Please don't forget to TURN THE OVEN OFF! I will be home at lunchtime. I will see you then. I'll miss you today.
Ever yours, Eponine

He pulled out a sesame seed bagel and found the cream cheese and settled down with that and a cup of coffee on the windowseat. The radiator hissed and rattled beneath the folded blanket that served as a cushion. The pillows propped up there were nice and warm as well. He shamelessly curled up with his breakfast and watched the rain.

His thoughts inadvertently headed back to the night before. At least his nightmares had the good sense to stay away most of the time! Why did his mind insist on dawdling over such thoughts about Eponine!

It had been a strange weekend.

He wondered if she was all right with everything that had happened. Her note was just like any other note that she'd ever left him. But it still filled him with exquisite, quiet warmth.

Julian watched the mist swirling in and about the naked tree-tops and gray stone buildings. People bustled by with umbrellas and brightly colored slickers. Although he would deny it if anyone ever caught him, he nearly glowed with happiness.

EPONINE STEPPED OUT INTO the chilling rain. Her skirt dragged on the wet front steps, but she didn't care. It felt too good to have the water fall all over her. It felt cleansing. It felt holy.

She took the hair stick out and let her shimmering red locks fall down her back. Her umbrella was in her bookbag.

It was only a couple of blocks between her apartment and the school, and as soon as she turned onto her street she saw him.

He was waiting, watching the sidewalk.

She slowed her steps, but he couldn't help but notice her there.

He stood straighter and smiled.

She blushed.

He looked away.

Before they knew it, they were standing in front of one another, blushing furiously in the rain.

"Mornin'," Julian said.

Eponine laughed. "It's twelve-thirty."

He shrugged. "No one woke me."

"I didn't have the heart to do it." She giggled into her glove. "You aren't *really* angry. Now come on, I have an errand to run. I want you to come with me."

She led the way downtown, toward South Mercer. She stopped in front of one of the high-priced beauty salons.

"'Nine. . . ? What are you doing?"

"Trying to undo some of this madness that I have wrought."

She gave him her bravest smile and tugged unconsciously at a curl that had fallen over her shoulder. Then she headed up the stairs and opened the door. Julian followed, his face carefully devoid of emotion.

Eponine grinned at the receptionist. "Hi, my name is Eponine. We spoke on the phone this morning?"

"Oh yes, wow, your hair is gorgeous. Are you sure you want it cut?" There was genuine concern in her voice. It was going to pain her to put scissors to that hair. "And that *is* the natural color, right?"

Eponine only nodded. "It is. It'll grow back. But those kids don't have that luxury. I want to do this. I really do."

The receptionist's eyes got misty and she smiled. "Right this way. Is your friend going to cut his hair, too?" She looked eagerly at the thick dark curls of Julian's ponytail.

"Oh, no!" Eponine looked a little horrified. "No, he just came for moral support."

"He has nice hair, too. But you're right, at least one of you should keep theirs."

Julian watched the exchange in confused silence.

The woman took Eponine back to the sinks and began to wash her hair. She combed conditioner through it and toweled it somewhat dry. Then she braided it, a thick, full braid that reached about to Eponine's waist. Julian watched the comb gliding through that silky hair and imagined it was his fingers instead.

"Would you like to do the honors?"

Julian jerked back to himself. "Me?"

The stylist handed Julian the scissors. He shakily opened them and slid Eponine's hair into the sharp steel jaws.

"Are you sure about this, 'Nine?" he whispered to her. "You know it won't be long again for a while. You'll never see it long again while you're here."

"It's not me," she whispered in return. "Take it, Julian. Take it and give it to someone who can use it."

"Wait, before you cut it, I have to *make sure* the hair isn't dyed. Locks of Love won't take it if it is."

"Don't worry," Eponine said with a smile, "I know the rules." She glanced up over her shoulder. "Julian."

He saw her grip the armrests of the swivel chair and take a deep breath. Her knuckles were white.

He nodded and she closed her eyes.

It didn't cut cleanly through in one try. He had to gnaw at it with the scissors a bit.

But at last the braid came free and he held it in his hands like the fragile corpse of a small bird. Eponine reached back and took it from him. She ran her slender fingers over the thick braided ridges and hummed. With eyes wet with tears, she carefully placed the length of hair into the woman's waiting hands like she was setting an offering upon an altar.

"It's not dyed," she said to her. And when Locks of Love checked it before they constructed it into a wig for chemotherapy patients, they would find out indeed, that it was naturally sunburst red hair that had never been dyed.

IT REALLY WAS A rather chic little bob. And once the rain hit it, it curled up at the ends, obliterating the style that the hairdresser had so carefully created. She didn't mind. She hadn't liked the style anyway, and with the donation of her own hair, the trim and styling had been free.

Julian had been her shadow all afternoon, dark and silent.

They walked along toward Canal Street for no real reason but to walk in the rain.

Julian stopped at a sidewalk vendor who was valiantly trying to stay open despite the cold and wet. He bought a piece of Tiger's Eye and slipped it into his pocket. He doubted Eponine noticed him. She was looking at herself in the beaded reflection of a nearby car window. She tossed her head and watched her hair settle back in place, curling just under her ears.

They turned aside and headed up Mulberry into Little Italy and found a little bistro for dinner. They sat alone on the wet veranda under dripping Christmas tree lights.

The waiter, a jolly portly man with incredible sideburns, brought them Chianti and a plate of fresh mozzarella and sliced tomatoes with basil and olive oil.

Eponine sipped her wine and watched the light really beginning to dim. It looked as if the sky were slowly going out.

"I like your hair," Julian said quietly. "It makes you look ... elvish."

"Did you just say it makes me look like Elvis?"

Julian laughed and gave her chair a playful kick. "No!"

She looked back out into the twilight.

"It looks good," he said with a sincere smile. "And it

was . . . beautiful what you did back there. Really took a lot of strength."

"I wanted to get rid of it, erase what I had done." She ruffled her bangs. "This was the best I could do."

The waiter brought them a plate of steaming, fresh-from-the-oven lasagna. He opened one of the large umbrellas over them and lit the candle in the center of the table. Then he bustled off whistling to himself.

Julian put his cold fingers on Eponine's wrist. "What are we going to do?"

"About what?"

"About the subject we've been avoiding all afternoon."

"Oh. I don't know."

"So far, I have learned that women in love go crazy and kill themselves."

She looked at him incredulously. "You need to cut back on the soap operas, mister!"

"Nah, that's strictly out of Shakespeare. I've been, uhhh, doing some reading while you've been out at school. Ophelia and Juliet." He whistled through his teeth. "That's enough to turn a guy off women all together."

Eponine nearly snorted Chianti out of her nose.

"Uhh, let me rephrase that."

She waved her hand and, as decorously as possible, coughed into her napkin.

"Anyway. . . ." He sat back from the table, stared up at the multicolored lights strung all around them.

"May I ask you a question?"

"Sure."

"What did you do to Jeremy?"

Julian shrugged.

"I am serious. The last time I saw him was Monday, and he called in sick today."

"Why do you care?"

"He's my *friend*, Julian."

He gave her a dry, derisive laugh. "Yeah, anyway. . . . I didn't do anything to him, not really."

He glanced back over at her and was surprised to see how cool her gaze had become. He gave her a self-conscious shrug. "I didn't do what I really wanted to do to him!"

"Which was. . . ?"

"Break open his chest. Then yank out a couple of ribs and gouge his eyes out with them."

Eponine's eyes widened, and her fork paused halfway to her mouth.

"Well, you asked."

To his surprise, she began to laugh. He blushed.

Their waiter brought them tiramisu and cappuccino.

It was delicious.

"I'll get it, tonight," Eponine said and went inside. Beside the cash register all the way in back was a bevy of baby pictures. She picked one up. "Your grandson?"

The Signore Sideburns laughed, and it shook his round belly. "Yes, yes. My favorite, but don't tell anyone."

Eponine giggled. "You should let him come to work with you one day. I'll bet he's a great cook, and he looks like he's got a lot of business sense."

"All he likes are his computers," the man told her, his black moustache dipping down over his frown.

"Let him get his hands dirty," she said with a wink. "I think he'll change his mind."

"You do?"

"I promise."

He grinned. "You're a good girl. An absolute angel!" He kissed her on both cheeks. "You make sure that boy treats you right, you hear? And come back as often as you like. Maybe my grandson will be here."

"Good night," she told him, taking a handful of peppermints. "I'll come back soon!"

THEY WALKED HOME THROUGH the mist, shivering. They both still carried umbrellas but did not use them.

"Do you ever feel like the rain cleanses your soul, 'Nine?"

She laughed like wind chimes and slid her arm around him.

"I have heard people say that when it rains, it's the angels crying."

Julian stopped and thought about it. "You may be right."

She turned to him, puzzlement clear on her face. She looked at him, at the sky, then back to him.

"Sorry," he explained, "just imagining what an angel's tears could be like on Earth.... And the rain.... Sometimes, the rain comes just at the right moment and washes the world and makes it new. When that happens, I'd say there might be a few angels' tears in that. At least, I wouldn't be surprised."

"Are you feeling washed and new, then?"

He tilted his face up and closed his eyes, feeling the stinging cold drops on his eyelids like pinpricks. He took her hand.

"Yes," he whispered. "Aren't you?"

He opened his eyes to find her basking in the raindrops as well. He thought he saw tears on her cheeks as well.

"Eponine?"

She threw her arms around him and pressed her face against his.

Yes, they were tears. He could feel them, hot after the rain, coursing over his cheeks. She cried against him, every teardrop holding a tiny spark, a glimmer of . . . something. He felt tears rise into his own eyes, mixing with hers, and the rain.

They clung to each other, crying in the rain, oblivious to the traffic and the noise and the people and the cold.

They parted, and Eponine began to bubble over with laughter.

"We are quite a pair," she said and began to shiver. "But let's go home and get something hot to drink. And I could use a nice long soak in a good warm bath!"

Julian laughed. "Aren't you wet enough already?"

"Careful, or I might pull you in, too, mister!" She shook her finger at him and then laughed. She wrinkled her nose at him. "Maybe not. Ewwww, wet Vengeance! Kind of like wet dog!"

"Oh, you are gonna regret that!"

"Only if you can catch me!" She sprinted away.

"I know where you sleep!" He cried and charged after her.

Their laughter echoed away, quickly absorbed by the sounds of the city.

A sidewalk puddle on Mulberry Street shimmered with raindrop ripples and glimmered with something else.

A LITTLE GIRL WALKING home tugged on her mother's coat. "Look Mommy, the rain is stopping. The angels must be happy again!"

Mardi Gras

THERE WAS SOMETHING ABOUT Tuesdays. . . .

It was fast becoming the children's favorite day of the week.

It was a day they knew they would be going to the Art League. A day they knew Eponine would be there. And a day that seemed to hold its own special magic.

This was one of those very special Tuesdays.

It was Fat Tuesday.

THEY ENTERED THEIR CLASSROOM to find a world of gold, purple, and green, representing wealth, justice, and faith. Beads were hung everywhere, and an enormous King Cake was resting on Ms. Branch's desk. A feathered mask waited at every student's place.

Eponine had enlisted Julian's help and had even managed to get him to put on a mask and drape a few beads around his neck. She had decked herself out with a score of golden spangles and a purple dress with the most amazing sequined, beaded, and rhinestone-set emerald green vest anyone had ever seen.

It was tacky. It was *incredibly* tacky. But somehow, she looked delightful in it. No one wanted to ask from whence it had come.

Eponine grinned and the room sparkled.

"*Laissez les bon temps rouler!*" she shouted. *Let the good times roll!*

They tore into the King Cake and flung beads at one another.

Jeremy poked his head into the room and was dragged in. Julian stiffened, his shoulders sliding back and his jaw setting. But Jeremy didn't notice him at all since Eponine was shoving a piece of cake into his hands and dropping beads around his neck. He bit into his cake and spat out a tiny baby doll made of plastic.

"Jeremy buys next year's cake," Eponine cheered.

She danced around him in a circle, clapping her hands. She had on a gold sequined headband, and it made her look like a flapper from the 1920s.

Julian shook his head and laughed despite himself. *She's a handful, that Eponine.*

But Jeremy didn't stay long, as he had a lesson to prepare for the afternoon and it was time to go to the Art League. He had been coming into school almost every day, but his attendance had sharply declined again. Julian tossed a toothy smile in his direction as he left the classroom. He was rewarded with a pinch on the arm.

"Are you coming with us?" Eponine's face was absolutely

covered in glitter. Julian couldn't help but laugh as she attempted to look serious and stern at him.

"Yeah, why not," he said with a snicker. "I would love to get a chance to draw you like this!"

She was taken aback, and her soft and glimmering brows came together in confusion. Then she smiled. "Just when I think I know you. . . ."

THE CLASSROOM WALLS WERE covered in glittering pictures of floats and krewes and masks, which meant the entire school, by the end of the day, was covered in glitter.

In music class, Eponine taught them songs in French. Julian stared coolly at Jeremy.

Jeremy held onto his patience and avoided Julian.

Ms. Branch sighed as the final bell rang. "Their parents are either going to love me or hate me for this. These kids are in for one major crash when they get home tonight."

Julian laughed. "Aww, it builds character."

They both stayed and helped clean up the classroom . . . it looked as if the whole of the French Quarter had been through it.

OUT IN THE MANHATTAN twilight, the party really began. Bars and clubs were packed with people and hung all over with shiny beads. Eponine had an idea. She refused to speak of it. instead, she took Julian's wrist and tugged him off toward Lexington Avenue. She told him he wasn't allowed to remove his mask.

It was called the Acme Bar and Grill. It specialized in Cajun cuisine. Tiny and brightly painted, it was a hole-in-the-wall type of place that was frequented by locals of the Lower Village. Tonight, it was the center of attention.

Tables had been set out on the sidewalks, and live zydeco music from the basement lounge rocked the floorboards. They managed to score an inside seat and get the very last of the jambalaya for the night. But by seven-thirty, it was obvious that no one wanted to eat. So the tables were stacked against the walls, and the band came upstairs.

It was a long, narrow place, but the band set themselves up around the bar, leaving only a sliver of room for the bartenders to serve drinks.

The floor was a warm, worn wood, the kind so conducive to dancing.

And dance they did.

People flooded the place, taking up all the space they could. The band played everything they knew, from Dixieland jazz to waltzes to reels. Many of the Acme's regulars were Louisiana natives, and the music flowed in their veins. They never missed a step. And those who didn't know how to dance . . . a mint julep and a few minutes of feeling the rhythm, and they overcame their shyness and gave it a go anyway. After all, it was Mardi Gras.

It took a little more than a drink and a song to ease Julian away from his post by the wall.

He was, at first, content to watch Eponine get passed along the columns of dancers in the Virginia Reel and to see her hitch up her skirts and stomp in time to the Slap Dance. He even smiled when an older gentleman gracefully spun her around in a quick-time waltz. But she caught his eyes every time she neared him. Those eyes, blacker than night, which shone behind his metallic golden mask. She beckoned him to join her, with her short hair bouncing in waves around her ears and the silly purple feather fluttering as she was spun in the arms of another dancer.

She was electric.

All around them, toasts went up, cheers and prayers assailing their ears.

"This here is the night of joy!" the bandleader cried out between songs. "This is the night to forget your troubles. You ain't got no past, you ain't got no worries, you ain't got no future, what you got is just tonight. And tonight, tonight is joy, *ma cheres*. We be partying tonight!"

They began again and she spun on her toes, her arms outstretched and her fingers wide. Julian thought he saw one of her strands of beads break. Tiny spheres of gold flew away from her in all directions. The drunken revelers chased after them, finding traditional golden doubloon coins in their hands.

About a dozen women joined Eponine in a frenzied dance that barely followed the rapid beat of the music. It seemed that the band was having a hard time keeping up with them. They laughed and threw their heads back, neatly coifed hair coming undone and make-up smearing, but no one seemed to care.

The light was at once both faded and bright, and Julian saw Eponine as if through a haze. She was dark and voluptuous with piercing black eyes and waves upon waves of flowing hair, her ripe and lush figure barely covered by a linen wrap as she twisted and leapt barefoot in the tall grass. He saw a wreath of grapes and wheat and roses upon her brow. He shuddered and closed his eyes. When he opened them again, she was walking toward him, leaving the women behind her. She was pale and ethereal, but vibrant. She seemed dressed in the prismatic white light of the sun. Her kaleidoscope wings reached out and enveloped him, drawing him close to her. He was mesmerized by the shifting colors and the mad flowing of patterns one into the next. He stumbled forward and fell against her breast.

"Dance with me," she whispered.

The dance floor cleared a space for them with ease. The band played a waltz. His feet knew the rhythm; how could they not when the pulse of the music beat in his very bones . . . one, two, three . . . one, two, three . . . one, two, three. . . .

She was light and nimble, stepping just right. Her eyes never left his. He felt as if they were dancing in a bubble, the faces of the humans around them nothing but shadows. All around him was light, scattered rainbow prisms leaping in the corners of his vision.

Why doesn't anyone notice this? He wondered. *They can't all be that drunk, can they*?

But the people at the Acme did notice. They noticed a beautiful girl, full of energy, full of smiles, and full of grace. She danced like a rainstorm: wild, furious, and free. Stunning bolts like lightning flew from her, bringing a surge of joyful pleasure to all they contacted.

The waltz, which had seemed to be never-ending, finally concluded with a flourish, and he found that he had spun Eponine into his arms and was holding her quite close against him.

They both panted, and he realized his mask was literally dripping with sweat. He went to pull it up off his face but she stopped him.

The band leader raised his bow.

"It's midnight, chil'rens!"

Still out of breath, Eponine nodded to him and let go of his hand. As Julian slid the mask away from his face, even the close, warm air of the Acme was blessed relief. Those who were wearing masks tossed theirs aside, and another cheer went up.

The band leader waved for silence again. "Fat Tuesday, is over. It's Ash Wednesday, now. Let's all say a prayer and go home."

He bowed his head, and most of the assembled did as well. But instead of intoning some spoken petition, he began to play a song. It was a mournful melody. One of the others began to sing in French, but Julian couldn't catch all the words. It was about lovers separated by darkness and death, only to meet again in the bayou mist at midnight between Mardi Gras and Ash Wednesday. And they would walk together to the Saint Louis Cathedral to throw open the doors for the believers to come inside and atone for their sins.

Eponine laid her head upon his shoulder, and they swayed in time without moving their feet. He closed his eyes, and he could see the heavy New Orleans fog crawling along the old cobbled pavement. He could smell chicory coffee and beignets coming from the Café du Monde just across the square from the Cathedral. He could hear horses' hooves and carriages rattling home after a night of revels. The glamour of Mardi Gras faded into somber Lent.

He opened his eyes. The place was nearly deserted.

The band was just about done packing up, and the crowds had vanished. Worn-looking employees were busily trying to reorder the place for the next morning.

Eponine was grinning at him. She had on her purple crinkly dress and crazy green-spangled vest. Her hair was still bright red and in messy Marcel-waves topped off by a gold-sequined band with a now-broken purple feather.

"You look like you've seen a ghost," she told him.

"I've seen something. . . . How long since the music stopped?"

She shrugged. "I wasn't paying any attention."

He blinked several times, feeling as if a thin film coated his eyes. They walked outside together. It was foggy, and all the streetlamps and headlights were surrounded by a glowing halo.

He looked at her; she was still shimmering. He caught the traces of a faint trail of light just behind her. All around them, people on the street still hollered, and they passed bars where parties still raged. Everyone noticed her and, it would seem, saw her light. They waved, others bowed. She blew them sparkling kisses and kept on her merry way into the night. He shook his head, laughter making a soft rumble in his chest.

She drew her head up and gave Julian a haughty smile.

"When the Angel of Joy says 'let the good times roll,' she means it."

Front Page News

THE WHOLE OF GREENWICH Village was absorbed by the news. Papers sold out within hours of their delivery, and every resident was glued to the television at five o'clock.

There was a man preying on young women in the University and Village areas.

He had assaulted and raped six girls in the past week and a half. Four were still in the hospital, two in critical condition with both head trauma and multiple stab wounds.

Julian was not eager to expose Eponine to that, but he was growing restless and bored. Even Eponine seemed a little stir crazy. In the chilly weeks since Mardi Gras she had grown a little withdrawn and even a bit aloof. The weather was dreary, and an anxious, fearful mood hung over the Village. Even Julian was feeling depressed. Since the trouble had begun, shortly after Mardi Gras, they had not ventured out after dark, and even during the day he walked her to and from school.

But tonight was Thursday; it was still early in the evening and rather mild. A lot of students would be out since NYU didn't have much in the way of Friday classes. Julian wanted desperately to get out of the house.

"I just want to go out for coffee, okay? Over on MacDougal, that Italian café we both like?" He gave her his most charming smile.

Eponine shrugged, "Sure, why not? It's not like I have any plans."

At least she agreed to go do something.

They strolled down toward Broadway and beyond it into the taller, more ornate buildings of the Central Village, most of which were occupied by the classrooms and offices of NYU. Up in the bright windows of the Student Events Building on the corner of Mercer Street, various clubs were gathering for their weekly meetings. Down along the glittery sidewalks, the frightening face of the man at large glared sulkily from behind the glass of the newspaper boxes. It seemed everyone was carrying the composite sketch of the wanted fellow. But Julian and Eponine moved along without seeing it. They had not given too much notice to the whole affair; at least they had been trying not to notice. He thought it better for Eponine's sake if he kept her somewhat in the dark about the evils of the world. He had no idea she'd been keeping up with the entire set of events from the first attack to the most recent.

Someone was playing acoustic guitar in Washington Square Park. Eponine paused; it was a very good rendition of "The Sound of Silence." Julian would never admit to enjoying Simon and Garfunkel, but he was inwardly happy that she'd stopped to listen. He tossed a gold Sacagawea dollar into the guy's open guitar case, and they continued on their way.

The café was across from a row of boutiques; several of them were still open.

"Go on ahead, Julian. I'll be out here," Eponine told him and became mesmerized by the sale tables out front. He was happy to see her acting like herself again.

Julian nodded and jogged across the street. There was a couple sitting at the front table just inside the shop, sipping coffee with tall pillars of whipped cream and watching the little TV that was on the counter. The news was on. Julian was contemplating his beverage ... hot chocolate or cappuccino. The hot chocolate this place carried was Ghiradelli's from San Francisco. He'd never been to the city but thought, *If you can judge a place by its chocolate, San Francisco must be paradise!*

There was someone else ahead of him in line, a tall young man in an olive-green, army-issue trenchcoat.

Julian gave him a nudge. "Hey, if you don't mind, I know what I want to order, and there is someone waiting for me. Do you think I could go ahead of you?"

The guy turned and stared; his eyes were watery blue and he looked quite tired.

You could sure do with some coffee, fella, Julian snickered to himself.

The man glanced over Julian's shoulder and out the glass front door of the store. Julian followed his eyes and saw Eponine talking with a salesperson near a rack of 1950s rhinestone cocktail jewelry. Julian noticed that the couple was staring at him as well. The woman leaned over toward her date and whispered something to him. The man looked Julian and the other guy in line up and down and nodded.

Julian shivered.

"Yeah, man," the guy told him, smiling, "no problem."

Julian smiled back, trying to hide the wariness that edged its way into his mind. "Thanks."

He made his way to the counter and ordered a hot chocolate. He noticed a huge chocolate chip cookie on the table of the rather nosy couple. They were now no longer talking or looking at the TV but just out-and-out staring, first out the window, then at him. He asked for a cookie to go along with his order, the most undercooked peanut butter cookie in the café. He thought Eponine would like that. He glanced nervously at the couple, who were *still* staring. The guy who had been ahead of him in line was now just outside the door smoking a cigarette, and Eponine was still at the boutique table. The sales lady had gone back inside. He was eager to leave the coffeehouse. A bead of sweat trickled down between his shoulder blades and hung there for a moment. He felt . . . exposed, vulnerable. It made the hair on his neck stand on end.

The couple abruptly stood and left the shop, leaving their coffees only half finished. Julian jumped at the harsh sound of their chairs clattering on the mosaic tile floor. They shot Julian a look as they passed him. His gaze met theirs, and he was shocked to read what was written in their eyes. Expectation, fear, anguish. Resentment, disappointment, and more fear. The man held the woman tight to his side. She buried her face against his shoulder.

What do you want from me? Julian wondered.

They turned left out of the shop and disappeared in a hurry.

"That was weird," Julian murmured and turned back to the counter to get his change.

He noticed the television.

They were showing the composite sketches of the rapist.

He felt as if ice water had been poured down his back.

No way, he thought frantically.

Julian heard Eponine's voice. She said his name.

Not "Julian," not even "Vengeance," but *his name*.

He forced himself to turn around slowly.

The man with the cigarette was gone.

Eponine was gone.

He tore out of the store, leaving his hot chocolate and cookie on the counter and a dazed shopkeeper trying to hand him his change.

"Eponine!"

Instinctively, he turned to the right and dashed past a few storefronts. Between two moldering brick buildings, he spotted an alleyway. Toward the rear of the alley he saw a basement entrance, the top of the railing beginning only a few feet above the pavement and vanishing into the blackness of the stairwell below. He ran for it.

He heard the struggle before he could see it. The figures were a mass of writhing shadow in the darkness before him. But the sound of tearing fabric and a young woman's cries were all that he needed to understand the situation.

In a red-tinted blur, he had his hands on the man's shoulders. Something flashed in the low light, and he felt cold air against his stomach. His shirt began to cling wetly to him there, but he paid it no attention. He was looking at the assailant face to face, now. Watery blue eyes and cigarette smoke on the man's breath.

It was the same face. The face from the newspapers and the television. The face ahead of him in line. The face from which the couple in the café were fleeing.

In a heartbeat Julian understood. But they had run.

He was going to fight.

This despicable excuse for a human had laid his revolting hands on Eponine and on six other innocent young women. And now, he was going to pay.

The darkness coiled in Julian's breast and he allowed it, reveled in it. With every breath, it gathered, flowing into his blood. He savored the metallic tang that came into his mouth and relished the tightening of his muscles as they prepared to unleash months of pent-up rage. His eyes crackled with the surge of energy that filled him, filled every fiber of his being. The cloistered tortured memories swelled through him, boiling hot and searing him from within. He embraced them, gazing into their depths for the first time in . . . he could not remember when. Brutal, bloodstained, and alluringly powerful, these visions beckoned to him, seduced him. He gave in. He wholly became the fearsome avenging force that hid beneath his human facade. He knew he must have looked like a demon to this man.

Julian smiled.

He hauled the man out of the stairwell, pivoting on his heel and slamming the weak little mortal's body into the pavement. The man's head cracked audibly. He was stunned, but he did not lose consciousness. Julian was beside his prone body in one long stride and crouched low over this creature that gloried in taking his sense of strength and power from the pain of his victims. The cocky grin faded from the man's face as he looked up into the blackness of Julian's eyes. The devil's eyes held more mercy than the eternal darkness of those fathomless depths.

"You want to see power," Julian growled. "I will show it to you."

He took one of the man's hands in his own and gripped it like a vise. "May you feel the pain that these very hands have wrought."

The man cried out and tried to pull away. Julian held firm, his fingers like stone. His face was expressionless as the man began to dig his heels into the ground and try to scuttle out from beneath his assailant. Julian exhaled a long, measured breath, his tempest-dark eyes half-closing. His hands pulsed fiery cold. He squeezed; there was burning ice in his touch, both melting and scorching the flesh beneath it. The man swore and tossed his head from side to side.

Julian was relentless. He let go of one hand and the man let out a sigh, then brought his arm around as if to attack.

Ignoring his motions, Julian pressed one palm over the man's face, digging his fingernails into his forehead. "May you intimately understand the fear, the humiliation, and the suffering you have caused."

The man flinched quite visibly away from his touch, but Julian was faster. He easily strolled through images of this man's victims. Screaming, bleeding, pleading girls who were crushed before this man's wintertime touch like fragile flowers. The disturbing sights and sounds washed over Julian like water, leaving no trace. Julian absorbed them easily, then turned the tide, sending wave after wave back into this man's mind. He gave him the violation, the pain, the terror.

Now the man howled. Julian let go of him and clamped a hand over his ugly mouth. The man shuddered and writhed on the dirty sidewalk. Julian sat back on his heels and watched for a long moment. A teasing sensation of pleasure licked at him like a flame.

He saw the knife lying forgotten. It was a kitchen knife with a very long blade. It should have been used for cooking: to cut up vegetables and meat for a stew, to slice off thick rounds of store-bought cookie dough, to divide a fat deli sandwich, to do *anything* in the world but rend human flesh. Blood oozed down the blade, beginning to congeal in dark maroon blotches.

He took hold of the handle, clasping both hands over it as if in prayer. It would never be clean again, that blade.

Julian looked at the man. The blue eyes were rolled back and he was trying to cover his face with hands that were now shriveled and burned.

"May you yourself lose what you have thoughtlessly taken from those girls."

Without taking his eyes from the contorted and distressed face, Julian stabbed the knife down with one swift arc just below the man's belt buckle. He felt the knife tip tear through fabric and flesh and finally scrape the pavement. A violent wave surged though the man's body, then he went utterly still. Julian rose and roughly kicked him.

"I hope you regain consciousness before you die, you sick fuck."

The familiar red haze cleared, leaving him momentarily disoriented. Then full realization hit him, and he rushed back to the stairwell.

He had her in his arms in seconds. She was in bad shape. Her hands were cold and her fingers stiff. The front of her coat was soaked in blood.

He closed his eyes and exhaled a rough and shaking breath. He rocked her gently and wondered what to do. She was breathing, but it sounded weak and strained. The world, which had seemed so defined and sharp moments ago, now swung away from him, spiraling out, growing large and empty. He felt alone at the bottom of that alleyway, lost in a forgotten canyon. He had to get her help; her life depended on it. As did his.

If she dies now.... His body shook and he shied from the thought. He stood easily with her in his arms and headed for the street. He kissed the top of her head with tears streaming down his cheeks.

"You are going to be all right, 'Nine, okay? What's that song you sing from *Les Miz*, about the rain? But you're not going to die, 'Nine, you're not! I promise you, I will not let you go."

I can't let you go. You are the only thing that holds those memories at bay. I saw them tonight, 'Nine, I saw them and they scared me. You can't leave me alone with them. They'll devour me. You can't leave me, Nini, you can't leave me!

He had to stop for a moment. His shaking legs wouldn't carry him any farther. She shifted against him, pressing her face against his shoulder and knocking her little woven hat askew. He crouched down and held her in his lap while he tried to fix her hat. Blonde curls spilled down over her ears.

His breath caught painfully in his chest. It wasn't Eponine! He gently tilted her back and looked down into her face.

In the wan street light he could see she had golden hair and a perfectly oval face without a trace of freckles. She opened her eyes; they were hazel-green. She smiled at him.

"My avenging angel," she whispered and passed out again.

He stood quickly and brought her into the better light of MacDougal Street. There was a police officer at the intersection of Bleecker and an ambulance just coming to a stop in front of the café. The EMTs rolled out a gurney and left it beside the rig while they consulted with another police officer.

Like a sliver of the very night itself, Julian made his way unnoticed to the gurney and laid the girl down. Her eyes flashed open, and she looked up at him again. Terror flared and then she smiled. Julian smoothed her hair and stroked her cheek.

"You are going to be safe now, I promise."

She nodded and reached up and squeezed his hand. "You saved me."

"Shhh, just be still now, all right?"

"I can see you." She reached her hand out, groping for something just beyond his body. "I can see your wings; they're black."

"Hush," he whispered and carefully brought her hands back to her sides.

"Thank you." Tears glistened in the corners of her eyes. "I won't forget you."

"Yes, you will," he told her and gently stroked her eyelids. "You are going to forget all about me. Now just go to sleep for a bit and dream good things. No one is going to hurt you ever again."

"My avenging angel," she whispered again with a sleep-drenched voice. "I love you."

"You're safe now. Shhhh."

Her breathing slowed to a deep and regular pace, and Julian backed away. He leaned into the entryway of the café where the University rapist had just recently smoked his last cigarette.

The EMTs came around the corner, and pandemonium ensued. They were checking her vital signs and loading her into the ambulance while barking at the cops to find out how she'd gotten there.

Julian buttoned his coat, covering up the bloody rips in his clothes, and went back into the café. The hot chocolate, cookie, and change were still sitting on the counter. He ducked into the bathroom and washed his hands. He still had no idea where Eponine was. But he forced himself to breathe slowly and splashed water on his flushed and blood-spattered face. He smoothed his hair and went back to the front counter. The employee was there, looking pale and nervous.

"What's going on out there?" Julian asked him. "I ran out to ask my housemate if she wanted anything else besides the cookie, and the police told me to go back inside. I never did find her."

He wondered how much time had elapsed. The hot chocolate was still fairly warm. He took a sip. The guy behind the counter shrugged.

"Something about the rapist, the police said."

Julian nodded. "You think they are going to make us stay in here?"

The employee shrugged again. "Who knows, but you're going to have to go somewhere. I am closing for the night. I am not going to deal with this shit. I told the police I didn't see anything after the guy left this shop."

Julian nodded again and took his cup and cookie. "Well, I'll get out of your hair then. Keep the change."

He was amazed at how calmly he lied as he stepped back into the night. It seemed colder now, darker.

He saw Eponine.

She was across the street, standing with two of the sales ladies from the boutique. One had a portable phone in her hands. The flashing red and blue lights bathed their faces in a fierce and unearthly light.

He didn't realize he had dropped the paper cup of hot chocolate and the cookie and was walking across the street until he came face to face with her. She was eerily still, staring off past the lights of the police cars and the ambulance. Her eyes were cool and strangely emotionless. She was standing so stiffly that her knees twitched occasionally.

Without a word, he hugged her.

He wrapped his arms around her, pulling her body close to his. The gash in his belly burned at the crush but he didn't care. He inhaled her scent and buried his face in her hair, kissing the top of her head. Silent tears soaked through her woolen beret.

He clutched her so tightly that she could hardly breathe.

"Are you all right?" His voice was a ragged and deep whisper beside her ear. Terror and panic raced through him, threatening to drag him from sanity. He held her tight.

She nodded.

"I thought it was you, 'Nine." He squeezed her closer, feeling as if he could not bring her close enough to him. His hands fanatically moved over her, her back, her shoulders, her arms, as if he had to feel every inch of her to be sure she was indeed safe and sound. She stood stock-still and let him enfold her into his embrace. She felt if she were to release her muscles for even a moment, that she would shatter like glass.

He relaxed somewhat finally and then just hugged her desperately and cried into her shoulder.

"He's dead, isn't he? You've killed him?" Her voice was so soft, even Julian barely heard it.

He nodded.

"Good."

He looked down at her. Her face was resolute and cold. She was not smiling, nor crying, nor even looking the least bit afraid.

"Now, let's get home before to police decide they need to talk to us."

He let her pull him alongside her as she turned and headed toward busy Houston Street.

"Don't worry," she told him quietly. "They won't know us from that couple who left the coffee shop right before everything happened. I have made sure of it."

"Aren't you the least bit afraid, Eponine? I thought for sure that he had you, that he had taken *you*."

She put her arm around him as they crossed Broadway and made for Third Avenue.

"Perhaps I was, a little." The tremor in her voice led him to believe that she had been more than just "a little" afraid. "When I saw him watching me, I went into the store and told the people to call the police. I knew who he was. I recognized his face from the TV and the newspapers. I watched him take the girl," her voice broke, "but there was nothing I could do but call for you and hope you'd get there in time. I knew you would." She paused and looked up at him for a long moment. She took off one glove and licked her finger. She then wiped a bit of dried blood from alongside his nose. She gazed a long moment up into his eyes, and he felt her begin to relax just a little. She put the glove back on, slipped her arm though his again and continued on. "I have faith in you, Julian. I could never be afraid with you here."

Once home, Eponine made short work of the cut across Julian's stomach. The gash wasn't deep at all, but she put peroxide and about a dozen Band-Aids on it anyway. Then she took him to his bed.

He let her lay him down and pull the blankets around him, smoothing them over his body. She laid his hair across his pillow. He watched her do all of it. She had done such things for him before, but he had never seen it. Never seen how her face shone with happiness to be near him, to take care of him, to touch him. He allowed himself to be helpless before her. He let her do whatever she wanted to.

He looked at her, studying her face. She *had* been afraid, he knew. She had been terrified, but she was pretending to be brave. She was giving him the best show she could, trying to calm him, to settle him down, to make him feel safe.

"It doesn't bother you at all that I killed him?" he asked finally, when Eponine had finished her ministrations.

She didn't stop combing out his hair with her fingers. "You have killed thousands upon thousands of people; don't be silly."

She had a point. He fell still and silent again.

She smoothed the blankets out for the third time. "Does it bother you that you killed him?"

Julian thought about his answer. "I thought he had taken you. I admit I was . . . excessive."

"And when you found out it wasn't me, you felt . . . remorse?" She had no judgment in her eyes.

"I hated him, 'Nine. It went beyond the simple act of vengeance. I wanted him to suffer for hurting you."

She nodded again and took his hand. "But what you did was right. I won't say it was *good*, but it was the right thing. It's your job, after all."

He sighed heavily, and she smiled at him. He was warmed by her touch. He found himself smiling back. The thought of her safe and whole, untouched by those vile hands, sitting beside him instead . . . it made him happy. He closed his eyes and pushed his brimming emotions aside. All he wanted was to be here now, and think of her.

He felt something cold slip onto his finger.

Eponine laid his hand across his chest. She had put his ring on. "You're beginning to understand what it means, I think."

THE NEWS ALL OVER town was about the rather brutal slaying of the "University Rapist." It made the front page for three days while the police searched for leads in the case. They found none. The only eyewitness was the seventh victim, who could say only that someone had rescued her, but that her assailant was already dead when it happened. She couldn't identify the Good Samaritan who came to her aid.

"He seemed like an angel to me," was all she could say.

The trail went cold, and the police gave up searching. They didn't really want to find the slayer of the sexual predator. They made much noise rallying against "vigilante justice," but in the end, nothing came of it. The city slipped all too easily back into its routine, and the matter became history.

JULIAN RESISTED THE VERY powerful urge to follow Eponine everywhere she went in the ensuing days. The first day she went back to school, however, he got up early so he could see her out.

What he found was that Eponine was far ahead of his game. She was long gone and had left a note.

Don't worry about me. I have faith in you.

He held the paper in his hands and read over those simple words.

Julian sat in the warm windowseat with a cup of coffee. He read her note again, then examined his ring.

It was beginning to make sense.

He was frightened, but he smiled.

MARKET DAY

WEDNESDAY WAS "DAIRY DAY" at the Union Square Farmer's Market. And also there were the usual regulars that Eponine loved: the bakers and the beekeepers.

She had a little wicker basket that she brought to the park when she went shopping there. She'd risen early to beat Julian again. Things were safe and settled now in the city, but he still worried. The thought made her smile. He was a marvelous bodyguard! But that did not ease the fear in her heart.

Sometimes, deep in the night, her dreams passed close to his, and she could taste the blood in the air. She was afraid for him. And when he meted out vengeance against that man, the scales tipped away just a little. The man was a rapist; he deserved what he got, there was no arguing that. But the city reveled in the brutality of the act. Humanity loved Vengeance just a little too much.

He had slipped before, not so long ago. It was recently enough that there were still plenty of people who kept shadows in their eyes, long after they'd witnessed the atrocities. He'd slipped, but they had brought him back. He had never been the same after, and now. . . . Vengeance was perilously close to that chasm once more; she could see it as plain as day.

If he fell this time, it would be so much worse. It spelled the very possible end of humanity, or at least humanity as it had existed thus far. She was fairly sure that the race would live on. Humans were tenacious if nothing else. But it would be a world of fear, of hatred, of anger, and never-ending cycles of wrongs and retributions. Some parts of the world already lived that way, and this very city that she so loved had paid the price once already. That was when they all knew that Vengeance had to be stopped. Joy was one of the few who believed he still could be healed. And now she stood alone between the angel she knew and the madness that was consuming him. If she failed, she knew she would be the first of her kind to die. Joy cannot live where fear holds sway. She was in far over her head. She was going to need some help.

The basket slid down her arm, and she remembered where she was. Shaking free of the terrible thoughts that plagued her, she headed decisively toward the beekeeper's booth. She bought new candles, thick and golden and smelling richly of honey—candles full of light to banish bad dreams. She bought some cheese for the week and a bag of mozzarella curd to nibble on the way home. At the bakery booth she got some sourdough bread and cinnamon rolls, but they were just out of her other favorite Farmer's Market treat, strawberry bread.

Disappointed, she wandered over to the flower-seller and debated bringing a fresh bouquet home with her to brighten up the dreary late-winter day. She had been suffering a major attack of the doldrums and hoped some flowers would help chase away her blues.

The hairs at the back of her neck pricked, and she brought her face up from the hot-house roses and glanced about. She idly stroked meaty tulip petals that grew up out of decorative terra-cotta pots alongside amaryllis and paperwhites. But still the sensation lingered.

She was being watched.

Casually, she gave the area a once-over. Nothing and no one out of the ordinary. But the eyes were there.

Then her gaze met the intent stare of the watcher. Up on the embankment over the newsstand was a young woman. Her legs dangled at least fifteen feet above the ground as she perched on the retaining wall that held the hilly north side of the park itself back from the street below. Resolutely, Eponine walked up the stairs into the park proper and made her way to the dark-haired girl on the wall.

From this side, the wall and was an easy climb. Eponine laughed to herself over how much more impressive it had seemed from the pavement to see her up there. She sat down beside the girl and they remained side by side in silence for some time.

The young woman smiled and took a brown paper sack out of her backpack. She brought out a thick slab of strawberry bread and a little container of fresh butter from the creamery booth. She tore the slice in half and handed it to Eponine with a small plastic knife. The little tub of butter was set down beside them, and she began to smear her half of the bread with half of the butter. She took a big bite, dipping her nose into the butter, and smiled.

"Well, I did take the very last piece of the day," she said, apologetically. "And the very last focaccia, too."

Eponine nodded and buttered her own piece.

"Thank you." She smiled at the girl, feeling her heart lighten a little as she began to eat. She offered the girl some cheese curd.

Laughing, she showed Eponine her own half-empty bag.

"May I ask you something?" Eponine said, finally.

The girl polished off the last of her bread and took a swig of milk bought from the same booth as the butter.

"Sure," she answered, wiping the milk-mustache away with the back of her hand, then wiping her hand on her plain green cotton skirt. She kicked her black Doc Marten boots against the wall.

"Why were you watching me?"

The girl's eyes were nearly as black as Julian's and swept over Eponine's face and form, seeming to take in the air that surrounded her as well. She laughed again and offered the milk bottle to Eponine. Eponine took a tentative sip and handed it back.

"There are two of you." The girl's voice crackled with amusement. "I hope you know about each other, because if not, it's going to be hell trying to find one another in a city this big."

"What are you talking about?"

The girl gave Eponine a cock-eyed grin and a wink. "You're like him, the one I met the other day. Well, about a month ago now, I guess. But it was on the subway on the way to the Met. You both have the same feel, the same auras . . . but yet, not the same."

Eponine listened, quite intrigued.

"I must sound like a total fruit." She shrugged. "But I see what I see, and you and he are two of a kind. A kind I have never seen in real life, well, not like this, *in the flesh* and all. He was an amazing one, with a face so beautiful and a soul so powerful and so *dark*. And those eyes. . . . But, uhh, anyway, I'm not sure if I could help you find him if you don't know who he is. Well, how many gorgeous creatures radiating that kind of aura *could there be* strolling around Manhattan?"

"I know who he is." Eponine's voice sounded hollow.

"Good," the girl beamed. "That makes my job easier. It's often difficult to keep track of our other selves, you know."

Eponine found herself nodding.

"Let me see your hands." The girl reached over and held her own hand out.

Eponine reluctantly removed one glove and placed her hand into the girl's, who flipped it over and peered down into Eponine's palm. Her wry smile grew into a grin.

"Just as I thought," she mused.

"What do you see?"

The girl's eyes came up in a flash and met hers. "Nothing you don't already know." She clasped Eponine's hand between both of hers.

Eponine drew back and put her glove on. "That tells me nothing," she said, testily.

"Oh, no," the girl said. "It tells you everything."

She glanced over Eponine's shoulder and began to gather up her things.

"I have to go," she said, smiling. "It was good to meet you."

"But I don't even know your name!"

"Call me Phina."

"Okay, Phina, my name is. . . ."

"Shh! I don't want to hear it. Some things aren't meant for *people* to know."

"I'm not going to tell you *that*, silly!"

"Next time, then," Phina winked at her. "I have to go. Some-one's waiting for me."

"Wait, but I haven't given you anything in return!"

Phina waved her off and got up, brushing the dirt and crumbs from her skirt and wrapping her gray wool coat tighter around her.

"No," Eponine stood as well. "You shared your strawberry bread with me. Not to mention the milk and butter. I won't be in debt to you! No gypsy tricks."

A slow smile spread over the girl's face. "You're a smart one," she laughed. "No debt. All gifts. I ask for nothing in return."

Eponine nodded and offered her hand to shake. Phina took it and gave it a quick squeeze.

Eponine bowed her head, "*Parika tut.*"

"You're welcome." And Phina bounded away, her blue cartoon character backpack bouncing on her shoulder. She called back, "Say hi to your friend for me, would you?"

She waved and trotted down the stairs. Eponine watched as she reappeared in the midst of the afternoon traffic on University Place, as fearless as any native New Yorker. She met up with a young man in a long woolen coat of the very darkest blue and the two of them headed south toward the university. Before she was lost from sight, Phina turned and waved once more. Eponine could tell it would not be the last time she saw Phina.

"I think I've made a friend," she mused.

REBIRTH

THE AIR IN THE room was taut, like the claustrophobic press of an approaching thunderstorm. It leeched into Julian's dreams and pulled him out of sleep. It was a quarter to six and still dark. The city sounds, usually quiet at this hour, were truly muted now.

Julian lay still, feeling the heaviness of the blankets clinging to his chest. He was aware of them pushing down upon him, adding to his own weight; he felt as if he were being pulled into the bed.

He could scarcely breathe.

The winter was dragging on, hard and cold. April was just around the corner, but the world was still cold and grey. Even the intrepid daffodils that bloomed in the parks and sidewalk planters were pale and washed out, their elegant heads drooping and sad. And Eponine . . . as much as she fought it, the last grasp of winter held her tightly. Like a flower, she turned her face toward the sun at every possible moment, but the sun often hid behind steely clouds stained on the undersides with exhaust and frustration.

Eponine. On Mardi Gras, she had shone like a star, but the night of Julian's murder of the "University Rapist" had changed her somehow.

She's seen me for what I am, finally. She knows. And it's changed her, changed how she feels. . . .

He remembered New Year's Eve and the fight that had ended in kisses. . . .

Stop it! Why torture yourself with what cannot be? She doesn't love you; she can't love you.

He forced himself to think about how angry he was at her at that moment. How her moods were so subject to change, how irritating and petty she had become, how all she wanted to talk about was how long the winter was dragging on and would it ever be spring again?

She is my winter these days; this whole assignment is like winter to me! Bleak, grey, interminable! And to what end? Since our first week here, she's made no mention of why we've come. All except for "enjoying the snow." Well, I am done enjoying the fucking snow now! Enough with the snow!

Her snappishness was beginning to affect him, and thinking about it enraged him anew.

"That's it." He climbed out of bed, fighting the leaden sluggishness of his limbs. "I am going to go get an answer from that girl right now. And if she pulls an attitude with me, there's gonna be tears!"

A noise came from Eponine's room.

Strange, he could hear it clearly while every other sound still felt muddled to his ears. She was tossing and turning; the rustling of her bedding was startlingly loud. It seemed she was having a nightmare.

That's . . . not right. Eponine never has nightmares.

She cried out, and he found himself halfway past the kitchen before he even realized he'd left his room.

She gasped and sputtered. It nearly sounded as if she were choking.

Julian threw open her door. It hit the wall, leaving a doorknob-shaped dent in the plaster, and bounced back, leaving a ring of pain upon his hip. He was knocked off balance, but it didn't slow his steps. He was at her side in an instant.

Her arms reached madly about and then flew to her throat. Julian tossed her comforter aside and grabbed her wrists.

"Eponine!"

She wrenched herself free with surprising strength.

Slowly, the cool dawn light was beginning to fill the apartment. In the dimness, he could see something dark looped around Eponine's neck. Her face glistened with sweat, and her head rolled from side to side. He leaned closer toward her, gingerly reaching for her throat.

It was *her hair* that was tangled there. Her bobbed, once-red hair, now grown again and hazelnut brown. It was longer than he had ever seen it before, spilling over the edge of the bed in waves. It was caught around her neck in a thick twist and tangled in her fingers. He took both of her hands and pressed them with all his weight to the mattress.

"'Nine," he whispered urgently, "Nini, you need to wake up!"

She only fought harder against his grasp.

Then the morning light finally crested the masonry peaks of the canyon of neighboring buildings and flooded the bedroom with light. Julian's eyes were dazzled, and he felt Eponine relax in his grip as the sunrise poured over her. She sighed, deeply, and Julian felt her tension ebb with his entire body. It was as if whatever dream demons had held her captive had melted with the dawn. As if by that cue, the rest of the morning sounds swelled to an orchestra of birds and traffic and the laughter of children. The scent of cherry blossoms and green, growing things permeated the apartment.

Eponine uttered a soft cry of pleasure, and the air around them was suddenly alive with fluttering. Julian instinctively dropped to the floor and was amazed to see the room filled with butterflies. They swirled on silent, colorful wings through the glittering golden sunrise. It was like a living mobile, dipping and twirling. There had to have been at least two dozen of them.

He slowly pulled himself to his elbow and peeked over the bed. He squinted against the light. He saw Eponine, but yet, it wasn't. She was herself, he realized.

Her body, Julian saw, was formed of illumination, her prismatic wingtips brushing the walls.

No illusion this time.

"Joy. . . ." His voice failed as she turned her eyes toward him. He knew them, those brilliantly violet eyes. ". . . oh . . . God. . . ."

And then the light burst forth, a shimmering wave that knocked him to the floor. He fell back, his head hitting the hardwood boards with a crack that made black diamonds swim in his vision. The great rush of light raced past and over him like a tidal wave.

He lay there, stunned.

What the fuck just happened?

He scrambled into the living room, but it was empty. The windows were shut. The door was shut. There was not a single butterfly in the apartment. Eponine also was nowhere to be seen.

"Eponine? *Eponine!*"

He ran to his room but it, too, was empty. In a daze, he wandered back into the kitchen and stared blankly at the automatic coffeepot busily going about its business without a care in the world. He took a cup and drank it black, burning his mouth. He didn't care. He downed a second cup.

He began to pace. He paused in Eponine's doorway and somehow did not drop the coffee cup. He would find it later balanced precariously on the back of the sofa with no recollection of having set it there.

Eponine was in her bed. At least it *looked like* Eponine, looked like her body at any rate.

Julian crept forward, not wanting to look, but incapable of drawing his eyes away from the forlorn shape that remained upon her bed. It was only a shade, an ashen figure that seemed as if it would disintegrate at the slightest touch. An ugly thing, a little mortal body created of dust and clay and totally devoid of the sparkle of life that had once animated it. Her merry eyes were shut and slightly sunken, her jovial lips slack and listless, her rosy face dull. Julian recoiled, realizing that he was looking upon her soulless husk, the temporary home of her divine being. Eponine was as dead as any mortal could be, her soul of Joy flown into the sunrise with a passel of butterflies.

But, why?

He backed away and shut the door behind him.

Something tickled the back of his memory. He couldn't place it and found himself pacing again. His feet came to rest in front of the computer desk, and his eyes fell upon the calendar.

Of course! He felt both relieved and apprehensive at once.

It was the first day of spring.

She was the spirit of Eostre, Primavera, Persephone ... she was the very embodiment of the Maiden, the lifeblood of springtime ... she was what she was: Joy incarnate.

Joy always got restless around the first day of spring, especially when it had been such a hard winter. But now the world was perfectly balanced: day and night, light and dark. From this day forward, the days would grow until the Solstice when the wheel will turn again toward the darkness of winter.

But why did she leave her body behind?

Julian had no real answer for that, only that the strain of the assignment must have been much harder on Eponine than he had ever imagined.

What could she be tackling that is so damn tough?

He deduced, finally, that she must have been called back. Perhaps she had some heavenly duty to perform on this first day of spring, although Hope had handled the ceremonies plenty of times on her own.

Maybe she has failed. Maybe this is it; she's gone and they're sending someone to take her place.

Julian's whole soul ached with a sigh. He wished deep in his heart that when Eponine awoke again, there would still be Joy in her eyes.

WAITING IN THE GARDEN

IT WAS LATE.

But the dream was so nice.

And so familiar, although she could not say why.

The waking world seemed so distant, so cold. She could not remember ever feeling so reluctant to wake and face the day. But then again, she could not ever remember having such a perfectly wonderful dream.

She nuzzled deeper into her bed, pulling the warmth around

her. Just a little longer; yes, she'd stay just a little bit longer. It was *so* very nice.

The sky was brilliantly blue, and the sun warmed her. She had the greenest grass at her feet dotted with golden yellow daffodils.

But a shadow was always skittering just behind her, marring her perfect happiness. Once in a while she heard voices, distant and muffled. They sounded so dull and discordant, so lifeless and sorrowful. She was at once both appalled and moved to tender sympathy to hear them. But they often faded before she could follow them to their source, or else she was distracted by something shining in the distance. The dream flowed on like a shimmering stream: bright, delightful, and never-ending.

It rained in her dream, rain like kisses upon her naked flesh. There was something she was supposed to remember, about the rain. Rain... like tears... but why should she be thinking of sadness?

She could not even remember why she was there, or how long she'd been. She was supposed to be elsewhere, but she had taken a break. She'd been overwhelmed. She was unsure of herself, of her feelings. She'd been granted a respite, but from whom or what, she did not immediately recall. But she felt better, rested; she would go back soon. Back to wherever she had been, back where to the rain was. What was it she was supposed to remember about the rain? It washed away pain.... Someone was in pain. Someone she loved. She was supposed to be his rain, but it was all going badly. She was off track; she was ruining the assignment; she was risking his soul with her failure.

Spring had come, this she remembered. Spring had come, and she had used its power to break free, to slip away from the world. Yes, her reprieve had come with the first light of spring, the year in balance, in harmony. More than rest. Yes, she wanted rest, but she came for guidance! Now she remembered! Yes, she wanted guidance! She was confused; she was concerned.

She'd had a question. It had been related to the other question she had, about the rain. She had sat in her meadow for ages, it seemed, waiting for her answers. Many times she forgot that she was waiting, and lived in each moment like she always had. But there was something missing. She needed to know about why it had rained, but gazing up into the prefect sky, she saw no clouds. What was it she was supposed to remember? What was it she was supposed to ask? Was it about a ring? Warmth filled her when she thought of it. Must have been something about a ring. Or the rain.

A dark spot moved through the golden light. It was something soaring high above her, a black silhouette with raven's wings. She chased after it until it was lost over a horizon of clouds.

Come back! Come back, I love you!

There, the rain must be coming from there. Cold, winter rain. So dark, so sad. She was waiting for her answers. The questions, she didn't know, but questions there had been. She was waiting for the answers.

She sat down in the field, heady with the sweet smell of blooming clover, and resolved to wait there until she could figure out what she should do.

She drew her knees up to her chest and wrapped her arms around them. She expected to see her skin freckled, but it was not. It was blank.

She was alone. There were no answers.

The shadow didn't come back for her, and she was afraid.

HE HAD GONE OUT to look for her.

Not anywhere in New York City, but the place he guessed she was most likely to go.

It was vast, golden, infinite. He didn't linger there. If he were caught, there would be trouble. It was neither his time nor his place to be there. The repercussions would be severe, he knew, but he didn't care. She was worth running that risk.

But he hadn't found her.

Julian knelt beside her bed with his hands clasped in prayer. His head rested upon his folded fingers, and he dozed fitfully in the flickering candlelight.

She had been gone too long.

He watched spring burst into bloom from her bedroom windows. All around the city, colors began to emerge as the days grew longer and brighter and warmer. People smiled more, and he could see joy in their eyes. He could see *Joy* in their eyes.

She was there, present in every one of them, but not with him. She was gone from him. Perhaps it was he who had failed, and now he was being punished somehow.

She wouldn't forget the assignment, would she?

She wouldn't forget him, would she?

She wouldn't possibly leave him behind without even saying goodbye. . . .

He steadfastly guarded her lifeless body.

Once, he thought he saw her kaleidoscope wings shimmering in the slanting morning sun beaming into the apartment. He rose on leaden legs and stumbled toward her. But the breeze that crept under the slightly open window slowly spun the crystal prism that hung there, scattering the image of her into a thousand rainbow pieces.

Come back! Come back, I love you!

He slumped back to the floor and wrapped his arms around his knees and waited. She would return, he knew it. She had to return. She was not finished here. She wasn't going to leave him alone. But the days rolled on and she did not return. He was afraid.

SALVATION

THE TANTALIZING SMELLS OF breakfast tempted Julian from a deep and sluggish dream. He felt as if he had been asleep for days, but had not been able to rest. His muscles ached furiously, and his shoulders creaked. He rolled over and jolted awake to find himself curled up on the rag rug on Eponine's bedroom floor.

His head throbbed. He couldn't quite recall why he had been sleeping there. He remembered that Eponine was having a nightmare, and that he had gone to her and. . . .

He sat up.

His stomach rumbled painfully.

There was someone else in the house. *Of course* there was someone else in the house.

Wait, no. There *shouldn't* be. He was alone. He was waiting for Eponine. Yes, Eponine was gone. But where had she gone? Julian wracked his mind to remember. The memory taunted him from that dismal, awful place where all his stray thoughts went to hide. He decided not to chase it.

He leaned upon her bed and pulled himself to his feet. He was weak-legged and lost his balance, falling forward into her plush comforter.

The church bells all through the neighborhood were ringing.

It did nothing to ease his pounding head. He felt as if his eyes would burst or bleed.

He sat up and looked around the room. Yes, he was alone.

That thought gave him pause as his eyes took in the neatly made bed upon which he sat. He could see where he'd rumpled up the covers.

His ears perked up at the sound of sizzling and the renewed scent of cooking . . . this time it was bacon he smelled. Weakly, he shambled to the doorway. The wall behind the door was marked with a large ding in the plaster shaped like the doorknob. Funny, he thought he would have remembered Eponine's mentioning that had happened.

The television in the front room was on quietly and showing a grand Catholic Mass from what looked like the Vatican. On the table was a steaming plate of biscuits and a pitcher of orange juice. Eponine was singing along to her CD player.

He closed his eyes, daring not to hope that she was really there, singing and cooking breakfast like on any other morning. Singing to the Bangles, of all mundane, beautiful things.

He laughed and looked at her. She was wearing a robe and her favorite pajamas. Her hair was in one amazingly long braid that bounced playfully over the backs of her thighs as she moved through the kitchen. He came up behind her and realized she had headphones on. He stood beside her as she obliviously stirred the thick gravy forming in the bacon pan.

She turned and yelped to find him hovering right at her elbow.

"Well, Happy Easter, lazybones." She turned the CD player off and tossed the headphones onto the counter.

"Easter? Already?"

She rolled her eyes. "I suppose this means that you're not going to be able to tell me what happened, then?"

He gripped her forearms and looked directly into her face. It was she. Same freckles, same eyes. Just her hair.

"What's gotten into you, Julian?" She squirmed a little.

"Eponine, what happened to your hair?"

She blushed. "I don't know. But in my dream it was long, too."

"Your dream? What was it of?"

"I'm not sure. It was stupid, really. Flowers, a stream, a raven, I think. I must have been asleep a long time. I was one big ache when I got up today. Have I been sick? You'd tell me if something was wrong, wouldn't you? The last thing I clearly remember was going to the Farmer's Market and meeting Phina. I told you about her, right? Other than that, there are snippets here and there. Of you, of the city, of the usual things . . . but it was like watching everything through a stained glass window, or a kaleidoscope."

He listened to her, open-mouthed as recollections tumbled over him.

A kaleidoscope. Her wings are like a kaleidoscope.

"Julian?"

He threw his arms around her. "You came back."

She stood still and awkwardly received his embrace. "Um, was I *gone*, Julian?"

He took a minuscule step away and gave her an incredulous laugh. "'Nine, it was the first day of spring."

She was confused. He could see her struggling to catch and keep hold of fleeting memories. Suddenly, a light dawned in her eyes.

"Oh, *that*." She forced a laugh. "But I mean, it's not like I *went* anywhere, I mean it's not like I . . . ."

Julian's mouth pressed into a pale, thin line, and he nodded slowly.

"No, Julian, I couldn't have. I couldn't. . . ."

"You did," he said gravely.

"But I *couldn't have*!"

"Three days, Eponine. Almost four."

The color drained from her face. "*Three days?* That's how long I was asleep? But that's impossible. . . !"

He shook his head. "You weren't just asleep. You were gone. Three days. I know. I counted every hour. I never left your side."

"Never left my . . . oh. *Oh!*" A shiver ran through her, and she pulled away to take the gravy off the heat. "Well, we'd better eat. Seems like we both need it."

And eat they did. Between the two of them, they polished off every last bit.

THE APRIL SUNLIGHT WAS warm on their faces. There was no trace of winter anywhere now. Daffodils and jonquils seemed to flourish in every planter they passed.

They found themselves in Washington Square where children were eagerly hunting Easter eggs, and parents sitting on blankets watched them with cameras and smiles.

Eponine and Julian sat together near a family of squirrels that were trying to decide what to do with the dyed egg they had found.

She laced her fingers through his and leaned her head upon his shoulder. He squeezed her hand and rested his cheek on the top of her head.

"I was really worried, 'Nine," he whispered. "So much has happened in such a short time, I don't know what to think. About this assignment, about us. Where did you go? Why did you leave?"

"Did you really wait there for me all that time?"

"Of course I did. I'm your guardian, remember."

"Did you really think I wasn't coming back?"

"Yeah, pretty much. But you haven't answered—"

"Did you go looking for me?"

"Yes."

"Even though you know that's not allowed?"

Julian nodded, not willing to speak aloud his incrimination.

"Why?" She turned to look him in the eye.

"I had to. I had to know. I mean if you thought you'd failed, if you had lost faith in the mission, I wanted to tell you to keep trying, that I would help you as much as I could." He licked his lips and forced himself to gaze steadily into her eyes. "You have to tell me, Eponine. What's this all about?"

"You were such an absolute gentleman about it, you know. Like the Steadfast Tin Soldier. Even if you did break some rules, it was in good conscience."

"Damn it! Why do you insist on changing the subject every time I bring it up?"

"Don't you realize by now that there are some things you cannot know? There are some things I cannot tell you?"

"So, there are secrets between us?"

"Not secrets, Julian. It's hard to explain."

He sat back on the bench. "I understand, now. I understand your mission. Damn it, why didn't I see it before? It was so obvious! I feel like such an idiot!"

"Julian, no. I don't think you get it, not entirely. And you are not an idiot. It's all very complicated; even I don't fully realize the half of it, I'm sure. And running off like I did certainly didn't help things. And for that, I'm sorry. I jeopardized everything right then, but there were questions that needed answering."

"Did you get the answers you needed?"

"To a few, yes. But not all. I think I have even more questions now, though."

"Why couldn't you tell me, Eponine? You should have just said something."

"I couldn't, Julian. There is no way I could have told you and still held on to the purpose of this mission."

"Of course not. Of course not. I forget that I am just the guardian around here, just the babysitter while you dash about and do your holy duty. This explains why I couldn't find you, though. I guess I should have gone up to the Upper East Side and knocked on his door, but you being in your true form and all, who knows what I would have walked into. . . ."

"Julian! That's not true!"

He chuckled drily. "Eponine, I'm not blind. Tell me, what did he do to earn the likes of you? How did he get to be your mission? What is he to the Divine that he gets *you*?"

"Julian. . . ."

"I know, I know, you can't tell me." He put his arm around her shoulders and drew her near. "It's just as well. I have realized that I would really rather not hear some things actually spoken out loud."

"No, let me explain!"

"Eponine." Julian took her gently by the chin. "Listen. Some things are bigger than you or me. I have ruined myself, my chances, my being. I don't want you to tell me, okay? I don't want to know. I think it is best for everyone involved if I just stay out of the picture. I think I have done enough damage to your assignment as it is."

"I should have never gone! What was I thinking?"

"We all do what we have to. 'Nine, I understand."

"No, you don't, and that's the problem!"

"Shhhhh." He placed his hand over hers. "Eponine, I am trying my best here. It's hard for a man to admit defeat, even harder for an angel. You know that; you've heard the stories."

"I am going to make this up to you, Julian. I swear it."

One corner of his mouth twitched into a half-hearted smile. "Don't make promises."

She looked away and thought better of saying another word. Failure loomed more menacingly than before.

I don't understand why I can't just tell him. I went looking to You for answers, and You only sent me back here. Now what?

They sat in silence for quite some time, watching the families and the squirrels and the sparrows.

The sky was clear blue with not a cloud in sight. The wind blew softly, just enough to freshen the pleasantly warm air. The sun drenched the multitude of springtime colors and drew the sweet scent from the faces of the upturned flowers.

"We're still friends, Julian. I don't want you to forget that."

"Of course not."

"I'm serious! I don't want you going on this 'I'm just a body-guard' tear! You're not; you're more. You're my friend, Julian. You stayed by my side for three whole days."

"We all do what we have to."

"Some of us do more."

Julian closed his eyes, blotting out the sting of her words as they missed their mark.

She kissed his cheek. "Thank you for being you. For being who and what you are, my guardian. My salvation."

He clenched his jaw, stopping any trace of tears that threatened to form. He had to let her go; he had to let her fulfill her mission. He was there to protect her. He was never supposed to get involved.

The season of renewal was in full bloom. Life, it seemed, had been rescued from the winter, brought from the dark of the year into the light, but yet shadows remained.

QUESTIONS AND ANSWERS

IT SEEMED WINTER HAD one more trick to play on Manhattan. But it was a pleasant one.

In the midst of a fresh spring morning, tall thick clouds like whipped cream tumbled in from the north. They dusted the city with a powdered-sugar layer of snow.

Eponine discovered a familiar face that morning down in the Costume Institute: Phina, the gypsy girl from the Farmer's Market. They had recognized one another immediately, and Eponine was treated to the grand tour of the Institute's exhibits, including a healthy dose of gossip and background information on nearly every piece.

"Why don't you stay for lunch?"

"That would be marvelous! Oh, there's something I need to tell you."

Phina tilted her head to one side and regarded Eponine with a perplexed smile. "What would that be?"

"My name's Eponine."

"I take it you aren't giving any secrets away by telling me that."

"You should know better! Just like the Romany, my kind have three names as well. The name for the masses, the name for our families, and the name for the One who stands above all."

"Makes sense. Just wanted to make sure I wasn't going to get, oh, I don't know, smote or anything with you telling it to me."

"You are totally in the clear."

"Good to know. Let me go find Alphonse, and we'll catch lunch."

Eponine followed the two employees right into the basement cafeteria of the Metropolitan Museum of Art. Alphonse was the Costume Institute's librarian. He had been born in France and had lived in a small town a few miles outside of Paris most of his life. His accent was still rich and thrilling, and he enjoyed wearing flamboyant neckties.

"All he needs is the beret and he'd fit every French stereotype there is," Phina whispered to Eponine as Alphonse switched from discussing the terrible wine Sardi's was serving to his favorite topic: Who is secretly gay in Hollywood? To hear Alphonse explain it, it was everyone.

The girls giggled into their end-of-lunch cappuccino.

"Well, we'd better head back. We have to get back to work in time to take our coffee break." Phina stood and stretched and reached over to bus Eponine's tray as well as her own. One of the docents strolled by with a security guard, and they overheard them discussing how the snow had started back up again.

Eponine's eyes lit up. "Oh, we must go and see it! It'll be the last snow of the year!"

"You go on, baby-cakes," Alphonse replied. "I had enough of snow this winter."

Phina laughed. "Just let me finish my coffee. I'll meet you up there."

Eponine nodded and dashed out of the cafeteria.

Phina turned back to her friend and shook her head. "That girl, I swear. . . ."

"She acts like this is all new to her."

"It is," she told him with a smile. "Where she's from, the world is nothing like this."

OUTSIDE, THE DAY WAS perfect and shimmering. The sun broke

though the meringue-like clouds in broad, colorless beams of light. It looked like the pictures on the postcards of "heaven" that the Christians at the mall liked to hand out. The slight layer of snow on the ground was already beginning to melt, and just a few thick flakes were falling here and there from the dissipating clouds. Farther into the park, a few flurries still shimmered along the horizon. It was breathtaking.

Eponine stood beside Cleopatra's Needle once again and watched the snow-streaked sunlight make its shifting way across the dark stone.

"So we meet again, in the snow, old friend." She patted it with her bare hands. Her fingers were already growing red and chapped from the chill in the air. She crammed her fists into her pockets and rubbed her thumbs across her knuckles in a futile attempt to warm them. She looked about for Phina, but the girl was nowhere to be seen. In her brief relationship with her, Eponine had caught on that Phina would appear when and where she was needed, but otherwise was a gypsy at large. There was no real sense in waiting for her now. After all, the snow was melting, and Eponine had no doubts that Phina could find her easily enough.

She set off, as usual, toward Belvedere Castle.

It was just enough snow to frost the daffodils and plum blossoms and wet the grass underfoot. Just enough to sparkle in the midafternoon light and lend the world that air of quiet. Just enough to put that smell in the air, the clean and slightly bitter scent of snow, so unlike anything else on Earth. That snow-smell today was blended with the aroma of flowers and fresh-cut grass.

Eponine thought she would weep.

She climbed the balustrade where she had found Julian that one morning, a day that seemed forever ago, but was really just five months past. A few people milled around, taking pictures and admiring the snow. She took a bench beside a tall and thin young man. He was quite handsome, with high cheekbones, long curling hair, and hazel eyes that reminded her of the woods of The Ramble.

He had on a black leather jacket with his hands pushed deep into its pockets. His legs stretched out straight before him as he leaned back against the bench, just studying the sky. His eyes flickered over her as she came to sit, and he smiled shyly, without showing any teeth.

"Is it all right if I sit here?" she asked, but he was nodding before she'd even finished speaking.

She returned his warmth with a little grin of her own and sat.

"So." She tugged her denim jacket around her a little closer. It was drafty up on the battlement. "Do you come here often?"

He raised an eyebrow at her and laughed. "Uh, no. I am just visiting New York."

"I like the Castle."

"So do I." He was blushing a little.

"Have you been up to Fort Tryon Park? They have an entire medieval cloister rebuilt up there. The Met has a museum in it."

"Hmm, no, I didn't know that. I'll have to check it out."

Eponine giggled and realized she was sounding like a complete and utter moron. She closed her eyes and felt the sun and wind on her face. Long moments passed in companionable silence.

Finally the young man cleared his throat. "Can I ask you something? I usually don't ask questions like this to people I don't know. . . ."

Eponine very slowly turned to look at him. His long legs were tucked under him now and he leaned slightly forward, his elbows on his knees. A rather frazzled bit of hair was pulled loose from his ponytail and danced about on the errant breeze. He tucked it back behind his ear in a nearly unconscious gesture.

"I've been doing a lot of thinking lately, you see, and I'd like to get an unbiased opinion on something that's been really nagging at me."

Eponine chewed her lip and put on a bright face. "Sure, ask away. Let's see if I can help."

"That's really great of you to talk with me. I didn't think New Yorkers would be so . . . friendly."

"Well, I am not quite your average New Yorker. What is your question?"

He sat back again, his forest-colored eyes skittering over the treetops, picking out the buildings along the Central Park skyline. He let out a deep sigh and finally turned back to Eponine. He gazed at her for a long moment, but his scrutiny did not make her uncomfortable for some reason.

"Well, uhh, I wasn't raised particularly religious, but my mom's family is pretty serious about it, Baptists, and all. And my girl-friend used to be Catholic, but now she's pagan and pretty serious about *that*. And well, it's all rather confusing. I mean, there are *hundreds* of religions, so who is to say which one is right? I mean, do you believe in God?"

Eponine gave him a sincere smile. "Yes, yes I do."

"But really, do you actually *believe* in God?"

"Wholeheartedly."

He paused, his eyebrows drawing together. He nodded quietly. "You do. I can see that. But *why?*"

This time it was Eponine who gave him a quizzical look. "Why? What do you mean, *why?*"

"Well you can't just have blind faith!"

"No, of course not!"

"So . . . *why?*"

"I . . . can't really explain why. It's like . . . well, if you'd been adopted but never met your birth parents . . . I mean you'd still know your mother exists. She *has to;* you're alive."

He shook his head. "Yes, but that's pure biology and nothing else. You can't be saying if there were no God then none of us would be here? I mean, what about evolution? What about . . . *a lot* of things?" he asked.

"I don't know about you, but *I* wouldn't be here."

He laughed. "Let me guess. You are some sort of Christian who thinks you are specially chosen by God to be on the planet?"

Eponine laughed. "I am not really *Christian.*"

"But you seem to be telling me that you believe you were chosen by God to be here on Earth."

She thought about an answer that wouldn't confuse him, but nothing simple came to her. "It's a little more complicated than that, but *basically*, yes."

He blinked and waited for her to say more. "That's it?"

"What else is there? I mean if you come right down to it, every person alive on the planet was chosen to be here, chosen to be who they are where they are when they are. If you think there is no Divine plan in all of *that*. . . ."

"Wow. Well, I wish I had your faith."

"It's not faith, really. It's just my life. Well, this part of it, anyway."

He sat staring at her, open-mouthed, then chuckled. "Of all the people to have randomly come and sat down next to me. . . ."

Eponine winked. "Fate's funny that way, isn't it?" She giggled. "There's a girl I know, her whole life is like that. One big twist of Fate."

"I don't think I'd like that."

"But, really, when you look at it, that's all life is. For any of us. Even me."

"Even you, hmmm? God's special chosen one?"

She knew he was teasing. But it was strange how close he had come to the mark.

"Well," she said, reveling a bit in her own too-close-to-the-truth joke. "I wasn't *exactly* chosen. I volunteered."

"Volunteered? I guess it's like my girlfriend says, when you achieve enlightenment you can choose to go into Nirvana and become one with the universe or come back into the flesh and live again as a teacher. That's the theory behind Jesus, Buddha, Mohammed, and the other great religious figures." He laughed softly to himself. "Not a bad gig. Get to run around on Earth, commune with all the other mortals. We're not a bad lot, us mortals, don't you think?"

"Nah, you're all right." She rose with a smile and stretched. She was cold, and the snowclouds were beginning to darken and threaten rain. She gave him a dazzling grin. "Keep your chin up. A person's true character is seen in a crisis. Especially a crisis of faith. Listen to your heart."

"Thanks, I will." He went back to gazing out toward the Great Meadow, lost in his own thoughts.

For a moment, Eponine's own words haunted her as she thought of Julian and of her mission. *A person's true character is seen in a crisis.* She had seen Julian in a few. She'd so far seen him panic and run, and she'd seen him kill. Was there more to his soul than that? As an angel, he was the Divine embodiment of Vengeance. He was a hunter and a ruthless killer. He was great bravery in the face of injustice and terrible odds. He made Eponine's heart flutter when she thought of him. But he was ill: sick at heart and fading quickly. The world did love him too much, that she could see; and his illness was growing like a cancer. Only she stood between what remained of his soul and the great chasm that threatened to take him. He had fallen once, and violence had blazed across the Earth, vengeance meted out upon the innocent, misguided revenge seeking to wipe out whole peoples from the world. All under the banner of great justice. The world had never been the same. Battle lines were erased, and now no one was safe from the new wars that waged daily in the streets of some places and in the hearts of many men. The taste for blood and vengeance grew strong in the souls of humanity. Eponine trembled. And she had volunteered to put herself in the middle of it. *Volunteered.* Because she loved the world ... and because she loved Vengeance.

She smiled at the young man still sitting on the bench. He looked for answers, but she had none to give him, only more questions. *Just like Julian ... I have no answers for him, only more questions. If only he would learn to look within himself, he would find what he needed. The truth is in all of us; it is all of us. "To thine own self be true."*

The young man glanced up, and Eponine wondered if she had spoken aloud, or if he were becoming attuned to the voices of divinity. "What did you say?"

She smiled. He was close, tantalizingly close, to the awakening of his spirit and the end of this journey. Another journey would be waiting, but it would be one of discovery, not of searching. "I said, 'The truth lies in each one of us.' There is no answer I can give you. Never trust in God more than you trust yourself, though. I mean, don't go waiting for answers to come to you from on high, because they won't. Even I am denied that privilege. The only way to find the answers you seek is to look inside yourself. You cannot know true peace until you know your own soul. 'To thine own self be true.' And it's a lot harder than it sounds."

"It always is."

"But if the journey were easy, you could never appreciate the destination."

"Sounds like you've been talking to gypsies."

"As a matter of fact, I have. I have to get going now. It was nice talking to you, Caylen." Eponine waved and headed for the spiral staircase in the nearest tower.

"Wait, how did you know my name?"

She glanced over her shoulder back at him. "I have it on very good authority."

Eponine blew him a kiss, and the sun broke free of the cloud cover, illuminating the stone terrace and raising the temperature several degrees in mere seconds. The light bounced across the film of water that had once been snow. A puddle at Eponine's feet threw feathery gold reflections all around her, shimmering across the curved walls on the stairwell. She waved and, in a flash of shifting light, she was gone.

The young man went to the wall and looked down over

the edge. He watched Eponine dash back in the direction of the museum. She seemed to draw rainbows in her wake. He felt ... *rejuvenated.*

He waved in return, but she did not see, and he settled back down onto the bench. He stretched his legs out and slouched down into his jacket. He hadn't told her his name. And if she'd asked, that was not the name he'd have given.

"Evidently," he murmured to himself, "you have it on *very good* authority."

DREAMS

THE WEATHER OF LATE had been strange: First there had been warm, wonderful days, then it had snowed, and finally, a rainstorm rolled in that lasted half the week. It was disconcerting, and it made them both restless.

"April showers bring May flowers," Eponine told him with a winning smile.

Julian had grunted in reply.

The principal of the Ukrainian school had called to tell Eponine that Mrs. Devareaux was coming back from her maternity leave and she wasn't needed as a teacher's aide any longer. But since the children seemed to love her so, she was welcome to help out whenever she pleased.

Julian not-so-secretly reveled in the fact that she was home more often. Although she hadn't spoken of him, Julian knew that she was still exchanging e-mails and the occasional phone call with Jeremy. But he somehow felt better knowing that she wouldn't be seeing him regularly, no matter what her protestations of innocence were. He was still battling with himself whether to honor Eponine's mission and stay out of it, or to bring matters to a head and cut her off from all contact with Jeremy.

Why was I sent? Why did I have to bear witness to this? Who is that little blond runt that he gets Eponine's love as his own? This is not fair.

But he had caught Eponine looking at him on more than one occasion. He wasn't at all sure what it meant, but he knew if he got caught in the middle, the assignment would be a failure. He resolved to quash his affections for Eponine. Not only was he seriously impairing her heaven-sent mission, but he was crossing a line of propriety, of decency! There was no possible way for Joy and Vengeance to have that sort of relationship. But he could not forget the way she sometimes gazed at him. It made him ache to put his arms around her, but he did not. He put duty before desire. So far, it had been nothing more than the occasional lingering look, but Julian felt something underlying it. It felt like the weight of the air before the rain: a pressure, a waiting. All too soon, he feared, the storm would break.

IN THE DREAM, THERE was a storm.

Julian knew it was a dream with a simple surety that filled him with a profound sense of freedom and irresponsibility.

Lightning crackled, and the world went suddenly ultra-bright. Then, as if being sucked away with that wayward current of electricity, all the lights in the apartment went out.

He stepped carefully into the main room and was amazed to find that outside the windows, the city was pitch black as well.

"Julian...."

He could hear her voice, but had no idea where she was.

"I'm here," he answered.

He stood still and listened. From somewhere in the distance he heard the faint but steady *tick-tick-tock, tick-tick-tock, tick-tick-tock* of the little brass wind-up clock on Eponine's bedside table.

She touched him and he jumped. Her hand ran up his arm; her fingers were very warm but brought on goosebumps all over his skin.

"What are you wearing?" Her voice shivered with giggles as her hands tentatively touched his chest. She withdrew, her laughter fading into confusion when she felt nothing but his flesh. "Uhh, Julian...?"

He took her hands and held them easily in one of his; the other ran the length of one arm until it crested her shoulder. Her bare shoulder. It was wet there.

A look of consternation passed across his face, unseen in the total darkness. "Were you in the shower?"

"The bath," she replied, and he could hear her blushing.

"But it's the middle of the night...."

"But it's *your* dream, mister. How should I know what weird fantasies you've been having about me?"

He let go of her and backed away, expecting to run into the back of the sofa but finding nothing in his path.

"It's late. Come on; you'll catch your death." A flicker of golden illumination lit up her face. Behind her, he could see the doorway to her room all aglow with beeswax candles.

In the front room, there was nothing. The hardwood floor beneath his bare feet felt like stone, and it had suddenly become very drafty. He wrapped his arms around himself and wondered where his shirt had gone. He shivered visibly, and she came nearer to him. She was wrapped in a robe now; a simple, sheer thing, but it seemed to be keeping her warm.

"Julian, come on. I don't want you to have to stay in your room all alone with the heat and power out." The silver locket gleamed in the hollow at the base of her throat, just between her collar-bones. It throbbed slightly with her pulse. He reached out and touched it, remembering the night the power and heat *had* gone out.

"Is this what it's like," he whispered, "to be able to reopen a memory and step inside?"

She closed the small remaining distance between them and wrapped her arms around him. He felt the soft press of her body against his, warm and wrapped in silk. He felt . . . safe.

"It's *your dream*, silly. You can do anything you'd like here."

"But it's never been like this before. I have never dreamed like this . . . not like *this*. . . ." His own pulse thudded throughout his body, and he drew back again, suddenly self-conscious of the effect she was having on him.

The room beyond was bright and inviting; the darkness they were in was growing colder by the instant. She tugged at his wrists. For one moment, he felt rooted, frozen to the spot, but then he melted and flowed along beside her, not quite walking, not quite floating, but just *gliding* along.

She closed the door behind them with a quiet sound and regarded him with a shy smile. In the candleglow, her robe was nearly transparent. Her hair hung in one long river of chestnut brown, pooling on the floor at her feet. She had her hands clasped behind her and her eyes cast down. Her bed, which was usually blue, was now made up with ivory satin sheets and pillowcases with a matching comforter as thick as a cloud and shimmering velvet blankets.

Eponine glanced up, slightly confused at her surroundings.

"Is this what you want?" she whispered, wringing her hands at the small of her back.

"I suppose it is. After all, it is my dream, as you keep telling me."

She met his eyes with a mischievous glint. "You could have anyone, you know. Anyone at all."

Her face shifted into that of the gypsy girl's.

"Anyone at all." She spoke with Phina's voice as well.

He then saw her become Love, who was renowned for her beauty . . . and then Wisdom who was serene and severe . . . and then Peace who was golden and nearly childlike . . . Honor with her head held proudly . . . Hope who had hair like a sunrise that fell in huge ringlets . . . Charity with her clear, silvery eyes . . . and even Death, whom he loved like a sibling, with her hair blacker than his wings. . . .

"No. . . ." He closed his eyes and shook his head. They were there before him, one by one, all looking so human, all looking so lovely, and all looking *quite* feminine. Dressed in the same gossamer robe Eponine had been wearing, they had appeared before him in forms as human as his own.

"Then what is it that you want?"

He was tempted to say simply, "You." But the honesty in his heart won out. "I don't know. . . ."

"Come to bed, then, Julian." Her voice was sleepy and slurred.

He opened his eyes and found himself standing in her bedroom. Streetlamps cast long shadows across her walls, mottled by the tree branches that were now teeming with new leaves.

He was wearing nothing but boxer shorts.

Eponine propped herself up on one elbow and looked at him with sleep-glazed eyes. She wore her favorite flannel pajamas of clouds, fitting in so nicely with her sky-themed bed.

"Well?" She sounded at once both mildly irritated and fairly worried. "Julian?"

"Come to bed?" The words sounded thick and stupid to his ears.

"Yes. I mean, unless something has happened I can only imagine that's what you came in here for."

Mechanically, he shuffled to the other side of her bed, kicking one of her shoes and curling up the edge of her braided rug. He pulled her covers back and climbed inside. It was warm, so warm and so soft. Yes, he felt safe.

Eponine rolled over and cuddled up to him. "Goodness, you're cold!"

She rubbed her hands over his arms and chest. With her feet, she drew his legs against her own, entangling them in silken heat. He lay still, staring up at the stippling of light dancing across the ceiling. Eponine nestled her head in the crook of his shoulder, and he absently slipped his arm beneath her and rested his hand on her hip.

"Did you have a nightmare?"

His arm reflexively tightened, holding her even closer to him. He shook his head.

"Then what was it?"

"Promise me something," he whispered, his eyes still staring blankly up at the shadows on the ceiling.

"Julian! What's the matter?"

He turned his head, shocked to find her face so close to his. She was fully awake now, and he could feel her heart beating, outpacing her little clock. Fright and worry were etched clearly on her face. He put his other arm around her and made a soft sound at the back of his throat. He enfolded her to his chest and felt her breath on his bare skin.

"Promise me you won't dash off anywhere in the morning. Can you do that? Can I wake to find you here? Here with me...?" His voice broke off at the last bit.

"Of course," she murmured. "Of course, I will. I'll stay right here until you wake up. All the way until noon if need be."

He could hear the smile in her voice and found himself smiling in return. He hugged her tight for a moment.

"Thank you," he whispered into her hair.

"Now, tell me about this nightmare."

"I'll tell you in the morning."

"Are you sure? It had to be pretty bad to get you to come in here."

He shook his head and found that there were tears threatening to spill from his eyes. He couldn't find the voice to explain it to her.

"It wasn't a nightmare."

The memory surfaced, suddenly and with vibrant intensity, of her silk-clad body pressed up against his, merged with that lingering, hungry look in her eyes; the one she couldn't hide moments ago, half-asleep as he stood there in her room, nearly naked. And she was warm. So much warmer than he had ever remembered her being. She draped one leg lazily across his shins, and he drew his breath sharply. She had dozed back into sleep, a little smile on her lips. A little, devilish smile on her lips as she lay there with her arms and legs wrapped around him.

"It was a dream. . . ." His pounding heart finally slowed, and he felt too the pull back into slumber. "A dream. . . ."

BELTAINE

JULIAN DRIFTED TOWARD WAKING.

With a smile warm on his lips he turned to his left, expecting to see Eponine. Knowing she'd be there, because she had promised him she would be.

It took him a long moment to realize that not only was the rest of the bed empty, but that it wasn't even *her* bed he was in. He slumped over onto his back and let out a frustrated groan.

It had been last week. *Last week.*

That day he had opened his eyes in the broad midmorning light, almost afraid to turn his head, to look and see if she was still there. She *had to be.* She'd promised him she would.

She had been.

Her chin was tucked down toward her chest and her knees were drawn up, nudging his left hip. One arm was curled alongside her face and the other was draped across his shoulder. Her amber eyelashes shivered against her cheeks, and she looked up at him.

"Good morning," she whispered, a blush rising to her cheeks.

Julian had been able only to smile in return. He had awakened beside her at last.

And it had been last week. But every morning thereafter, he expected to see her, even though he didn't sleep anywhere but his own bed. She had given him an open invitation to join her to sleep whenever he pleased, but as of yet, he hadn't indulged. He could not let himself. The mission would be in pieces if he did; he knew that now. He could not do that to her. He could not ruin her chances like that. So instead he battled new dreams, new visions. Eponine in translucent silk, beckoning him to her bed. If she stood close by him and he caught her scent . . . he remembered the first time he'd noticed it. It had been the very second day they'd been on Earth. He should have known he was doomed from the beginning! He should have opted out, when it had been so early still. Any of his brethren could have taken his place: Strength, Justice, Honor, any of them. But he hadn't known the mission, then. He hadn't known she was to love one of them. He didn't realize he would have to sit and watch it all unfold in utter and terrible agony as she and Jeremy courted ... and to what end? He refused to think it, although his mind already cast up images for him. It was sheer torture! Worse than any suffering he had devised! It would have been his most brilliant master-work of vengeance, if only he wasn't doing it to *himself*! In a way, the terror-filled visions he used to have were easier to deal with. When blood-soaked nightmares invaded his mind from dark and forgotten corners of his memory, he knew what to expect. It was a familiar pain. But this wound was fresh and raw, and all he could do was to continue to pour salt into it and mock his own pain. The harder he tried to douse his love for Eponine, the stronger it grew.

A small knock at his door roused his attention from his contemplations of going back to sleep. Anyway, he knew it would mean only waking in hope followed closely by disappointment, as usual.

"Yeah, 'Nine," he called, cheerily. "I'm awake. Come on in."

Her head popped into the room. "If you're coming to the park with me, you'd better get dressed. I plan on grabbing breakfast on the way, and I still have to stop and get some flowers."

"What are you...?" He yawned widely enough to make his jaws creak. "What are you talking about?"

She rolled her eyes, playfully kicked the door open, and leaned against the jamb. "You've forgotten, haven't you?"

"Oh, no, baby, I'd never forget our anniversary!"

She laughed and her eyes darted about the room, looking for something to throw at him, no doubt.

"You *have* forgotten."

"Well, I know it's not your birthday." He flashed her his trade-mark rogue's grin.

"It's May first." She paused, expectantly. "Beltaine?" Again, nothing. "In the park? Maypoles and flowers and all that? I told you I was going, and you said you wanted to come? Ringing any bells yet?"

"Ding-dong."

"*You're* a ding-dong," she wrinkled her nose at him in mock chastisement. "Now, are you coming, or no?"

"Sure, why the hell not?"

"Because that's exactly what you said last night, and here it is the next morning and it's already gone from your head."

"Nah, I'll go, I'll go." He tossed back his covers and got out of bed. "Let me just throw something on, okay? How fancy is this thing?"

"It's a bunch of pagans wrapping ribbon around a big phallic stick in Central Park . . . how fancy do you *think*?"

EPONINE HAD BROUGHT A blanket and a picnic lunch. She had fresh cheese and French bread from the Farmer's Market along with green apples and grapes. Nearly a hundred people were milling around a high meadow nestled just off The Ramble, north of the lake.

There were several small groups practicing some sort of choreography and others reading papers in a tight knot. Most of the rest assembled there were lounging on their blankets, mats, or the bare grass eating lunch and weaving flower garlands. Eponine had two thick bouquets of dyed mums and a dozen pearl-colored roses. She tossed Julian one of the bouquets and set to work weaving her own garland. He watched her, fascinated, as she deftly entwined the stems into a sturdy headpiece.

She noticed his scrutiny and blushed a little. "What?"

"You're very talented." He frowned at the wilting and broken flowers in his hands. The dye was turning his fingers blue. "Help?"

"Like this." She gave him fresh flowers and showed him slowly how she'd plaited the stems together. Then she took his hands in her own and went through the motions, guiding his fingers with hers.

Julian felt his mouth go dry. He was trying to be a good student, but his fingers felt giddy and numb. All he could think about was the feel of her hands enlaced with his. Her work slowed, and she gave him a flirtatious sidelong glance. They sat for a moment, gazing at one another, up to their wrists in flowers and tangled in one another's fingers.

"Excuse me."

Julian jumped and scattered flower petals all over his lap. His knuckles popped as he quickly pulled free of Eponine's hands. Out of the corner of his eye, he saw her flinch at the interruption and cringe as he wrenched himself away.

The young man dipped his head in a nervous bow. "I am sorry

if I startled you, but we are looking for people who would like to participate in the ceremony."

"Oh, go on, Julian. It'll be fun!"

"Just me?" He didn't like the idea of that.

"I just want to run the maypole," she told him.

Julian gazed skeptically up at the boy, who looked barely out of high school. "What would you want me to do?"

"Well, uhh, actually," he flushed slightly, "I was wondering if you'd hold the sword?"

Julian's eyes lit up. "You got yourself a volunteer. What's your name, kid?"

"They call me Puck around here."

"Right. Well, around here, they call me Julian." He stood and reached out to shake Puck's hand with his blue-tinted one.

Puck laughed. "Well, right this way. Let me introduce you to Birch and Branwyn and Clio!"

"You'll be all right, 'Nine?"

"Just fine." She tossed him the garland she had made.

IT WASN'T EXACTLY AS exciting as he had hoped.

The High Priestess, who was Branwyn or Clio, he couldn't remember, gave him very detailed directions that amounted to "hold the sword, stand where I point, don't say anything." Then she handed him a red and black sarong and told him to remove his shirt and wrap the fabric around his waist. He opened his mouth to protest, but caught sight of Eponine lounging in the tangled roots of an oak tree just off the meadow, watching him. She was wearing a flower garland of her own. He sighed and pulled off the short-sleeved Henley he was wearing and tossed it aside.

At least it was a nice blade, heavy and well balanced with a thick pewter pommel and a hand-and-a-half grip wrapped in black leather. He stood still as stone and enjoyed playing the "guardian of the circle" for the first half-hour. But it was hot out in the meadow. The sun was bright and for the most part directly overhead. He wished he'd thought to bring sunscreen, but he hadn't exactly planned on being shirtless in the middle of a meadow for the better part of the afternoon.

They did a little pageant for each cardinal direction and element, said a thousand blessings, and ritually married the High Priest and Priestess. Then they uncast the sacred circle, and the outer circle of participants broke off and surrounded the three maypoles that had been set up. Julian stood behind the High Priest and Priestess, holding the blade skyward and looking impressive. Eponine was wearing her blue and white tie-dyed sundress and was fairly easy to spot, especially with that sweeping cascade of hair behind her. There were two other women with hair nearly as long, but not remotely as lustrous and beautiful as hers.

She ran with abandon with her feet bare and her hair streaming out from beneath her floral crown with a bright green ribbon in her hands. Over, under, over, under, over, under, and around and around. The group grew smaller and more concentrated as the ribbons wove down to the pole. Eponine was among the last left. She tied her ribbon into a big, floppy bow and rejoined the outer circle that was beginning to re-form.

The officiates of the ritual gave the final blessing and dismissed them all back to the impromptu picnic area for the traditional "cakes and ale." Julian finally lowered the sword. His muscles ached fiercely, and his skin felt taut. Puck came with the scabbard and took the blade to be put away with the rest of the ritual articles. He invited Julian to sit and eat with them. Julian nodded. His head hurt, and he figured eating would be a wise idea. He wondered where Eponine was. With the organized part now over, the ritual dissolved into a party and a little bit of chaos. The noise was hurting Julian's ears. But he ate a mouthful of the wheat loaf Puck handed him and drank down the entire cup of honeyed beer.

It wasn't long before Eponine found him. She had his shirt in her hand.

"Are you ready to go?"

Her words filled him with unbelievable relief. "Oh, yes, *very*. I am really tired."

She pursed her lips and bumped him playfully with her shoulder. "Not *too* tired, I hope."

"I just want to go home and go to bed, I think."

"Okay," she said with a cat's smile.

She took his hand and led him back down the path they'd hiked from the subway station.

"It was a nice ceremony. You did a great job."

"Yeah, fantastic amount of skill, you know. Me hold sword. Me stand here and guard. Grrrr!"

Eponine laughed and nudged up against him again. It stung.

"I think I got a little sunburned, 'Nine."

"I'll put some aloe vera on it when we get home, okay? That'll make you feel better. I'll rub it all over."

He nodded, glossing over Eponine's unintentional entendre like usual.

THEY WERE JUST GETTING to the Astor Place station when Julian realized he was far from feeling well. What had he eaten . . . the bite of bread and the big plastic cup of beer. He couldn't remember breakfast clearly at all. The rocking of the subway car and the combined scent of axle grease and wilting chrysanthemums was making him queasier by the minute. He was happy to get back outside, even if it was into the bright, after-noon sunshine.

"Do you want to get some lunch?" Eponine asked him, and for some reason she sounded as if she wanted him to say no.

He shook his head, his stomach lurching at the thought of food.

"All right, then. Home we go." Her eyes glittered tantalizingly, and he wondered what she was so happy about. But it would have to wait. All he wanted now was to lie down and rest.

Once inside the apartment, he flicked on the A/C to high and went into the bathroom to throw some cold water on his face. Eponine watched him go and dashed off into her room.

"You know, Julian. . . ."

"Hmmm," was the best answer he could manage as he care-fully peeled his shirt off his reddening shoulders.

"Beltaine is the biggest fertility holiday of the year. It was banned *for centuries*." She laughed, "Rated R for strong sexual content."

Eponine's "Five Sisters" incense began to fill the place with the heady scent of sage, lavender, and myrrh. And although it was still daylight, she had lit several candles and placed them in a close ring on her nightstand.

"It was a big deal once upon a time. The day when the maidens of the village went out into the fields with the young men and became women. Now, we don't have any fields . . . but I do have the requisite fire. Not quite a *bonfire*, but I think it will do." She shyly crept out into the main room. "Julian?"

The bathroom light was on, and the door was open. She

peeked in and was surprised to see herself blushing darkly. It spilled from her cheeks and down her chest, making a blotchy dark pink line between her breasts and spreading across her belly toward her hips. She suddenly felt embarrassed for wandering around the apartment in the nude. "Julian? Where are you?"

He didn't answer. It was ruining her plan; she wanted to have him just walk in on her naked. She figured that would toss aside his misguided impressions that her mission was all about Jeremy. Forgetting her momentary modesty and tossing her careful plans aside, she went straight to his room. His door was open, and he was lying across his bed, shoes still on and shirt still in hand.

She crossed her arms and sighed. "Wow. I guess you really were tired, weren't you?"

She stripped him of his shoes, socks, and pants and turned him to lie properly on the bed. She ran her fingers from his ankle all the way up to his shoulder, wondering if her caress would wake him. But when her fingertips brushed the skin of his upper body, her smile dipped down in dismay.

"Oh, boy, you are going to have one wicked sunburn." She sighed again. This was not going in any way according to her vision of it. "I guess I had better put some clothes on and go get you that aloe, then."

She bent over him and placed a soft kiss on his lips. Then she pulled just his topsheet over him and quietly left the room. She gave him one last, forlorn glance over her shoulder, which was also slightly burnt.

"Ah, well, I guess there will be other Beltaines. I was just hoping to celebrate this one with you."

She sighed and shut the door with a barely audible click.

PLEASURE IN PAIN

SHE ANSWERED THE CRY she had been expecting but dreading.

Julian had been asleep for a couple of hours, long enough for her to run down to the store for supplies and draw a cool bath filled with tea. She had taken a few minutes to run a Google search on sunburn remedies and was now stocked with aloe, baking soda, cornstarch, vitamin E lotion, and plain black tea.

He had cried out in surprised pain, and she was beside him in an instant. In the deepening shadows of the late afternoon,

Eponine could see that he was as red as a boiled lobster from his forehead down to his hips. He was sitting up, breathing roughly, with eyes wide.

"Nini." His voice was strained.

"Shush, now, just relax." She flicked on the light and recoiled from the blisters beginning to form on his flesh. He flexed his shoulders and the skin split in several places, oozing thick, clear liquid. "*Oh, fuck!*"

Julian stared dumbly at her, totally unwilling to believe what he had just heard come out of Eponine's mouth.

"Get up! Come on, let's go!"

With strength that shocked him even more than the expletive, Eponine pulled him out of bed. She yanked his boxers down and dragged him to the bathroom. He swore a blue streak as his tortured skin tried to stretch and bend, hardly even noticing he was now completely naked. Without so much as a downward glance, Eponine all but threw him into the bathtub, which was filled with cold tea. Julian howled and she shook a few cocoa-brown pills out of the ibuprofen bottle and pushed them into his mouth.

"Swallow," she said sternly, pressing his upper body beneath the water carefully. "My God, you're burning up. . . !"

He gagged on the pills; their coating was rapidly dissolving in his throat. Eponine let him sit up again and quickly brought a glass of water to his lips.

Julian downed the entire cupful. "More, please! I'm so thirsty. . . ."

"Hold on." She was dipping towels into the tea water and draping them across his afflicted shoulders. "Stay right there."

She rushed from the bathroom and returned with a large, plastic Disney mug. Julian growled. Brer Bear, Brer Fox, and Brer Rabbit were cavorting among vines of red roses and obviously mocking his pain. But he snatched the cup from her and held it to his parched lips with both hands, gulping the water down most audibly.

"More! Please!"

Eponine filled the cup at the bathroom sink and Julian downed that as well, not even noticing the usual metallic taste of the unfiltered water from the pipes. He looked at her over the white plastic rim. She was soaking wet in her navy blue sweatpants pulled up to her knees and a gray ribbed tanktop. Her floor-length hair was coiled in back in a bun the size of a round French bread and held in place with three long chopsticks. He finished the glass with a gasp and handed it to her.

Eponine returned it to him filled, and he sipped it more slowly this time. She knelt on the wet tiles beside the bath and caught her breath. Her heart was racing, and the adrenaline was slowly ebbing from her body. Julian was beginning to shiver. Goose-bumps broke out across his flesh and he grimaced, gritting his teeth against crying out. Eponine lifted the wet towels. They were already hot to her touch from their contact with his burns. She saw the blisters beginning to recede slightly, the skin around them not quite as taut and strained as before. She dipped the towels in the cool water and draped them again across his shoulders. He hissed through his tightly clenched jaws. He had never known such pain. Somewhere in his mind, he sought to remember this sensation for future reference, if he ever met someone vile enough to deserve such torture.

"'A pain only my enemies should know,'" he quoted, humorlessly.

The Advil began to dull the jagged and cutting edges of his pain.

"I'm cold, 'Nine. Can I get out now?"

"Sure." She helped him to his shaky legs and ever so gently draped a towel over him.

Julian stood dripping on the fluffy bathroom mat, trembling with cold but also disturbingly warm. His skin was a mass of shrieking, raw nerves that felt every fiber of the terrycloth towel. Eponine softly patted him somewhat dry and led him across the kitchen to her room. There were towels already spread over her comforter, and she sat him down atop them. Nimbly, she smeared thick, cold, green gel across his chest. It smelled of menthol and fresh-cut grass. The sensation was both cooling and warming, and he relaxed a little. She laid him down on his stomach and, with the most tender care, worked the gel into his blistered back.

Although it hurt like hell to move at all, he reached his hand out for hers. Her fingers were sticky with aloe vera when he squeezed them.

"I feel like I have ruined something," he whispered. "Something important. . . ."

"Shhh. Don't worry about anything right now."

"Eponine . . . Joy. . . ."

"No, don't try to get up." She put her hand firmly on the small of his back, where he wasn't burned. She left a tingling residue there that reminded him he wasn't wearing a stitch of clothing. He was rather abruptly glad that he was lying on his belly. His cheeks flushed, but he doubted she could see it under the sunburn.

He glanced around the room and saw the pitcher. Eponine followed his eyes and immediately poured him a glass of water. He gingerly raised himself up enough to sip at it.

Eponine stroked the top of his head. She chucked. "Well, at least your scalp's not burnt like mine is."

"Well, thank heaven for small favors, then, hmm?"

She laughed aloud at that. "I think you're going to be okay."

The streetlamp just outside her window hummed into life and filled the room with a flat yellowish light just as the last of the sunset was disappearing.

"I'm still tired. And a little cold."

She tucked one of her lap blankets from the sofa around his waist, covering him to the feet.

"I can't stay here," he protested.

"You will too stay here. Right here where I can keep watch on you."

"Okay, I concede the victory."

"That was too easy, mister."

"I am not feeling quite myself right now, in case you were wondering. I am covered in blisters and naked on my roommate's bed. Not *exactly* how I thought to be spending tonight."

Eponine winked, "Weren't banking on those blisters, were you? At least not *before* you went to bed."

Julian's head shot up and he bellowed in agony, forgetting all about the meaningful glare he was intending to cast toward her. Eponine clucked her tongue and gently spread more aloe gel onto his back.

"I wish I could heal you," she whispered to him. "But all I can do is give you some happiness to make you forget how much it hurts."

He raised an eyebrow at her, and it made his forehead sting. He had found a reasonably comfortable position with his arms crossed over his chest and his head turned to one side. She slid down beside him, keeping about an inch distant the entire length of his body.

"Now promise me that you're going to stay calm and in

control. Else you'll open up those blisters again and this will be all for naught."

"Eponine, what are you thinking of...?"

"Just promise me, will you?"

"Okay. But, I still don't...."

She kissed him then, solidly, cutting off the last of his words. A wave of electric pleasure surged through him, raking his ravaged skin. But the sensation faded into a sweet lull of warmth that slowly began to fill him, body and soul. Her mouth was soft but insistent against his lips, and he had to fight himself to stay still, to let her work whatever magic she was attempting.

He found himself drifting.

Dreams closed in around him like a downy blanket. And in that sleep-soaked world of shifting colors, he was whole and unhurt. He could lift his arms and pull Eponine close against him. He could hold her tightly and kiss her in return. Her body dissolved in his arms, becoming as incorporeal as mist, but left within him both a pervading sense of comfort and an even deeper feeling that he could not readily name. He was thirsty again. Thirsty to the bottommost reaches of his soul, it seemed.

From somewhere across the great divide of consciousness, he could still feel her lips.

Eponine clung close against him, her lips pressed against his, eager to soothe his distress, and her own. She could feel him slipping away from her, deeper into sleep. And as much as she wanted to draw him back to waking, she knew she must let him rest if he was to heal.

But before he slunk totally away into the dark, he lifted his arm and wrapped it tightly around her. She swallowed his groan of pain and breathed ecstasy into his mouth instead. His body twitched from head to foot, and he was gone into the depths of sleep. She tumbled into unconsciousness herself with a pleasant shudder, her lips still softly touching his.

Then all was still.

TEMPER, TEMPER

EPONINE GAZED LISTLESSLY AT the dawn slowly filtering through the apartment, turning the place first somber gray, then softly gilded. She hadn't slept much, far too aware of Julian's suffering to be able to rest. He lay still and peaceful in her lap, his sleep a thin veneer over the pain of his skin. He'd be well enough again soon; she would see to that. Already the blisters were but a memory. She'd smoothed cool aloe gel over his shoulders all night long.

Slowly, Julian pulled himself back into the waking world. He'd had a wonderful dream of being a small black cat curled up in a purring furry ball on Eponine's lap. Coming fully into consciousness, he found that his head was pillowed against the small roundness of her belly, and his upper body was lying across her lap.

She looked down at him as he stirred. "How are you feeling?"

He grumbled and rubbed his eyes, flinching at the shooting pain from moving his shoulders. "Thirsty. . . ."

"Still?"

"Mmm-hmm."

"Come now, sit up a little and I will give you some water." She poured a fresh glass from the pitcher that was still on the bedside.

Julian downed it in one long draught.

"More?"

"Not just yet." He carefully pulled himself into a seated position and wished he could lean back against the pillows. "Was that all really yesterday? All of this that happened?"

Eponine laughed. "Oh yes, you had better believe it."

"I am feeling like I am missing something. . . ."

She toyed with an errant lock of his hair. "Nope, not really. We came home and you zonked out. I woke you and put you in the bath and then brought you to bed."

He glanced over at her and noticed the dark circles beneath her eyes. "You haven't slept, have you?" He reached for her hand and found it a little sticky with aloe. He remembered grabbing her fingers the previous night, as she massaged the healing gel into his shoulders. He saw the nearly empty aloe vera bottle on the nightstand between her clock and the pitcher. "You've stayed up all night for me."

"Well, what was I supposed to do?"

His eyebrows arched and he felt very deeply touched. "Oh, 'Nine, you didn't have to do that . . . but . . . thank you."

"Oh, silly, you're welcome. What do you want to eat for breakfast?"

"Something cool and fresh . . . do we have any fruit? I am craving fruit really bad."

"Heavens, perhaps the sun *did* bake your brain!" She laughed at his scowl. "I think I have just the thing. Do you want me to bring it in here, or set up in the kitchen so you can watch TV?"

"May I eat in here?"

"Of course."

"Will you sit in here and have breakfast with me?"

She chuckled. "Yes. Are you done with the separation anxiety?"

He colored and looked away. "Out in the front room is fine."

"Now, Julian, I didn't mean. . . ."

"I said the front room was fine." He pushed the covers down, then abruptly pulled them back over his lap. He blushed darker than his sunburn. "Where are my clothes?"

"In your room. Shall I get them for you?"

"Please. I don't like the idea of strolling around naked."

"Yes, sir, Mister Modesty, sir!" She slid from the bed and paused in her doorway. "But, I mean, it's not like I have never seen you naked before."

"When?" Julian raced through his memory, but with so many gaps, he realized that anything could have happened in the previous twenty-four hours and he would have no idea.

"Uhhh, last night? When I bathed you, for starters. And it's not like we really *wear clothes* back home. . . ."

"And it's not like we really have bodies *quite* like this at home and . . . never mind! Just bring me some sweats or something, would you, 'Ponine?" Sweat stung his scalded flesh and he felt vaguely nauseated. Why did she have to insist on being flirty *now*?

She giggled. "Oh. yes, I see why you like this!"

"*Like what?*"

"Having the upper hand over a superior foe," she said with an impish wink, "and watching the poor soul *squirm!*"

"That's a horrible thing to say! I don't take delight in the suffering of others!"

"Goodness, you really are in pain. Where in the world has your sense of humor gotten to?" Her gaze flickered over him and she smiled.

"Damn it, Eponine! Must you make this as difficult for me as possible? You like to see me suffer, is that it? Tease me and torment me, put yourself on display like I can *have you* and then dart it away like some cat toy? And on top of all that, you expect me to have a sense of humor about my situation? I have had enough, Eponine. I have just had enough!" Rage seethed through him, prickling his skin, but he could not care. He welcomed the pain;

it obliterated all thoughts of *her*. He snatched up one of her throw blankets and wrapped himself in it and stormed from the room.

"Julian. . . ."

Once in private, he threw the blanket out into the hallway and slammed his door.

"I can take care of myself," was the muffled statement that came from his room.

Eponine was suffused with anger and utterly at a loss over what to do about it. She kicked his door as hard as she could, tears spilling down her face. "You *ruin everything*!"

He heard her run back to her room and slam her own door.

"*I'm* the one ruining everything? This is *not* about me," he shouted in her direction. "I am not the one playing Poke the Bear with the goddamn angel of fucking Vengeance!"

There was quiet in the house. Far down the hallway, he heard the heavy metallic *bang* of the stairwell door. Silence closed in. He felt like a heel.

"Hey, Eponine?" He opened his door a crack. Her bedroom stood open, and there was a small pile of cloud-print flannel near the door. "Uhh, 'Nine?"

You've done it now, he chided himself. *She's gone, probably run to Jeremy, and that'll be the end of things for you. At least that means the assignment might be over with sooner and you can get home where you belong.*

Regardless of her angry outburst, there *was* something he'd missed yesterday. *Something important.*

But for the life of him, he couldn't place what it could possibly be. And now it was too late. His chance had passed, and she was running to the arms of another man. A man who was her destiny here on Earth. Julian was powerless to stop her, or change the course of events that were marching forward toward an inevitable conclusion.

Julian slumped down onto the sofa and immediately leapt to his feet as he rasped his scalded skin against the upholstery.

He howled in pain, but there was no one to hear him.

SHELTER

IT WAS FOOLISH OF her to be upset, she knew. Julian was laboring under a very misinformed notion of what the two of them were doing there. And as much as she wanted to, Eponine could not bring herself to explain everything to him. Each time she tried, her tongue dried up in her mouth and she was unable to speak. Her plans to lay his worries to rest had been shot down by the most intense sunburn she'd ever heard of. So Julian was left free to leap to his paranoid conclusions, which he had done with exquisite dramatics.

Outside, the sun was now bright enough to make her squint, and it was starting to feel a touch humid, hinting at the sweltering summer that was soon to arrive.

He doesn't know, she thought to herself. *You can't very well hold it against him if he doesn't even know what's going on!*

She took off her denim jacket and draped it over her shoulder bag. The back of her neck was already damp with sweat beneath her hair.

And he's not well, you know that. Besides the problems he came here with, he's had a lot of sun. Shame on you for leaving him back there!

She argued with herself all the way down the block, but never turned back toward the apartment. She stopped at the steps of the Ukrainian school and very much wanted to go in. But she thought about trying to explain her mood to her students and suddenly didn't think it was such a good idea. Her temper had run out of momentum, and now she stood staring dumbly at the gray granite façade of the school building.

"Eponine? Is that you?"

She looked over to the front doors to see Jeremy standing there, his bookbag and a sweater in hand. He trotted down the stairs with a grin on his face.

"It *is* you!" He came just shy of hugging her. "How have you been?"

"I've been all right."

His face clouded, "You sure? You look a fright."

"Gee, thanks. I didn't sleep well last night."

"Are you *sure* you're okay?"

She nodded and smiled at him. "Fine, I'm fine. What are you doing out of school? Isn't there class today?"

"My afternoon class is out on a field trip, and I have the rest of the day free. Was just heading out to Kiev to drink some coffee and contemplate how to fritter away my afternoon. Care to join me?"

She glanced back down the street then nodded. "Sure. Yes, definitely. I need to get out of the house today."

THEY SAT AT A table in the back corner beside the window with two cups of coffee and a basket of toasted challah between them.

"Something's bothering you, I can tell," he began, gently.

She dipped her buttery crust into her coffee and ignored him.

"Eponine...."

She favored him with a warm smile. "I appreciate your concern, but really, I'm okay."

The waitress brought them their food. Apple pancakes for Jeremy and boiled cheese pierogi for Eponine. They ate in silence.

"So, you want to catch a movie?"

"Movie?"

"Yeah, I don't know what's playing, but we could walk up to the theater at Union Square and see."

"I think that'd be fun, actually."

The waitress brought the check. "My treat," Jeremy announced. "Now, now...."

"I insist ... but ... only if you tell me what's wrong."

She sighed and did not look amused in the slightest. "Honestly, Jeremy, it's none of your business."

He took fifteen dollars out of his wallet and left it on top of the tab, covering both the food and the tip.

"I knew it," he muttered, gathering up his things.

"Knew what?"

He handed her bag and jacket to her and opened the exit-only door that was near their table. He waited until they were outside and walking up Second Avenue.

"What's bothering you. It's Julian, isn't it?"

"I don't want to talk about it with you, if you don't mind," she said, her eyes on the pavement.

"Actually, I *do* mind. You're starting to scare me, 'Ponine."

"*Scare you*? How in the world do I scare you?" She gave him a wary glance.

"It's just sounding like a classic case of abuse here." Jeremy wrestled with the impulse to put his arm around her shoulders.

"*Abuse*? You've got to be kidding me!"

"No, I'm not." He didn't reach out, but he gazed over at her for a long moment, feeling caught between anger and tears. He nearly walked into a newspaper box on the sidewalk.

Eponine laughed. "Oh, don't worry about it. It's not what you think."

"Has he ever hit you?"

"*Julian?*"

"Who else?"

"No, of course not." *Well, except that one time when he threw me up against the wall, but that's different. And it all ended up okay, anyway.*

"You are lying to me."

She stopped. "No, Jeremy, Julian has never hit me."

"Why don't you come to the school anymore?"

"The principal called and said I wasn't needed since Mrs. Devareaux was back."

"I meant before that. I heard Julian called the school and said you wouldn't be there for a few days."

"That's true; he did."

"Why?"

"Because I was unable to call, myself." She began walking again, not liking at all how the conversation was going.

"Why couldn't you call?"

"I *wasn't able.*"

He nodded his head, slowly, as if sifting through her words to find her true meaning. He said nothing more until they got to the movie theater. Once there, he bought tickets for a movie that sounded fairly good to them both, and they went upstairs.

IT WAS A GORGEOUS late afternoon when the movie let out. Eponine and Jeremy strolled though Union Square Park, wandering back toward the Farmer's Market. Eponine bought a piece of honeycomb to suck on.

"So, tell me about him."

"About who?"

"Julian. You know, I haven't seen the guy much outside of his threats to my personal safety on my own front stoop."

"That was *hardly* a threat."

Jeremy's glare was cold. "Oh? You don't think so?"

"Nah. He has a temper, but he wouldn't hurt you."

"He's a fucking bully, Eponine, and I don't know why you put up with that!"

"Hush, now." She laughed a little self-consciously. "There is very little I can say to make you understand him. You two will never get along."

"I'm serious, just because he isn't *physically* hurting you. . . ."

"Jeremy, you don't understand him. I do."

"Can't you hear yourself?" He had wandered over to Broadway and was hailing a cab.

"What are you doing?"

"Taking you home. And making you dinner."

"Jeremy. . . ."

The cab came to a stop and Eponine looked dubiously at it. He touched her arm and looked into her golden-flecked eyes.

"Just for a little while," he said softly, with genuine concern in his voice.

"Just for a little while," she agreed. "Someplace private and quiet where I can try and explain. . . ."

He nodded and helped her into the cab.

AFTER A LIGHT DINNER of chicken stir-fry with jasmine rice, they sat on his couch with glasses of crisp white wine.

"So, explain," he said, leaping into the hanging conversation that had not been touched since they'd left the park.

Eponine's head perked up and she blushed. "Well, so much for a subtle lead-up."

"I want to know, 'Ponine. Because right now, I am not about to let you go back there."

"Jeremy Peyton!"

"I'm serious. You don't have any idea what you sound like. He hurt you today, somehow. And it wasn't the first time, nor will it be the last."

"It was stupid. We fought. Friends fight, Jeremy, even good friends. It happens."

"Not like this it doesn't. You've gotten all defensive since I brought it up. Doesn't sound like a normal little argument."

"But that's all it was! And really, I deserved it!"

"You *what*?"

"That came out wrong. What happened was that I said something stupid that I shouldn't have. I really goaded him, and he's sick, he got all sunburned, and I should have been more patient but I wasn't and I really pissed him off and he got all huffy and slammed the door, and we were yelling at each other. . . ." She stopped to catch her breath and realized she was sobbing. Not for the reason Jeremy thought, but because the realization that she had left Julian alone when he was ill and upset and obviously *needed her* finally hit home. "And we were supposed to have a good time for Beltaine but it got all ruined and it wasn't his fault at all. It was mine because I didn't remember the sunscreen, and there's all this stuff going on that I can't tell him about and now it's all a mess and you think he's abusing me and he's not, but I can't make you understand him or what he's like because it's only going to make things worse because I can't explain *anything* to anyone right, and now you *really* hate him and *that's* all my fault too, and he is just going to *kill me* when he finds out I was here because he is going to think something is up between us and he's going to get all chivalrous but really he's burning up with jealousy inside but he won't say anything because he thinks I need to be here with you and . . . and I don't know why I am telling you *any* of this. . . !"

Her voice faded into deep, gulping sobs, and Jeremy put his arms around her.

"Oh, God, Eponine. I had no idea."

She shook her head. "No, no! See, this is what I meant! You don't understand. I *love* Julian."

"Of course you think you do. Over ninety percent of abused women choose to stay in their relationship, and those who leave end up going right back to their abuser."

She took a deep breath, calming her crying. "Julian *doesn't* abuse me."

"Yes, he does. I think he physically threatens you and psychologically controls you. He's jealous and possessive and very violent. You've said it yourself; you said it just now. That's *not healthy*, Eponine!"

Eponine leaned back against the sofa and put her wine-glass down on the end table. She rubbed her temples and sighed heavily.

"Listen, I *know* it might *sound* bad, but that's really not what it's like."

"Uh-huh," Jeremy said, unconvinced.

"I'm serious!"

"So am I!"

She shrank back into the cushions, and Jeremy softened. He scooted closer to her and ran the back of his hand across her cheek.

"Look at you. You're afraid."

"I have had a long day is all. I'm tired of arguing."

"Well, you can stay here as long as you'd like."

Eponine sighed, feeling her head was too heavy to lift. It was a long cab ride from the Upper East Side back to Astor Place.

"Is this just a ploy to get me in your bed?" She smiled to hear Julian's trademark cynicism flow so easily from her lips.

"I'll take the couch. It has a fold-out bed."

She arched an eyebrow at him, but he wasn't joking. His gilded hair fell across his eyes, and his smooth, high forehead was now pinched with worry.

"Eponine, you are so beautiful, so loving, sometimes I feel like you shouldn't even be on this planet with the rest of us jerk-offs. Especially with *him*. He doesn't deserve you."

To Jeremy's surprise, she laughed. "Oh, I know he doesn't. Not yet. But I am trying to change that."

Jeremy shook his head sadly. "I really think you should see someone."

"Don't worry about me, Jeremy. I think he and I both needed a night apart to cool off. Thank you for making that possible."

"You're welcome. Just promise me you'll think about this."

"I promise."

"He doesn't love you, Eponine."

She blinked at him, sleep hovering in the corners of her vision.

"Don't speak of what you don't know," she told him and shakily stood. "Can you show me where I'll be sleeping?"

"You'll stay?"

"It's too late to go home now. I'm too tired."

He nodded and put his arm around her, leading her to his bedroom. He pointed out the bathroom and switched off the light.

"If you need anything, I'll be right here, okay?"

She nodded. "Thank you. I appreciate the hospitality."

He gave her a warm kiss on the cheek. "I care a great deal about you, 'Ponine. I just want to see you happy."

"I *am* happy, believe it or don't. I can't help but be what I am."

He looked confused and gave her a hug. "Get some sleep, sweetheart. You look like you really need it."

He shut the door, and she crawled across the bed. It was the same size as her own but felt so much bigger. It was cool and flat and so utterly unlike hers!

She suddenly missed Julian terribly. But Jeremy's words had some truth in them. It seemed that whenever they got close, the two of them, something would happen. There would be a fight, or a misunderstanding. Julian seemed convinced that her mission included running off with Jeremy. And now . . . oh, if he found out where she was . . . that would seal it. There would be no healing him from that heartbreak. But what could she do now? She was on her own in this and still at a loss. Eponine burrowed into Jeremy's thin, thermal blankets and lay awake under their light weight for a long while.

What if Jeremy were right? What if she was trying to pull something from Julian's soul that did not even exist? It was a thought too dreadful for words. It would imply things she could not bring herself to think about. . . .

She sang to herself in a soft whisper in the dark of Jeremy's room, trying to lull herself to sleep. She heard him pull out the hide-a-bed with a slightly rusty squeal, then the light switched off and all was quiet. Her voice cracked and faded, and she dozed off with tears glinting on her eyelashes.

Jeremy listened to her from out in the front room. His chest felt like a lump of ice.

Damn you, Julian, for making her cry. You don't deserve her tears. You don't deserve that kind of love. I wish I could go to her . . . but she doesn't want me, just you. She loves you, and you don't even seem to notice. . . .

CLOSE TO THE EDGE

"YOU'RE STILL ASLEEP? GOOD God, sweetheart, it's nearly one in the afternoon!"

Eponine rubbed her eyes, then burrowed her face back into the pillow. Broken dreams still haunted her memory, and she struggled to catch them. There was something important there, an urgent message.

Warm hands pulled the sheet from around her head. "Come on, now. I've been out to my class and back already. . . ."

She could see herself in a dark room in the dream. Before her was an open door into a place filled with light and sound. Yes, the message was there! If she could just take the two steps through that doorway, she'd have it!

The door swung shut and the wide, bright swath of light collapsed down to a single thread before vanishing.

"Eponine, wake up."

There was no turning back now. Sleep had gone. She fought to stay in that dark room in her mind and groped for the memory of the dream. It was elusive, but she nearly had it in her hands. It was *right there*.

"Oh, my God...!"

Her eyes snapped open at the sound of Jeremy's voice, and Eponine forgot the room, the dream, and for a moment, even where she was. Confusion set in, and she stared uncomprehendingly at Jeremy for a long while. He was saying something about her hair. He was sitting on the bed...*his bed*, she realized...holding a lock of her hair at arm's length.

"...remember it being red? I mean I *thought* I did, but I could be wrong.... Was it always this long?"

"Yeah," she lied. "It's been this long for a while now. And the red was only a rinse. It washed right out."

Jeremy looked at her, a little dazed. "Funny, I don't remember it being quite this long...."

"Oh it wasn't *quite* this long, but it's been a while since you've seen me, you know." She smiled and he nodded.

"Are you hungry?"

Eponine giggled. "Are you trying to fatten me up or something?"

"Let's get some lunch."

"I really ought to get home. I have a bad feeling."

"Nonsense!" He slid closer to her and gave her a charming grin. "Okay, okay. So we'll get food in your neighborhood then, okay? That way I can treat you to lunch and walk you home. Sound like a deal?"

"You're not giving up until I say yes, are you?"

He shook his head. "So, where do you want to eat? Veselka...Dojo's...Lexi's Mexican...Tres Giovanni...?"

"Well, let me get cleaned up a little and I'll think about it."

He left the room so she could freshen up in the attached bathroom and straighten the clothes she'd slept in.

THEY TOOK THE CROSSTOWN bus to Lexington Avenue and the Six subway line to Astor Place. They agreed on Veselka's for lunch.

"I really miss seeing you, 'Ponine," Jeremy said, suddenly

feeling shy. "School's not the same without you there. The kids don't smile as much."

"Don't say that. I am sure they are fine."

"They miss you."

"I'll come visit soon, I promise."

He nodded and sipped his coffee. He grimaced and poured in more milk and sugar. "Veselka's coffee is too strong!"

"'Black as a moonless midnight' says the menu," she told him with a mischievous giggle.

It amused her to think that Julian knocked back that coffee like it was water. She was taken with an icy chill at the image of his face. She pushed the rest of her eggs and kashi aside.

"I think I need to get home now."

"Aww, but 'Ponine, it's early yet!"

She smiled and squeezed his hand. "I need to get home, Jeremy. But thank you for a wonderful couple of days. You've been a big help. I don't know what I would have done without you."

His face lit with a thrill of euphoria. "You mean that, don't you?" He took both of her hands in his and kissed them. "'Ponine, you have no idea how much I adore you. You know if you ever need me. . . . "

"You'll be there. Yes, I know, Jeremy, dear, I know. But really, I must be going now."

"I don't want you to go back there. He'll be angry. I am worried about you."

She laughed and pulled her hands free, drawing her fingertips across his palms. "Fear not. If it's one thing I know how to do, and know how to do *well*, it's handle Julian."

"You have my cell phone number. Day or night, it's on. I'll come get you, no matter where or what time, do you understand?" He rose and put his arms around her in a strong hug.

"I know. Thank you." She pulled back and felt a pang of guilt at leaving him there with the corners of his eyes beginning to glisten and a simpering smile on his face. "I have to go."

It seemed like a force of will, but he reluctantly let her go. "Take care, 'Ponine."

"No problem, Jeremy. None at all. See you soon." She blew him a kiss and walked quickly from the restaurant.

Out in the street, it was a busy afternoon. Traffic was starting to accumulate and children of all ages were getting out of school. She rushed past the Ukrainian school but didn't see any of the students she knew. Which was all right by her; she felt the pressing need to get home right away.

She waved to her doorman, who made some protest at her having been gone all night, but his words echoed, unheard, in the empty lobby as the heavy stairwell door swung closed behind her. She paused in the hallway in front of her apartment, a little afraid and even more ashamed to go in.

What *would* he say?

She put the key in the lock and turned it, shocked to find that it wouldn't budge. She twisted it harder and turned the whole knob beneath her hand. The door was unlocked.

Strange.

She remembered she hadn't locked it behind her when she'd stomped out the previous morning, but this was impossible.

I've been gone a day and a half. Surely Julian must have come and gone by now. . . .

Perhaps he was down in the basement doing laundry. They never locked their door when they were still in the building.

She stepped into the short front hall and shivered. Something was not right.

"Julian?"

The door to his room was closed and hers was still open a bit, with her pajamas piled on the floor just inside. The plate she had been intending to use for breakfast was still sitting on the counter. Nothing in the apartment had been touched at all in the past thirty hours. Something was definitely wrong.

"Julian!" She knocked on the door to his room. There was no answer.

She opened the door and was shocked to see him lying in bed.

A bubble of relieved laughter escaped her, "Julian, this is *extravagantly late* to be in bed, even for you!"

He didn't stir. The air in the room was heavy with the cloying scent of illness. Eponine threw the door wide and ran toward him. Shadows flickered near the edges of her vision. She thought she was going to faint.

His skin was raw and burnt painfully red, but it also looked pallid at the same time. He was both feverish and clammy at once with cracked lips and deep circles beneath his sunken eyes. A sweet odor of infection lingered around his broken blisters, and he emanated a scent of sickness and fever.

Eponine collapsed to her knees, not even feeling them strike the hardwood floor.

"*Julian!*"

His chest rose sharply, then slipped back into its shallow and nearly imperceptible movements. Her heart thundered into her ears. At least he wasn't dead. She hadn't been sure when she had first seen him.

Cold fear gripped her inside, freezing her to the spot. Julian stirred and tried to speak. Fresh blood seeped out of what was already caked on the splits in his lips. His forehead puckered, then smoothed, but he did not look any calmer, any more relaxed. Eponine forced herself to stand. She brushed back his hair and felt his forehead. He was hot, hot from the burn and from a deep and high fever. She reached down beneath him, behind his neck and between his shoulder blades. There wasn't a drop of moisture there. He wasn't sweating. That was a very bad sign.

She ran to bring the pitcher and glass from her room. Carefully, she lifted his head and brought the cup of water to his lips. It dribbled down his chin. She had to get him to drink!

She rushed to the kitchen and banged a tray of ice into a big salad bowl. Back in the bedroom, she slid slivers of ice into his parched mouth. She swore even his *teeth* were dry.

"Oh, God, Julian, don't die...." But she felt the eyes on her. Unseen eyes and the hush of silence. In her mind, she could see Death. Saw her as Julian's sister, pale and dark and silent and waiting. Eponine did not acknowledge her presence there.

She pressed more ice between his lips. He choked once, and his eyes flickered open.

"You're too late," he rasped. "You blew it. Get out."

"Julian!"

He slid back into sleep, and Eponine fell across his chest, crying helplessly into his blankets.

"You won't die, you won't! This isn't finished, yet, Julian!"

She swung her legs up beside him, cramming onto the narrow bed with him. Taking the ice chips and slipping them into his mouth became an automatic motion for her. She lay there and fed them to him until the sun set, hours later.

The phone rang, and she heard Jeremy's voice on the answering machine asking if she was all right and giving her the number of the battered women's shelter down in the East Village.

She stayed beside Julian, lying on her side to give him the

most space in his bed, and fed him more ice. She got up at one point in the night like a sleepwalker and brought him the little jar of Carmex lip balm from the pocket of her trenchcoat that was hanging in the hall closet. She dabbed his lips now and again between rounds of ice.

"I never should have left. What's wrong with me? Why did I lose my temper like that? I think you're a bad influence on me, mister." She let herself smile a little at that. "Now, if only I am being a *good* influence on you, then we'd be in business."

She stroked his forehead. She thought that perhaps he felt a *little* cooler. She hoped he did, anyway.

"Don't leave yet," she whispered. "It isn't time to go."

She glanced up at the thick, nighttime shadows that had gathered around the bed and hallucinated the eerie, fathomless eyes of Death in all of them.

"It isn't time to go," she repeated, no longer sure to whom she was speaking.

VOICES IN THE DARK

"HE'S DOING BETTER THAN I thought he would," spoke the first voice in a quiet and measured tone.

"He's not even half through yet," was the answer, a woman talking. Her voice was quiet as well, but chilling rather than calming. "And I am already here. They should have sent Love to do this."

He laughed, the first speaker. "Now you know he can't stand Love. She gets him into almost *all* of his troubles. Besides, he doesn't trust her."

The woman paused and made a sound in her throat. "This isn't looking good. She had better come back soon."

"Will you take him?"

"Probably not. You know how grouchy he'll be. Besides, I want to watch the fun. He's *really* angry with her."

"You don't like Joy much, do you?"

"About as much as Vengeance likes Mercy."

"That's hardly fair to say," he said, sounding very much like the eldest brother trying to placate his squabbling siblings. "I have seen you two work very well together."

She scoffed. "Only when some mortal needs a little *frosting* on his death. And half the time she gets involved where she isn't invited and ruins things. All those damnable near-death experiences and that blasted 'drowning euphoria' rumor!"

Julian tried to raise his head but found he could not move. The voices sounded so close and so familiar, but he couldn't place them. Nor could he figure out what these two people were doing in his room.

"Don't be so hard on her."

"She just *doesn't think,* and that pisses me off."

"She's not Wisdom," he laughed. "Besides, I don't think you could do her job."

"I could if I had to."

He snickered, loudly. "Oh, I'd love to see that. You'd *explode.*"

"Anyway, Justice, don't you have somewhere you need to be? I'm trying to work, here."

"I thought you said you weren't taking him. . . ."

"I might have to if she doesn't come back soon, capricious little tart . . . trolloping about with that mortal. . . ."

"Now, now. . . ."

"Julian?"

He heard Eponine's voice. That, he knew.

"Julian!"

He sensed her nearby. She was upset. She smelled like someone else's house.

"*Julian!*"

Oh, you're worried about me, now. *Where've you been since yesterday morning?*

He looked around him, surprised to see his room in a flat wash of grayish illumination. His heart leapt to see the shadowy woman in the corner. She wrapped the very night around her and gave off great waves of cold. She stared mutely at him with a hint of a smile on her pale lips.

Beyond the thin veneer of shadow, Eponine was trying to get him to drink. She fed him slivers of ice. He felt them, cold and wet, in his parched mouth. The woman in the corner rolled her eyes. She strolled toward him and made a *tsk-tsk* sound toward Eponine. She smiled at Julian, and he wanted to go home with her. Home, she'd take him *home,* wherever that was. . . .

But Eponine would stay.

And there would be a great many problems. She would be there, with Jeremy, all alone. And Julian would never again know the magic of her kiss and the gentle pleasure of drinking coffee with her at Veselka's.

He looked between Eponine and the silent, dark woman. He was angry with the both of them, one for staying away too long and the other for arriving too soon.

"You're too late," he shouted, blood rising into his face. "You blew it! Get out!"

The woman raised a thin, black eyebrow at him and chuckled softly. Eponine's head shot up, but she didn't dare look away from Julian's face. She burst into tears but kept feeding him ice.

"You won't die, you won't! This isn't finished yet, Julian!"

Eponine was beside him, close by. He felt comforted. With her there, the world was so much brighter. But she'd upset him; she'd hurt him. The voices had whispered about her running off with someone else. . . .

Yet she stayed beside him, spreading tingling medicine on his cracked and stinging lips and always slipping little chips of ice into his mouth.

Her hands must be so cold.

"Don't leave yet. It isn't time to go." Her whisper was closer now, right against his ear with a warm, moist breath.

The room was dark now, the weird dull light nearly gone. But Eponine's body was rigid, her eyes darting about, wild and restless.

"It isn't time to go."

Julian looked up and saw the woman's face at his bedside. She was but a shadow in the dark, like a reflection in a windowpane. He wasn't afraid of her. He knew her. She was a friend. She was *family*.

"Let's go home, now. Leave him here; he needs to stay." The male voice had returned, and Julian could see a tall and broad-shouldered man just behind her. He smiled down at him. "Don't worry. We haven't forgotten you."

The man slipped his arm around the woman's willowy waist and drew her near.

"If she has to come down here and get you before your time is up, Vengeance, I lose a serious bet. So stay healthy, okay? And for God's sake, look both ways before crossing the street!"

And then they were gone.

He shook his head and felt an ice cube slide down his cheek and nearly into his ear. It jolted him awake instantly.

Fever dreams. . . .

Eponine was propped up on one elbow and barely staying on the bed. Her other hand was lying on his chest where it had fallen trying to feed him another chip of ice. Her eyes were closed, and her head nodded. She wavered uncertainly on the edge of the mattress. Careful of the pain that motion brought him, he pulled her elbow out from under her and let her sink into a better position. She stirred and unconsciously took another ice cube from her bowl and put it in his mouth. Her fingers as they brushed his lips were indeed cold. He gasped, and she reached over and brought him the cup. He managed to sip at it and not spill much. Eponine's eyes were still closed.

Julian took the bowl off the bed and dropped it on the floor. The ice was mostly gone now anyway, melted or consumed. The fingers on Eponine's left hand were dead-pale. He thought of the woman at his bedside in his dream and came to a thundering realization.

It was Death. And for some reason Justice had been with her.

I almost died. The thought was ludicrous, yet chilling. Yes, he could die. The body he inhabited *could* be killed. And then . . . what? He'd go back home, he assumed. But what about Eponine? Would she stay and finish whatever assignment she was on? More than likely.

He glanced down at her; she was snoring a little in the depths of dreamless sleep.

You let me slide to the very edge, but then you brought me back. I am not sure what to make of that. But you hurt me, Joy, when you walked out. When you ran to Jeremy, instead. I don't care if it is your mission. You left me when I needed you, and you left me for him. That hurt. And I don't let that go lightly.

He listened, but there was no one else in the room. He wondered if there ever had been, or if he really had summoned them out of his fevered mind. His two closest kin: Justice and Death. But for the moment he was alone, with Joy. He took her chilly hands in his still all-too-warm ones and joined her in sleep.

LOOKING FOR TROUBLE

IT WAS THE BETTER part of a week before Julian was feeling like himself again. The fever had passed by late the next morning, but the scalding sunburn lasted for days.

He often woke at all hours of the night to find her there, rubbing healing lotions and balms into his tender flesh. It irked him.

She's just trying to get back in my good graces.

He withdrew, speaking little to Eponine.

It's not going to work.

If he hadn't been so terribly and deeply thirsty, he would have refused the fresh, cool water she constantly had on hand for him. She was irritatingly pleasant and understanding during his bouts of temper, which were becoming more and more common. He began to wonder, when she said that she was going to the store, if she were secretly meeting up with Jeremy. She always came back with the items she had said she was going to get, but it seemed to take longer than usual.

Jeremy called only a few times that week, to check up on how things were going. Eponine told him. He said he was worried about Julian's health and wanted to make sure they didn't need anything.

What we don't need is your meddling, Julian thought.

IT WAS WEDNESDAY NIGHT, and Julian was stir-crazy.

His back and shoulders were healed enough to wear a shirt, and he decided to head out for the night.

Eponine was just giving him a dinner update as he was brushing out his hair in the bathroom. He tied it back with a black hairband that had a pewter Celtic knot charm on it.

"I see you're up and about this evening." She leaned in the bathroom doorway, one oven mitt on her hand and the other tucked beneath her arm. "We've got about a half hour until the casserole is ready."

"Well, don't worry about it."

She smiled and looked him up and down. He was wearing a nice shirt and black Dockers instead of jeans. "Are we going out, then?"

He took out the electric razor and gave his face a once-over. It stung to shave, but he truly despised stubble.

"We? No." He tossed the razor back into the drawer and pushed past her, out into the front hall. He took down his black nylon flight jacket, the one that always made Eponine laugh because of the fluorescent orange lining, and carefully shrugged it on. "*I* am going out. I don't know what you intend to do. And honestly, right now, I don't care."

He shut the front door and paused in the hallway. He listened to the stunned silence he'd left behind him. Then it began. A small, choking sound of carefully contained sobs. He smiled. Step one.

He wandered off down the hallway and punched the elevator button. He felt pretty good, better than he had for several days.

OUTSIDE, THE LATE AFTERNOON was balmy but cool. The streets and sidewalks were crowded with people coming home from work, class, or whatever they'd been doing out in the bright Manhattan day. Julian strolled through Washington Square Park and headed into the Village. He was making for the area around Bleecker Street where all the bars were. If he remembered correctly, most of them had early evening specials on the week-nights for the University kids. He walked up and down the quaint, narrow streets, weaving a path along them between Bleecker and West Third. He passed the dark alley where he'd killed the rapist.

Julian surprised himself with the level coolness with which he surveyed the scene. The concrete there was still stained; an old shadowy puddle sunk just into the pitted surface. His soul-rending emotional storm from that night was a memory, and a hazy one at that. He smiled slowly. He'd done a good job that night, top-notch. The Boss would have been proud. . . .

He thought for a moment of Eponine, standing out on MacDougal Street with the red and blue lights of the police cars and ambulances flashing across her skin gone so pale with fright. Then he remembered why he'd come out to this part of town. He walked out of the alley and across the street. A big sign out on the sidewalk proclaimed it to be "Ladies' Night" at Off the Wagon. He poked his head in and surveyed the place. At one of the booths along the wall opposite the bar, he saw a familiar face. The gypsy girl, whose name he'd been told was Phina, was chattering with a few other young women over pint glasses of cider and a couple of baskets of fries. She caught his gaze as he walked in, and smiled warmly. She waved him over and scooted over on the booth's bench to make room for him. He gave her a nod and returned the smile, strolling over to the table. Step two.

"I didn't think to find *you* here," he said with as much suavity as he could muster.

"It's our girls' night out," she replied.

"Oh, then I'll leave you to it." It looked as if someone kicked Phina under the table.

"Ah, no, no, you can stay. Julian, isn't it? You're Eponine's friend." Her tone made it clear that all her information about him had come from Eponine herself.

He gave her a questioning look. "Well, *Phina*, for a girl who was worried about knowing people's names when she shouldn't. . . ."

She looked a little abashed and quickly turned and introduced Julian to the rest of the table. It turned out they were all graduate students and had come directly from their classes to meet for their weekly night out.

They sipped the one-dollar pints at Off the Wagon until seven o'clock, then usually headed over to Madame X or Fat Black Pussycat to finish out the night lounging on plush sofas with martinis. Julian was invited to wander with them. He was enjoying their discussions about politics, sex, art history, and the gossip from the Met Museum, where three of the five of them were interns. He also could not help but notice Phina's eyes upon him the whole time. He didn't feel like prey, but like an artifact. She was studying, tilting her head to catch his words when he spoke, watching his gestures and expressions. It was both flattering and unnerving at once.

They ended up at Fat Black Pussycat up on West Third where it met Sixth Avenue. It was a dark and foreboding place with a barebones interior that would have been as welcoming as the quaintly dilapidated Off the Wagon if the lighting had been better. Phina's friends laughed and led him behind the curtained doorway.

It was dark and smoky there and looked like an opium den. Mismatched antique furniture was everywhere, and the only light came from a smattering of little beaded table lamps. Large pieces of wrought iron and masonry were mounted on the exposed brick of the walls. It was a secret and decrepit and beautiful place. He sat beside Phina on a burgundy velvet couch that was balding on the arms and smelled sickly sweet of dust and rotting silk. The group of them smoked clove cigarettes and listened to the eclectic music and didn't say much. Finally, Phina's classmates began to take their leave. It was getting late, and there was work in the morning, classes, papers, and the usual drudge. One girl, a tall,

stylish blonde, hung on until the last. And after a silent exchange
with Phina, she gave Julian a wide and sly smile and told him how
nice it was to meet him.

"I will see you in class tomorrow, Phina. Maybe lunch
afterwards?"

"Sure thing, Kate."

Winking, Kate disappeared through the heavy drapes, and
Julian was left alone with Phina.

She laid her head against his shoulder flirtatiously and looked
up at him. "So, what brings you here?"

He could hear all the different meanings behind that question,
but chose not to answer. To his surprise, Phina laughed.

"She really ticked you off, didn't she?"

Julian glared down at her and made to pull away, but she
snaked an arm around his waist and held him tightly.

"Not so fast. You came here to find me for a reason. I want to
know what it is."

"How do you know I came out looking for you?"

"Because I see things sometimes. And I see a lot about
you . . . and about *her*."

"I would rather not talk about her with you, if you don't
mind."

Her laughter was dark now. "I see how it is. But no matter. I
know what you want. At least I know what it is you *think* you
want. . . ."

She pulled her knees beneath her and rose up a little, bringing
her lips to his. She kissed him lightly and easily, then settled back,
sitting on her heels.

He exhaled slowly. The sensation of her warm and soft mouth
had been pleasant; well, it had not been *unpleasant*, but it was
sorely lacking.

She gave him a perplexed look and shrank back a little. "Let
me guess; you don't like the way I kiss?"

"That wasn't how I remembered it being. . . ."

"I take it you mean how you remembered kissing Eponine?"

Julian nodded, dumbly, then flushed and shot her a glance full
of ice.

"It's not going to feel that way with me," Phina explained,
simply. She rolled onto her hip and tucked herself beneath his
arm, drawing it around her shoulders. "I'm not like her. Not like
either of you."

"Well, you are certainly unlike everyone else I have met here."

She smiled at that. "You could say I am *unique*."

"You're . . . something, all right." He suddenly felt out of sorts.

She nuzzled against his side and gave him a smile with a feral gleam. "The smoke in here is just killing me. Let's head out."

She hopped off the battered velvet sofa without waiting for him and tossed a couple dollars on the low table. He found her outside, having nearly to jog to keep up with her quick strides.

"Where are we going?" he asked.

"I am going home. You may join me if you'd like." She cast another come-hither smile toward him and turned down LaGuardia toward the towering and ugly student housing at Washington Square Village. She turned to speak to him only when they were finally in the elevator. She pressed the number thirteen button. "Good of you to join me."

"You didn't give me much choice, just sort of took off."

She shrugged and leaned a hip against the elevator wall. "And did I handcuff you to my wrist and drag you along?"

"Like you *could*."

She raised her eyebrows at him. "Rowr, I like a dangerous man."

Julian laughed. "You have *no idea*."

The doors opened, and she headed to the left, disappearing into one of the dozens of identical gray doors. But this one had a long scroll painted with kanji hanging from a wide red ribbon. Inside, the room glowed with the soft reddish-gold light of dozens of strings of multicolored Christmas tree lights. She popped open a Coke and tossed him one as well.

"So," she said, taking a swig of soda and leaning onto the battered kitchen countertop.

He put his unopened can down and came toward her, pulling her into his arms. He tried to fight through the numbness that settled across his flesh like a cloak. She tilted her face up and kissed him, far deeper than he expected. He pressed her against the cabinets and felt her breath hitch and momentarily stop. She went faint, and he steadied her quickly.

"Phina?"

Her eyelids fluttered, and then she was staring at him with an intensity and strength that unnerved him.

"Get out."

"Excuse me?"

"I like you. And I like Eponine. And I am not going to be a part of some petty revenge plot."

"Now, see here. . . !"

"If you wanted to play, if you wanted a tryst, that'd be one thing. But you just want to hurt her. I don't play *that* game. A hundred others, but not that one."

"And you saw that, didn't you? In the kiss. . . ."

"And you saw *nothing*. You felt nothing. I just had the experience of a lifetime, and you felt *nothing*." She crossed her arms and laughed. "Well, well, who's got the revenge now?"

Black rage flooded Julian to the core, and he shook. Phina, at least, had the sense to look concerned about her safety all of a sudden.

"Get out of my house." Her voice was grave, and she was no longer smiling. "I want to consider you a friend, Julian. So please leave here while I still do, okay?"

"Tell me what you saw."

She slid past him and opened her door. She glared silently at him for a long moment, and he grudgingly made to exit.

"Phina, please, tell me what you saw."

Her face softened, and she looked on him with pity. Julian felt his temper spark and flare anew.

"Ask Eponine." Phina gave him a shove and slammed the door on his heels. He heard about three locks slide in place. They'd be nothing for him to break through, but he felt something else there, too. A shielding. He found he could read the ward easily: *Let none who mean to do harm be able to enter here.*

With such unspecified wording, he knew he'd never be able to break it in his current state of mind. And it was strong, unbelievably strong. It would seem Phina was a rather powerful witch.

Daunted and fuming, he trudged toward the stairs, slamming the door hard enough to shake the building.

INSTANT KARMA

IT HAD GOTTEN LATER than Julian thought.

He swept down through the park, nearly getting run down by a speeding cab on West Fourth. The cabbie brought the car to a screeching stop, and Julian leveled an inhuman gaze at it. His frighteningly black eyes regarded the cab and the driver, and then the vehicle's radiator blew, billowing steam out from under the hood. Outside the NYU library a slightly battered-looking dog suddenly turned on its owner, dragging the guy right down to the sidewalk.

On the West Eighth Street corner, there was a man closing in on a late-night jogger.

Dumb woman shouldn't be out here alone. She collapsed to the pavement with a colossal charley-horse. The man, however, paused, concerned, and went to the red emergency phone to call for help.

Julian tapped him on the shoulder. "Good call. You get to live, *for now*... this is the coronary you were about to have...." He snapped his fingers in front of the stunned man's eyes and turned away.

On Broadway, he tripped a student hurrying toward the University. She fell forward, scattering a binder full of papers into the slimy gutter out front of the liquor store.

"Shit!" She pulled herself to her knees and looked sourly at the soggy papers. "I don't have time to print this out again. It's due by midnight!"

"Then you shouldn't have plagiarized it in the first place," he told her and walked on.

All around him, little wrongs righted themselves, but in the most vengeful manner possible. Like a sheen of oil over the water, bitter threads of darkness spread throughout the Village. A girl calling to tell her parents a lie about where she was dropped her cell phone in front of a truck. A girl borrowing her roommate's brand-new boots without permission got her heel caught in the metal grating of the stairs beside her building. Not only was the boot ruined, but she was stuck. She began to cry but Julian ignored her.

A guy jaywalking was nearly hit by a car, and while he stood there laughing at the driver who had come to a shrieking halt mere inches from his legs, he was hit by a man on a bike. The SUV behind the stopped car gunned its motor, hopped the sidewalk, and hit a fire hydrant, sending water spouting everywhere. The water ruined a card table full of illicit bootleg CDs. It washed away the wedding ring that had fallen out of an adulterer's pocket.

Julian stood out front of his building with a quarter of the city's bad karma running through his blood. There was a subtle flickering in the windows of the front room, what Julian figured was candleflame dancing on Eponine's nightstand. The dew was falling, making hazy soft circles of light around the streetlamps. He shivered and went upstairs.

The apartment was quiet, and Eponine's door was open halfway. He smelled the warm honey-scent of her candles and watched the shadows chase each other on her walls. It did not bring the usual smile to his lips. He opened the door silently, and blew out the candles. He impulsively pulled the tasseled bookmark out of *The Secret Garden* and tossed it under her bed. Somehow that childish act soothed him slightly.

He slid back to his own room and shut the door, locking it soundly behind him.

JULIAN WAS AWAKENED BY a muffled thump and a quiet string of swearing. It was nearly three in the morning and his television was on, but the sound was muted. From the look of it, *Cowboy Bebop* was just ending on Cartoon Network. The doorknob shuddered and he heard a soft knock.

"Julian. . . ? Julian, are you all right?"

He slunk to the door and leaned against it. He could hear her breathing just on the other side. He closed his eyes, and he could *see* her with her cheek pressed against the wood and her palms resting on the knob. She looked tired and worn; her face was tearstained. For an instant, he wanted to open the door and let her fall into his arms. But he shook the idea away.

"Go away," he growled. "Don't you have *anyone else* you could be bothering?"

"Julian, I'm worried about you."

"Yeah, *now* you are. . . . How about the other night? Weren't so worried then, *were you*?"

He heard her gasp and back away from the door.

"Having an attack of the morals, are we?" He mocked the tone of voice she often used with him.

"Laugh all you want," she said thickly through tears. "I deserve it, I'm sure. But if you won't hear my apology, then that's your guilt to bear."

He opened the door suddenly. "I got strong shoulders, babe."

And he slammed it in her face. He fell against it and slid to the floor. This was madness, and he knew it. But he couldn't stop himself.

"Julian, I need to speak to you ... I *need* to. ..." She dissolved into tears again, and he pounded his head against the door.

"*Don't ... you ... ever ... stop ... crying. ..?*"

"No," she whispered. "I fear I'll drown myself in the sea of my own tears just like Alice."

It was on the tip of his tongue to ask what she was talking about, but he heard her door shut softly.

"There, now, that wasn't so hard." His voice sounded harsh and brittle, aloud in his silent room. "She'll cry herself to sleep or lie awake with a heartache until dawn. Then she'll make breakfast, and things will be just the way they always were."

He sighed disgustedly and heaved himself across his bed, wincing at the crush of his weight upon his still-tender sunburn.

"Yeah, *right.*" He pressed the heels of his hands against his eyes, trying to push back the migraine that was threatening to form. "My God ... we're so *fucked.*"

He thought of Eponine in Jeremy's apartment. She'd stayed the night there. Had she slept in his bed? Had he stayed there beside her, breathing her scent, dozing off to the lullaby of her heartbeat? And hadn't he intended to be doing that and so much more with Phina at this very moment?

Shut up, shut up, quit thinking that! Just leave all of it the fuck alone! I was fine for an eternity without her. I'll be fine now!

He would do his duty, just do his job. Make sure Eponine didn't get killed while she was on Earth. It didn't matter if she left him for Jeremy or some other useless mortal.

But she went to him. After everything that's been between us, knowing how much it hurts me, she went to him. ...

He pulled the covers up over his head. Yes, some thoughts were better left untouched.

But in the stillness of his room, the voice of his soul began to weep. He silenced it fiercely, and all was quiet once more.

He rolled over and watched the opening credits of *Dragon Ball Z* flash over his TV screen for a moment. Then, he thumbed the remote, and all was dark as well.

FUTILE

EPONINE WAS SITTING ON the front steps of the Met when the museum opened. She wasn't sure what she was hoping for, but a little companionship and an open ear were an excellent start. She walked directly to the counter just inside and to the right of the massive front doors. Eponine smiled at the girl sitting there with rhinestones on her barrettes and cat's-eye glasses.

"I'm here to see someone," she told the girl.

"Who are you here to see?"

Eponine bit her lip a moment and hoped she had the name right. "Delphine Nabokov."

The girl nodded and flipped open a book on the desk. "Do you have an appointment?"

"No."

"Is she expecting you?"

"Without a doubt."

The girl nodded and chewed the eraser of her pencil as she punched an extension on the phone. She spoke briskly into it then hung up. She scribbled something on a sticker and affixed it to a laminated yellow badge. She hadn't bothered to smile once.

"She'll be right up. Here's your visitor's pass."

Eponine clipped the small badge to the neckline of her blouse.

"Hey, 'Ponine, *mishto avilon.*" Phina jogged up past the coat check. She was surprisingly dressed in blue jean cut-offs and a paint-spattered T-shirt. "I got it from here, Stacy, thanks." She gave Eponine a jerk of her head and made off toward the Egyptian end of the museum. "You sure know how to warp the truth eight ways from Sunday without ever telling a lie, don'tcha? *Expecting you* . . . yeah, I guess I was."

Eponine nearly had to run to keep up with her. "I'm sorry. If this is a bad time, I'll go."

"Nah. It's fine. I was about to go down to the cafeteria for coffee with Alphonse. . . . I've been here for two hours already, and we're *still* not done." She swore. "Sorry, you caught me on a really bad day. Don't know what it is, but I just can't shake this funk I'm in. Seems like everyone else is catching it, too."

She flipped off a security guard who tried to stop them from going downstairs to the roped-off Costume Institute. "I *work here*, asshole! Same as you, you flashlight-toting, wish-you-had-a-gun rent-a-cop, except I don't get paid!"

Eponine blanched. Phina never hesitated to say what was on her mind. In fact her honesty was usually quite brutal, but this went beyond her usual tartness. "She's having a really bad day. . . ."

"'PONINE!" The voice echoed sharply from around the corner.

"Uhh," she gave him a thin smile. "Have a nice morning...." And she nearly tumbled down the wide granite stairs that led to the basement galleries in her hurry to catch up. She ran into Phina, who had turned around at the foot of the stairs and was coming back up with Alphonse, the Costume Institute's librarian.

"*Bonjour, amie,*" Alphonse said to Eponine, pausing to give her a kiss on both cheeks.

"*Bonjour, Alphonse, comment c'est va?*"

"Never better," he grinned and put his arm around her. "Oh, I like this one. She speaks such beautiful French!"

They rounded the corner, and Phina gave the security guard another lewd gesture. "You gonna remember us when we come back down, buddy?" He pointedly ignored her. "Senile old coot."

Alphonse put his other arm around her shoulders and pulled her close. "Oh, Phina, you're such a *bitch*. That's why I like you, *bébé.*"

Eponine sighed to herself, *Oh, please don't encourage her! Not today, anyway....*

They threaded their way though the onslaught of school groups and finally to the stairs that led down to the employee cafeteria. Alphonse bought them all cappuccinos while the girls searched out a seat.

"Don't you *dare* put sugar in this, girlfriend," he said to Phina.

She glared and stuck her tongue out as she dumped four packets of sugar into the heavy paper cup. Eponine sipped hers plain while Alphonse regaled them with gossip from the department as well as his favorite topic: Who was gay in Hollywood this week.

"Okay, *ma cheries*, I am heading back upstairs." He gathered the empty coffee cups to toss out.

"Will you cover for me for a few? I got the feeling I need a little alone time with girlfriend here."

"No problem." He gave both the girls a kiss on both cheeks. "Just be back from your break in time for lunch, *oui*?"

"*Oui,*" She gave Alphonse a wink and then turned her dark and intense eyes on Eponine. "So . . . what's up?"

"I need to speak to you. It's about Julian."

Phina sat back. "*God fuck it*, I *knew* you were going to say that! Listen, 'Ponine, I don't care what he said to you, *nothing happened* last night!"

Eponine's mouth fell open. "Julian was with you last night?"

Phina's eyes turned nearly black, reminding Eponine all too well of Julian. "He didn't tell you, did he? He didn't say a word, that bastard. . . ."

"Tell me what happened!"

"It was really nothing. He ran into me and some classmates at a bar and ended up coming home with me." She noticed Eponine suddenly go very pale and touched the girl's wrist. "No, *really*, it wasn't like that. I mean it *could have been* but . . . *shit* . . . let me start over. . . ."

"No, no," Eponine shook her head to try to stop her tears, but it was to no avail. "It doesn't matter. If it's you he's after. . . ."

"That's just it, 'Ponine, it *wasn't* me he wanted. He was angry with you, very hurt, and all he wanted was to make you jealous, make you suffer like he did when you went home with that guy . . . the musician, with the blond hair . . . but all he kept seeing was *you* there; he never saw me."

"He told you this?" Eponine gazed down at the backs of her hands.

"No. He . . . he . . . kissed me."

"He *kissed* you?"

Phina nodded. "Yeah. And I had the vision, so I threw him out."

"You *threw him out*?" Eponine's head whipped up as if it had been yanked on a string. Her eyes were wide and worried.

"Hell yeah, I threw him out. It was *my house* he was in!"

"Well, then he must care *something* for you."

"What makes you say that?"

She gave Phina a dark laugh. "Because you're *still alive*."

Phina met Eponine's gaze and said nothing for a long moment. Then she nodded, as whatever knowledge she had, or at least *thought* she had, clicked into place with what she'd just been told.

"Well, *foutre*, 'Ponine. I'm sorry, I didn't mean to make this mess any worse. . . ."

"You didn't. It's just a mess, with or without you. I wish I could tell you more. Maybe you could help me sort it out."

Phina nodded. "Was there anything else?"

"No," Eponine whispered, unsure of what more to say.

"Okay, I gotta head back over to work. They'll be missing me." She roughly pushed back from the table, making Eponine jump at the screech of the chair on the linoleum.

"Are you angry at me, Phina?"

"Nah. Well, not really . . . not *rationally*, anyway. I'll be okay. Things will be fine; you'll see. Maybe I'll make you a charm. Yes, I think you two need some help."

Eponine actually laughed. "If I can't manage with the help I already have, then I am *utterly fucked*."

EPONINE SAT IN THE cafeteria for a few minutes longer. She drifted right past the sale table just outside the doors at the foot of the stairs. She wandered the Museum like a sleepwalker, the noise and motion seeping into her senses as if through a thick fog. She found herself in the park, with no real recollection of having gone outside.

She was on the path to The Ramble and let her feet take her where they thought she should go. It was no surprise when she rounded the corner of the trail and came face to face with the spring. It bubbled up from the earth there and poured into a small, shimmering pond that drained slowly into a creek running haphazardly though The Ramble and vanishing somewhere along the manicured edge of Central Park proper. She didn't know what happened to it, but she had heard tales of a vast network of underground pipes that funneled the many natural springs in Manhattan through the city and out into one of the rivers. But that was all forgotten as she became entranced by the head of the spring there at her feet. She sank to her knees in the spongy earth and cupped her hands. She dipped them into the chilly water and brought them to her lips to drink. The water tasted sweet and loamy, like fertile soil and trees, like life.

This spring had been her first experience on Earth, and she thought perhaps she was returning to it now for some degree of solace. But there was little to be found.

The water tumbled along the pebbles and chattered to itself in a language long forgotten by humans. She had thought she understood it when she first came, but now it was lost. Lost like the chirping of crickets and the trills of sparrows. It was all just noise now. When had it stopped being music? When had she stopped hearing the words?

Wrapped in a veil of worry, Eponine went back out into the park and looked at the faces of those around her. They were dim, no longer surrounded by shining coronas of light. They didn't turn to look at her as she passed. They didn't inexplicably smile whenever she was near. She hurried down the concrete paths, a growing sense of paranoia creeping upon her. She thought that the world was growing smaller, dimmer, as if she were going blind, deaf, and insane all at once. And now the people looked, but their faces wore the tight masks of indifference and disgust that Julian had once told her he saw when he looked at humans.

As if it's a thin coating of varnish . . . keeping what they perceive as "bad" out and what they think is "good" in . . . but all it really does is suffocate them. I don't think you can imagine that, constantly seeing humanity trying to smother itself in disinterest. . . .

She blinked in the harsh glare of sunlight at the bottom of the park. She lethargically made her way to the subway station at Rockefeller Square and headed home. The ride was soothing in its familiarity: the strong scent of axle grease, engine fumes, and spilled soda; the rhythmic clatter of the wheels that occasionally screeched and shrieked on the tracks; the rolling rock of the cars that nearly put her to sleep. At least *that* hadn't changed. . . .

The big tiles of the beavers in the Astor Place station swam into view, and she rose to her feet and was pulled along with the crowd to the light and air above. It was still broad daylight, but the world seemed pale and dreary, like the wan sunlight after a storm.

Eponine shambled into her building and up the stairs. She was in no hurry, felt neither delight nor trepidation. She knew Julian was not there. She was failing him, failing them both. Perhaps this would be how it began, the world slowly dimming until it was no more, until *she* was no more. She looked down at her hands; they seemed solid enough. Would she wither first, or just vanish like a wraith? The hallway loomed long and dark, and she pulled herself to the door. She had risked so much to bring back a sign on the first day of spring and had received nothing for her trouble but the strange miracle of extraordinarily long hair. Failure was all around her, and it would be only a matter of time before that inevitable tragic end claimed them both. But it was for Julian she mourned, rather than herself.

Once inside, she saw that her hunch was correct. His bedroom door was open, and his overcoat was gone. Nothing was packed, but she got the distinct impression that he had left for more than just the evening. She stared vacantly at the kitchen table and for a moment hallucinated a note.

"I need some time to think, a few days to cool off. Don't worry, I haven't left you. If you need me, you know how to call."

Then she saw him crumple the paper and stuff it into his pocket.

She shook the image from her mind and idly wondered if it was a vision like the kind that Phina had.

The apartment was growing dim, and Eponine decided it would be prudent to lie down before the headache that was forming behind her eyes burst fully upon her.

She left the kitchen light on for Julian out of habit.

LOSE YOURSELF

IT WAS A CHURCH. At least, it *looked* like a church. Spooky vapor wafted around the grounds, and a black and red banner hung from a wrought-iron, finialed banner post. Julian read the banner, *Limelight*.

The beat of the music was so loud, he could hear the individual pieces rattle in the lead casings of the stained glass windows. An endless stream of black-clad club-goers flowed through the doors to the throbbing darkness within. He followed them. And inside, he was assailed with the vicious pulse of the music. He felt it dully in the center of his chest and for a moment, his heart forgot its own rhythm. Behind his eyes, in the hollow of his bones, in the thick arteries in his legs, anywhere with a space large enough to form an echo, vibrated with the overwhelming beat. It was mindless. It was a thing of impulse without intelligence, existing in a forgotten primal realm that spoke to the base nature in humans. It had no words, no melody, just a pulsing throb and a storm of surrounding noise.

He put his overcoat and satchel into the coat check. The evening was far too warm for the coat, but he'd brought it along anyway. He had no idea where he was going to sleep, but he thought the coat would make a nice tarp or blanket if need be.

He pushed through the milling crowd and toward the dance floor. It amazed him to see just how many different fashion statements could be made with only the use of black clothing. He saw vintage lace and leather and T-shirts and plastic and all manner of silver accents in the form of zippers and pins and chains and jewelry. Long hair, shaved heads, spiked, dyed, braided, curled tresses adorned the heads of the clubbers.

They danced as if they were hypnotized; they danced as if they were on fire; they danced standing stone still and looking at their hands. White make-up and glow-in-the-dark nail polish came alive under the blacklight.

Julian was entranced.

He stepped into the somewhat more open space of the dance floor and breathed deeply. Cigarette smoke stung the inside of his nostrils, but he welcomed the sensation. It reminded him of brimstone, and he found that he was smiling. The rhythm of the music wrapped itself around him, reaching back into his body to show him how to move. And he swayed to the beat, his arms snaking around him. From someplace outside of himself, he saw that he fit in among them with his black jeans and T-shirt that clung to his already sweaty chest. He pulled the tie out of his hair and let it swing loosely around his shoulders. He moved first jerkily, then smoothly, as the drumming of the pulse commanded him.

Finally, he could no longer ignore the burning in his throat. He stumbled to the bar, finding his legs surprisingly clumsy when not under the spell of the music. He slouched onto a barstool and asked for a ginger ale.

The man behind the counter was tall and barrel-chested and had tattoos instead of hair. Julian gave him a knowing nod of the head. The guy was a bruiser.

"That seems pretty tame for a guy like you."

He tilted his head just enough to see the wisp of a girl at his elbow. She was draped in gossamer black tulle over a corset and tiny velvet skirt. Her dyed black hair was pulled up into two sprightly pigtails and shimmered with deep blue highlights. She gave Julian a pixie smile.

"I'm having a rough night," he said, gravely. "Besides, what could you possibly know about a guy like me?"

"You just strike me as someone not to be trifled with."

"I strike a lot of people," Julian said without a trace of humor, but the girl laughed anyway.

"My name's Eurydice."

He turned to look fully at her and didn't believe her for a moment. But he supposed it wasn't any sillier or any less pretentious than Joy calling herself Eponine.

"You can call me Julian."

"*Julian.*" She flashed that smile again. "So, can I buy you a drink?"

He sighed. "I suppose you could." *If it means you'll leave me alone.*

She leaned against the bar and laid her head back, giving the barkeep her best grin upside down.

"A pink and a green, please!"

He grunted in reply and tugged one of her pigtails. He brought back two drinks, one was glowing pink and the other green.

"Yours is a Midori Sour," she said. "I don't remember what's in this one besides vodka and grenadine . . . but *something* makes it glow under blacklight."

Julian gave the glowing green drink a dubious look and took a sip. It was sweet. It made his tongue curl and his molars ache. He put it down.

"I hope you won't be offended, but that stuff is *awful.*"

She giggled in a lilting scale and downed the rest of her drink before taking his glass. "More for me, then."

He wondered where she was putting so much alcohol. Her small frame looked barely robust enough to handle plain water.

"You might like this instead." She pulled an incredibly tiny flask from the front of her corset. "Hope you won't mind that it's warm."

"And what could possibly be worth drinking out of a bottle that little?"

"Something you don't need much of." She unscrewed the stainless steel cap and sucked a drop from the flask. She closed her hazel-blue eyes for a moment and then went both pale and flushed at once. It was as if all the color in her body leapt to her cheeks, leaving the rest of her freakishly pallid. "Try some. But you gotta keep it on the down-low. This stuff isn't exactly legal."

Curious, he took the warm silvery flask and tried a taste. It was pungent and a little like the flavor of licorice. He knew it in an instant— absinthe. At once sensation flooded his mouth, nerves leaping where the fluid had touched. He felt light; he felt tall. He took another sip and the colors and sounds became brighter, more vibrant. He would have gone for more, but Eurydice plucked the bottle from his fingers and deftly replaced the cap.

"Save some for later!" She swayed a little when she laughed. The flask disappeared back into her scant cleavage, and she threaded her arm through his. "Dance with me. I want to see if you move as dangerously as you look."

She stopped in the middle of the dance floor and put her arms up over her head and rolled her slender hips. Her body undulated in a seductive, serpentine path. Julian rocked on his feet and watched her. The music was more urgent now, or at least seemed to be. The songs melded into one another, some pounding and loud, the others more delicate and sad. Eurydice wrapped herself around him at times, sliding against him, then dancing away again. He ignored her, focusing on the thunder in his veins.

She caught his eyes and took a drink from her flask. He watched the color transformation happen again and the dark centers of her eyes suddenly double in width. She offered the bottle to him, coming quite close. She pressed the curve of her hip into the hollow of his and held the little flask to his chin.

"Last drop," she urged him breathlessly.

It occurred to Julian that she was trying to do more than make him drunk. But he took the last bit of liquor from her and enjoyed the heady rush of icy fire that raced through him.

Is this stuff supposed to make me love you?

"Let's get out of this place. . . ." She had her head pressed against his chest, and Julian had a brief fear of deafening her with the roar of his heartbeat.

He followed her out, stopping to collect their belongings from the coat check.

"I live really close by. I come here almost every night. Remember that. . . ." She was quite shaky on her own two feet by this time, and Julian put his arm around her to steady her.

She directed him across Sixth Avenue to a turn-of-the-century apartment building only a few blocks west.

"Do you think we could stop and rest a minute? I don't feel so good. . . ."

He bore more of her weight and doubled his pace. "Which floor are you on?"

"Six," she said in a voice that was tinted with nausea. They stumbled together into the dim lobby. It was nothing more than a ten-foot by ten-foot stairwell landing. "Up."

Julian looked for an elevator, but in vain. He sighed and lifted little Eurydice in his arms and carried her up the stairs. She felt so light and fragile, he thought he might crush her.

She rallied when they got to the top floor and demanded to be put down. She pulled her house keys out of her little jet-beaded purse and gave him a wink.

"My dark knight, so chivalrous to see me home safely. Would you like to come in?" She ran her finger down the length of the key and seductively pressed it into the keyhole, banging her slender hip into the door behind it. She turned the knob and miscalculated the timing, nearly falling onto her face as the door swung open. She gave him a little self-conscious laugh, then closed her eyes and shivered. Her shoulders began to slump forward, and Julian darted out and grabbed her before she collapsed.

He easily scooped her up in his arms again. The apartment was a tiny studio with her futon in a corner opposite the mini-kitchen. The bed was shrouded with more of the shimmery black tulle she was wearing. He laid her down gently and took off her shoes. It was disturbing to see how her feet were still bent into the agonizing arch of her boots. Then he rolled her over onto her side and loosened the ties of her corset. She was breathing evenly, but her face was deathly pale. The silver flask fell out of her corset and rolled off the futon. He went to what would have passed for a kitchen in a moderate hotel, found a clean glass, and filled it from the water-filter pitcher he found inside the refrigerator. The appliance was regular-sized and looked monstrously huge in the small space. He set the glass on the floor beside a book and left a bottle of multi-vitamins near the head of the bed. Then he tossed a threadbare patchwork quilt over her still form and stroked the fine, soft hair at her temple before silently retreating a few steps from her bedside.

He felt a subtle, simple pleasure from seeing her home and tucking her in. A soft glow at his solar plexus seemed amplified by the absinthe that had been in Eurydice's flask. It occurred to Julian that this small delight must be what drove Eponine to do what she did for him. Except that—he closed his eyes and he could *see* it—the light it brought her was a thousand times what he was feeling. In a licorice-scented haze, he could suddenly perceive that light, that extension of her very essence, and how it gave strength back to her. In the space between heartbeats Julian understood how Eponine brought joy and light to those around her but also thrived on the happiness she bestowed upon others. And he had refused to be happy with her.

Well, no wonder. . . .

Then his thoughts derailed, and he stood absorbed in confusion there on the battered hardwood floor of the strange girl's apartment. He needed to move. He needed to walk. The burning fluid seemed to be having an opposite effect on his body than it had on hers. But then again he had not mixed it with the amounts of regular alcohol that she had. He cast one last glance at the girl. She had curled up on her side and looked much more just asleep than unconscious.

He shut the door behind him and ensured that it was locked, feeling strangely protective of the diminutive young woman who lived alone at the top of this century-old tenement. Eurydice, alone in the darkness of Hades, separated forever from Orpheus's song. He grieved for her, this stray kitten of a girl, but he knew her path lay far from his. He checked the door again and descended the stairs in silence.

Back out in the after-midnight world of Manhattan, Julian paused, unsure what to do next. He was far from tired, so he walked. His body ached for the music once more, but he had no desire to go back to Limelight. He shifted the satchel so it rested against his lower back, crammed his hands into the pockets of his coat, and turned north.

His mind wandered as it often did when he walked like this, strolling aimlessly to escape the tumult that would otherwise drag him down. He found himself in Times Square.

THE CITY THAT NEVER SLEEPS

NEW YORK CITY WAS the Golden Paradise of the sleepless. It was an insomniac's dream—although, of course, if one were actually insomniac, dreams would be few and far between.

It was past two o'clock, and Times Square was still bustling enough to be considered busy in a regular city in America, although by its own standards, it was quiet and tame.

Julian's stomach rumbled, and he strolled into Roxy's for a burger and some cheesecake.

He sat upstairs by the window for a couple of hours, just drinking coffee and watching the people below. He wondered what their lives were like outside the brief glimpse he caught of them. Were they happy with their job? Did they love their spouse? Had they fought with their mother? What kind of sheets were on their bed? Julian laughed to himself. His sheets were plain black. But Eponine's were snuggly and covered in stars.

He drained the rest of his coffee and told himself to stop thinking about her. He left actual cash on the table and went downstairs. He expected to feel exhausted, but instead, he was still full of the same nervous energy that had been with him all night. The effects of the draught in Eurydice's flask were still clinging to him, slightly. He felt strangely tall and was compelled to duck when going through a doorway. Sound and light still had a peculiar sharpness to them, and it was starting to grate on his nerves.

At this point in the night, the streets were dead, even up in Times Square. The lit-up billboards flaunted themselves for no one but him. It was that magic hour when the night crawlers were slinking away and the day dwellers hadn't woken yet. This was the quietest he'd ever seen Manhattan. But he could keenly sense that the city was not sleeping, only resting its eyes for a moment. Very soon, the world would come alive with folks going out to start their days.

A blue and white NYPD car glided nearly soundlessly along. The occupants gave Julian a scrutiny he could feel through the tinted windows, but rolled on, leaving him to his own devices. A cab zipped by at an outrageous speed, passing the cop car as if it were standing still. In any other place, the cop might have given chase. But at four o'clock in the morning in Manhattan, the police didn't seem to care. Julian wondering if cabbies ever got pulled over for anything in this city.

He passed through the Square, leaving its day-bright lights behind him and plunging into the shadowy chasm of Broadway. The last time he'd been in Times Square had been New Year's Eve . . . but he didn't want to think about that.

Why does everything *in my life here have to revolve around her?*

He trudged on, head down and hands in pockets.

You know the answer to that. . . .

Shut up. . . !

Now he was arguing with himself. Not a good sign.

By the time he reached Columbus Circle, the tide had changed, and the early-morning folks were beginning to move. He sat on the edge of the fountain at the entrance to Central Park and watched the traffic begin to accumulate. It wasn't much at such an ungodly hour of day, but it was mildly intriguing to see it begin to build already, even though the sun would not be fully up for at least another hour and a half.

He wandered into the park and was immediately enveloped in the deep quiet darkness of wilderness. His feet hit the paved paths and his mind was gone again, strolling the murky depths of his thoughts.

He knew where he was headed. And as if he could scent her on the wind, he knew Eponine had been there recently as well. Drawn, as he was, to the spot where their feet had first touched Earth.

He passed a few joggers out in the pre-dawn, but paid them no mind.

What in the world is Joy doing here? And why does she need me? Strength could have baby-sat her, Justice, Honor. . . any of them. But I was chosen, he sighed. *Some sort of revenge on Vengeance.*

The dew fell heavy this morning, clinging to everything around him, and he was again happy he had brought his coat. He wished he could remember what he'd done with his hair tie, however, as the dampness was causing his hair to curl and creating a havoc of wet tangles.

He heard the stream long before he saw it, although the birds were already awake and chattering. Eponine had once told him that she knew the words to their songs.

Stop thinking about her. . . ! She isn't for you!

He followed the stream to the pond and walked along the edge of it to the tiny waterfall. The rocks and roots made a natural stair to the spring above.

Julian stood there with the morning beginning to break through the trees and the water sighing at his feet. Thoughts churned in his mind, swirling and carrying on like the water at his feet. He sensed an insight there. Why was it the two of them? What did God know that they didn't?

Besides everything. . . .

Eponine's smile, Eponine's laugh, Eponine's scent, Eponine's skin, Eponine's eyes, Eponine's hair, all of it from nape to floor . . . those were the thoughts that pressed on his mind, not the terror and the gore and the cries of bloodlust. How had it come to that?

HE WATCHED HER STEP out of the light. It distracted him from the rough texture of the fabric wrapped around his body, pressing the coarse and ugly hair on his legs into his flesh. He was sitting on the ground, despising the damp creeping through his jeans and into his very bones. He looked up from the contemplation of his hands to see her pale foot.

His breath caught as the light grew very bright, obliterating the lines of her body as she was wrapped in dreary mortal flesh. And then she was standing there, ankle-deep in the water that tumbled over the little fall into the pond just below. She had on a long skirt made of blue plaid flannel and carried a pair of hiking boots in her hand. She reached out for his help, but he didn't move. In fact, he laughed as she stumbled out of the stream and fell hard into the moldering leaves on the ground.

"Wow," she said, brushing herself off and giggling. "Would you look at that? My toes are blue ... how pretty."

He put his hands over his face and groaned. It was going to be a very long year.

SOMETHING CRAWLED ON HIS nose, and he sat up with a grimace. His head ached and his tongue felt ... *hairy*. He found himself sitting there in the same spot where he had been in his dream memory. He swatted the spider away from his nose and spat out the bits of underbrush in his mouth. It was still early morning, so he knew he hadn't been asleep for very long.

The dream was still clear in his mind. So clear, in fact, that when he noticed the girl sitting on the large rock beside the pond, it didn't startle him immediately.

But when Julian woke sufficiently enough to recognize her, his heart leapt into his mouth.

The Test of Faith

SHE SAT THERE IN pressed khaki pants and a simple white cotton blouse, looking every bit the wholesome girl-next-door. Her sun-streaked, honey-blonde hair was up in a ponytail, and she had pearl earrings on.

Julian sat there in stunned silence.

"Good, you're awake. I don't have much time. No one knows I am here," she told him, quietly.

"*No one* knows you're here?" He couldn't help but laugh at that.

Her brows furrowed. "You know, I don't have to help you at all! But your sister sent me."

"My sister?"

"Well, brother now, I guess." She rolled her crystal-blue eyes. "I have no idea why Justice has decided to be male. He's been a woman since . . . oh, well, *the dawn of time!*"

"Faith . . . you're babbling."

"Anyway, I can only imagine you know why I am here. . . ."

"I am drawing a total blank why *you'd* be here, honestly."

"Vengeance, you have lost your faith."

"In *what*, sweetheart? All the good in my miserable soul?"

She ignored his biting sarcasm. "I'm serious. You have no idea what's at stake here!"

"Then tell me! Somebody please tell me what the *fuck* I am doing down here, because I sure as hell don't know! Oh, wait, you can't tell me. It's probably against some rules somewhere."

"It is, in fact. But I know how much you care for rules," she said sarcastically.

He looked a trifle chastened, but gave her a wide grin. "Heard about that, did you?"

"But I am breaking a rule or two, being here, sort of. I mean you *are* in a crisis of faith here, so *technically*. . . ."

"Faith, I still believe in God."

"There is more to faith than religion, you know." She gave him as close to a sly smile as she ever could muster. "Did you know that in Japan, they need seven deities to express the concept of joy?"

He nodded.

"And did you know that the only woman among them, the one considered to be the strongest, is the goddess who represents the joy in finding true love?"

He nodded again, not sure what she was trying to say. Faith leaned forward, expectantly.

"What are you getting at? Y'know, for someone who is short on time, you are sure beating around the bush."

She stood up, irritated. "You are *still* a jerk, you know that? I think maybe they *should* let you fail . . . but then I guess this world would be even more screwed up and make my job even harder. And I have a hard enough time keeping up with your havoc as it is!"

"What are you talking about?"

She gave him a cool gaze. "You really don't know, do you? You really *are* just as self-absorbed as the others say."

"Faith. . . ."

"Don't you watch the news out here? Read the papers? Hope is pulling her hair out! You are *ruining everything!*"

He recoiled. He had no real idea what she was talking about, but she was truly upset.

"You don't remember any of it, do you?" She stopped pacing and crouched down before him.

"I remember darkness. And . . . headaches. But that's normal for me," he shrugged and offered her an insincere smile.

"Vengeance," she reached out as if to stroke his hair but stopped herself, looking decidedly unwilling to touch him. Her hand hovered near his face for a moment, and he roughly batted it away.

"Say your piece, Faith, and go home."

"I came to help you." She stood stiffly and reached into her pants pocket.

"And you have been of the utmost assistance, *thank you.*"

"She deserves better than you, you arrogant bastard."

"Aren't I lucky you're not the one who decides those things."

She dropped what looked like a scroll wrapped in red ribbon at his feet. "Get your act together. You have no idea what you're doing to her, and by that, the rest of the world."

He nudged the scroll with his boot. "What, I don't get a cookie with my fortune?"

She rolled her eyes. "The fact that you can even *see* the scroll means you have a tad more faith in her than you think you do. That's a good thing. I guess everything isn't totally lost after all. Let's just see if you can read it, or understand it." She laughed at him. "Hope still believes in you, but you know how she is." Faith made a cross-eyed face at him and stuck out her tongue a little.

"Well, I'm glad *someone* out there still believes in me."

"And Justice, but you know how he gets when there's money riding on something. And it's a big one, too."

"Just who is he betting against, anyway?"

"Me. Along with Love and Death," Faith said smugly. "I said you'd never make it. After all, Joy isn't Patience."

"Was there anything else?"

"Concerning you? No. But I have to go appear to a guy up at the Cloisters. You were on my way so I thought I'd stop by."

"It's graciously appreciated," he told her drily. His stomach rumbled.

"You better put a leash on that thing. Does it do tricks?"

"Yeah, you wanna see?" He opened his mouth and made to stick his finger down his throat.

"Oh, *grow up!*"

"*Ye of little faith*," he told her mockingly.

She waited for a moment, obviously expecting something further from him. Then, with an exasperated sigh, she turned back toward the spring.

"*Thank you?*" she prompted.

"It was nothing, I assure you," he replied with a wink.

She shook her head and slowly disappeared in a haze of light and mist that was carried up through the treetops and out of Julian's sight.

He stared at the little scroll still sitting in the mulch between his feet. When he first went to pick it up, he found that his fingers passed right through it. Metallic-tasting fear coated the back of his throat. He took a deep breath.

So, is it true? Have I lost my faith in Eponine . . . or is Faith just trying to win her bet?

Just consciously thinking of no longer believing in Eponine stung him. Gentle, capricious, willy-nilly, silly ol' Eponine. In love with an idiotic mortal and hell-bent on carrying out her God-given duty. But yet, she'd kissed *him*. That had to count for *something*. She'd kissed him more than once. And each time it was light and life and peace and utter contentment. When he'd kissed Phina, it was warm and not terrible. Her lips were soft and velvety, but not charged with that unexplainable tremor of energy he felt whenever he touched Eponine at all. It could be that it was because Phina was just a normal mortal. Well, she was a mortal. Why was it so different with Eponine?

Without thinking, his hand burrowed into his coat pocket and pulled out the crumpled note he'd nearly left for her. Why hadn't he told her where he was going? Why was it so important to his anger that she be fretting at home over his safety and wondering when, or even if, he'd be returning? Would it mean she cared for him more than she cared about Jeremy?

"I need some time to think, a few days to cool off.

Don't worry, I haven't left you. If you need me, you know how to call."

It had seemed a silly thing to say. A silly thing to tell her what she already knew. She knew he was coming back.

Realization then forged a painful path to the center of his mind.

She had faith in him.

He, on the other hand, had been hurt and angry when she had disappeared.

Because he didn't think she would come back. He expected that she would, but did not believe in his heart that she would come back to *him*. Especially not from Jeremy's arms. Not when it was her assignment to love that boy. To be for him, whatever she's been instructed to be. And be ... *what* ... for Julian? He had no place in her mission. He was her guardian. Nothing more, nothing less.

And now where was she? Had Eponine run away back to Jeremy's apartment?

His fears told him that she had. That she had used this chance to get free of Julian. To finish what she had begun on the night he was so sick. Perhaps it had been her way to try to sneak out without his knowledge, to spare him that little bit of pain if she could. She could be there at Jeremy's now, be there because Julian wouldn't know it.

But he knew it wasn't so. If he knew Eponine at all, she was waiting for him at home.

He closed his eyes, and he could almost see her sitting alone in the dark curled up on the windowseat and looking for him. He felt terrible for putting her through it.

Julian stood to leave. It was damp and dreary now by the spring. The bright morning seemed to lose a bit of its color, somehow. He brushed the debris off his clothes and, almost as an afterthought, bent down to pick up the scroll.

He held it in one open palm for a long moment, then tucked it into his pocket with the note he had written for Eponine.

"Don't worry, I haven't left you."

He headed back out into the rolling green of Central Park, but it too seemed to be lacking some sparkle. The birds sounded tuneless.

Just goes to show what two hours' worth of sleep on the damp ground gets ya.

He went looking for a quiet place where he could get some challah toast and coffee.

Someplace out of the way where he could look at the scroll and think what the hell to do next.

THE ORACLE

"BY THE PRICKING OF my thumbs something wicked this way comes. . . ."

Phina froze on the fifteen-foot ladder with the cold shivers running down her spine. It was never a good situation when lines from *Macbeth* invaded her mind unbidden. The employee door thudded closed, and she saw through the maze of ladders and dropcloths a pair of Doc Marten-clad feet, black jeans, and a dark overcoat.

"What the hell are *you* doing here?"

Julian paused, momentarily confused by her total lack of surprise. "Looking for you."

"*Great*. Do I look like the shrink to the supernatural here, or what?"

"I have no idea what you're talking about. But if you are going to be a bitch about it, I'll just leave." He glared up at her, arms folded tightly across his chest. "Don't you even want to know how I got in here?"

"Not particularly." She touched up the trim she'd been painting, then pressed the lid back onto the can. With the brush in her mouth, she scampered down the ladder. "I am, however, mildly curious to know where you've been."

Julian bristled. "What, has Eponine been looking for me?"

"Um, *duh*. . . ." Phina tossed the brush into a bucket of water with a few others. "So where *have* you been?"

"Damn, what is it with you women? It's only been what . . . twenty-four hours?"

"Twenty-four hours? You expect me to believe that?" She wiped the paint off her hands with a battered towel. "Drop your gear over there. This sounds like a discussion that needs some coffee."

THEY SAT AT A table in the back part of the dining room, which was trying to make itself presentable with overstock prints on the walls. The fact that it was connected to the rest of the banal cafeteria made the attempt just as ludicrous as the random fountain in the center of the smoking section.

Phina sipped her cappuccino and nibbled on her half of the giant Rice Krispies Treat. She listened to Julian explain, again, that he'd left his apartment the morning before and had spent a sleepless night wandering Manhattan, then finally dozed off for a couple hours in Central Park's Ramble.

"How long does Eponine think I have been gone?"

"*Think* nothing. That's what I keep telling you! You left while Eponine was here at the Museum sitting here in this same ruttin' cafeteria talking to me, and that was Tuesday . . . *last* Tuesday. It is now *Thursday*. Not two days after, but *nine* days. Are you getting this, Julian? You have been missing for *over a week*."

"It's impossible! Last night I went to Limelight and then wandered around. That was Tuesday . . . today is Wednesday."

"Not only is it Thursday, but it's *next* Thursday."

"See, now you're just *trying* to piss me off." He ran his hand down his rather prickly cheek. "Does this look like *nine days'* worth of stubble to you?"

"Okay, *fine*, forget about what *gorram* day it is! Why did you break into the Met to come find me?"

Julian sat back. He chose to ignore her vicious mood and took the scroll out of his pocket. It was still wrapped in the red silken cord. He'd fiddled with it for an hour, but could not find a way to get the damn thing open. He set it on the table and waited.

"Are we playing charades, now?"

"You can't see it, can you? Well, that's just *peachy*."

"No. I can't see it . . . but I . . . I *sense* something is there." Her eyes lost focus for a moment, but she was looking right at the scroll. "It's a gift . . . and a challenge. . . ."

"Tell me something I don't already know."

"You know, my cousin gets paid for this, and all I am getting is *your shit*. And *I* even bought *you* coffee. Oh, where did I go wrong?"

"Will you just cut the melodrama and help me? Please."

Phina's eyes settled on his face, and he relented to her gaze. A seer's gaze.

He closed his eyes and exhaled. She saw the darkness, the shadows, the river of loneliness that swirled and eddied around him. He stopped her there, throwing up a wall to her sight. It was an old wall, made of heavy stones piled one atop the other and covered with moss and mold.

Let me in, she urged him.

I can't. There are some things mortals can't see, not even unique ones like you. I wish I could show you, though. Maybe you could explain some things to me....

She laughed aloud. "What in the world could *I* explain to *you?*"

"More than you know," Julian whispered.

He put his hand on her wrist ... *Delphine, her full name is Delphine Avalon Nabokov; her mother still calls her Delia. She has no siblings but a cousin named Cassandra who lives in Nashville....* "This." Julian shook himself free of the stream of knowledge he was riding through Phina's mind. "I want you to explain this."

With his hand still on her wrist, he held the scroll in front of her face and watched her eyes. She saw it.

"Where did you get it?"

"That's not important."

"Sure, it isn't.... That's fine if you don't want to tell me, but it makes my job a little harder."

"It came from ... a cousin. She brought it from home, I think."

"'Home.' Okay, then." Phina nodded and looked at the scroll. He could feel in her mind that she openly refused to touch it herself. And from her, he saw an image of an ornate lantern. He saw himself through her eyes being held aloft in a dark sky by an ambiguous winged being. He was being carried toward the lantern.

"You have angels watching over you," she whispered in complete sincerity.

Julian laughed. He laughed so hard he let go of her hand and fell forward onto the table. His stomach ached, and tears collected in the corners of his eyes.

"I'm sorry," he gasped, "but you have *no idea* ... Phina?"

She was gone.

He hurried back though the museum and found her once again on her ladder, blithely painting the trim where the display case met the ceiling, and paying him no mind.

"Phina...."

She began to sing "Greensleeves" rather loudly to herself.

"Phina!"

She glanced down at him over her shoulder, then continued with another verse.

"I can wait."

"This song has fourteen verses, you sure you're that patient?"

She dripped paint on her leg and wrinkled her nose. "Dang, lost my place, guess I had better start over."

"Phina, please. . . . The scroll . . . ?"

"I can't help you with it, Julian."

He sat down on the spattered and battered office chair.

"You want my advice? Just go home. She's waiting for you."

"I can't," he whispered.

She turned on the ladder and straddled the very top, her feet looped through the supports.

"Why can't you?"

"There's something missing. . . ."

"Offhand, I'd take a wild guess at your sanity."

"Very funny. I meant *besides* that. I am missing something, something about why we're here. And I know I missed something on Beltaine. And it seemed to really hurt Eponine's feelings. We got into a stupid argument about it, and she left."

"And then you got mad at her for leaving so *you* left."

"I am getting in the way of her mission! I thought I was doing her a *favor*!" He yelled up at her, surprised by his sudden vehemence.

"Oh, come off it! That's just a convenient excuse for you to use because you're too stuck on this self-righteous victim mentality to look her in the eye and ask her what's going on!"

"I don't know what else to do, damn it! And she should have fucking known better before she decided to come out here with me! She knows what I'm like! How can she carry on a romance right in front of me and think I am not going to care? If she's miserable, it's her own fault!"

"Well, let's just all have a pity-party for you then! Poor Julian, the little victim!"

He was on his feet with his hands on the ladder before Phina could blink. He gave it a violent shake, knocking the paint can over. She righted it before too much spilled and slammed the lid back on it. Then she hurled her brush down at him, striking his cheek and leaving a smear of navy blue across it.

"You hurt me and you'll regret it, mark my words. Do you hear me? Upon my grandfather's grave, may you live and die alone."

She might as well have slapped him hard across the face. He let go of the ladder and hung his head. He heard her climb down.

"Julian, go home."

He felt her hand on his shoulder. She wasn't afraid to touch him.

"I can't." His voice had gone hoarse again. "I can't face her. I can't face this."

"Julian, you *have to*. For no other reason than that she deserves that kind of respect from you. You owe her that much."

He shrugged away from her touch. "You don't know a thing about it."

"Then you're a coward. Get out of my museum."

He opened his mouth to reply, but the words died in his throat. His anger dissolved at the sight of Phina's shadowed eyes. He could hardly believe this was the happy-go-lucky gypsy he'd met on that early morning subway ride. Something was wrong here; something was very wrong.

"I'm going." He backed away from her, heading toward the employees' entrance that would take him back to Fifth Avenue.

Eponine was waiting. Something was wrong. It had been *nine days*.

When had he lost those days? In the club? In the park talking with Faith? Somewhere in between?

"It doesn't matter now, Julian. Just come home!"

His eyes surged over Phina, but she just stood there with the paintbrush in her hand and her eyebrows raised at him.

"Did you just. . . ? Oh, never mind." The door slammed behind him with a hollow bang in the concrete hallway. He ran along the corridor, past the huge black-and-white photos of the Museum over the past hundred years.

He didn't stop running until he slipped between the closing doors on the 6 train heading downtown.

BROKEN

JULIAN FOUND HIMSELF IN the dim hallway of his building. It had been a dull afternoon; the quality of light was blank and lacking sparkle. He attributed it to his foul temper. But the hallway actually spooked him a little with its utter lack of sensible lighting.

"Gotta talk to the doorman about calling maintenance," he muttered as he patted his pockets down for the keys.

He let himself into the apartment, opening the door with deliberate quiet. It was pitch black inside. He shuffled forward, reaching for the hallway light. He felt the switch, and it was flicked on already. The door swung shut behind him, making more noise than he would have liked and cutting off the rest of the weak illumination from the hall.

"Who's there?" Her voice was brittle and high. "Julian?"

"Who *else* would it be? Unless you've given someone else keys to the apartment. . . ." He stopped himself from speaking further. He did not come back to upset her. "Eponine. . . ?"

"I'm here."

"Why is it so *dark* in here? Turn on a light or something."

"The lights *are* on. All of them."

He could see that they were, somewhere beneath the shade of darkness that cloaked the room, that seemed to be cloaking the city. It wasn't a dark that humans could see, but they could *feel* it. It explained Phina's mood, that was for sure.

He moved toward Eponine's voice, searching through the dimness that clouded his eyes. He was reminded of his dream, the dream that had brought him to Eponine's bed the week before Beltaine. It had been dark and cold in the dream, but this, this was far different.

"Eponine, what's going on? Where are you?" But he saw her blurry outline in front of the pale window. Yes, sitting on the window seat, right where he'd imagined.

"So you can't see either?"

"It's dark. *Freakishly* dark. I mean, I have seen *dark*, but this blows it all away. . . ."

"I thought I was going blind. . . ."

"When did this happen?"

"I don't know. I woke up the other day, and it was like this. At least I think it was the other day. . . . I can't tell anymore. It never changes in here, day or night. It's always dark. I can't see anything."

"Well, why didn't you get out of here? Go stay with Phina . . . or . . . somebody. . . ."

She sighed. "Well, I wanted to be here when you came back, but then you never did. So I thought I'd go looking for you. But I found out that it didn't matter where I went. The dark followed me."

"It *followed* you?"

"Yes, it follows me. It follows me, Julian, everywhere I go. I think I'm dying. I have failed. It's over, the mission, the dream, your soul, my life. . . . I failed. I failed you. I failed everyone: all of us, and all the people here on Earth. But it's you that it hurts the most. I tried so hard, but I can't get through to you. I thought I could, but I just can't. I'm sorry, Julian, I'm so sorry!"

He was just in front of the window now. He could feel her there; she was trembling. But in his mind's eye he could see her clearly. Her eyes and cheeks were hollow and empty, her flesh dull, her hair ragged. Her fingers clutched desperately to one of her woven blankets that she had wrapped around her, and those fingers were like the dried-up twigs of winter. And in this vision, he could see the tips of dirty gray and tattered wings hanging limply among the fringe of the blanket. Hanging broken and forgotten from her stooped back. He shuddered and drew back. She began to cry. What frightened him the most was how *natural* it sounded.

Oh my God. . . .

He realized he was looking at Joy transformed. He was looking at Sorrow.

Sorrow was a ghost, a greedy leeching thing that skulked around the shadows of the living. It was born in the same instant as Joy. It wandered the world alone with the likes of Grief and Despair. It longed to sink itself into Joy, to possess her, to claim her, to turn her from a being of light to a creature of darkness. Vengeance, strangely enough, had a charitable view of Sorrow. He knew what it was to live in the shadows and be fed on the depravity of human nature. And he knew that Sorrow's maneuverings were usually just some misguided attempt to find happiness, to reclaim the part of its soul that now lived in a world of glitter and dreams, to pull itself upward into the ranks of angels. For Sorrow was neither angel nor demon, just a shade. A powerful and often noble shade, one invoked during the "Sorrowful Mysteries" of the rosary, but it was a shade nonetheless. It lived as Joy's shadow forever. If it was one thing Vengeance understood, it was the desire to *belong*.

But that didn't mean he *liked* Sorrow. No more than he knew the other angels didn't *like* him.

"Joy!" He was loath to touch her. "Joy, talk to me, Joy!"

"There hasn't been joy here in ... quite some time." The voice was hollow and seeped in melancholy.

"Snap out of it!" He grabbed her shoulders then, surprised to feel them so substantial and so human. He blinked and saw the room and his beloved roommate. The darkness was gone, the visions of Sorrow, all gone from his angelic sight, replaced by drab mortal vision. He had never been so thankful for such a thing.

"Eponine!"

"Julian. . . ." Her voice, sounding a bit more like herself, drifted out between choking sobs. "I'm sorry, I'm sorry! I tried everything I could. It's no use, Julian. Your darkness is more powerful than I am. I thought I could but I can't. I can't. I am so sorry, Julian. I'm sorry. . . ." She broke down into hard, grating sobs.

"Well, just calm down, 'Nine. Everything is going to be okay . . . okay?"

"This is a terrible mess, and it's all my fault. I promised I would do this! I promised everyone I could! And now it's over. It's over! I thought I could do this but I can't!" She hiccuped violently and nearly fell out of the window seat.

Julian pressed his body quickly against her to steady her. "Eponine, no, it's not like that. You can do it. You can. I . . . have faith in you."

Her breath hitched again, and he felt her nod, still quite hysterical. "You shouldn't! I failed. Even God won't talk to me. No one can help me, but I wouldn't give up, I couldn't give up. . . . I thought I could do this. I thought I could help you, I thought I could save you!"

He wrapped his arms around her, doing anything to stifle her heart-rending sobs. "How long have you been crying? The whole time I have been gone, haven't you?"

She nodded and gulped down a breath. "I thought you had gone for good," she whispered. "You were gone for so long. You were so very angry with me. I said, 'This is it,' and kept waiting for the news to announce that wars had begun, that terrorists had come back to New York City, or gone to San Francisco or Boston. . . . I thought you were gone forever, that you had finally fallen into the pit . . . and I had pushed you right over the edge."

"No, 'Nine, how could you think that? You've done so much for me, so much more than anyone else would have done." He thought about the bet his siblings were running. He held her closer, putting his shoulder beneath her cheek, and whispered into her ear. "I remember your fingers on my lips that night. And a thousand pieces of ice. Your hands were so cold." He reached out and took hold of her fingers. They were cold now, but it was a death-chill. He brought them to his lips anyway and gallantly kissed her knuckles. "You didn't push me to the edge. You brought me back, 'Nine. My time was almost up, but you brought me back. And it's been my own fault. I have been pushing you out. I'm so stubborn, 'Nine; you know that."

"Yeah, I do," her voice trilled a little with humor.

"'Nine, tell me, did anything happen when you were with Jeremy that night?" He felt her stiffen beside him and fall silent.

"You have to ask? After all of this? You have to ask?"

"Never mind. I'm sorry. Forget I said it." He wished he'd kept his mouth shut. "I think you should lie down. Come on." She didn't fight him as he gathered her up into his arms. She felt fragile, almost as light and tiny as Eurydice had been. And she was crying again, but the sound was strange. Julian brushed his chin against her face and found her skin to be dry. Eponine had run out of tears.

Faith was right. She deserves better.

Julian laid Eponine down on her bed and drew her covers up over her. The darkness still hovered in the corners of his vision, thinner now, but not vanished entirely. He could see her inner light there inside of her, buried deep. It wasn't gone, but it flickered like a candle's flame.

"Just rest now, 'Nine. Get your strength back."

"I have jeopardized so much."

"Shhh. Be still, now, be still."

"Julian," her voice betrayed her bone-deep exhaustion. She was fighting to stay awake.

"Not now," he said as tenderly as he could manage. He stroked her eyelids gently, as she had done to him on many an occasion when he was claiming insomnia. "Go to sleep now."

"I'm afraid," she whispered urgently. "The nightmares will return. I don't want to go alone."

"Well, I can't come with you."

"Yes, you can!"

"Hush, now. Just sleep. I'll be right here."

"No, Julian . . . no, I don't want to sleep . . . I . . . can't . . . I don't want to. . . ." And then she was out. Her body twitched once, and she was very softly snoring.

He waited for a few long minutes, then, satisfied that she was indeed very unconscious, he slipped out of her room.

Outside, it was late afternoon and the already deep shadows cut fierce lines across the streets. He had an idea to cheer her and raise the spirits of the entire city in the process. He nearly ran to the newsstand on Second Avenue.

"Let's hope there is still a chance," he murmured to himself. "I just gotta keep the faith."

CHANCES

"JULIAN! JULIAN, I'M FALLING! It's dark! Julian! Stop it, stop it! I want *Julian*! You can't help me, Jeremy! Julian! I'm sinking! Please, help, *please*!" It sounded like a dream she'd had before. This was the nightmare that had plagued her all week, when she had bothered to sleep, at any rate.

Her arms flailed out, desperately reaching for him. With eyes still closed, she caught a wrist in her hand and *knew* it was his. Knew it with the surety that a child would recognize her own mother simply by touch. She clenched it tightly for a moment, drawing it close to her chest.

Julian blushed slightly as she clasped his hand to her breasts. Beneath the lace-edged tank top she wore, he could feel her skin damp with the cold sweat of fright and her heart hammering there beneath her ribs. He gently pulled his hand free of her and wrapped her up in his arms instead, propping her against his body. He could feel the shuddering weakness in her as well as that brittle fragility that Sorrow had brought.

"I've got you, 'Nine," he whispered urgently. He rocked her slightly and petted her hair. "Shhh, don't you worry; Julian's here. Julian's here."

He glanced around the room. Night had fallen some time ago, and the place was as dark as ever. But the flames of Eponine's beeswax candles danced on her bedside table and her dresser, bringing some cheer to the room. He knew she might be upset when she saw what he'd done, because it would mean that he had left, but at the same time, he figured the surprise would make her happy enough to forget that part.

"Julian...?"

"Yes. I'm here, 'Nine."

She sighed sleepily and sounded like she was trying to pull herself free of her maddening dreams. "Julian...."

"Right here."

She pressed her face against his chest and lay still for a long moment. He could feel his heartbeat echoing in her. He thought she had drifted back into sleep.

"You aren't angry with me anymore?"

Her question surprised him. Not just the question itself, but that she was awake enough to ask. "I was never angry at you."

"You don't hate me?"

He felt tears sting his eyes, but forced a mirthful little laugh to his voice. "You have to ask?"

She was silent a long moment, considering his reply. "This has not gone according to plan at all."

"What hasn't?"

"This whole thing. The two of us here. I mean, it's not what I expected to have happen at all."

"Listen, Eponine, you didn't do anything wrong. Shit happens. That's life in the big city, as the people here say."

"Not just that. Everything. I never thought, never in a thousand lifetimes. . . ."

She trailed off, but he could make out her eyes glimmering darkly in her pale face. She was looking at him. He thought that in his mind he could hear the conclusion to her words: *that I could love you.*

Julian looked away from her, eyes squeezed shut.

"Okay, 'Nine, I don't know what they told *you*, but the message I got about this assignment was to keep you out of trouble. That you had something *spectacularly important* to do here, and I was to make sure you got it done. Nothing more."

"They told you that, did they?"

"As a matter of fact they did." He was growing defensive.

The "mission" was growing very tiresome. It was ripe with the sort of inaction and indecision that made his flesh crawl with nerves. It was a wonder that he hadn't gone completely ballistic seven times over since he'd set foot on Earthly soil. But having Eponine was such a balm to him. When she wasn't trailing after that insipid *boy*. But a mission was a mission, and who was he to argue? Eponine had to do what she was told.

And he realized that she was becoming "Eponine" to him. Not "Joy," not her true name, but "Eponine." Because Eponine lived in this apartment with him. Eponine had her head against his chest. Eponine made him breakfast and made him laugh. Joy was to be shared with all of Creation, but Eponine was his and his alone.

He put his arms around her and blotted out any and all

thoughts of sharing her with Jeremy or anyone else. His and his alone.

I never thought, never in a thousand lifetimes . . . that I could love you.

"I was worried," her voice was a sweet intrusion, "not just about our task here, but about you. There is so much at stake here, so much more than anyone realizes. Sometimes I think I am the one who needs to keep *you* out of trouble, mister." She smiled then, a tiny crack of a smile, but a smile nonetheless. Julian couldn't see it, but he knew it was there; he could hear it when she spoke.

"Well, most days you do a pretty good job."

"Most days? Pretty good?"

"Did you really think I was gone for good, Eponine?"

She went quiet again, and again Julian cursed himself for speaking when he should have held his tongue.

"I don't know. I feared the worst. You were gone for so long. . . ."

"Nine days, or so Phina tells me."

"Nine days. . . . Yes, I suppose that's about right. Where were you?"

"No idea. Honestly. I thought it was overnight. I went to a club and Times Square and out to the park. I met Faith there while I was sitting by the spring in The Ramble. But who knows where the time went." He touched his face, still amazed at the utter lack of beard there. Perhaps Faith had plucked it out of him. Or maybe he had strolled out of reality himself. He thought of how surreal that night had been, how never-ending it had seemed. Perhaps he had just seen a patchwork multitude of many nights strung together.

"I thought you had gone. I thought for sure that I had lost you. That I had ruined everything. And there wasn't a thing to be done about it."

"You didn't think I had *abandoned* you, you thought I had *fallen*," he whispered. He sighed darkly.

She nodded. "And I thought if I felt bad enough, took enough blame, that the guilt would burn away the wrong-doing."

"You didn't do anything wrong. And besides, you know it doesn't work that way."

"Sorrow crept up on me and I let it, I welcomed it," she said in a tiny voice. "And in that darkness, the only healing is pain."

"And you know that's not true, either." He kissed the top of her head.

She glanced up at him, a faint smile touching the corners of her mouth. "Sometimes we have to visit our own dark sides, to really see the light." She sat up a little on her own.

"Julian, I did run from you. I ran straight away from you. I didn't know where I was running to, but it ended up being to Jeremy. And I let him keep me, because I was spiteful and hurting. I had tried to give you a gift and blamed you when it was really just plain bad luck that ruined my surprise. I knew you'd be wretched and miserable all alone, so I left you. But I didn't think . . . I never thought all of this would ever happen. . . ." She began to cry again, but not with the self-deprecating tears of before.

"I know," he said soothingly. "I know you did it to spite me, regardless of your ties to him. So I went and spited you in return. I hated you in that moment for running away like that. Hated you for acting like that . . . and I realized you were acting just like me . . . and, well, you can guess *that* illogical progression."

She chuckled even as she wiped her tears away with the back of her hand.

"So," she said. "Things are going to be okay, then?"

He nodded. "Eventually, aren't they always?"

"Now *you* sound like *me*," Eponine laughed softly.

"Well, I think somehow that's better than you sounding like me."

The light in the room was soft and fluttering and seemed to cling to them.

"So," she began, sounding nervous, "we have established that you don't hate me. And that we are no longer angry with each other. And you know, or at least you *should* know that I harbor no ill will toward you for this whole mess. The very last question that remains is: Do you forgive me for what I have done?"

It seemed so strange of her to ask such a thing. "Why are you asking? There is nothing that needs forgiveness. But if you want to hear it, then of course I do, 'Nine. Don't be silly. I forgive you."

Then it struck him. Had he *ever* actually said that to anyone and meant it? "Forgiveness" for him meant retribution, meant evening the score, and even then it was a matter of leaving the situation in the past, forgotten. Actual *forgiveness* was a thing like apologies, something he had had no use for.

"Even though I did something cruel, intentionally to hurt you?"

I never thought, never in a thousand lifetimes. . . .

"Yes." He found his throat tight and thick-feeling. "Oh, God, yes, Eponine. *Of course* I forgive you."

The candlelight glimmered off Eponine's tears. "I wish you could see yourself, Julian." And for the first time, she sounded like herself. Her soft brown eyes opened and closed in slow, sleepy sweeps.

"Don't ever leave again. I couldn't bear it." Her tears were pure and heart-felt, not tainted with Sorrow's touch.

"Only if you promise the same to me." Even as he spoke, he couldn't believe he was actually saying the words.

She relaxed, and began to slide into a blissful sleep of peace. "Oh, yes, my love. All the days of your life, I'll be yours. For a year and a day. Forever and a day."

His blood thundered in his ears. He wanted her to repeat what she'd just said. He longed to hear the words again. But she was done for, finally released into the sleep that had been eluding her for over a week.

"You must be tired. Your ear is right over this jackhammer in my chest, and you aren't even stirring."

He gently lowered her to the pillows and saw the smile on her rosy lips. The shimmer of the streetlamp illuminated the room softly, and he could see that she was indeed profoundly asleep.

He reached into the pocket of his jeans and found his note and the scroll.

He left the note unfolded on the bed and toyed with the scroll as he slipped out of his clothes and kicked off his shoes. He nestled under the blankets beside her. Although he was sure that her nightmares would not return and that Sorrow had fled, he still felt compelled to remain near to her in case she woke later in the night.

He lay there next to her, close but not touching, breathing her scent and her warmth, with the scroll twiddling between his slender fingers. She fretted in her sleep, and without a conscious thought Julian rolled over, draped his arm around her waist, and made a soothing sound. She quieted at once and cuddled up against him. Julian stopped fidgeting with the scroll and tried to collect his wandering thoughts.

His heart was still pounding loud and hard in his chest, but at the same time he was filled with a sublime peace. Eponine's arm wrapped around his, and she held him firmly with a soft smile on her lips. Julian slipped his other arm beneath her head and cradled her shoulders.

He took a long slow breath and found himself smiling.

"It *is* going to be all right, 'Nine."

The red silk cording slid from the scroll in his now-still fingers. Carefully, he unrolled it with one hand. There were words inside, but the candlelight was too fitful for him to read them.

"I don't suppose it's important, now, is it?"

A glow began to emanate from the little slip of curled-up paper. The words showed stark and black against the illumination. His mouth dried up, and his eyes widened.

Then he laughed. He laughed so hard it shook the bed and roused Eponine. She opened her eyes drowsily and looked up into his face, startled. Then she grinned warmly and laid her head in the crook of his shoulder, and drifted back into contented sleep in no time.

He caressed her cheek with the tip of one finger.

"I think I am beginning to see," he told her. "Well, at least I think I am beginning to see that there is something there to look at."

He closed his eyes and fell into lush unconsciousness.

The scroll slipped from his fingers. It was beginning to fade out of existence.

In the soft light, a few words could be seen before the little scroll winked out into nothingness: TO THINE OWN SELF BE TRUE.

OH, WHAT A BEAUTIFUL MORNING!

"JULIAN!"

He jerked awake immediately, ready to fight. "What's wrong?" Which translated in his mind to: *Who needs to die?*

"How did all of this get in here?"

He blinked in the streaming sunlight. *What the hell happened last night?*

He realized he was in Eponine's bed, and there was nearly a marketful of flowers in the room. Thick puffs of hydrangeas in pink, blue, and lavender. Mixed bouquets of miniature roses and lilies, and mums with long fingers of silver-green eucalyptus leaves. Dozens of full-sized roses with heavy blossoms that nodded on slender stems. Wildflower bunches of snap-dragons and irises. All were wrapped and ribboned in florist paper, and they lay on the floor and the vanity and on the dresser and side table in frozen puddles of beeswax.

"Oh, *that*...."

"Yes, this!" She was standing before the window with her long hair falling in waves and tangles to her knees in her little gray tank top with the white eyelet lace and a pair of what looked like his flannel boxer shorts. But what he noticed most of all was the smile on her face. "Where did this come from?"

"I went and got it for you. Yesterday afternoon." The memories hit him with the force of a hurricane's gale. Of holding her while she cried, of the realizations that he had come to, of the scroll and its words that would not let him be. He looked down at his ring. *Well, sometimes you need to be reminded to treasure the things you see every day, I suppose.*

"*You* did this?"

He blushed a little. "Yeah. While you were asleep, the first time."

"Before we talked?"

Julian nodded. "Yes, I suppose it was."

Without warning, Eponine threw herself at Julian in a colossal bear hug.

"I guess I was correct in my assumption that it would make you happy?"

"You amaze me, you really do." She was sunshine in his arms.

"Well, I am glad to have been able to help."

Eponine's face clouded over. "Last night was strange. But I think it's okay. Do you?"

"I think we're getting there."

"How's your sunburn?"

"Itching like hell and peeling."

"What do you want for breakfast?"

"Hmmm, Veselka's or Dojo's."

"And leave all the flowers behind?" Eponine gave him her best pout.

"I thought it would be fun to go outside, you know, together."

"I have an idea!" She hopped off the bed and gathered several of the bouquets into her arms. She sat down on the floor, tore the paper and ribbons away, and began to weave the flowers' stems. She created a floral crown for herself.

"You want one too? It'll be like Beltaine all over again." She blushed furiously at her own words and melted into giggles.

"Nah, I think I'll let you be the flower princess. You want first shower or should I take it?"

"You go ahead; I need to brush out my hair first. I won't wash it today, else we'll be here 'til half-past lunch!" She giggled and set her garland aside. She reached for her brush and began to work the snags out of her hair, starting from the bottom.

Julian watched her for a moment then headed across to his room. He saw the lamp on the floor and set it back on the end table. Outside, a sheet of thick and rainy-looking clouds stretched over the tops of the tall buildings. But the early morning sun streaked in underneath, illuminating the bottoms of the clouds and lending a strange horizontal feel to the light. It was captivating. Julian couldn't remember ever seeing a prettier dawn.

"Hey, 'Nine, come look outside. The light is just trippy this morning," he said.

She leaned in her bedroom doorway braiding her hair. "What, you aren't naked yet? Get in the shower. I'm hungry!"

"Did you see outside?"

"Yes," she said, still smiling. "It's lovely, and I was about to call you in here to see it, myself."

"Well, good. Now what was it you wanted about me and being naked?" His rogue's grin sparkled across his face.

Eponine brandished her hairbrush at him. "Don't make me break this across your backside."

He winked. "Tease."

He gave her a hip shake that sent her into fits of giggles and sauntered to the bathroom. He closed the door behind him and listened to her laughter filling the apartment. It was so good to have her back.

"You better not use all the warm water, mister!" she called in with a bubbly snicker.

He opened the door a crack and peeked out at her. He was surprised to find her standing right there.

"And if you even make one smart-mouthed comment about being naked, hot, and wet...."

"Would I do such a thing?" He gave her his most innocent and charming smile.

"Yes, now hurry up! I am *ingesting a kidney* here, I am so hungry!"

"You could join me . . . it would take less time."

"I somehow doubt that, very much," she snickered and shut the bathroom door. "Hurry up or I'll come in."

"Ooooookaaaaay," he said, taking off his clothes with exaggerated slowness and making it plainly obvious he was doing so.

"I'll come in . . . with ice water."

He heard the freezer open and shut, and the familiar rattle of the ice trays.

"All right, all right," he laughed.

The hot blast of water felt good against his skin. He felt invigorated and alive. He thought of an afternoon wandering the East Village with Eponine and found himself grinning.

It was like the world was new. There was so much potential that it felt like the first day all over again.

Today is the day I really start searching for that truth in myself. Gotta know it to be true to it. She thinks she's failed; to hell with that! She'll succeed. I don't care what it takes to make her succeed, but I will do it. Even if I have to walk her down the aisle to wed Jeremy. From this moment forward, this is all for her. I will live to make her happy.

I LOVE NEW YORK IN JUNE, HOW ABOUT YOU?

EPONINE SEEMED TO BE the same as she ever was from all outward appearances, but she often sought solitude more than she used to. She dutifully massaged lotion into Julian's itching, peeling, and finally healing skin, morning and night. But she seemed most content to remain indoors with her books and her music, rather like she had when they had first arrived. Her eyes were dreamy, and her thoughts wandered.

Julian found himself going out to the store on his own, something he had never done before. But Eponine still did most of the cooking, although she was bent on teaching Julian some of the basics at least. She went out walking alone in the morning or the afternoon, ate dinner with Julian, and sometimes watched a little television with him. More often than not, once dinner was done, she shut herself up in her room playing her Loreena McKennitt or U2 CDs and reading until she fell asleep.

He fretted secretly over her, often listening at her door, trying to discern if Sorrow had fled for good or was just hiding, coming out to torment her while she was cloistered away from prying eyes.

"What have you been doing in there?" Julian had asked her one morning.

She'd given him a kittenish smile and patted his cheek, telling him not to worry. "Just thinking, that's all. There's been ... a lot, lately. Just trying to sort it all out."

"Yeah, there has been that. I worry a little, that's all."

She smiled at that. "Don't." Her laughter chimed as it always had. "Just give me some time, Julian. Just give me some time."

Jeremy called during one of these nights, and Julian did not quite understand why he got so particularly huffy about not being able to speak to Eponine.

"She won't see anyone, not even me, so kiss off," Julian said, and hung up. Mission or not, Jeremy was an irritating little twerp.

But it surprised Julian the most when Jeremy called again, about a week later, and was even more insistent than before.

"Tell her I just want to say a few words to her, speak to her for only a moment."

"Listen, mister, I don't know who you think you are, or what kind of rights you think you have. . . ."

"Who do you think *you* are?" Jeremy yelled, suddenly. "You have no right to keep her there, away from everything in the world! You're all but holding her *prisoner!*"

Julian sighed. *If it weren't for Eponine's insistence that you be left alone, if it weren't for the fact that she is here for you, you'd be dead now.* "Have you ever thought that she is keeping *herself* in seclusion?"

"I couldn't imagine why."

To stay the hell away from you! "She has her reasons, I am sure, but she hasn't been sharing them. Not with me, anyway."

"Perhaps she's finally wised up to your possessive and controlling ways."

Julian sucked his teeth a moment. *I would love to rip your heart out of your chest and show it to you while it's still beating. It happens, you know. I've done it before. Quite fascinating.* "Listen, you got a message for her or what? Because I am about to hang up now."

"As if I would trust *you* with any message for her."

Julian didn't even bother to reply. He just tapped the "end" button with his thumb and waited, counting with a smug grin on his face. The phone rang again in twenty-two seconds.

"What's the message?" he asked instead of saying hello. "And you had best tell me, because if you start feeding me that crap about how I abuse her and what-not, not only am I hanging up, not only am I having your number permanently blocked, but you are going to find it hard to even pick up a phone in the very near future."

"Is that a threat?"

"*The message.*"

"Fine. Tell 'Ponine that graduation is Friday. For the kids at school. They'd like to see her."

"I don't know what kind of an ass you think I am," Julian began, irate that Jeremy would think he'd keep such an obviously important thing from Eponine. But he refused to concede to any of Jeremy's paranoid ramblings. "And I don't care."

He hung up the phone and pulled the cord out of the wall.

Eponine wandered out into the kitchen, looking drowsy.

"I thought I'd make some tea," she said softly. "Would you like some?"

"Hey, 'Nine, uh, someone from school called to tell you that graduation is on Friday."

She dropped the box of chamomile tea. "Already? Is it really the first week of June?"

"Yup. Time flies whether you're having fun or not."

WITH HER HAIR CUNNINGLY braided and coiled up *fraulein*-style, Eponine was able to hide its substantial length under a colorful kerchief from India. The children were too overjoyed to see her to really notice such a thing.

She walked into the school's auditorium with Julian by her side. She shimmered from her gold-threaded hair-wrap to her mirror-sewn gypsy skirt, while Julian was like her shadow in all black and gray. Much to his surprise, the children were nearly as happy to see him.

The two of them sat in the center of the row with the students as the principal addressed the entire assembly. She spoke about each grade's achievements for the year and finished with a prayer. Then she merrily clapped her hands, announced that the school year was over, and the refreshments would be served in the court-yard. The children leapt to their feet and surged forth, reuniting with their parents and tugging them outside to be first in line for the cookies, cake, and punch.

Once outside, Ms. Branch's second grade class swarmed their beloved teacher's aide.

"We haven't seen you in *so* long. . . !"

"Poninny we *missed you*. . . !"

"Tell us a story!"

"Sing us a song!"

A few parents nodded, smiling. "So *this* is Eponine?"

She beamed at them and blushed. "It's good to meet the parents of such wonderful children. They have been an absolute joy to teach!"

Tabitha tugged on her skirt. "This is a *very* special day, isn't it?"

Eponine smiled indulgently. "Of course it is, sweetling. You're a third grader now. That's quite an accomplishment."

"Not that. You brought *Julian*," she whispered and pointed to where he stood like a brooding raincloud in the midst of the late spring sunshine.

At the mention of his name, he glanced up and raised an eyebrow. Tabitha shyly waved, then buried her face into Eponine's side.

Julian chuckled and strolled over. "What's all this about?"

Eponine put her arm around the girl's shoulders. "I think Tabitha here wants to thank you for coming."

"She does?" He looked confused.

The child peeked up at him with wide eyes. "I wished that you would come to us one more time. Because we only got to see you on *really* special occasions."

"You . . . *wanted* to see me?"

She nodded and gave him a sweet, shy smile. "You showed us the New Year in Chinatown . . . and wore a mask with us on Mardi Gras. We missed you."

He looked at the little girl with Eponine's arms around her, giving them both such trusting smiles.

"You are better with children than you think," Eponine said..

Tabitha broke away and gave Julian a sudden hug. "Thank you, Julian! I am *so glad* you came to see us!" Then, bashful again, she ran off to find her parents in the throng.

Eponine simply grinned at him with amusement dancing in her eyes. And Julian suddenly wished that she could have children of her own.

What a mother you'd make, 'Nine. Yours would be the happiest, most well-rounded, well-read, well-adjusted, tolerant, loving, joy-filled children on the block. I wish that someday you'll have that chance.

"'Ponine, you made it after all!"

A nauseous shiver ran through Julian's body, and he caught the split-second warning glance Eponine threw him before she went to greet Jeremy.

Jeremy threw his arms around her and hugged her tight, casting an icy glare over her shoulder at Julian. Then Jeremy gave her a kiss on the cheek, never taking his eyes from Julian.

"I am so thrilled to see you here and in one piece." He finally looked at her with a broad grin on his face. "Here, there are some parents who have been just *dying* to meet you. You interested in doing any tutoring this summer? How about some babysitting? We have *so much* to discuss!"

He pulled her away from Julian and toward the center of the group where several families were already waving.

"I won't be but a minute, Julian!" She turned away and began a series of introductions before he could even reply. Julian let her go. He closed his eyes, breathed deeply, and counted to ten.

Jeremy stood beside her looking quite satisfied with himself. He rested his hand on Eponine's lower back and cast Julian several meaningful glances. Eponine didn't even notice him. She was raptly chatting with the parents of her beloved students.

Julian laughed to himself. *You seem to think this means you've won some sort of battle here. But I can really see that you've lost. Eponine loves those children more than she could ever hope to love you, asshole . . . more than she could ever hope to love me, either. You don't even realize how good you have it, you bastard. She's yours already. You don't need this charade. At least I came here without ulterior motives.*

"See, Mumma, *this* is Julian. He didn't know he was a prince until Eponine loved him, and now she has a curl of his hair in her locket. *I've seen it!*"

He looked down and smiled at Tabitha, who was quite unabashed now that she held her mother's hand tightly. He crouched down to look her in the eye and gave her shoulder a gentle squeeze.

"Is that so, little one?"

She crossed her arms over her skinny chest. "Yes, *it is*. Eponine *said so*."

He thought at first to protest, then laughed and ruffled her hair instead. This was something new. "I know it is. I was just teasing." But his mind tracked back, trying to remember what she'd told him about the stories she told in her classes. He couldn't recall that one, but he felt Eponine's warmth in the child when he touched her.

The afternoon was winding down. Eponine had gotten herself involved in many conversations with the children and the parents. Julian sat on a bench and ate chocolate-dipped strawberries and just watched her. She was telling each and every parent the particular strengths and interests that their child had displayed with her in class and how best to develop them.

Finally, she began to walk among her students and say goodbye. She handed them each a little cloth bag that Julian knew held a tiny sliver charm: a miniature locket with a few strands of her hair coiled inside.

"You ready to go?" She came toward him, looking happy but drained.

"Only if you are."

"Yes, it's about time. Can't hang about forever." She gazed wistfully at the school as she walked out with Julian. She didn't try to find Jeremy to say goodbye. And Julian did not care to remind her to do so.

"So," Julian asked, "do you think you'll want to tutor and stuff this summer?"

"I'd love to, but it would be selfish of me."

"Why?"

"Because I have said goodbye to them. They'll have the summer to forget me."

"They aren't going to forget. You know that, right? They won't ever forget you, 'Nine."

She sighed and gazed along the street with a sad smile on her face. "I know they won't. But if I teach during the summer, then I know I will want to come back in September. And after September . . . well, November is so close behind it. . . . I wouldn't want to leave them like that. I want to give them some time to heal. They don't realize yet that they'll never see me again."

Julian stopped and took her by the shoulders. "Of course you'll see them again. What are you saying?"

"But not like this. . . ."

"Who knows? But regardless, you *will* see them again. If only in their dreams."

She nodded. "It's pretty out. You want to walk around the park for a little while?"

"With you? On such a beautiful afternoon? Hmmm, let me think about it. . . ."

She pinched him.

"Okay, okay! Why, yes m'lady, I'd love to walk a turn about with you."

They strolled quietly toward Washington Square.

"Do you think they'd know me in their dreams? Do you think they'd really remember?"

"Eponine, even if they all live to be a hundred and ten, those children would know you *anywhere*."

Eponine smiled. "You always know the right thing to say."

Julian gave her a quizzical cock of his eyebrow. "*Sure* I do."

She giggled at him.

"Oh, Nini, like *anyone* could forget *you*. . . ."

He let her walk on ahead a little, watching the afternoon sun gild the edges of her outfit and light up the wisps of hair that framed her face.

I wonder if it would be better to forget I ever had these moments with you, than to live without you forever more. And as much as it would be so much easier, I know I could never do it. You are too deep in my heart now. I wish to God I was your mission, Joy.

THE SACRED AND THE PROFANE

THE SUMMER SOLSTICE PARTY being held out at Limelight was the talk of the entire Village. Although Eponine was dubious about a church turned into a dance club, she agreed to accompany Julian.

Eponine stood in the thick shadow of the reddish stone façade of what had once been an Anglican church. The silken banner rustled in the warm evening breeze, occasionally resounding with a whip-crack snap that made Eponine wince.

"Are you listening to me?"

She jolted back to the present. "Sorry, I drifted away there. . . ."

Julian paid their way in and sighed, retracing his thoughts

back to where he thought she'd still been keeping up with him.

"You see," he said, steering her through the milling black-draped throng, "the problem with this whole vengeance thing is that it's so ... *reactionary.* I mean, you have Event A which causes Emotion B and requires Reaction C so that there is balance again. Cause and effect."

He guided her with one hand cupped beneath her elbow to a small cluster of antique smoke-saturated sofas that lined the corridor running parallel to the dance floor. It had once been part of the nave.

"It's not like joy, where someone can experience it at random moments all on his or her own. You know, like a rose, a dragonfly, a sunset, a song. No, no human being wakes up one morning feeling *avenged.* No one just walks along the sidewalk and suddenly becomes *vindicated.* Something *has to happen* to another person."

He looked at her, a frown cutting across his face. "You aren't hearing me at all, are you? You aren't even trying."

She swung her eyes toward him in a swift and nearly feral motion. She was obviously distressed.

"Look, do you want to go home?"

"No, no, it's all right, I'll be fine. But I just want to take a look around. I have never been in a church that wasn't a church anymore."

"Then why don't you go give yourself the grand tour and bring us some drinks?"

"Okay. I can do that. What would you like?"

"Something dark," he muttered. "Bring me a Guinness."

EPONINE RETURNED TO THE seemingly endless corridor with two frothing pint glasses of stout. She looked a little dazed, but nimbly steered her way toward where Julian was waiting.

"Did you see it all?"

She nodded.

"Did you get lost?"

She nodded again and gave him a tired smile. "But I found something very cool," she said. She handed him his glass. "I found a little side bar, over by the baptismal font. They have a bunch of local stuff. This is from a place the bartender called The Belgian Beer Bar. He says this is 'Monk's beer,' the darkest they've got. Look, Julian, no light can escape the surface of this beer!"

He raised an eyebrow at her and burst out laughing. She was really trying to have a good time.

"Come, sit down, 'Nine."

She curled her legs beneath her on the couch opposite his. She looked pale and sweet, like a dream, in her filmy burgundy silk skirt with the shimmery vintage scarf tied over it and the lacy little top she wore. She was dressed *correctly*, but she didn't fit in with the rest of them. She was just *too happy* to be goth. But she was beautiful nonetheless.

Julian looked up. "I am so thrilled to see you here," he said with a quietly flirtatious smile.

"You remembered!"

Eponine's eyes widened and her nostrils flared as a tiny girl tossed herself across Julian's lap. Her bobbed blue-black hair skimmed the tips of little ears that seemed slightly pointed. To his credit, Julian looked equally confused and uncomfortable.

He took a deep breath before letting go of the sofa's armrests.

The giggling fairy of a girl glanced around and, spying Eponine, looked delightedly unimpressed with her. "Oh, is this your girlfriend?"

"She's my roommate," Julian answered through clenched teeth.

"Oh." The girl looked perplexed as she tried to decipher what sort of footing to put the term "roommate" on. "Well, then, my name's Eurydice."

To *her* credit, Eponine only smiled placidly. "*Enchanté.*"

"Come on, Julian, let's go dance." The little corseted creature scrambled out of his lap and smoothed down her cobweb skirt. "I want to get some fun in before they turn off the music for the ritual."

"Ritual?" Eponine looked interested.

"Yeah, this really dumb thing they do every year." She rolled her eyes. "It's *so* overrated. I mean they act like it's the Witches' Ball or something. I mean *really*."

"What do they do?"

"How should I know? Candles, roses ... the usual fluff. Ringing bells at midnight." She shrugged. "Oh, Cruxshadows! Let's go, let's go!"

She tugged on Julian's arm, and he slapped her hand away.

Tears glistened in Eurydice's eyes. She took a furtive sip from the slim flask that hung on a chain between her miniature breasts.

"Go dance, Julian," Eponine said, coolly. She smiled a little; it was a rather bitter smile that seemed out of place on her cherubic mouth. "I think I'd actually like to see that, you *dancing*."

He glared, and she drew herself up.

You have no right to be jealous, 'Nine. Oh, no, you of all creatures in this world have no right to be jealous.

But she was. It was obvious. And it charmed him.

He smiled at her with the corner of his mouth and gave her a wink. "As you wish, my lady."

Eponine stood. "Good. I think I'd like to have another look around. Perhaps see the grounds. You know, have some fun before midnight when the ritual starts." She tossed him a glance over her shoulder as she glided away.

You're leaving me here with her. You're ditching me. I can't believe it.

A thought caressed his mind, lightly, like the touch of a feather. *Talk about revenge, no? I have learned from the best.*

I'm going to get you back for this, you know that, right?

Tsk, tsk, so . . . reactionary.

So you were listening.

Of course I was, silly. Now go have fun and come find me later.

EPONINE STRODE THOUGH THE tall, iron-banded oaken doors. It was an amazing place full of red bricks and silvery masonry. The place smelled dimly sweet of mildew and dust. A morose garden ran along the side of the building between its moldering walls and the rusty wrought-iron fence that trimmed the sidewalk. But around the back of the place she found a hidden treasure: A stone well sat in the center of an overgrown garden. It was pleasantly unkempt, and rambling flagstone paths crisscrossed beds of roses and plots of ivy-covered hedges. At the end nearest the church building was a large brass bell mounted in a sturdy but beautifully carved wooden frame. Beeswax candles burned on the lip of the well and on a number of simple stone benches throughout the yard.

The throbbing music sounded like distant thunder, far removed from this elegant little space. Eponine closed her eyes and drew in a deep breath. Yes, it felt right; it felt calm and serene and sanctified.

The bell began to toll. She looked up to find a young woman wearing an elegant black kimono stenciled with red and golden roses. The girl solemnly rang the garden bell twenty-one times. She stood still and statuesque, waiting. But the music throbbed on, and no one came outside.

She sighed, her shoulders slumping slightly. "I don't think they are coming."

Then she went to the well and drew a little ladle out of the bucket on the ground. Standing over the grass, she poured water over her fingers, then into her palm. She sipped the water from her hand, spat it out, rinsed her hand again, and then tipped the ladle back so the remainder of the liquid flowed back down the handle. She put the ladle down and smiled at Eponine.

"You're welcome to join me," she said, blushing a little under her light, geisha-like makeup.

"You're Shinto," Eponine said, amazed.

The girl shrugged. "Somewhat. My parents, both Wiccans of sorts, met while they were both studying abroad in Kyoto. It's an odd mix, but it's how I was raised."

"That's wonderful!" Eponine bowed. "*Shinsei na.*"

The girl bowed in return, more formally. "Oh, no, not me. You are *kami no megumi.*"

Eponine smiled and waved her hand. "We shouldn't argue over who is holier than whom; it seems rather odd to do that in a church yard."

"Odd, but rather appropriate," the girl laughed. "Shall we?"

Eponine nodded and the girl clapped her hands loudly three times.

"In the cold of winter, we found hope in the promise of spring. And now in the warmth of summer, we feel the darkness coming upon us once again. The year turns round and we are back to the beginning once again, the beginning which is both the middle and the end."

Eponine felt a hand on her shoulder, but she didn't flinch. She knew Julian's touch. She felt as familiar with his human hands as she did with her own.

"Am I too late?" he breathed into her ear. She detected the faint odors of cloves and licorice on him. "It's a ritual all to itself in there. No one has remembered to come out for this. They'll be lucky to remember their own names. Eurydice's potion is strong stuff. It seems like everyone brought absinthe tonight."

The girl began walking the circle she'd made with the candles. She picked each one up and blew it out as she passed.

"Though the fertile season is at its fullest, the year turns. Fields will ripen, leaves will turn, snow will come and the Earth will sleep in winter again. Snow will melt, buds will bloom, and the Earth will dance in spring again. Come summer and bear us away. Come darkness and bear us away. Come guardians and keep us safe. Come ancestors and bring us wisdom."

"Come angels and bring us joy," Julian said, reverently.

"Come friends and bring us love." Eponine touched his hand on her shoulder with gentle fingertips.

The girl smiled. "May our eyes be opened to the magic that surrounds us always. May the *kami* remind us of the Divinity that dwells in us all."

She blew out the last candle and clapped her hands three more times. In the distance, above the bass that rattled the little panes of stained glass in their leading, the Jefferson Market Library's tower clock tolled the final strokes of midnight.

"Should we have gotten gifts to exchange for this solstice, 'Nine?"

"I honestly don't know." Her breath hitched, and it looked to Julian as if she were about to cry.

"What's wrong?"

"The days slip by so fast," she whispered. "So much faster than I ever remembered. November will be here again so soon."

It was quite dark now in the garden, but Eponine's tears glittered like opals, casting shivering reflections on her cheeks. The girl went back to the bell and rang it twenty-one times again in long, soulful tolls.

"Don't think about that now. You, of all people, should know better than to destroy the magic of the present by worrying over the future." He touched his fingertip to one of her tears and drew the dewdrop of light into his mouth. It sent a shudder through him to taste it, to glimpse the vibrant, but fleeting, vision of how her heart would break to leave this lovely little humble planet. He saw how her heart would break to leave him as well.

"Eponine. . . ."

"I have a gift for you, after all, Julian." She rose up onto her toes and kissed him.

But I have nothing for you.

Don't be silly, you are enough for me. You are everything for me.

It's so simple to say that here and now. Shadows dabbed at the edges of the enfolding corona of light that surrounded them. He wrapped his arms tightly around her, savoring the feel of her body pressed against him, how her breasts were soft and firm at once, how her ribcage was a little bit lopsided, how she stood with more of her weight on one leg so one hip rested higher than the other.

Her laughter rippled across his soul. He wanted her so badly. He pulled away from her, and the illumination became an illusion and faded like a dream. The girl and all the candles were gone. The music still pulsed like a heartbeat from behind the once-sacred stones. An orgy of dance was mounting between those walls that had been so stoic.

"You want to dance for a bit, then maybe go get some coffee and watch the sun come up?"

Eponine stared up into his eyes, looking on the verge of tears again. "You didn't like my gift?"

"Well. . . ." He felt the heat rise into his face. *I wish I could accept it, Eponine.* "It's not that, well, not really. I mean, well, I don't know what I mean, but I think I would like to see you dance."

She thought about it for a long moment. "For you."

Her eyelids slid closed and her head tilted to one side, listening. She rocked in the rhythm of the throbbing music, her long skirt rustling softly like sparrows' wings.

Julian took a minute step back and watched her. She used the flow of the song to guide her motions like a fish uses the current of the stream, like a reed uses the breath of the wind.

She kicked aside her pretty Chinese silk slippers and danced barefoot on the mossy stones. Pinpoints of light like a hundred fireflies surrounded her. Within the former church, night-loving children heralded the shadow half of the year with misunderstood pleasure as they wallowed in their own despair. But outside, Eponine danced in the courtyard, a being of light, proving that there is never any real darkness if one has joy in one's heart.

Julian was ever-awed by her and moved to hold her again. "Would you take your gift back again?"

She paused, gazing up at his face. "What do you mean?"

Screw the mission, I am here now. I am the one she needs. He slowly pressed his lips to hers.

They were caught up in a moment of frozen time where there was no light, no shadow, no sound, no motion, only the soft, urgent sensation of their mouths locked together. The spell dissipated and fluttered away in a hush.

Eponine gazed shyly into his eyes. "Happy Solstice, once again, Julian."

"Happy Solstice, 'Nine."

"Yeah, coffee sounds good. Coffee sounds real good." She was breathless.

"And in honor of the coming of the dark part of the year, I think we should get some chocolate. Kiev makes a mean dark chocolate truffle cheesecake with Oreo cookie crust."

"That sounds almost *sacramental* for a night like tonight. Let's go!"

Julian smiled to himself, although he found it was touched with a little sadness.

Yes, winter is returning, but I can still hold spring in my arms for a little while longer.

As American as Apple Pie

"I HAD THE MOST curious dream. I was on a train, an old-fashioned, elegant one like the Orient Express. I was lounging in this sleeping car, in a box bed with tasseled drapes all around it." Eponine gazed off into the horizon. The setting sun was shimmering reddish-gold on the crests of the tiny harbor waves. "All the fringe was dancing to the beat of the train, clickety-clack, clickety-clack."

She bobbed her head slightly to the rhythm of her memory, which made Julian a tad ill as it ran counter to the lurch and sway of the boat.

He watched her watch the gilded clouds; high and puffed from the morning's thunderstorms, they rose up like cotton candy columns. But it was blessedly clear now, as evening was fast approaching. Eponine had insisted on going out on the Circle Line cruise, even if rain precluded the Fourth of July fireworks.

The sun slid behind a tall nimbus tower, and the light broke into a halo of broad prismatic beams behind it. Eponine gasped.

"Then what happened?"

"What happened when?" Her voice was hushed, distracted, and her eyes were transfixed upon the natural spectacle of the sunset.

"In your dream."

"Dream?"

"The train, Eponine?"

"Train? Oh! Yes, the train! Uhh, I had a book. Yes. It was that new one about Sappho, I think. I was reading the book, and someone brought me tea. Yes. It was Earl Grey tea. Very strong. I remember asking for some milk for it."

"While on a train."

"Yes. A Victorianly marvelous train."

"And that's it?"

She tore her attention away from the golden death of the day. "Isn't that enough?"

"But what *happened*?"

"I drank the tea. It was in a Royal Dalton teacup. Old Country Roses, a classic."

Julian laughed and shook his head. "As long as there are stars in the sky, I don't think I'll ever understand you, 'Nine."

Her graceful brows drew together as she looked back out across the water. The ferry rounded Ellis Island, and the brilliance and fire of the sunset flared up behind the Statue of Liberty. Lady Liberty gazed fearlessly into the glaring light, holding up her own torch in salute or defiance, Julian couldn't decide.

"Wow," he breathed. "It looks like a postcard."

He watched the golden radiance play across Eponine's cheeks and forehead, turning her eyes to topaz and her hair to rich auburn. She glanced at him over her shoulder, slightly freckled and a little sunburnt beneath the sleeves of her blouse, and seemed surprised by his scrutiny.

She smiled playfully. "Are you enjoying the sunset?"

The ever-shifting surface of the water bathed her flesh in a swirling illumination that suited her perfectly.

"Immensely," Julian whispered and grinned. He reached around her trim waist and took hold of the rail just beyond her hip, trapping her cozily between his arms.

The sun peeped through a slender break in the clouds like a glimmering eye peering down at them. Eponine stood a little stiffly; uncertainty crept across her face.

Julian wavered. *Should I move?*

But he could not bring himself to distance himself from her. So he stood there, hands on either side of her gripping the worn wooden rail. Her shoulder blades pressed against his chest.

He could feel so intimately every breath she took and shakily released.

Wait, is that her trembling, or is it me?

"Why are you holding me like this, Julian?" Her words were husky and she sounded almost scared.

"Do you want me to stop?"

She turned to face him, an action that startled them both equally. She blushed brightly for a moment.

"No, I don't." Her gaze was intense and, although she faced away from the setting sun, her eyes still shone like gemstones.

He tilted his head forward and to the side, and she lifted her chin ever so slightly so that their lips met.

A delicious shiver ran through him, and he let go of the railing and wrapped both arms around her fiercely. There were no songs, no visions, only the flood of sensations that coursed through his blood. His ears rang and he felt terribly light-headed.

Can't do this, can't do this, can't do this. . . .

Just as softly as they'd met, their lips parted and Julian opened his eyes just in time to catch the last dazzling glimpse of the ruby sunset as it surged from beneath the clouds just above the horizon. Eponine turned her head and saw the very last drop of daylight swallowed up by the New Jersey skyline.

We are both doomed. Totally doomed. Doomed, doomed, doomed. Every second I am with her, I am jeopardizing the whole reason we have come down here. What happened to that Zen-like acceptance I was so sure of before? Every time I touch her, it shatters like glass; it just disappears. And what am I left with? Lust and longing and the undeniable sense of betrayal. Every time I touch her, I betray the trust she has put in me, the trust to be her guardian, her protector . . . not some lecherous imp. This has got to stop. We are both doomed.

"It won't be long now," she murmured.

"'Til what?"

"The fireworks. It *is* the Fourth of July, silly. Aren't we here to see fireworks?"

He desperately wanted to feel guilty for sabotaging her emotions like this. But there was nothing in him but desire. He was still dazzled from the sunset and her kiss.

A fiendish grin broke out across Julian's face, and he gave her a tight, flirtatious squeeze and a wink. "You mean there's *more?*"

HOT AND COLD

THE AIR CONDITIONING WAS out. Julian woke sweaty and sticky in a tangle of his sheets. He heard the fan in the main room still whirring. Usually it served to more evenly distribute the wonderfully cold air that came from the air conditioning unit installed under one of the front windows. But this morning it made only a warm and humid breeze throughout the small apartment.

"'Nine," he moaned.

"I've already called down. The repairman is on his way, they tell me."

He dragged himself out of bed and cringed at the thick, damp bunching of his usually loose cotton pajama bottoms.

He stopped dead in the doorway and felt his jaw hang limp.

She was sitting on the coffee table in a plain white nightgown trimmed down the front with pin-pleats, pearly buttons, and eyelet lace. She had the big salad bowl at her feet and was rubbing ice cubes over her arms and chest, then leaning in front of the fan. Julian thought of his sunburn and how she'd fed him ice cubes to try to keep water in his system. But this was an application of ice (quite literally) that had never occurred to him.

"Staying cool?" He tried to sound flippant and casual, but he could see she detected the strain in his voice.

"Attempting to," Eponine sighed. "How are you? You don't look well. Would you like some water? I made some iced tea. It's a lovely mint blend. I was thinking it was too early for iced tea, but I've drunk half the pitcher myself already."

"Sure, tea sounds good. My mouth feels all syrupy and thick. Urgh."

"Help yourself to some ice; I have more in the trays for the tea."

She brought him a pint glass of sweet, cold tea and Julian downed it in mere moments.

Eponine laughed, "More?"

"Nah." He wiped his mouth with the back of his hand and set the glass down. "You're a wonder, thank you."

Impulsively, he threw his arms around her and pulled her close in a quick, tight hug. Although her flesh was cool to the touch, his skin crawled at the contact with another warm body. Eponine squirmed.

"Oh, Julian, you're sweet and all, but it's too hot to be cuddly right now." She pulled away, but gave him what could have passed for a coy smile. "Perhaps you should take a cold shower, and we can go find someplace that's air conditioned. Then you could hug me all you want."

"On the condition that you go wearing that."

"Absolutely not! But how about my white sundress that's *almost* like this?"

"Deal," he said over his shoulder as he dashed for the bathroom. This was a dangerous game, but it thrilled him. "You're not going to renege on me, are you?"

"You mean go back on an offer of air conditioning and possibly some breakfast, with you? Has the heat addled your brain? Of course not!"

"I meant more the . . . oh, never mind, I'll be right out."

* * * * *

THE DOORMAN ASSURED THEM they didn't need to be in the apartment for the air conditioning people to work. Repairs were being done on the eighth floor, and their unit would be next. Eponine smiled brightly and thanked him, then skipped out into the glaring July sun in a cloud of rose-scented powder and body glitter. Julian caught up to her, and they agreed on Veselka's for breakfast. He enjoyed the fact that the staff didn't bat an eye when the two of them ordered cold borscht and iced tea for breakfast.

"This is nice," Eponine said with a soft smile. She tore up her fresh-baked challah bread with the ice-cold butter but didn't seem to mind. "These are the things I will miss. Sitting here in our favorite restaurant eating breakfast with you."

Julian slurped up the last of his cool soup and pushed the bowl away. He swept the crumbs of his own challah into a small pile in front of him, then blew them across the table. Eponine giggled, but Julian didn't share her merriment.

"Okay, sourpuss, what's wrong?"

He didn't answer. Eponine slid her chair around and rubbed her shoulder up against him like a cat might rub against its master's ankle.

"Well, here I am, ripe for the hugging!"

He sighed. Temptation roared but he reined it in.

"Julian! What's with you? You couldn't keep your hands off of me at home!" She actually sounded hurt.

He gently pushed her away and looked into her eyes. She was hurt. And concerned. He sighed.

"This cannot happen, 'Nine."

"What are you talking about?"

There was so much at stake. He didn't know where to begin. "What do you see when you look at me?"

She blinked. Obviously that was not what she was expecting to hear. "What do you mean?"

He took her by the shoulders, but softly. "What do you see, 'Nine?"

"I see you, silly."

He sighed, again. "That's not what I mean. I mean what do you see *about* me, what do you see *in* me?"

"Someone fierce and passionate and brave and strong."

Julian nodded and sat back in his chair, letting her go. But she caught his hands and held them tightly.

"I see someone who has learned so much more than he ever thought was possible for him." She brushed his fingertips against her silken cheeks and Julian, with hardly a conscious thought, made sure to keep his hands quiet so she could move them easily. She smiled knowingly and let go of him. "See what I mean?"

"No." He crossed his arms and glared sullenly at her. *How can I get her to understand what I am asking? I wish I could just ask her flat out: Am I worth losing everything for?*

She rose and leaned over, her long braid sliding over her shoulder and pooling into his lap. "Yes. I just wish you'd admit it." She kissed him softly on the cheek and stood, stretching.

Julian's mouth hung open, and he wondered if she'd heard. Of course she hadn't. Even Eponine never peered through his carefully crafted walls. He would not let her. There were things that Joy should never have to see. His soul was one of those things.

"Come on, let's take the long way home and look at the street vendors on St. Mark's."

Eponine was already at the front counter paying by the time Julian got up from the table. Although it was still plenty hot outside, he felt a chill. Goosebumps danced across his flesh, and he was trembling. He caught Eponine in the threshold and hugged her.

"While we have air conditioning," he said. *While my resolve is shot,* he thought.

Eponine shivered, but she was smiling. "You are a puzzle, Julian. But one I am enjoying figuring out."

I could give you much to ponder, my sweet Eponine, but for now, let's take these little moments as they come and try not to think about tomorrow.

ARMS AND AMOUR

WELL, AT LEAST IT'S air conditioned. Julian strove to ignore the stifling and cloyingly sweet scents emanating from the enormous flower arrangements in the gigantic stone urns set throughout the museum lobby. Everywhere around him were bustling people and noisy children, their voices echoing madly in the high-vaulted stone interior. This was not the solace Eponine had promised at the end of that hot and gritty walk nearly ten blocks down Lexington Avenue from the 6 line. The wait seemed endless as security guards checked every bag, purse, and parcel. He was glad Eponine had left her little backpack at home and stuffed everything she needed into her pockets or his.

"So, where to first, my dear?" He tried to sound interested. Eponine was in her element here, he could tell. He had never really been inside the actual museum. *I suppose it's rather humorous that I've dined in the employee cafeteria, but I've never seen the exhibits.*

"Not sure. Hmm. Let's begin at the beginning. The ancients. We have Greece on the left and Egypt on the right. I propose we go see the Temple of Dendur first. I think you'll like it."

"I'll follow your lead." He stepped aside and swept his arm toward the entryway behind the small ticket counter. "My lady...."

Eponine flushed and giggled. "You rogue." She put on her grandest airs and swept past him and into Ancient Egypt.

ADMITTEDLY, THE TEMPLE WAS a greater affair than Julian would have thought, occupying its own room in the museum. The room contained a reflecting pool and a collection of statuary, and was all glass on one wall. He smiled wryly to see the sunbathers there on the little knoll between the windows and the road.

"What an odd place this is."

"This room?"

He laughed. "This world!"

Eponine smiled. "It's my favorite."

"The world or the room?"

"Look over there." She pointed to the cool limestone wall that separated the Temple room from the rest of the Egyptian wing. She smiled even more brightly as the color drained from Julian's face.

He blindly walked forward, led by the captivating stares of the statues before him. It seemed that their eyes followed him as he approached. There were six of them, enormous and carved of some mysterious dark stone, six figures of a lion-headed goddess seated on a throne. Her breasts were bare save for a broad carved necklace, and her hands, smooth female hands, rested lightly on her seat. But rather than lounging at her ease, she seemed poised to rise or strike suddenly.

Julian closed his eyes and inclined his head as a long sigh escaped him.

Eponine was a warm presence beside him.

"I knew you'd like to see her," she whispered reverently.

He nodded, feeling the hot throb of adrenaline-filled blood in his heart. Yes, see her, and allow her to see him with her eyes of eternity. He had been hers once, in the ancient muddle of the world, before pantheons were so neatly divided. His being was so close to her fiery heart. Just as Eponine's soul was one with the Goddesses of Springtime, so did he belong to her: Sehkmet, the harbinger of pestilence, the very soul of vengeance.

He shuddered and released another pent-up breath. He bowed to her image, deeply, from his waist. He felt her eyes, relentless, unflinching, burning. A hand caressed his cheek, a soft hand, a woman's hand, but with the thick black claws of a lioness that raked carefully across his flesh.

Eponine remained beside him, her face placid and patient. "Ready to move on?"

Sehkmet sat still and lifeless six times over, eyes blankly staring into the Temple behind them.

"Yeah, sure. Where to next?"

"I don't want to rush you, Julian. I know how important this is," she said.

"No, no, it's fine. She's gone . . . for the moment. I said my hellos and she said hers."

"Well, you should really enjoy what I have to show you next, then." She gave him a little wink and led him slowly from the Egyptian Galleries and back into the Main Rotunda. Before them a huge staircase swept up to the second floor, but Eponine pulled him into the opening to the right of the massive stairs.

Julian raised a questioning eyebrow at her, but Eponine only pointed to a sign that was hanging above one of the many sets of gallery doors.

The Gallery of Arms and Armor.

He hardly waited for her, eagerly pulling open the heavy glass door. The gallery was a long hall with gleaming white walls and bright skylights. A mannequin cavalry rode down the center of the room. Warriors in full regalia sat astride war-horses in burnished armor. Along both walls were smaller side galleries, their glass cases filled with all manner of weaponry. Brilliant banners reconstructed from England, Scotland, Wales, Japan, Korea, and China undulated slowly in the domed recesses of the gallery's ceiling.

He felt Sehkmet's powerful touch again as he flew from display to display, eager to see it all, yet tortured at being unable to put the weapons in his hands, to feel the blood course over his fingers. Eponine was somewhere behind him, her face alight at his rapture, telling him where she'd be waiting for him. Julian pressed his nose to the glass of each vitrine and tripped the alarm on the statues countless times. How long had he been there looking at every helmet, every katana, every musket, every dagger, every spur and boot-heel?

Finally, eyes weary and bleary, he pulled himself away. He felt wrung out but at the same time strangely elated. The light had faded; it was afternoon. Where had Eponine told him to meet her?

He wandered back out into the center chamber done up to look like the nave of a church. Across from him were signs declaring the galleries for seventeenth- through nineteenth-century art. He stumbled through overdone Rococo drawing rooms that stank of rotting silk like the inside of Limelight. He took a broad, winding stairway to the second floor. Upstairs he found himself in a long, wood-paneled hallway that pitched upward and was full of boring black-and-white, artsy photographs. Below, in a world of glittery afternoon sunlight, was a garden of white marble statues. Beyond that was another glass wall and the thick black point of the Cleopatra's Needle obelisk that stood amid the trees just behind the museum in Central Park. The only way down from the floor he was on was by way of a back stair that switched back upon itself a half dozen times in the short distance to the ground floor. More furniture.

No, Eponine wouldn't be here.

Julian wandered silently among nineteenth-century nymphs and goddesses cavorting in pure white stone. *Ah, poor, misguided Victorians. And you meant so well, too. Just goes to show that money can't buy taste.*

A heady scent of sweet mildewed air conditioning permeated this room. It was more cloying than the flowers in the lobby had been. He ducked back into another long gallery and found himself at the edge of the tall chamber full of church relics.

"Damn it!" His voice echoed around those holy icons and brought more than a few cold stares from the other museum patrons. He tugged the black elastic band out of his hair and rubbed his fingers severely across his scalp, trying to ward off the headache born of frustration that was threatening to consume him. He turned with a snap and headed resolutely toward the Great Rotunda. He would have to wait by the information desk for her. It was the only museum exit, wasn't it? But he knew she'd slipped out other doors previously. She'd crept out into the park before. And what if she'd found Phina? Julian had no idea how to get to Phina's basement department. The only stairs he saw only went up!

He stormed past the glass vitrines of senseless trinkets and idiotic pieces of stone. A small doorway on his right caught his eye. It was a brick archway that led into a small pillared room. He paused and curiously peered into this strange little place. It was all brick inside, rough hewn and stepped in a most bizarre manner. He realized this gallery was positioned beneath the Great Stair. Huge pieces of pale stone were mounted against dried blood bricks. Humble embroideries and simple garments were housed between glass plates that were set between the pillars so one could get a view from all sides. Crystalline lights hung from delicate wires above his head, lending a clear but hushed illumination to the strange gallery. It was like none other he'd seen in the museum. He liked it. He liked the way it felt.

He was so caught up in the study of a rosary carved from ancient Roman glass that he didn't notice the girl who came to stand beside him.

"Isn't it interesting how old systems of belief are incorporated into new ones? This glass was originally blown for beads and bowls in a temple of Venus."

"You don't think it's sacrilegious at all to have turned it into a rosary?"

"It's only been re-sanctified with a new meaning, although it is a little sad that the original artwork is lost."

He nodded. "That sounds like something Eponine would say."

"Oh, it does, does it?" The girl rubbed her shoulder against his. "How long you been in here, mister? I've been all over the museum hunting for you!"

Julian looked down at her and smiled. "I found you!"

"You? Found me?"

"Did you see the swords?"

"Yes, Julian, I saw the swords."

"*All* of them?"

"Enough of them to suit me just fine, thank you." She grinned, then rose up on her toes and gave him a gentle kiss.

He stepped back, nearly striking his head on the brickwork behind him. "What's that for?"

"You're very beautiful when you're happy."

"Beautiful?"

"Handsome, then. Most fetching, ever-so-becoming, easy on the eyes. . . ."

"I get it, I get it." He laughed and stood still while she cozied up to him.

"These linen shifts were worn by the original missionaries who sought to solidify the Christian belief in Constantinople. See the blood stains?"

"Huh, guess it didn't go over well."

"What, you don't remember? Constantine had quite an imagination for revenge."

"Ah, Constantine—the world has never seen his ilk again. I'd have liked him better if he had just stuck to his guns and not did that whole last-minute, politically savvy, death-bed conversion thing."

"He got what was coming to him in the end. Everyone does." She gave him a sideways glance.

"Are you implying something, Miss Allegresse?"

"You remembered the last name I picked!"

He shrugged. "Hard to forget."

"You are a man of wonders, Julian."

"And an angel of what?" he whispered low to her.

"I am not concerned with that at all right now."

"Oh, no?"

"Nope." Her smile was secretive.

"I see. I feel like I should be worried ... but over what I am not sure...."

She met his eyes with a hint of some fearless sparkle. "Thank you for coming to the museum with me today, Julian. I trust you had a nice time?"

"Indeed. The pleasure was all mine, m'lady. It was ... it was ... good ... to see your world."

"My world? You spent all day babbling to Sehkmet about the weapons!"

He blushed darkly. "You know what I mean."

"You see a lot more of my world every day than you'd care to admit. Sometime I'd like to see some of yours."

"No." He took her hands and brought her fingers to his lips. "No, you wouldn't. It would destroy you. Joy has no place there."

He dropped her hands but did not let them go as a handful of people meandered into the gallery. They wandered in one side and out the other, finding nothing to catch their interest there.

Eponine squeezed his hands. "I am stronger than you think, Julian. I wish you'd believe me." *Everything depends on it.*

He leaned toward her and tentatively kissed her. It was thrilling in this dim and secret place, surrounded by bricks and relics. Throngs of people came and went over the Grand Staircase above their heads. He pressed his lips to hers with more urgency as the tremors of Sehkmet's fire filled him again. But this wasn't bloodlust; it was a different passion.

He tore away. "No, Eponine, I can't. We can't...."

"Why not? Tell me why and make me believe you."

He crossed the strangely appointed space in a few strides, finding himself on the outward curve of an alcove that boasted a large and impassive mosaic of the Virgin Mary.

She offered him no solace.

"Julian. It's time to go. The museum is closing."

He nodded and turned to make for the exit. She caught his wrist.

"Don't lock me out, Julian. Please. If you knew how much this meant to me...."

"How much what meant to you? The museum? Or this little flirty game you seem to be playing with me?"

"It's no game." She fought the overwhelming urge to look away, instead keeping her warm gaze on his elegantly sculpted face. He really was quite a handsome devil. She leaned against him and pressed her face against his neck, gently kissing his throat.

"Stop," he whispered, but he put his arms around her. He held her close and savored her scent, her heartbeat, her trembling breath, until the security guard appeared and walked them out the front doors into a hot Manhattan evening.

THE PRIMROSE PATH

"WE'RE NOT GOING TO have a fight." Eponine had one arm wrapped around the upright near the subway car door. She was reaching toward Julian with the other.

"Says you." He blatantly ignored her and instead concentrated his gaze on the "Learn English now!" poster, which repeated its slogan in eighteen different languages, most of them translated incorrectly. *Learn English instantaneously. Understand a minute of English. Quick assimilation of American tongue. Understanding of fast American. . . . No wonder so many foreigners think Americans are morons.*

"Julian, I'm serious! You're being ridiculous." The train jolted, and Eponine lurched forward.

Out of pure reflex he caught her arm and with amazing grace came up to her side. He grasped the bars around her and held her against the upright with the press of his body so she could not fall. He realized what he had done, and was torn between his desire to protect her and his need to remove himself from her immediate presence. She chewed her lip and gazed up at him. The train clattered to a stop at the station, and she allowed herself to be pushed against him.

"We're not going to have a fight," she said smoothly. "I won't allow it."

He grumbled something to himself, then said, "Ours is the next stop."

He held her as the train jerked forward, but she clung tightly to him when he tried to step away.

"Eponine, let go."

"I don't want to."

"What's wrong with you today? All afternoon you've been all *clingy*."

She sighed and let her arms fall away from his hips. "Sorry. I didn't realize it was actually bothering you."

"Thank you." Julian straightened his shirt and fiddled with his ponytail. He avoided looking directly at Eponine, who was gazing listlessly out the window into the dim graffiti of the subway tunnel. *We can't do this, Eponine. Can't you see it? Regardless of the mission, I am me and you are you, and it would never work!*

They rumbled and squealed into the Astor Place station, and Eponine mechanically stepped out onto the platform as the doors opened. She drifted past the Kmart entrance and allowed herself to be caught up in the press of people trudging up the stairs. It was still bright and hot outside. Julian watched as she crammed her fists into the little pockets of her gray vest and hunched her shoulders forward. She paused at the corner until he caught up. They walked in silence past the tables of hemp jewelry and three-dollar T-shirts on St. Mark's. She didn't even glance at the sale rack of the small used clothing store next to Dojo's.

"You want to go look, 'Nine?"

"No, not today."

"You want to stop into Dojo's for something? Iced tea and cold sesame noodle salad? Sound good?"

"You can if you want. I'm not hungry."

Julian was gripped with the fear that she would slip into twilight depression again, that spectral Sorrow would take her once more. "Eponine...."

"It's all right, Julian, I'm all right. I guess I just have to come to the understanding that ... that you may not ... feel for me what you once did. Perhaps I waited too long." She shrugged. Her eyes were blank and teary. Hers were the eyes of grief, of despair, of all hopes dashed. She was wandering away from him, heading for their apartment.

"'Nine...?" His voice was small, and he doubted she could hear him.

She turned. Perhaps it was not his voice she heard, but his intentions. She stood there on the sidewalk, a girl in a green sundress and twill vest with an inordinately long braid. The late afternoon sun was beginning to cast long shadows around them. She looked to be standing upon the edge of a narrow island of shadowed stone set in a sea of light. She still shimmered, even in her sadness. Her dark eyes squinted to look at him, a figure of darkness with the bright western sky behind him.

"What do you want, Julian?"

"I don't know." His voice was rough and hollow like the wind across desert sands. He made a tentative step toward her, as if she were a wild creature that would shy at his approach. "Eponine, I don't know. All I know is that I smile when I am around you. I don't think dark and bloody thoughts when I am around you. And I know it's not just your power of happiness; it's something more than that. At least, I *think* it is. I could just be getting tricked. . . ."

She raised an eyebrow but made no reply.

"And then I start thinking, if this is a trick, it's the best damn trick anyone has ever played on me. And maybe when we're done, they'll all say, 'Look at Vengeance, the grinning fool!' But right now, I don't care. I don't care who thinks me foolish, and I don't think this is a trick. I think you are more aware of this mission than I will ever be, and I have to let you make the call here. If we ruin everything, then we ruin it. But I . . . I think I . . . trust you, 'Nine, trust you not to let me come to that sort of harm."

The sun dipped behind the buildings, and everything shifted into a hushed dimness.

"So what are you saying, Julian?"

"Don't speak like that," his words aching with sorrow, "don't speak to me like I am a stranger. You'll break my heart."

"I wasn't aware you had a heart to be broken."

"'Nine. . . ." He took another step, and another. She stood still, and her gaze never left his face. He stood right in front of her. Although only inches separated them, he felt as if there were an infinite chasm there, that he would fall headlong into nothingness with one more step. Her face was the Virgin Mary's of the museum: cool, impassive, patient, waiting.

"So, what you're saying here is that *right now* you don't *think* you care what everyone says about you where I am concerned. And *right now* you think anything between you and me might disrupt the assignment, but you are willing to take that risk."

"Yes."

"Then what's stopping you?" Her question dumped ice water over his sense of satisfaction.

"You know what. All excuses aside, trivial or otherwise, you know damn well that I can never indulge in anything of the sort. Not with anyone, and most of all not with you."

"Says who?"

"You know that as well."

"Do I? And for that matter, do you? Do you really know? Or do you just *think* you do? Have you just made up convenient excuses in your mind to cover up the fact that you're really just a coward?"

Julian's jaw dropped. He was filled with the urge to haul off and backhand her, but his limbs were frozen in shock.

"I thought so. You know, it's ever so easy to kill someone, but to *love* them? That takes real courage." She shook her head. "Looks like you aren't going to be the laughingstock back home. It'll be me. I tried so hard. I put every ounce of my soul into this. But it wasn't enough. And now ... what? What happens to us now? What happens to the world if I really and truly have failed? I am afraid for it, Julian, and afraid of it. Goodbye, my dearest. I don't think I'll ever see you again." *Because if I really and truly have failed you, I will be one of the first to suffer, one of the first to die.*

"Where are you going?"

"Home." She turned away again, and he truly felt the gulf between them, deepening with every step she took.

"Fine," he said, his flesh tingling with the familiarity of anger and retaliation. "Don't bother leaving the light on for me, okay?"

"You mean at the apartment?" She spoke without looking back at him. "That wasn't the home I was talking about."

He ran toward her and spun her around forcefully by the shoulders. "Don't you dare leave me here! Don't you dare leave me, 'Nine!" he shouted.

Julian's body shook as cold sweat trickled between his fingers. His heart pounded fiercely, and tears began make zigzagged tracks down his cheeks. The brilliantly scarlet rays of sunset pierced the gaps between buildings and trees, making a rosy patchwork on the sidewalk. He held her with his arms so rigid and trembling that he thought they would fall from his shoulders. The thought of her turning away from him was like a black abyss of terror, leaving him alone. He felt as if he were slipping down into it, a whirlpool of dark water. He could see no light there. His soul would smother there, and he would be forever gone, forever changed. He who was so unaccustomed to fear was seized by it, keeping it at bay with his iron grip on Eponine.

A soft touch on his face brought him back to the present, standing there clutching her like a madman in the dusky evening on St. Mark's Place with cautious locals skirting about them. Eponine, despite being pinioned at the shoulders, was wiping his tears away. He eased his hold and felt his knuckles creak.

"I'm sorry. . . ."

"Shhh." She pressed her fingertips to his lips. "Julian, you are so good at being divine. Why don't you try and just be human for a little while?"

"You say that like it's the easiest thing in the world."

"It *would be* if you weren't so stubborn, mister."

"If you only knew what that stubbornness was holding back," he laughed. It was a single sharp sound, but it soothed his temper. "Eponine. . . ."

She gave him a gentle smile.

Let it go. Her voice pierced the darkness of his mind. *These walls you've built, this burden you carry, let it all go.*

He threw his arms around her. How good it felt to hold her close! It was as if the waking world had no more meaning.

"Please stay," he whispered urgently into her ear. "Please tell me you really weren't going to walk away from me like that. I don't care if you have to lie, just please tell me you weren't going to go!"

"Well, I meant it when I said I should just go home, but I hoped to the heart that'd you'd call me back, that you'd give me a reason not to go. I knew you would. I knew you wouldn't let me leave."

"And if I hadn't called to you?"

"Perhaps I wouldn't have been able to go through with it after all. Perhaps *I* am the coward."

"There isn't a cowardly bone in your body, and I sometimes wish there was, you capricious thing, you!" He hugged her tight and kissed the top of her head.

"Are we made up then?" She wriggled away from him.

"Yes."

She leveled him with a long, steady gaze. "Mind if I pick a new fight, then? Since that always seems to happen when we kiss. . . ."

But . . . the mission, your assignment. . . . He folded. If any love between them stood the ghost of a chance, he was going to have to trust her. They would sink or swim together. He leaned toward her and met her halfway. He was hesitant at the first, but the scent of her skin, the sweet taste of her mouth, and the glimmer of delight that swept through his body and soul overwhelmed him. *I'm going to that special hell for this. And I don't care. She's worth it.*

The light was there, a soft reflection of the electrified vision he'd had when first he'd kissed her months earlier. In the back and forth between them, how often had their lips met? Julian thought he could keep count, and maybe he could, but not in this shimmering dream he shared. All was glowing warmth, different from the sunset-drenched heat and humidity in which they stood.

He heard a catcall hoot, and it shattered his reverie. A huddle of men across the street were shouting at them and making their opinions of what the two of them should do next extremely clear. Eponine blushed deeply but laughed. She smoothed down her sundress and gave Julian a bashful glance. Julian fumed and took a menacing step toward the other sidewalk, but Eponine stopped him cold with a single touch on his forearm.

"Don't worry about them. They aren't getting any tonight."

"How do you know?" he growled.

"Silly, make it so. *You're* the Angel of Vengeance."

He caught the sweetly fiendish undertones in her voice and smiled. He closed his eyes for a moment and sent his punishment. "That's one group of guys who ain't gettin' it up anytime soon. I don't think there is enough Viagra in the world that can help them now."

"Good," she smiled. "Now take me home."

IN HIS KISS

JULIAN SHUT THE APARTMENT door behind him. The room was cloaked in the gloaming twilight. He stood there with his hand on the doorknob for some moments while Eponine swept into the kitchen, flicking on lights as she did and singing softly to herself.

"Julian?"

He shook himself out of his reverie and looked at her blankly. She was holding a plate of sliced nectarines.

"I thought you could nibble on these while I got dinner ready," she said.

He stepped forward. "Let me get dinner tonight."

She laughed. "Sure. I am in the mood for pizza."

"I was actually thinking Chinese," he told her with a smile. He knew by heart the number of the local Chinese place that delivered. He ordered kung pow chicken, Szechuan beef, and extra steamed rice.

Having made the call, he retired to the couch and sat beside Eponine. She was snuggled into her favorite corner smiling at him. She took a piece of fruit from the dish and ate it as daintily as it was possible to eat a dripping slice of ripe nectarine.

Julian watched hungrily. "You got some juice on your chin."

Her tongue darted out, trying to catch the spill.

"Uhh, not quite."

She was quite amusing to watch as she tried to lap the clear amber juice from her chin.

"Here, let me." He slid over to her and drew his fingers across her jaw. He brought his fingertips to his mouth, savoring the sweetness. He knew her mouth would taste that rich and lovely. With a shuddering breath, he reached for her, drawing his hand around the nape of her neck. She acquiesced easily, her eyes sliding closed and her lips flushing red and parting slightly. Julian could smell the heady scent of summertime fruit upon her as he leaned in to kiss her.

The intercom buzzer rang, and Julian nearly leapt out of his skin. Even Eponine jerked with the grating sound.

"Our dinner," she said in a winded, shaking voice.

"Right." Julian glumly rose from the sofa and hit the doorman's intercom. "If it's our dinner, send them right up. Thanks."

He slumped against the wall. Eponine gazed at him from the back of the sofa, her head cradled on her folded arms and a wistful smile on her face.

THEY ATE CROSS-LEGGED ON the floor by candlelight and serenaded by Eponine's favorite Beethoven CD. Pushing the red and white pagoda boxes aside, Eponine reached again for the plate of nectarines.

"Here." She took a slice and held it out to Julian. "It'll cleanse your palate."

"What's that mean, anyway? To cleanse one's palate?"

She shrugged. "I guess it takes off the aftertaste of what you just ate. But I know I could use something cool on my tongue. We just ate the two spiciest things on their menu!"

Julian laughed and reached for the proffered fruit. Eponine dodged his hand and pressed the nectarine directly into his mouth. He coughed in surprise and managed not to choke. The nectarine was indeed a balm to his burning tongue, and the proximity of her fingertips so close to his lips made him forget all about his dinner. He caught her gently by the wrist and held her gaze.

"Eponine," he murmured. "What are we to do?"

"Have another nectarine." She had another slice ready in her other hand and purposely missed his mouth. "Oh, you've got juice all over your lips, my dear."

His brows furrowed. "Don't tease like that."

"Oh? How should I be teasing, then?"

He released her and wiped his mouth with the back of his hand. He couldn't help but imagine that syrupy sweetness upon Eponine's lips if he were kissing her. He shook his head to clear the image and opened his eyes to find Eponine sitting back on her heels with a look of serene patience on her charming face. The CD ended, and the sounds of a New York night rose to fill the silence.

"Why are you gazing at me so?"

The subtle rise of one shoulder was all the answer he was given.

"You know I am a wicked soul. Don't look at me like that."

She smiled, nearly laughing. "Wicked? You? Don't be silly."

"We're not going to have a fight." He realized he was repeating her words from earlier in the evening.

"Julian, you aren't wicked. In my eyes, you are quite noble."

"Noble?" He scoffed. "You can't possibly mean it."

She rolled her eyes. "Noble and pig-headed. We've been over this a hundred times. Why can't I convince you?"

He didn't meet her eyes. "Just stop. We are heading down two avenues of discussion I don't with to talk about."

He felt her silken touch against his cheek and knew his resolve was near to the breaking point.

"Julian, your duty is a harsh one. But you never shrink from it. You do what you are bound to do with honor and courage and a great deal of nobility. You don't take pleasure from another's sufferings, and you try your best not to let revenge get out of hand. You enforce the balance. Often it takes blood. Where Justice ends, you take up."

"Of late, there has been too much," he said in a pained daze, "too much hate, too much blood, too much need for me, just . . . *too much.*"

"I know," she whispered. Her fingers curled into his hair, pulling it loose from its tie and letting it spill over his shoulders. Her nails massaged his scalp, and he tingled from head to foot. "Trust me, my love, I know. But let it go now, let it all go. Just relax for once, stop worrying. About me, this assignment, the world. It's not important right now."

"But—"

"I said, stop worrying! You don't need to be the strong one right now, carrying the weight of the world on your shoulders. Just be here, in the moment. Enjoy this time. It's so precious, and we have so little of it."

She was right. This was not the time to worry about such things. He relaxed, realizing just how much tension he was carrying.

"Can I tell you something, 'Nine?"

"Anything."

He glanced up with a shy smile. "I know. And that's what I mean." He took her hands and drew them out of his raven hair. He held them tightly and saw that he was trembling. "You are the best friend I have ever had."

"Oh, silly. . . ."

"No, don't dismiss it like that! I'm serious. I don't think anyone has ever cared this much about me. Ever."

"Julian, I'm *sure.* . . ."

"Not like this." His voice was a hoarse whisper. "Not like *this.*"

I never thought, never in a thousand lifetimes. . . .

Their lips met with a singularly gentle grace. Both paused for a moment between heartbeats, then heat washed through them. Eponine felt him breathe into her a small shudder, a measure of release, of yielding. She could sense trust in his kiss. Trust, and so much more.

Like the first time they had kissed, the world swam away in waves of shimmering light and wishes. Dreams rode butterfly wings and came to rest in his heart. He found his fingertips upon her neck and felt the pulse there beating a rapid staccato. He drew her closer, sliding his hands down her back. She melted against him, her flesh rippling with delightful little helpless shivers.

Passion boiled into his dreamy state, and Julian pulled the

down vest off her shoulders. Eponine obligingly moved her arms to let him remove it. Her hands dug under his T-shirt until she could run them along the smooth skin of his back. She could feel the firm shape and motion of his muscles between his ribs and her hands.

His mouth broke from hers and feasted upon her blushing neck and shoulders. Her breath was so very warm and moist at his ear, carrying with it the faintest trace of her voice. He heard the joy there in those near-silent non-syllables. He bit her tender flesh just below her ear, and she gasped, digging her fingernails into his shoulders beneath his shirt. He shrugged it up to his armpits, and Eponine pulled it free, tossing it somewhere in the direction of the television. Her palms explored the whole of his upper body now, sliding across his dampening chest, back, and shoulders, kneading his flesh with her tiny, sharp nails like a pleased kitten.

A low sound that might have been either passionate or menacing rumbled from Julian's throat, and he unceremoniously pulled the hem of Eponine's sundress up over her head. She made no argument, only fell back against him in earnest once he had sent her dress to lie with his shirt on the floor somewhere in the darkness beyond the edges of the candles' glow.

The sensation of her bare skin against his nearly undid Julian. Never had he felt the satin caress of another's body.

I never thought, never in a thousand lifetimes. . . .

He stroked the curve of her spine from the nape of her neck to her waist. He was confused by her underclothes, the mass of straps and hooks that she wore across her chest. He fumbled, and she took her hands off him only long enough to help. He managed to free himself of his jeans one-handed, his mouth fused to hers the entire time. With both of them unconfined by the majority of their clothes, he pushed her to the floor and sought the sweet depths of her mouth again.

She shuddered and pressed her hands against his chest, pushing him away.

"Eponine, what is it?" His body ached with restraint, and his voice was rough. His lips felt raw and throbbing. He didn't want to stop, but he could see the concern so clearly written in her eyes. "What's wrong?"

"Julian," she whispered, her eyes darting to the open door of her room, "not here on the floor."

HUMAN NATURE

HE WAS STUPIDLY UNSURE of what to do. As many times as his thoughts had wrapped around the idea, he had never expected to actually be in any position to act on it.

She smiled softly and would not meet his gaze.

"It's all right. This doesn't have to happen. Not now, not ever...."

But there was something in the way she spoke those words that told him: *of course it had to happen.* He understood her meaning, however; she wasn't about to force him any more that he'd ever think of forcing her.

She lay quite still beside him with her head pillowed upon his shoulder and her two small hands pressed together almost as if in prayer, resting on his chest. As he closed his eyes, his adrenaline-filled blood still roared in his ears, screaming with frustrated desire.

Give in. Why don't you just give in? You've been strong for so long. It's time to let go now.

He tried to shake those maddening thoughts from his mind, but they encroached, climbing deeper into his skull. He snapped open his eyes and was astounded to see Eponine's lips moving. He wasn't *thinking* those things, he was *hearing them.*

"I mean," she whispered, with real trepidation in her voice, "are you saying that after all of this ... that you don't want me?"

His mouth went utterly dry, and his heart heaved. He sat up, collecting her in his arms.

"Is that what you think?" His voice was that of the wind, soundless, but he was sure she could hear it. He rocked her a little against him, feeling the tremor that lived in the pit of her stomach. He nuzzled the top of her head, pressing kisses into her hair.

"You couldn't possibly think that, could you?" He pulled her away and looked at her for a long moment. "I mean, *look at you.*"

She blushed deeply, coloring all the way down into her chest.

"No, Eponine, that's not it. I don't want to take what is not mine."

"It's no sin to take a gift freely given."

"I'm not for you! And you ... you are not for me."

"Yes, I am, Julian. I am." She reached out and wrapped her arms about him, burying her face against his neck. She could feel his pulse there, pounding alongside her cheek. His flesh felt scalding hot to her—not like it had been when he was so sunburnt, but heated from within. The scent of him was overpowering, and she drank it in with shuddering gasps of air.

Her mouth moved along his neck, feeling so very warm but making him shiver. She kissed his throat, his ears, the edge of his jaw. . . .

He cupped her cheeks in his hands and pulled her lips rather forcefully against his own.

She stiffened for a moment, resisting, and he nearly let her go. Then her body melted against his. His arms snaked around her and he held her tight, like a drowning man clinging to anything that would keep him afloat. He kissed her in lieu of breathing, it seemed, every kiss deep and urgent, giving him what he needed to live.

In a confused tumble, he found himself lying over her, his mouth taking fierce gentle bites of her breasts, her throat, and the taut, blushing flesh over her collarbones. She laughed. It was not a laugh of humor, but of rapture.

She wrapped her arms around him and held him tight. She wrapped her legs around his, letting her knees slip to the outside. Julian noticed and stared down at her, his eyes as fierce and black as the heart of a storm. He could see her pulse shuddering in her throat; he could feel it answered in her legs. She watched him, her own eyes wide and so dilated he wouldn't have been able to guess their color if he didn't already know.

He opened his mouth to speak but she put a finger to his lips. Then she drew his head down and kissed him deeply. Her mouth enticed his with warm, liquid kisses as the rest of her body opened to him as well.

He was wrapped in her sweetness, and it was nothing like his dreams. Her arms and legs and mouth and body enveloped him in warm and richly scented silk. The sudden quiet astounded him. After the passionate rush pounding in his ears, he found himself steeped in delicious silence. From somewhere far away, he heard what sounded like his voice, a clear, open sound issuing from what he could only assume was his throat, although he could not pinpoint any such sensation.

He saw himself standing in a cool light. Out of the shifting prismatic mist, he could see someone else. She was standing there, her head tilted, her lips slightly pursed with a look of complete bemusement upon her delicate face. She was neither mortal Eponine nor the transcendent Angel of Joy. She was somehow neither and both at once: a simply beautiful girl with stars in her eyes.

She held her open arms out for him.

She was only a few steps away, but yet seemed to be looking at him from across some deep divide. He shied away, unwilling to come too close to that precipice. But he could not take his eyes from her. She said nothing, but he could feel her calling him. Her voice was carried on the soft breeze floating above them.

"Julian...!"

He smiled at that. It felt like a pet name, a nickname only she knew. She grinned at him in return to hear his rough whisper.

"My Eponine...."

He took a deep breath. Thunder rolled softly in the distance. She was waiting.

He was afraid to fall.

But he reached out for her hands and took a tentative step forward. Lightning crackled across his vision, leaving a trail of glitter in its wake. His foot found nothing beneath it and he fell forward, tumbling through the shimmering cloud.

Terror left him. What had he to fear in this place?

He thought he would be lost, but that was silly. She knew where he was. She knew precisely where he was.

The wind came up around his ears in a deafening roar, spiraling higher and higher as he fell. Then he was caught up in her arms. She held him securely, bearing him up.

They clung to one another and plummeted toward a light as bright as the sun. He cradled her against him, protectively, but he knew at once that it was *she* who was keeping *him* safe.

She looked up at him with her star-bright eyes still shining.

"I love you."

His world shattered into shards of light, and all was still.

In that quiet, he found a tiny kernel of light and sound. It was candleglow, laughter, weeping, and lush leaves tracing patterns in the glow of a streetlamp.

It was silvery and heart-shaped, that kernel.

Eponine's eyes floated across his vision, above cheeks blushed like wild roses.

The world around him shifted back into focus, but still he felt light, weightless. Her arms around him, her warm and heavy legs kept him from bumping his head against the ceiling.

Everything seemed so bright. She smiled, suddenly turned terribly shy, it seemed. He wrapped wings around her that seemed made of night, not inky black, but shimmering with stars and moonlight. He released a sigh that he had not realized he had been holding. It escaped his mouth in a dim and fleeting shadow, replaced in the core of his being with a resplendent prism of light, a tiny kaleidoscope in the center of his soul.

He smiled, and laughter rippled out of him, sending rainbow arcs dancing around them both.

For the first time in the history of Creation, Vengeance knew Joy.

O BRAVE NEW WORLD ...!

THE LIGHT SLID IN, shifting and silky. Julian opened his eyes, having no idea of the time. Beside him Eponine stirred, her damp satin skin brushing against his equally naked side. His heart raced into his throat as he looked down at her, curled on her side with her back pressed close against his ribs. Her hair draped across the deep blue pillows and over the side of the bed, resplendent with a thousand shimmering highlights.

Julian propped himself onto one elbow and gazed down at Eponine. In one hand she had gently clutched a dark feather. Carefully, he drew it from her sleeping grasp and stared at it. Deep and dark as India Ink, but somehow richly blue, a breath away from black. It reverberated in his fingers, resounding with his own heartbeat. Yes, it was his.

"Good morning." Her voice was pleasantly slurred, lazy and indolent.

Julian looked down at her. "Are you ... are you ... well?"

"Yes," she murmured.

"And ... everything is ... okay?"

"Everything is *wonderful*, simply wonderful."

"Better than chocolate?" There was a hint of teasing in his tone. He idly twirled the feather.

"Believe it or not, Julian, there are some things in this world that are better than chocolate."

She stretched like a great cat, the lazy smile never leaving her lips. Her eyes glimmered with sunrise and mischief. She reached out and took the feather from his hand.

"That's *mine*," Eponine drawled. "I won this prize fair and square." She set the feather on her bedside table, just out of his reach. It glimmered there in the shadow of her replica Tiffany lamp.

She rolled over to face him and slipped her arm beneath him, sliding close against him. He shuddered at her proximity.

"Eponine. . . ." He looked away from her blissful face.

"Don't tell me you've gone shy, mister."

"There is no undoing what we've done here, is there?"

Her face darkened. "No. There isn't. Is that a problem?"

He sighed, memories crowding and clouding his mind. He felt shadows closing in.

"Julian . . . Vengeance, *I love you*."

His breath caught. "You say it so easily," he rasped, a note of disbelief in his voice.

"And why shouldn't I?" She lay there on her back looking up at him, her cheeks flushed and the curves of her breasts, belly, and hips rosy. Her ruby lips opened in a soft smile. "Oh, Julian." She ran a hand over his slender hip.

"Eponine . . . what do we do now?"

"Mmmm, what would you like to do?"

"I didn't mean *that!*" But he could feel his body aching for her touch, for her warmth, for *her*. "We shouldn't have begun this."

"But we did. And we must finish it."

He let himself sink back into her featherbed, removed her arm from beneath him, and unthinkingly cradled it to his chest. He kissed her hand, each knuckle and each finger down to her shell-pink nails.

Eponine smiled. "Tell me you love me."

"'Nine, I . . . I don't know if I can."

"Certainly. You don't need to tell me. I already know." She stretched out her index finger and playfully tapped him on the nose.

He suddenly hugged her fiercely, crushing her to his chest. The breath surged out of her in a high-pitched gasp. He ran his hands all over her body, over every curve, entangling his long fingers in her never-ending mass of hair.

"Eponine . . . Joy. . . . *Joy*." He wept. Glimmering tears from the bottom of his lonely soul spilled over his cheeks and ran down her shoulder. He loosened his terrible grip on her, and she tilted her face upward to catch and kiss away every tear. He brought his lips to hers, crushing them together against their teeth. He tasted his own tears on her tongue. He thought of the rain, and of absolution. Angel's tears. . . .

Julian's body pressed against hers urgently, and again, he was allowed entry to her sacred space. He fleetingly thought of Eponine's now-ruined purity. What becomes of fallen angels?

"If you think virginity is all that holds my soul aloft, then I am sorry for you. For what is true purity than to be joined body and soul to the one whom you most love?" She gave him a breathy laugh. "And who loves you most in return."

He gave her a slightly wry smile and paused in his endeavors. "I love you most?"

"I know you do."

Julian rested his forehead against hers for a moment, then sought her mouth for a gentle kiss. "You're far too good for me, 'Nini."

"Only because you have no real idea what true goodness is, silly. Let me show you."

WHEN THEY FINALLY ROUSED themselves, it was late afternoon. Deciding they were too giddy to cook, they shared a luxurious shower and headed out to Veselka's in a gilded mood.

Julian felt the eyes of everyone upon him. He held fast to Eponine's hand, knowing that their actions were written as plain as could be upon their glowing faces. Eponine skipped and laughed and tossed her long braid, grinning at her reflection in every single shop window they passed. Julian briskly walked beside her with pride etched in his eyes. Occasionally, he pulled her close to give her a kiss, unabashed on the sidewalk in full view of the early rush-hour traffic on Second Avenue.

They sat on the same side of the table toward the back of Veselka's, earning bemused and slightly envious stares from the waitstaff. The day sank into a honey-rich August afternoon.

Julian admired the clear golden light as it touched the leaves of the hanging plants in the windows and cast deep gray shadows across the sidewalk in front of rollerblading kids and people out walking dogs.

"Tell me," he whispered. "The world, it always looks like this to you . . . joyous and golden like this?"

Eponine smiled up at him, and the light gained a thousand more colors, shivering in rainbows that radiated from her dancing eyes.

"It's *never* looked *this good.*"

And she kissed him.

HARVEST MOON

EPONINE WAS RUNNING LATE. She was supposed to meet Phina down in the Metropolitan Museum of Art's Costume Institute at half past four. It was nearing a quarter to five when she rushed through the pallid gray door and down the very institutional linoleum hall to the library.

"I'm sorry," she said breathlessly. "I completely lost track of time."

"Don't worry about it. You aren't that late, though I admit I was worried since it isn't like you to be.... Eponine ... are those ... are those ... *hickeys*?" Phina's dark eyes widened in utter surprise. A line of small bruises encircled Eponine's neck like a strand of garnets: livid reddish-purple. Phina whistled. "I always figured Julian to be a biter. And you're not the least bit ashamed, are you?"

Eponine looked taken aback, nearly insulted. "Ashamed? Why should I be?"

"Well, some girls who aren't you might be, I guess," Phina said, suppressing her laughter. "I, however, am not one of them. I wear my battle scars proudly. Mmm, boy, he did a number on you!"

Phina took Eponine's chin in her hand and tilted her head to one side, then the other, examining the dark splotches and nodding her approval. Eponine blushed a little at her friend's study.

"Umm, shouldn't we be going?"

Phina giggled. "Sure thing. Let me go sign myself out. What do you feel like for dinner?"

THEY ENDED UP AT the Comfort Diner, which was next to the subway entrance at Eighty-Sixth and Lexington. It was a bit out of the way but well worth the walk: They truthfully boasted they made the best hamburgers in Manhattan.

"So he's finally given in, has he?" Phina dipped her thick french fires into a ramekin of ranch dressing with gusto.

"'Given in'?"

"To you. He's had you on his mind for quite some time now."

Eponine traced shapes in the ketchup on her plate with her own fries. She smiled dreamily. "Has he?"

"Like you didn't know, like you couldn't see it in his eyes?"

"I suppose I wasn't willing to fully believe what I saw. I suppose I didn't want to be . . . disappointed."

Phina sucked up the rest of her iced tea with a loud gurgle and signaled the waitress for a refill. "Well, it's been pretty obvious what your feelings for Julian are, and have been, since I met the two of you."

"Oh, really?"

"Yup. In fact I first met Julian when he was on his way to go put the fear of God, so to speak, in a certain boy on the Upper East Side, I believe."

The waitress brought Phina's tea and a refill for Eponine as well. They paused in speaking until she was out of earshot.

"That would be Jeremy," Eponine muttered, making artwork out of her ketchup now. "He's been the one snag in our relationship, Julian's and mine. It was wrong of me to get infatuated with Jeremy, but it happens. Everything was so new, and he is a very attractive and talented soul. But now he won't leave me alone. Julian seems to think there is something . . . mystic between Jeremy and me, but there isn't. Jeremy seems to think Julian is hurting me somehow, which of course he isn't, and he insists on calling and coming by to check up on my welfare."

Phina's eyes flicked over Eponine's marked-up neck. "Julian *isn't* hurting you, is he? Everything's consensual, right?"

"*Of course* it is," she nearly growled the words out through firmly clenched jaws. "I thought perhaps *you*, of all people here, would understand the two of us."

"Hey, hey, be calm now. I *do* understand, but I just want to make sure. It never hurts to make sure, does it? I won't ask you again, I promise. But you have to admit, to the casual observer, it does look kind of bad."

Eponine sat back and sighed. "I suppose you're right, but I mean, he can't help it. He's the ange . . . uhh, he is who he is. And I love him, Phina."

She smiled. "I know," she said softly, touching Eponine's hand. "I can tell. And I could tell when things were rough for you, too. Damn, I think the whole city could tell. And he loves you. He's scared to death of it, but he loves you. And I think he has for a long time, long before you two ever came to New York."

Eponine grinned in return. "You think so? We never ... talked much back home. Different lives, you know? Different worlds, almost. But I'm glad to be here with him now. I'm grateful for the time he and I have."

"I'm glad you two are here, as well. I feel very blessed to have gotten to know you." She checked her watch. "Aww, man, we got to go. They are starting as soon as the sun goes down. You ready?"

Eponine nodded and gulped down the remainder of her iced tea, flinching at the accumulated undissolved sugar at the bottom.

"Dregs?" Phina laughed and downed her own unsweetened tea. She dropped the money on their table and pulled Eponine out of the diner before she could protest having her dinner bought for her.

IT WAS A GORGEOUS late summer afternoon bordering on evening when Eponine and Phina arrived. In a secluded grove on the west side of the park near the Reservoir, a group of women had gathered. Phina introduced Eponine to her "little sister," Iris, and explained that she was attending the gathering for moral support.

"You see, Iris is the president of the Pagans at NYU club. This is their first open circle event, and she wanted to make sure we had a big enough group."

Eponine looked at the girl and smiled. "I am honored to be involved." She noticed the girl's large and brilliantly blue eyes. "I know you. I've seen you before ... yes, I remember! The tree lighting at Rockefeller Square, you had the sign that said 'Light the Darkness.'"

Iris blushed. "Yeah, that was me. I can't believe you remembered!"

"It would be hard to forget eyes like yours. Or that smile. Pleased to meet you."

"It had better be good, sis. She left her hot boyfriend at home to come to this."

"Phina!"

"What? Tell me I'm wrong! Tell me Julian is not a *total* babe!"

"Well." Iris stepped in. "This is the one of the few gender-specific ritual gatherings we are going to have. He can come to the next one. I'll be leading that, and I am not as particular as Raven is. But you know, it's the Harvest Moon and it's a give-thanks-to-the-Goddess thing, so yeah, it's all femme."

"To which goddess are you giving thanks?" Eponine asked her.

"The Great Mother Goddess, in general, but we all have our own visions of her inside of us. So for me, it's Aunt Brigid and Aunt Sehkmet."

Eponine smiled at the familial references; it warmed her soul. She liked Iris immensely. "Sehkmet? I think you and Julian will get along nicely."

"Your boyfriend follows Sehkmet?"

"In a manner of speaking, I suppose he does, but it's rather complicated. What about you, Phina? Which aspect of the Goddess fills your heart?"

"Bast," she replied unhesitatingly. "Bast is my mother, Inari my lover, and Elegba my traveling companion. But the last two are gents, and therefore were politely asked not to attend tonight's gathering. I'll make it up to them both later, but for tonight, it's a bonding evening for me and Mama Bast." She winked and made a motion like a cat licking her paws and cleaning her face. "*Meow...*"

The three of them laughed, and Eponine felt a twinge of melancholy, knowing that soon she'd be leaving them all behind. Iris led them all toward the circle center where a huge flashlight was beaming up out of an iron cauldron.

The women were assembling themselves into a ring. The sun had dipped below the trees, casting a purple shadow through the glade. The women, Eponine saw, were topless, and the flashlight beam threw strange shadows across a range of sizes and shapes of breasts.

Phina noticed her surprise and plucked the thought from her mind as easily as picking a wildflower from the grass at their feet. "You see, there is a law in New York City that anywhere a man can go topless, a woman can."

Eponine recalled seeing the bronzed and sweating chests of a handful of teenaged rollerbladers on the walk to the Reservoir. She smiled wryly and unbuttoned her white Indian cotton shirt. She folded it and placed it and her pale pink bra beside a nearby oak. Phina took off her own red scoop-necked blouse and tossed it beside Eponine's clothes. Her black lace bra was soon to follow. With their upper bodies shamelessly bared, they joined the circle.

Within the ring, a woman began a drumbeat while another

lit a smudge-stick of pungent dried sage. They chanted, sang, and danced until the moon, swollen and golden, crested the top of the trees. The pounding drumbeat ceased and reverberated in the stillness. Eponine held her breath; it felt like an ancient wood far from the center of one of the biggest cities on the planet. The noises of civilization were faint and far away.

A heavy honey-oat cake was passed along the circle as well as crisp hard cider, followed by a small stoneware bowl filled with cool water. The drums erupted once more, but this time the beat was more frenzied. They began to dance—not the ordered movements of before but more sinuous and carefree. Someone put out the flashlight and let the warm glow of the moon bathe the clearing. They sang nonsensical things made of long vowels and hoots and trills and clicks, tossing their hair about them in shimmering waves. Finally, they collapsed, giggling and panting, into the dewy grass. Slowly, they began to collect their things, chattering and deciding where to go for coffee.

"Did you guys have a good time?"

"Oh, yes, thank you," Eponine exclaimed. Her cheeks were flushed, and she felt giddy. She'd beheld some interesting visions in that circle, undulating her body with the warm-cool September breezes caressing parts of her not used to being free to the open air. "I have been to several pagan gatherings, but no two of them have been even remotely the same."

"That's what's cool about being pagan," Iris told her. "You guys want to share a cab back to the East Village? Maybe we can hit Veselka's for some coffee and treats."

Eponine grinned and nodded vigorously. She did indeed like Phina's "little sister."

EPONINE CAME IN VERY late. She was surprised to find Julian asleep. He was on his side with a book fallen out of his hands, and the lights still on in her bedroom.

She nuzzled up behind him, kissing his neck. He inhaled and smiled.

"Mmm, you smell good. Like sage and," he tilted his head up, brushing his lips against hers, "coffee."

She kissed him suddenly, amused to hear his breath catch and shudder.

"It looks like you had fun," he told her with a smile.

"It does?"

"'Nine, you're *glowing*."

"So, you aren't upset that I left you behind?"

"Not at all. Not when you come home like *this*."

Eponine laughed. It was full and throaty and joyous. "This is a beautiful world, and I am so glad to be here in it with you."

His smile was almost shy. "Yeah, I'm glad to be here with you, too."

"Come look." She pulled him out of bed and into the front room. The moon had shrunk slightly and dimmed back toward silver, but it was still like a great shining coin in the night sky. She opened the window and leaned out.

Julian came up beside her, laying his hand on her waist. "It's lovely."

"Will you miss it?"

"Honestly? Yeah, a little. I didn't think I would." He placed a soft kiss between her shoulder blades. "I saw you tonight. I dozed off and dreamed of you dancing with nothing but the moon on your skin and your hair loose. Phina was there; she winked at me."

Eponine laughed. "I like it here. But the time goes by so quickly."

"Don't think about it now." His face darkened, and he held her tightly. "I don't want to think about it right now, either."

"Agreed." She slipped easily into a comfortable embrace with him, and together they gazed up into the sky.

BALANCE

EPONINE CRIED OUT AND Julian was instantly awake. His fingers tingled, and a dusky, reddish light played about his hands.

"What's wrong!"

She didn't answer, only sighed and shifted, still, for the most part, asleep.

Julian looked at the clock; it was just about seven in the morning.

"'Nine?" He shook her shoulder gently, and she regarded him with a hazy gaze. She seemed all right, although Julian's heart was still in his throat. He took a deep breath and forced himself to be calm, to move slowly, and to dispel the deadly sparkle that trailed in the wake of his fingertips.

Eponine blinked slowly and seemed to be gathering her thoughts. When she finally spoke, it was with great effort. "The summer ... is *over*."

In the gathering daylight, Julian could see the calendar hanging on the wall near the window. Yes, there near the bottom of September he could see the bold notation: *Equinox, First Day of Autumn*.

"I'm still so tired, Julian," she murmured. "Can I sleep a little while longer?"

"Sure, sleep as long as you'd like." He gave her a flippant smile as he brushed the back of his hand across her cheek. But his eyes betrayed the shadow of worry, as much as he tried to hide it behind a casual sounding: "Are you sure you're okay?"

Eponine's soft, even breathing was all the answer he got.

"Great, for once *you're* still asleep and I'm wide awake this early in the morning." He shifted restlessly, trying to get comfortable enough to doze back off himself, but it was no use. He tried not to disturb Eponine with his tossing and turning, but he soon realized that she was dead to the world. Finally, Julian got up and went into the kitchen. He shut the bedroom door behind him and switched on both the coffeemaker and the TV.

The *Good Morning, America* set was all done up for fall with scarecrows and red, gold, and russet leaves. Julian sipped his coffee and tried to focus on the screen. They were making some sweet snack food called "haystacks" that looked highly edible, but he found he couldn't sit still. He was a bundle of energy, and pacing the small common area was only making it worse. He found it rather strange that he was wired so early in the morning and before he'd even finished his first cup of coffee.

Slowly, the thoughts floated upward out of the turbulent rapids of his mind. The balance had shifted. Today was the exact opposite end of the year from the first day of spring. It was the autumnal equinox. The darkness was growing; the shadows were lengthening; soon it would be winter.

No wonder she's tired; her season has ended. She lives and breathes with the turning of the year, and now, we have come into the winter half, and for some reason, I am bouncing off the walls. ...

"Oh ... *duh*." He laughed into his coffee. "Yeah, hey, Angel of Vengeance, Creature of Dark and Shadows, yeah, it's your turn to shine, er, well, *not* shine, whatever the opposite of 'shine' would be . . . *and* you're talking to yourself . . . not to mention *answering* yourself, oh yeah, Julian, you *have got to* get outside, take a walk or kill something . . . or something. . . ."

He paced uneasily, unwilling to leave Eponine alone. His memory of the first day of spring was vivid, but nothing so dramatic seemed to be heralding the end of the light half of the year. She was just sleeping.

Julian opened the bedroom door cautiously, not sure what he expected to see. But Eponine was still asleep, deeply but naturally asleep.

"I hope you aren't going to sleep until it's time for us to. . . ." He couldn't bring himself to say "leave." He couldn't even bring himself to think about it. He sat carefully on the edge of the bed and touched her arm. She was warmly curled up on her side, her magnificent hair braided and lying in a loose coil at her back. She looked every inch the angel she was.

Julian was deeply divided between his desire to remain faithfully at her side and the insistent and all-consuming restlessness that surged through his blood. He remembered that reckless sensation, the undeniable urge to roam that usually accompanied an undeniable urge to shout, to strike out, to feel slick, warm blood on his hands. But this feeling was not tainted with anger, or frustration, or pain. This was not the endless soul-tortured wandering of Christmas, nor the night he had walked until the sun rose only to find he'd been gone for an entire week. No, this was wanderlust, pure and simple. He felt awake and alive and wanted to feel the sun upon his skin and the wind, which he knew would hold a subtle kiss of the frigid winter to come, through his hair.

He quickly and quietly changed his clothes; that giddy, schoolboyish air was beginning to creep back into his being.

I won't be gone too long, he assured himself. *I'll be back before she wakes up.*

He nearly skipped to the door, where a last pang of guilt overcame him. He ducked back into the kitchen, made sure the coffee was set to stay hot, and cut up a few pieces of fruit. He made what he thought was a rather pretty arrangement on a plate, covered it all with plastic wrap, and placed it into the refrigerator. Then he took a page of Eponine's rose-scented notepaper and left her a message.

"Gone for a walk, sweetheart. I won't go too far or be gone for too long. You know how to call me if you need me. I'll bring you a surprise. ~J."

He momentarily scowled at the familiarity. "I can't believe I just wrote that."

But instead of crumpling up the paper and starting over, he took it into the bedroom and set it beside the little brass clock on the table next to Eponine's side of the bed.

OUTSIDE, IT WAS A clear, warm day with just a hint of crispness in the air. Julian headed for Veselka's with challah French toast and coffee out on the patio on his mind. He was too restless to enjoy the food much and left a hefty tip alongside his half-eaten breakfast. He found himself a few blocks north, peering into the garden sanctuary of Saint Mark's on the Bowery. The moment he stepped foot within the gates, he felt the subtle hum in the air that hovered around consecrated land. A few students lounged in the grass reading or practicing morning yoga. The doors stood open, and a few elderly women came and went across the shadowy threshold of the white-columned entrance.

"Well, well, well. How are you then, old man?"

Julian gave the small woman who sat behind a battered card table a suspicious side-long glance. She had all sorts of religious paraphernalia out for sale including candles, icons, medallions, and rosaries; nearly all of it looked homemade.

"Don't put on airs with me. I know you; it's as plain as the smirk on your face!" She was a wizened thing, with skin very tan and freckled, but with surprisingly white teeth, only two of which were chipped.

"Are you talking to me?" He strolled over and looked at her wares. "Aren't these a bit *Catholic*?"

"Bah, shows what you know." She pulled out a battered cigar box. "*These*, old boy, are the Catholic ones. Those on the table are *Anglican* rosaries."

"I didn't think Anglicans said the rosary."

"Shows what you know," she muttered again. "But I actually sell most of these kind as jewelry for college girls."

Julian nodded; the thing was beautifully beaded and about bracelet size.

"And they, of course, have a perfectly Protestant explanation for all the bits," she winked. "Thirty-three beads it comes out to, the supposed age of Jesus when he was crucified to save our sinful souls."

He snickered and realized that she was laughing conspiringly along with him.

"But we know better, don't we, old man?"

"*Who are you?*"

"They're not important, names."

"Do you know a girl named Phina?"

"Who doesn't?"

"I figured you'd say that." He picked up a cobalt-blue rosary. "How much?"

"For you, I will settle for a kiss."

"*A kiss?* You've *got* to be kidding."

"I am," she nearly cackled. "But I had you going there, didn't I?"

"How much?"

"Ah," she chuckled. "Say a prayer on it for me."

"That's all?"

"Well, while you're at it, you might want to say a prayer for yourself, too. And for her."

"You think we need it?"

"Well, the year has slid into balance again. Soon it will tilt, then balance again."

He waited. She did not speak further. "So, the prayer? You think we need it?"

"We all need prayers, old man, even you. Especially now. The turning of the seasons seems to weigh heavily on your soul— even though it has gone on every year before you came here, and will go on every year after you go."

"That's not what I am worried about."

"I know."

Julian raised an eyebrow. "Congrats," he scowled, "you got me to admit I was worried about something."

The woman laughed. "You worry yourself sick on a regular basis."

He dropped the rosary back onto the scratched-up table. "*Gypsies*, think you fucking know *everything*. . . ."

"Hush." Her voice was suddenly as sweet and fluid as melted butter. She put the rosary into his palm and gently closed his fingers around it. "Take it. Take it and go inside and say a prayer. And don't forget what Phina told you."

He knew exactly what she meant. *May joy be yours all the days of your life.* "But what if I can count all the days left in my life?"

"Then use them the best way you can. Not all of us have the luxury of knowing when we'll leave this Earth and what awaits us afterwards."

Julian laughed hollowly, "Trust me, it's not a luxury."

"It would be for me. Do you realize how much money I could make with that racket?"

He laughed, truly now, and his soul felt lighter. "All right." He tossed the rosary up and caught it, twirling it on his finger. "A prayer for you, and for her, and two for me, because I need it."

"You have everything you need, old man. Can't you see that?"

He glanced back at her over his shoulder, fingering the glimmering beads. He caught himself between making a crass comment and saying something pithy and eloquent. In the end, he could only think of Eponine's smiling face. She was right, that old gypsy woman, but he wasn't about to admit to her as much. Instead he just waved the rosary toward her with a sincere nod of his head.

"Thank you." He stepped into the blessed shadows of Saint Mark's.

INSOMNIAC

IT WAS PAST THREE o'clock in the morning when Eponine awoke. She heard muted keyboard clacking just above the barely audible sound on the TV. She slinked sleepily into the living room.

"What are you doing up, Julian?" she asked through a deep yawn.

He turned with a start from the computer. "Did I wake you? I was trying to be quiet."

Eponine slid down into her favorite couch corner and shook her head. "I just went to cuddle up to you, but there were no cuddles to be had."

"I couldn't sleep, so I started playing around online. Found this really excellent short story website. I was just posting to the forum on it."

"How come you couldn't sleep? Are you feeling all right?"

"Yeah, I'm okay." He finished his statement and clicked *Submit*. "I just, I don't know, I have been thinking too much I guess."

"'Thinking too much'? I'm afraid I don't understand."

He sighed and joined her on the couch. "'Nine, it's October."

"Very astute, my love."

Julian growled and grit his teeth a moment. "Yes, yes, you're very funny. But I mean, the year has gone by so fast, so much faster than I would ever have thought possible."

"Regrets?"

"No. Well, only, I guess, only that we haven't ... more time."

"More time? What would we do with more time?"

"I don't know about you, but I would love to travel. See the Golden Gate Bridge, the Grand Canyon, redwood trees, Disney World, the French Quarter ... and that's just here in the States. I haven't even begun to dream of what there is to be seen overseas!"

Eponine laughed, "So if you were able to stay here, you'd go places?"

"Well, yeah. You've been here before, but this whole Earthly life thing is still so new to me."

"I guess in my line of work I come into more contact with humans than you do. Well, maybe not *more* contact ... but, you know what I mean. ..."

Julian gave her a humorless chuckle. "Yeah, humans *like* to see you. They pray to see you. There isn't anyone who likes to see me. Not humans, not other angels, not even. ..."

"Don't talk like that! Don't you dare talk like that!" She drew back, obviously affronted. "*I* like to see you. Doesn't that count for anything?"

"You like to see everyone. It's your nature, and you can't help it,"

Her jaw dropped; he could see that he'd cut her. It took her a moment to regain her composure and answer. "I can't believe you. I just can't! After all we've been through together! You sound like you did the first week we arrived! And here I was thinking how much you'd grown and changed and learned!"

Julian dug his fingertips into his temples. If there was something Julian hated more than anything else, it was seeing Eponine hurt, especially when it was he who had been the cause. "I don't mean it like that, 'Nine, I really don't. I just ... I guess I just have it in my mind that I don't deserve to be happy, that I don't belong anywhere ... and when I start to feel like I do ... then I begin to second-guess myself, my motives, and those of the people around me."

"You're second-guessing *me*?"

"Not because I doubt you, 'Nine, but . . . damn it, I make my own hell, and I know it. . . . So why can't I stop?"

"I don't know." Her voice dropped to a whisper, and she tilted her head over to one side in that unconscious gesture of hers that meant she was listening intently or thinking over something serious.

"That's why I couldn't sleep tonight. I kept thinking how close to the end of this I am, and realizing how . . . *happy* . . . I've been here, but then of course I've been enjoying myself, I mean I've been here with you and you are *Joy* after all. . . ."

"But there's more to it than that, isn't there?"

He caught the barest hint of pleading in her voice and gazed into her face. Her cheeks were sleepy-pale, and her eyes were red.

Is there? I wish I could tell you that there was, that you've changed me. But there is still so much I hide from you, so as not to risk hurting your beautiful soul. And I've realized that all I want to be is who I am when I am with you. And at the end of next month, that becomes nothing but a fond and tortured memory. I'll wake up from your spell and things will be as they always have been . . . except now I'll have something both to remember and to regret.

". . . Julian, are you even listening to me?"

"What?" He was shocked to find her in the kitchen with the whistling tea kettle in her hand.

She sighed, but with that ever-present smile on her lips. Yes, she was exasperated, but not angry. She handed him a cobalt-blue glass mug of steaming herbal tea.

"I was asking you if you wanted honey in your tea, but then realized it was silly of me to ask. *Of course* you'd want honey!"

He took the mug and sipped gently. Chamomile, valerian, peppermint, and just the right amount of honey. "It's perfect."

"I thought it might help you relax, get your mind off things so you can sleep."

Great. If my going to sleep hinges on getting my mind off this, then I won't be sleeping until the end of time. "Thanks, 'Nine, you always know the right things to do."

She grinned and sipped her own tea. "Now, will you come to bed?"

"In a little while. I want to finish this set of stories, see if the guy with the sunglasses actually ends up with the ice cream shop girl."

"Julian...."

He glanced up at her. She seemed somehow very frail standing in the bedroom doorway in her favorite cloud pajamas, which were starting to look faded and worn. She was absently wrapping her long braid around her wrist, uncoiling it, and then starting again.

I'm worried about you, Julian. If you truly believe that your time is so short, why are you wasting it fretting and worrying over things you are convinced you cannot change? "Come to bed. Everything will look better in the morning."

"In a little bit, really. The tea is making me feel pretty loopy. Won't be long 'til my head falls over onto the keyboard."

"Come in to bed before that, please? Elsewise you'll be a mother bear in the morning, and then no one will want to see you, not even me!" She wrinkled her nose at him and put out her tongue.

"No longer than an hour, how about that?"

"Deal." She put a little more hot water into her teacup and made for the bedroom. "You'll wake me when you come in to bed?"

"I don't think I'll be able not to wake you. You sleep as lightly as a cat."

"Okay, then, I'll see you soon."

"Yeah, good night for now." He turned back to the computer and punched up the timeline to see where he'd left off reading. He sensed she was still there, though, hovering, looking at him with her eyes gone dark and liquid with worry.

I can't help you if you won't let me in, he thought he heard her say. *There are some things, Joy, that maybe I have to do on my own.*

Don't shut me out just to cater to your ego, or some misplaced need to exact revenge upon yourself.

"I have to do this myself! I can't let you do this for me. I have to face up and...." He spun around in the chair, nearly knocking it over.

The living room was empty, and the bedroom door was closed.

Julian finished his tea, but it didn't quiet the rage of thoughts in his mind. So he sat and read about someone else's problems until the bleak morning sun turned the room gray. It was at least the third night that week he'd seen the sun set and rise again, and he knew it wouldn't be the last.

"I want to be healed. I want to feel whole. And just when it seems like that *might* even be possible, all I can hear is the ticking of the clock telling me my time is all but up."

Just then Eponine's alarm clock rang from the other room, and Julian nearly leapt out of his skin.

"Damn dramatic timing!"

He heard her stir and call his name. He opened the door softly and put on his best smile.

"You did fall asleep on the keyboard, didn't you?"

"Yeah, pretty much. Sorry."

"Was it a good story at least?"

"Yeah, actually, you should read them."

"Next time I can't sleep, I will." She winked. "You coming to bed then?"

"Nah, I'm awake now. I was thinking about some breakfast."

"Dojo's?"

"If my lady wishes, then Dojo's it is."

"You're in a better mood."

It's easier to hide it in the daytime. "You're right, things do look better in the morning."

"I'm glad. Perhaps I can coax you into a hot bath and a nap later on today. If you're going to be up all night again tonight."

"You didn't believe me for a second just now, did you?"

"Nope. But I trust you to know what needs to be done." She rose, stretched, and drew herself right into his arms. "Have a little faith in yourself." She kissed him softly. "And maybe you can get some sleep, hmmm?"

"Yeah, maybe."

"Now let's get changed. I'm starving!"

"As you wish." He bowed with exaggerated grandeur, and Eponine bubbled over with laughter.

DOWN ON SAINT MARK'S Place, the sun had lifted the evening's gray mist, and things looked brilliant in the clear light of morning. The day carried the first chills of autumn.

How does the saying go, "where there's life there's hope"? He caught Eponine smiling up at him. She was so dazzling, so animated, and so very much alive.

"Things are going to be okay, Julian, you'll see." She squeezed his hand.

He pulled her close and wrapped his arm around her shoulders. "I hope so."

It seemed a reasonable hope to cling to.

Julian allowed himself to smile, and was surprised to find passersby smiling back at him.

THIS IS HALLOWEEN!

JULIAN HAD BEEN DREAMING of ravens. Or crows. Or rooks. Or whatever they were, those great black birds of which his sister-angel, Death, was so fond. The ones that pecked out the eyes of the dead and learned the secrets of men's souls. The ones that guided souls through the labyrinth between the world of the living to the world of the dead, and sometimes back again. The ones that sat up on rafters and doorways and busts of Pallas and cried, "Nevermore!"

Beyond that, Julian learned these birds were tricksy creatures that never gave him a straightforward answer about anything.

But at least he was sleeping.

IN KEEPING WITH HIS nocturnal theme, Julian dressed as the main character from *The Crow* for Halloween. He'd liked the graphic novel and movie immensely. Eric Draven, brutally murdered along with his fiancee, returns from the dead as a dark and avenging angel. The movie was made all the more poignant by the death of Brandon Lee, the lead actor, at the end of filming. He died filming the scene of his character's death. It was quite up Julian's alley, even if Eponine did tell him that the make-up was all but silly.

When he strolled out in heavily gothic black leather and vinyl with his face painted white and black and his hair tangled around his shoulders, Eponine dropped her pomegranate.

"My lady Persephone," he rasped, "you've dropped your prize."

Eponine shivered into her blue velvet mantle, a near match for the one in the painting by Dante Gabriel Rossetti. She had been quite thrilled to find that she somewhat resembled his celebratedly plain model, Jane Burden-Morris.

Julian watched her reaction from beneath his brows. He peered at her, his head pitched forward and tilted to one side not unlike a bird.

"I can't tell if you are afraid, or not, my lady."

She laughed nervously. "It's strange. You are yourself, yet not at all. I think I have gotten so used to Julian, I had forgotten what Vengeance was like."

"Oh." He straightened. "Uhh, is that . . . bad?" He ducked into the bathroom and glanced in the mirror. In the darkness, his pallid face and heavily darkened features gave him both a start of surprise and a jolt of recognition. His coat hung from one shoulder, giving his reflection the appearance of black folded wings.

Except my wings aren't black anymore. Well, not just black anymore. He squinted his eyes and he could see himself, not painted pale, but smiling in that charming, roguish manner that made Eponine squeal with what looked like a cape of stars in the night sky draped behind him.

I hardly recognize you, Vengeance, m'lad. Once upon a time, you really did look like Eric Draven come back from the dead. Makes me wonder if James O'Barr didn't have a run-in with me once upon a time. . . .

"Are you ready, or still fixing your make-up?"

He caught sight of Eponine's smile over his shoulder and went back to brooding. He slunk from the bathroom, circling her as he headed for the front door, never taking his eyes from hers. He watched her rapture grow as she fixated on him. He had seen it before, when he was like the adder about to strike, dark and fascinating, entrancing his victims before taking what he wanted from them, often stealing his revenge from their very souls. But the vengeance was never for him, never brought on by his own desire for balance wrought with pain and blood. Instead he answered to a greater force of karma, or as some saw it, the iron will of God, Old Testament style.

He held her there with only his eyes and the barest hint of a cruel smile, held her firmer than if he'd used the considerable strength of his hands. He remembered the thrill of power that shivered through him when the moment was real and ripe, when he lapped up bloodlust like cream.

All Hallows Eve, when the walls between worlds are thin, indeed. But I never thought I'd be going out dressed up as an incarnation of myself. He laughed softly in that low manner that he had, which sounded so close to growling. *And she dresses as a part of herself, the springtime daughter, caught and hidden away by the darkness in the underworld. Rather appropriate.*

"Perhaps I should have dressed like Hades instead?"

"So you can ravage me?"

Julian dropped character with a snort of laughter.

"I'll tell you a secret . . . you don't need to be in costume to do that. Although it might be fun." Eponine winked and swept the hood of her cloak up over her head.

Julian nearly choked on his laughter. "Now, who's the bad angel?"

She gave him a long, languorous look. "I never said it wasn't me. I'm Joy, not Chastity. Now come on, mister, or we'll never make it to the parade *and* the Witches' Ball tonight."

THE CROWD AT AVENUE of the Americas was unruly. People had climbed onto scaffolding, fire escapes, and rooftops. Several even balanced precariously on the blue police barricades. Beyond the sea of heads, wigs, hats, and headdresses, the parade was passing.

Huge papier-maché marionettes of brightly clad skeletons danced past between slick black Rolls-Royces driven by devils and satyrs. An old-world style band swirled by in tattered capes playing flutes and pipes and drums under a black banner that hailed them as "Danse Macabre." It was a strange and beautiful sight. Julian smiled at the celebration of the darker side of humanity, brought out on this night before the lights of Sixth Avenue where the shadows lay strongest.

The crowd was soaking up this darkness as well. Danger prickled along the back of Julian's neck as he watched the police try in vain to control the masses. A bottle shattered at their feet, and Julian was quick to swing Eponine up into his arms before the wash of awful-smelling alcohol could wet her pretty silk shoes.

"I think we should get out of here, 'Nine."

"But we haven't even seen hardly any of the parade," she said. Her arms were wrapped around his shoulders, and she leaned her head against his.

"'Nine, this gives me a bad feeling. There is a riot brewing any moment; I can almost taste it." It was true, that metallic tang of violence was coating the back of his throat, creeping along his tongue into his mouth. He was certain Eponine would be able to smell it on his breath. "Come on, let's go to the Witches' Ball. I am sure Phina is already there."

She sighed, and he turned back along West Eighth Street toward the park, hoping to find a cab before they reached Broadway. The congregation parted for them, the dark angel with his maiden fair lofted easily into his strong embrace.

Julian snagged a taxi that had just been vacated, before the former occupants could get back in. The police had declared critical mass and were turning would-be spectators away in droves. He watched with grim satisfaction when the three girls ran after the cab as it pulled away from the curb and headed for Broadway.

THE WITCHES' BALL WAS held in a Victorian-era building on Fifty-Second Street. It was difficult to pinpoint what the building's original purpose had been. It looked in part like a small theater from the front, but inside, it was a maze of small and large rooms intersected by corridors and stairways.

"This place looks like it was designed by Escher," Eponine murmured in amazement.

"Great, how are we supposed to find Phina in *here*?"

"Hello, darlings!" Her familiar voice rang out from a carved wooden balcony above their heads.

"I should have known," Julian growled good-naturedly.

"How do we get up there?" Eponine shouted up.

"It's complicated. Let me come down and get you!"

"Leave it to gypsies to assume no one else has any sense of direction." He squirmed when Eponine pinched him. But it took Phina long enough to get down to the lobby that he was secretly glad she'd be leading them through that rabbit-warren of a building.

She emerged into the mosaic-tiled foyer in a flurry of kimono sleeves and with a friend in tow. He caught Eponine's attention immediately with his cream-pale skin and vividly dark eyes. There was something in his quiet discomfort that reminded her of Julian.

"Oooh, a *samurai*," she said to him by way of greeting. "Very nice costume!"

"*Ronin*, more like it," he said in return. He gave her a quirk of his eyebrows, making the intricate headband he wore shiver slightly. "Persephone? Not bad, yourself."

"*Prosperine*," Phina corrected. "Right out of the Rossetti painting! Fantastic!"

"And you." Julian looked her up and down with a wry grin. "You look like some sort of sword-wielding geisha."

Her companion laughed. "Good guess. You read *Blade of the Immortal*? You look like you have good taste in graphic novels, judging by your costume."

"Before we get too ahead of ourselves," Phina interrupted, "Patrick, this is Julian and Eponine. Julian, Eponine, this is the love of my life, Patrick Walker."

"You never told me you had a boyfriend!" Eponine sounded hurt that she was one of the last to know, but she glossed over her feelings with a heavy veil of curiosity.

Phina took Patrick's hand and gave them a secret smile. "It's very new. And we hardly get to see each other much since *somebody* moved back home."

"Hey, it's not my fault I am too brilliant for NYU and graduated early."

"And before you ask, again, *no*, I am *not* dropping out of school to go make costumes at the Grand Ole Opry," she told him, laughing.

"Is there anyone else here we'd know?" Eponine still wasn't on solid ground with Phina and her love-mate.

"Oh, yeah, Iris is upstairs and so is just about everyone from the full moon circle back in September. Come on, the DJ's pretty good."

She led them back through a narrow, domed hall and up a very industrial set of switchback stairs, through what looked like someone's living room full of tables of merchandise, along a kitchen corridor, up another staircase, and finally into a large room that throbbed with music and flickered with light.

Jack-o-lanterns with real candles threw gruesome shadows in the corners while all manner of mythical and historical figures swam in a haze of clove-cigarette smoke. They found Iris immediately. She was decked out in a battered brocade dress embellished with seashells, fragments of silver, and strips of paper inscribed with Tennyson's poetry in a flowing hand. Her completely blue eyes shimmered beneath silvery violet make-up, and her smile was infectious.

"Yay, you made it!" She hugged Eponine. "Ooooh, and you brought Eric Draven. *Rowr*, he is *much* cuter than Brandon Lee."

"Did I, or did I not tell you that Eponine's boyfriend was a complete hottie?"

Julian was glad for the white paint on his face. He hated blushing. "I bet you're Iris."

"Well met." She shook his hand, and he was surprised to find that her fingers could be so cold in such a stiflingly warm room.

"Don't I know you?" The whole group of them swung their eyes in one motion to the girl who had just spoken.

Eponine knew her at once; she recognized her dark eyes. She wore white and red Japanese temple garb paired with a silky fox's tail and a headband with black-tipped ears. "Yes, I saw you at the summer solstice at the club that used to be a church!"

"It *is* you!" Her face lit up in a dazzling smile. "My name is Naomi-Makie. It's a pleasure to see you again."

"I'm Eponine, and this is Julian. He was there as well. And this is Phina, her little sister Iris, and Patrick." She neglected to give him any further introduction. Again, no one else seemed to notice, but Julian knew too well the subtle signs of her bruised ego. It hurt her to have been excluded from Phina's good news.

"It's good to finally meet you," Julian said amiably. "Your ritual was beautiful, and I was honored to attend. But if you'll excuse me, I want a drink. 'Nine?" Before she could answer either way, he pulled her away toward the bar set up along one wall.

She stumbled along in his wake. "What's wrong with you?"

"With me? 'Nine, I have never seen you so ticked off. So what if she didn't tell you she had a boyfriend?"

"I told her about *you*." Tears were gathering in the corners of her eyes.

"I bet you haven't even seen her since they made it official."

She rubbed her nose and tried to stifle a sniffle.

Julian sighed, "Let me get you a drink. Would you like a cider? Looks like they have some on tap." He turned around, right into the last person he expected to see at a Witches' Ball. "Damn, they let just about anyone into these things, don't they?"

Eponine looked around him, surprise evident in her face. "Jeremy! What are you doing here? I didn't know you were pagan."

He gazed at Julian coolly. "I could say the same about you. I am here as an escort and that's all." His blue eyes shifted in the flickering light, looking like a swirling summer storm. He turned his phenomenal smile on Eponine. "But I must admit, I was hoping to find you here. I know how much you enjoy these sorts of things, exploring new ideas and the like, right? You look beautiful, 'Ponine. I am so glad to see you."

"I'm glad to see you, too. How have you been?"

"Eh, can't complain. Of course things at school aren't the same without you. The children really miss you. They wish you'd come back. So do I."

She laughed, a little self-consciously. "I'm afraid that's impossible, Jeremy, but I am really touched to hear it."

"Jeremy! Oh there you are...oh! It's Eponine!" Ursula, "Cosette" in Eponine's mind, had on a less-than-flattering pink leotard sewn with artificial flower petals and leaves. Her hair was teased out and covered with as much glitter as her skin. She also sported a pair of fairy wings that were too small for her.

Julian bit his lip to keep from laughing out loud. He noticed the small, feminine pentacle strung on the slender silver chain that hung around her neck. He flicked Eponine a glance he was sure she caught and understood, but she carried on as if he had done no such thing.

"This is my first Witches' Ball!" Ursula was babbling on about her recent awakening to the true power of womanhood.

Eponine smiled politely and nodded. A sudden, perplexed look crossed her face. "Oh, Julian! What happened to my cider?"

Jeremy's brows knit for a moment. "Let me get you one, 'Ponine." He cast a smug glare at Julian and turned to the bar while his date chattered on about the blessings of the Goddess.

Julian only rolled his eyes. "Excuse us, kids, but our friends our looking for us." He took Eponine by the elbow and steered her back to the group they'd left.

"That was rude," she muttered at him. "And are you going to let me decide where I am to go tonight at all?"

"Okay, I'll leave you to the wolves, sweetheart, but I thought I would save you from Cosette the Perky Pagan and your drooling lapdog, Jeremy."

"Not tonight, Julian! I don't want to fight. I want to have fun."

"Hey, I am having a great time." He winked and backed away from her, onto the dance floor.

The music was good, deep and pulsing like it had been at Limelight. It was easy to step outside of his temper, to feel the echo of the song in his body. He'd never known the simple pleasure of forgetting his troubles to the grinding beat of music before he'd come to New York. Before, he'd lost himself in the pounding pulse of his victims, the mournful cries of mercy he wrenched from the guilty to which he would forever be deaf and immovable. Of course, that had only led to more problems, which led to more escapism, which had, in turn, led to the headaches and blackouts. . . .

Something brushed against his leg, and his eyes snapped open.

"I couldn't let you dance alone." He wasn't sure if he had actually *heard* Eponine speak. But she was there, her body moving smoothly to the music, the silk and velvet of her costume caressing the curves of her hips as she swayed them. He put his hands on her waist, and the world drifted away. It was like making love to her, there, in front of everyone, the way his hands slid over her dress, stroking the velvet of her cloak, glancing against the warm silk of her underdress. In his arms she swirled and swayed, belonging to no one but him. He didn't feel possessive, though, only . . . only *certain*.

A heady sense of perfection swam through him.

Worlds could die and be reborn, and I could just be right here through all of it. And I wouldn't give a damn. I am right where I need to be, where I have always needed to be, where I have always wanted to be.

"Julian . . . Julian . . . the music has stopped. Julian. Snap out of it." He followed the thread of her voice like Theseus through the labyrinth. Eponine was flushed and smiling at him. Her hair was mussed, and her mantle was falling off one shoulder, showing a scattering of tiny, pale freckles like a constellation. It seemed jarringly intimate to be able to see her bare shoulder here in this crowded place. "The ceremony is starting."

He was still lost in euphoria and let her lead him into the spiral formation. He held onto her on one side, and Phina on the other. The chant began, soft and low, a flood of goddesses' names. As the line began to move, in and around one another like a great but slow-moving game of crack-the-whip, he heard an exuberant voice calling out the names in an overly excited sing-song fashion. From beside the voice, Jeremy's face swam in and out of his vision. But Julian's reality existed solely of Eponine's hand and her voice, gleefully chanting the names, sounding simultaneously like she was truly speaking of the divine and as if she were greeting old friends.

The chant got faster and more urgent, and the line moved quicker, the spiral squeezing tighter. Julian found himself with his left arm pinned behind him against Phina's body, Eponine pressed to his side, and Naomi-Makie crushed against his front. He could feel Phina laughing in her deep contralto through his back. Before him, Naomi-Makie was trying not to breathe down his shirt. She was blushing furiously, evident beneath her Noh-inspired makeup.

"Shinto isn't this ... *touchy*," she told him as if it were an apology.

"No worries," Julian said, feeling calmed by Eponine's presence beside him. "All in good fun, right?"

The tight knot unraveled with surprising force, sending people all around the room as they broke loose. The assemblage, for the most part, collapsed into a laughing mass onto the floor. Julian remained standing, although he felt drained. Eponine and Naomi-Makie leaned against one another, their clothing pooling beautifully around them on the parquet floor, and caught their breaths. It seemed that others were beginning to break off for "private worship." He stood over the two of them, staring cold and distant at anyone who might be interested in "worshiping" with them. Not surprisingly, Phina and Patrick were nowhere to be seen.

He helped the girls to their feet and whispered in Eponine's ear, "It's time to go."

He could feel the night turning, and he wanted to be safe and warm in his own place before he got called upon to chase down any demons.

Smaller groups were forming as well, holding hands around candles and jack-o-lanterns and wishing one another a happy new year. In the corner, someone had brought out a Ouija board. Beside them, a few couples were very obviously ringing in the new year, and others looked like they wanted a larger group with which to celebrate. Many eyes looked longingly on Naomi-Makie. Julian protectively put his hand on her shoulder and glared icy rage until the gazes and sighs vanished.

Naomi-Makie gave him a respectful bow. "Thanks. It's hard to be celibate at times like this."

Eponine looked stunned. "You are?" She blushed and looked askance, surprised by her own lack of tact.

Naomi-Makie didn't take it amiss. "For the time being. I like it this way. Besides, I leave to go to Japan next month, and I don't want to hassle with an attachment. Anyway, if I want to study at the temples, I had better get used to it." She looked a little nervously around the room. "I think if you two are leaving,

I might want to follow suit. I missed the costume contest, and it's looking like unless I want to try and call up Harry Houdini on the Ouija board, it's pretty much an orgy from here on out."

"Would you like to share a cab?"

"Thank you, but no, I only live a few blocks from here. Right near the Japanese Cultural Center, actually, lucky me."

"I insist we walk you home," Julian said in a tone that would brook no argument.

Eponine chuckled. "If the gentleman insists. . . ."

"What about your other friends?" Naomi-Makie looked genuinely concerned.

"Well, I know Phina can *always* take care of herself," Julian began, waiting for Eponine to nod agreement. "And if Iris is anything like her big sister, I am sure she'll be fine."

"All right, then. Let's try and find the way out of here."

NAOMI-MAKIE LIVED WITH HER parents in a narrow townhouse only a few blocks from a 6 train. Eponine and Julian stood on the dim platform together after seeing their new friend safely at home. They shivered in the cold, clean air, so different from the enfolding warmth of the ball.

"Does it ever seem sad to you that we keep meeting such wonderful people here?"

"I don't want to talk about it," he spoke quietly and through rigid jaws.

"I'm sorry. That wasn't very kind of me to say. But even I'm getting the blues about going home. I'm going to miss everyone so very much."

He couldn't help himself. "*Everyone?*"

Eponine sighed as the train rattled and screeched into the station. She waited until they were settled and moving before she looked Julian full in the face. "I give you full permission to handle Jeremy however you see fit."

He raised a smeared eyebrow. "Excuse me?"

"Take care of it. However you want."

"You realize what you're saying to me, don't you?"

She stared at the tunnel lamps zipping by in silence for a long moment. "Yes, I do. But it's about time I let go of your leash concerning this matter. Consider it your Samhain gift."

"'Nine. . . ."

"Don't speak to me of Jeremy any more right now, all right?

Or else we'll never get to finish what we started. And tonight is too magical a night not to. . . ."

He buried his face in her hair, drawing in her scent and finding the nape of her neck to kiss. He forced his vengeful thoughts from the forefront of his mind and concentrated on her. No one boarded their car, but Julian didn't think he would notice if they had. She stopped him from doing anything to her below her collarbone, but that gave him enough leave.

He would never forget holding her tight against him, her rapid pulse beating beneath the folds of velvet and silk, the train rocking them as he kissed her.

Even once they were home in their own room, he thought he could still feel the motion of the subway.

Julian finally gave way to sleep, long after Eponine had fallen still by his side. He slipped into a darkness rich and warm where nothing waited to torment or riddle him. If he dreamed at all, they were only dreams of her.

ALL SAINTS

"RISE AND SHINE! TIME for all heathens to be up and off to church!"

Julian growled and pulled the covers over his head. "You're cracked, girl!"

"Aww, come on, I want you to come to church with me. Please?" she begged.

"Why do you want to go to church?"

"It's All Saints' Day, a Holy Day of Obligation." She tugged the comforter down to his shoulder. "I want to go to the cathedral. Come along with me, please?"

He sat up and rubbed his temples. He smelled coffee from the kitchen and began to feel more awake. Eponine waited patiently for his answer.

"All right, it is obviously going to make you happy."

"You'll enjoy yourself." She slapped his knee and hopped out of bed. "I call first shower!"

"Hey!"

"Come catch me, then." She laughed and hastily wrapped her celestial print robe around her body and dashed for the bathroom.

BY THE TIME THEY reached the cathedral, Eponine was in more sober spirits. Ironically, the great white church was only a few blocks away from the site of the Witches' Ball. They were quite early for the Mass, but Julian bit back his grumbles about getting to sleep in for an extra hour or so. He silently knelt beside her on the padded kneeler and thought that Catholics had gone soft.

"*Padding*, hmph!"

Eponine laughed, quietly. All around them, women murmured the Rosary in a steady hum of low voices that tumbled over one another like the softly lapping waves of a lake. It was hypnotic but not unpleasant, and Julian was slightly disappointed when the services began. The bishop himself processed down the wide center aisle with a boy in robes swinging a censer of pungent incense. They rose, and Eponine listened, wide-eyed, to the readings. Julian's mind wandered.

"Are you coming to communion?"

He shivered and glanced around, surprised to find himself sitting in the third pew of the ornately decorated cathedral. Candles shimmered at the edges of his vision.

"Communion? Nah, I'll stay here and save your seat."

She gave him a quietly amused look, but made no comment.

Julian watched as she took her place in the line and had to chuckle as she chose the center. Of course she'd choose to receive from the bishop. Eponine stood before him with her head tilted back and her eyes raised toward the magnificently carved crucifix hanging above the High Altar. The bishop paused and gazed at her, recognition struggling in his features, but failing.

"The Body of Christ, my Child," he intoned.

"Amen," she breathed and received the Host reverently upon her tongue. The very same tongue that had intoned the names of the Goddesses the night before. But Julian saw no hypocrisy in her actions, only the purity of faith in all its forms.

She returned and knelt again beside him, folding her hands close to her chest and bowing her head, looking like a flower collecting its petals to itself as the sun fades into night. She didn't stir as the Mass was concluded.

"Eponine?"

She crossed herself and gave him a tired smile.

"Ready to go home?" he asked her.

"Not yet," she whispered. "I am enjoying the quiet, actually."

"Are you saying I talk too much?"

"No, Julian. But it's November now, and I just want some time to . . . think."

He nodded. But she didn't move, or speak. He sighed.

"You want me to do it now, don't you?"

She remained silent, her soft brown eyes fixed intently on the gilt tabernacle on the high altar.

"Eponine, answer me. You want me to go take care of Jeremy today, don't you? Right now!"

He kicked the pew, and she tilted her head toward him slowly. From all sides, the other parishioners glared. "Tell me that's what you want. I want to hear you say it."

"All saints must have their test. Of faith, of soul. You've never had a guilty conscience about this sort of thing before. Why do I need to give you permission to do your job? I thought I was doing you a favor in letting you have your way with him." She blinked deliberately. "Was I mistaken?"

Julian roared in frustration and stormed up the aisle. He paused at the door, oblivious to the icy stares of the rest of the people left in the church. Eponine sat still and composed on her knees in her pew. She'd taken the trendy, stretchy Buddhist prayer bracelet from her wrist. He watched her slender fingers slide over the moss agate beads as she murmured sutras along with the rosaries of the old women.

IT WAS A GLORIOUS autumn morning. The bright and clear light of the sun pierced the silky and moist-looking clouds. it would most likely rain in the afternoon. Near-rainbows clung to the clouds' edges, shifting and morphing as they skimmed the pale blue bowl of the sky.

Julian did not want to deal with the task that was set before him, but he felt he had no other choice. He'd known there was no other choice on Valentine's Day, when Eponine had brought home Jeremy's gift of roses.

Turning north, he made for a place he knew well and often visited in his more haunting dreams. A chill wind thrust fingers of cold down the back of his coat, and he reached into his pocket for his scarf. It was the deep burgundy cashmere scarf that Eponine had given him for Christmas. He wrapped it closely around his neck, savoring the velvety warmth of it and letting it soothe his whirling thoughts. He rounded the corner of Seventy-Sixth Street before he even realized it.

The place was just the same, only the stoop was now littered with bright golden leaves and smelled of damp masonry, another surety of impending rain. Julian hoped he could do what he was there to do before the weather turned wet.

Calling on his core of power, Julian easily penetrated into the building. Within, it was dim with the morning light, a mantle of sleep still shrouding the place. With eyes half-lidded, Julian easily felt the pull to his quarry's resting place. Effortlessly and silently, he mounted the stairs, coming to stand in front of a door he knew could only be Jeremy's. The knob turned easily in his hands, and the hinges did not dare to make a sound. The bedroom door was also as obliging, and Julian found himself in a plain but comfortable room that smelled of sandalwood incense and sex.

The little blonde girl Eponine called Cosette was lying blissfully asleep on her side, one arm tucked beneath her head and the other thrown across her lover's chest. Jeremy lay on his back, snoring once every third breath or so. One elegantly shaped hand covered Cosette's and the other vanished beneath the covers. It was disgustingly cute. Julian was reminded of the scene at the end of "The Little Mermaid" by Hans Christian Andersen, where the mermaid, now a human, is faced with the decision whether to kill her beloved and be able to return to immortality in the sea, or let him live on with his true love. She stands beside his marriage-bed with a knife in her hands, and only the blood from his heart can turn her legs back into fins. But she casts the blade aside and greets the dawn that heralds her doom, giving up her life so that he may be spared. Julian had scoffed when Eponine had read it to him.

"All she had to do was kill him? It's too easy! And the bastard deserved it, leading her on and breaking her heart like that!"

"But, Julian, that's not what the story is about. It's about true love and sacrifice."

"Well, if I were ever in that position, I'd gut the sucker; just see if I wouldn't!"

"Well, if you *are* ever in that position, we'll see what you end up doing."

He sighed in the gloaming of that room, remembering Eponine's words that night and this morning. *"All saints must have their test."*

"I'm no saint, 'Nine. I *should* just gut the sucker," he whispered to himself. Crouching down, Julian gingerly touched Jeremy's forehead and peered into the young man's dream. Although he was lying naked and satiated beside Cosette, he was dreaming of Eponine. She glowed like a star, twinkling and glimmering like a candle's flame. Julian stood discreetly at the edge of the dream, nearly forgetting himself in the shimmer of her radiance. Then, as easily as picking up a shiny stone from the bottom of a pool, he reached out and took the light. In its place, he left nothing—not a void, but a scattering of shadow so that nothing would seem to be missing. He stepped out of the dream as easily as he had slipped into the apartment.

Jeremy stirred in his sleep. One hazel eye slid open but saw nothing and fell shut again. His brow furrowed and he moaned, fussing in his sleep. Beside him, Cosette propped herself up on her elbow and gazed down at him.

"Hey, hey, you're having a bad dream. Shhhh." She rubbed his chest and pillowed her head against his shoulder.

"Ursie? That you? Mmmm, yeah, it was weird. Like I forgot something . . . or someone . . . but I can't even remember who or what or what it would have to do with."

"Well, of course you can't remember if you forgot," she said sleepily.

"Yeah," he laughed, dozing back off again. "Can't remember if I forgot. . . ."

Julian sat invisible and unmoving in the dark corner of the bedroom until their breathing was deep and regular. He looked into his hand and saw what looked like a small, crystalline marble. He opened his fingers and blew across his palm. The little sphere floated for a moment, then popped like a soap bubble. Jeremy twitched and made a sound. Julian waited, but heard no more. He slipped back out into the street as quietly as he had entered, leaving no traces whatsoever of his presence.

The sky was still crisp and bright with the promise of rain and trailing rainbow-edged clouds. He shoved his hands into his pockets and tucked his chin into his scarf. Julian shivered with a cold far deeper than what the weather wrought. He had just enacted the most cruel punishment he had ever brought upon a human. Although Jeremy would feel happiness and gaiety in his life, it would not ever be quite the same. He had met Joy, had kissed her, and fallen in love with her, and now that memory was gone. Julian had just irrevocably changed that boy's life, and the poor sod would never even remember there had been anything to change. It nearly made Julian pity him. Nearly.

EPONINE WAS STILL PRAYING when Julian returned. Only a few solemn murmurs resounded in the great church now. Sunlight streamed in through the stained glass windows like ribbons of watercolors. From the angle of the light, he was fairly certain that it was a rare time of day that the surrounding buildings didn't block the beams. He shook her gently as if waking her from sleep.

"Look," he whispered, and pointed to the wash of colors across the smooth white stone of the cathedral's interior.

She blinked uncertainly at him then followed his indication. As she turned to look at the patterns of colors, her eyes roved over his shirt, his cuffs, and his hands. There wasn't a trace of blood. The play of light and color dimmed and brightened with the passing clouds and swirled a little with the fickle light. She smiled, and the whole interior of the church glowed with amber and cobalt and ruby red. She threw her arms around him and kissed him on the cheek. He'd passed, with flying colors. She could tell by the pain in his eyes.

"Praise be to all that's holy, there's still hope!"

"I would like to know what in the hell you are talking about." His stomach rumbled loudly, echoing slightly in the vast church. "But I think you should tell me over breakfast."

She took his hand and walked with him outside. He squeezed hers tightly, as if she might float away and vanish as easily as the soap-bubble dream of her had.

But what Jeremy had had with her was an illusion and a dream. This is real. He paused and looked over at her, marveling at the fading rainbows that lined the clouds. She was chattering about how they were so much better than "silly ol' *silver* linings!"

No, this is a dream, and some day, someone is going to take her from me just as I took her from him. He sighed and put his arm around her shoulders. *If all saints have tests, then all angels must have battles. It would be a worthy fight . . . to get to keep her.*

Something You Should Know . . .

THEY STROLLED INTO TIMES Square in high spirits. The crisp November afternoon was giving way to the kind of sunset found only on the eastern seaboard: vivid, sharp, and utterly breathtaking in deep goldens and rich, riveting pinks. Streaks of clouds made indigo shadows across the dazzling skyscape of color that greeted their eyes between the sleek gray buildings. Slowly, the lights of the square came alive, looking tawdry and bleak next to the splendor of nature. Eponine clapped her gloved hands together, then buried them into her pockets.

"Certainly did get cold as soon as the sun went down! Do you think you will miss the weather?"

Julian exhaled deeply, watching the hint of steam grace his breath. Already his nose was dripping, and he could feel that his lips were cold. "Not really." He absently nuzzled his head against the cashmere scarf he wore and couldn't hide the little smile that tugged at the corner of his mouth. "Well, maybe a little."

"It's going to be all right, you know," Eponine brushed against his shoulder.

Yes, I know. We are going to be gone before it gets really cold here. But he knew that wasn't what she meant. "Let me ask you something."

"Sure."

"Do you have a sense of foreboding over the end of our time here?"

"Foreboding?"

"Yeah, I have been having these dreams, dreams that aren't dreams. . . . It's like I wake up from them and don't remember anything but this feeling of dread."

Her steps faltered slightly, but he didn't notice. "What else do you remember?"

"Not much. Just darkness, and headaches. Like what I used to dream when we first came here. I think it's the season, this whole winter business, like you and springtime."

"Maybe. . . ."

"Just seems weird. I thought once I was lying by your side, those nightmares couldn't get to me anymore." Julian paused and glanced down at her, fearing he'd said something that would hurt her. "But I guess even you can't help what comes from inside, can you?"

Eponine shot a look at him. "Julian. . . ."

"Don't fret, my little Eponine. I don't blame you. Would that I could show you everything that is in me, then your light could shine on all of it." He laughed drily. "But even when I want to, this little sliver of my self slides away and hides in the dark."

He could sense the tears forming in her eyes, feeling so warm and wet against her cold skin in the dry New York winter air.

"I'm not saying this to hurt you, 'Nine, but I know how much you want me to be honest with you." He sighed and gazed up at the scrolling marquee above the ABC studios. *This is such a cop-out, but what else am I supposed to tell her? I can't leave her to believe that she was able to wave her magic wand and turn me into a real boy . . . no matter how much I want to believe it. There is something there, something hiding in the shadows of my thoughts, I feel it encroaching little by little . . . and what it will do when it comes to the forefront . . . scares me.*

The words before his eyes began to make sense. He was reading about war, about terror, about death, about the world-wide cry for blood and revenge. He drew in a ragged and painful breath as the city lights began to fade from his periphery and a dark throbbing began at the back of his skull. Julian knew that sensation, that red-hinted glaze that covered his sight when the bloodlust was about to begin. He had nearly left it behind while on Earth, keeping it carefully sheltered except for a few occasions, so few he could count them: three, maybe four times he had allowed that part of his nature to emerge. That angelic essence clamored for release now.

Yes, we are so very close to going home, I can feel this mortality shedding from me.

He would step back into the spring, into the pillar of light, and Julian would be no more.

The pain came searing, red and black, through his head, and he felt the concrete slam into his knees, cold and unyielding. He shook violently, his stomach threatening to heave up the Godiva hot cocoa he'd drunk just an hour earlier.

It was a terrifying sensation, bearing the memory of amnesia.

As blackness blanketed his vision, he tasted the metallic tang of blood in his mouth and smelled the bleak and sour scent of panic.

Something had been wrong before he'd come. Something had been wrong *with him*. Faith had said as much, didn't she? That day in the park, when she'd met him by the stream and gave him the scroll. The scroll that echoed the words carved in his ring: *To thine own self be true.*

He suddenly realized it was because he had become someone else. Some*thing* else.

But the particulars eluded him.

He pulled his head up, searching for her. She stood a few steps

away from him, but her face was not fraught with worry. Instead
she looked at him with understanding and compassion.

"You know what's going on, don't you?"

Eponine nodded slowly.

"Jeremy isn't your mission. He was never your mission. It's
been me all along, hasn't it been?"

She nodded again, biting her lip.

"Tell me what's going on!"

She chewed her lip and fresh tears glinted on her silky lashes.
"I can't."

"What do you mean you can't?"

"I'm sorry."

He dragged his feet beneath him and stood on shaking legs,
both knees aching bitterly. "Then I'll have to find someone who
can."

He sounded so utterly calm to his own ears, belying the tumul-
tuous riot of darkness and pain in his head. He nearly threw
himself down the sidewalk, mind reeling, trying to get his bearings to Fortieth Street.

"Where are you going?" Eponine called after him.

*She asks like she doesn't know. But then again, do I really
know?* He lurched toward the corner, heedless of the traffic. He
knew where he was going. Jogging down Fortieth Street, past
the Majestic and down the stairs. He hopped the turnstiles and
fled onto the platform as the downtown C train was screeching
and clattering to a halt. He could hear Eponine behind him, her
voice echoing off the cheap white tiles that covered the walls and
floors.

He caught a glimpse of her at the top of the rusting, green-
painted stairs. He turned away and boarded the train.

"I'll be waiting." She didn't raise her voice, yet it carried clearly
to his ears. "I'll be waiting until you come home."

You're just letting me go?

You expected me to force to you stay?

The doors shut and the subway station slid out of view,
replaced by the dark and chilly tunnel that bore him downtown.

JULIAN HAD COOLED HIS heels considerably by the time he was
knocking on the door to 13-H in the Washington Square Village.
A shadow passed behind the peephole, and the door immediately
opened.

"Well, well, to what do I owe the honor of this visit?"

"Hi, Phina." Julian picked at the loose paint around the door-jamb. It was difficult, asking her this. "I was wondering . . . if you could help me out."

Her eyebrows arched, but she laughed. She took in his face and the air just surrounding him for a long moment, her eyes looking black as jet in the dim hallway. "I don't think I can help you."

"*Fuck!*" He slammed a clenched fist into the door; it resounded with a dull metal clang.

"That's a fire door, you know. Come inside. I'll fix some tea, and we can talk."

She stepped aside and shut the door behind him. The room was still gilded with the shimmering Christmas lights, and all around were Mardi Gras beads, Chinese lanterns, and posters of Pre-Raphaelite art. She and Eponine were very much alike.

Phina pulled a blue, green, and purple plush-covered inflatable chair out from the corner and told him to sit. Julian looked dubiously at it, but found it was remarkably comfortable. Phina returned with a dark blue teapot steaming on a banged-up Russian lacquered tea tray. She had two cups and two saucers (all four completely mismatched), a gold-edged sugar bowl, and a creamer in the shape of a duck. She also brought a plate of Walkers shortbread cookies and a handful of Hershey's Special Dark miniatures.

"Not sure if you are trying to impress me or scare me."

"You no like my things?" she said, in a heavy and obviously faked Eastern European accent. "I put gypsy curse on you!"

Julian sipped the tea she poured for him. It was Earl Grey, and very strong. "Would that negate any other curses already pre-existing?"

"No. And you're not cursed, Julian."

"Sometimes I wonder."

"Tell me why you're here."

He sighed and set the cup down on the worn faux-Persian rug. "I had this . . . *thing* . . . happen to me down on Times Square tonight. It was like a migraine, but with visions. Death, revenge, despair . . . and it all had to do with me. Eponine knows something about it, but she can't tell me, or won't. I thought maybe you could help, you know, being that you're *you*."

"That's not what I meant." She poured a little milk and added some sugar to her second cup of tea. "I mean why are you here. *Here*, as in the planet."

Julian nearly gagged on his tea. "What?"

"Why are you here?"

He curled his lip. "You assume I had a choice."

She only shrugged idly. "We all have a choice, even if we don't remember having made it."

He thought of a hundred lies, easy lies she might even believe. He looked her in the eye. "I was told I had to be here. I'm pretty sure it was penance."

"We're not so bad, are we? Us piddly little humans?"

"No, you're not."

"And you have Eponine with you."

He nodded, his gaze wandering over the riot of color that was Phina's room. "I did something wrong," he murmured. "I'm not sure what it was, but there was something wrong, something wrong with me. Then I was sent here, to watch over Eponine."

"But she can't tell you what the problem is?"

"I think . . . I think she may not be able to. I think she wants to, but she can't. I wish I knew why."

"Perhaps it is for you to figure out on your own."

"Don't you think I would have figured it out by now, though?"

Phina pursed her lips and ate a bite of chocolate, avoiding his gaze.

Julian laughed despite himself. "Okay, okay, point taken."

She glanced up, and the light in her eyes was both pious and wicked. "You are . . . a beautiful creature. I wish I could show you how you seem in my eyes, and doubtless how you must look to her. Your strength, even your ruthlessness, it's all counterbalanced by this exquisite tenderness. Very alluring. I understand completely why she loves you so."

He flushed hotly. "Madame Nabokov, if I didn't know better, I'd think you were coming on to me."

"Good to know you know better then, hmm?" She smirked. "Besides, we aren't meant for that, you and me. Although, no doubt you'd be a worthy tumble, your body won't stray where your heart doesn't lie. And it isn't me you love."

Perhaps it would be easier if I did.

"Besides, Patrick would break your legs," she winked. "So, Julian d'Sanguise, what would you have of me? Just hospitality and an open ear?"

He started a bit at hearing her speak his whole name. He had never heard anyone say it aloud. "Will you give me a reading?"

"Of course! Cards, runes, palm, aura, tea leaves?"

"You can do all that?"

She giggled. "Yes, dear. Grad school doesn't pay for itself, you know!"

"What would you like in payment . . . if I wanted you to read everything you can?"

"You don't have to pay me. Just . . . think of me fondly when you've moved on from here. Perhaps owe me a favor later." She winked again and pulled a carved teakwood box and an old hardbound book from a nearby shelf.

"You're a shrewd business woman."

She idly laid out some cards, picked them up, laid out some more, and ended up with the King of Swords in her hand.

"This will do for your marker." And she dealt a pattern of a cross and a line beside it. She turned over the cards; they were very pretty, looking as if they were collaged of shimmering fabrics and bits of things. "Iris is better at this than I am, but this is pretty obvious. I have never had so many Major Arcana in a reading. You are one important boy. Your time is close, that I can see. But there is a big decision for you. The Death card: change, renewal, but it hinges on you and what you do. The Hanged Man: a crossroads, something's waiting for you. The rest . . . I am not being allowed to see. The Heirophant . . . higher mysteries, secrets. Justice . . . blind, but fair, everything will work out the way it should. But details, no, there are none. I am specifically being shown that the details are not for my eyes."

"*Damn it!*"

She turned over the last card and laughed. "The answer you seek, you already have. Just open your eyes." She held up the card of zero, The Fool.

Julian clenched his jaws, making the muscles bulge.

"Don't take yourself so seriously! See, *The Fool*! Be like the fool!"

"Oh, shove it. Isn't there anything else you can try?"

She flipped over his teacup in a flurry and let the dregs dribble onto the saucer. She peered into the cup, and pointed him to the X inside and the heart nearby and the fish, showing a crossroads with love and good fortune on one side. There was an undecipherable clot of leaves on the other side. Her brow furrowed.

"See, I don't get to know."

He nodded. "Thank you for trying."

She began to clean up the tea, making sure to give him a handful of the Special Dark bars with conspiring smile.

"Julian, you are really much better off than you think," she called from the kitchen. "Give yourself some credit and listen to your heart."

The door shut soundly and she came back into the common room. It was empty.

"Julian?"

On the inflatable chair was a slip of her notepaper.

Thank you, Phina. I need to do some thinking. If I don't see you again, I want to thank you for everything you've done, both for Eponine and for me. I know we will both never forget you. And yes, if you ever need a favor, just ask me, I'll hear you.

~Julian

THE APARTMENT WAS DIM and smelled of her heady beeswax candles.

"Eponine," he called hoarsely.

"Julian!" She ran from the bedroom and threw her arms around him. "I'm so glad you're home. Are you all right?"

He could scarcely nod, so bone-deep was his weariness. Eponine guided him to bed and expertly undressed him.

She caressed his face, his chest, his arms until sleep began to steal over him in heavy waves.

Maybe if I let the nightmares out of my heart, maybe then she could protect me from them.

Eponine hummed softly. "Was Phina able to tell you what you needed to know?"

He didn't bother asking how she knew that's where he had gone. "What she told me, I already knew."

"Ah, well, at least she told you what you needed to hear, then." He would have glared, but he was too exhausted. Phina's words had rung true, and Julian could feel the weight of the impending future pressing down upon him. Yes, there again was that foreboding sense of dread.

"'Nini, there's something you should know."

Her face brightened. "What is it?"

"I'm scared," he whispered.

It wasn't what she had been hoping he'd say, he could tell, although he wasn't sure what she wanted from him.

"*Scared*? You?"

"I've never been afraid of the future, but I think there is something wrong with the past. For almost a whole year now, I've done nothing but live in the present, but all too soon I am going to have to go back and face it, face whatever it is I've done."

"Julian, it wasn't you."

"You know, don't you? You know what it is I am talking about."

She closed her eyes and gave a single, silent nod of her head.

"And all you can tell me is that it wasn't me? My very soul is being ripped apart, but it wasn't me?"

She took his hand and softly kissed it, lingering her warm lips over his ring. "No more of this tonight, Julian."

"'Nini...."

"Shhhh, hush now. You are right on one count: We haven't much time. We shouldn't waste it."

"But I want to know...."

She kissed him firmly on the mouth, quieting him. He pulled her close, returning her kiss fervently. It was his prayer.

"I want to know," he whispered again. "I want to know joy."

She smiled. "Here I am."

HISTORY

JULIAN, AS A RULE, did not like to be touched. He had never found any solace or pleasure in physical contact for as long as he could remember.

Whenever he was to touch another, it was to bring pain, death, vengeance. This had, on occasion, even brought him to a lover's bed. But there was no pleasure in it.

Whenever someone sought to touch him, it was out of fear or an attempt to subdue him, capture him, or push him away. There was definitely very little pleasure to be found in that.

But now, in the late autumn mornings, he awoke with Eponine by his side. Sometimes his arm was draped over her, his palm pressed against the slight roundness of her belly. More often, however, he woke up in her arms with her soft curves spooned close against his back, her arms wrapped firmly around him, cleaving him tightly to her. He had, at first, felt a momentary surge of panic before waves of comfort and contentment bore all traces of an ill mood far away.

He loved her, he knew.

Loved her only like one of her own kind could: like a friend, a lover, and a brother, all in one. Yet, for him it was more than that. They had an understanding.

They were both as old as the world. There had been but a few of them then, born with humanity, but creatures of spirit and magic. It was a world before religion and before the word "angel" was ever formed by human lips.

Strength, Joy, Vengeance, and Death were of an age, among the eldest of the angels, personified concepts to be prayed for or warded against. But the world quickly came to know others: Love, Hope, Wisdom, Faith, Compassion, Courage, Liberty, Honor, Justice, Mercy—these last three had split from the very heart of Vengeance, although he was hard-pressed to remember such a thing and spent a good deal of his time vehemently denying it.

No one was sure when Vengeance had begun to change. But it became horribly obvious that something was amiss when his memory clamped shut and he wandered the Earth in a reddened haze with his sister Death close at his heels. Destruction and blood flowed freely in his path, and he returned to his realm with no recollections, only blinding headaches.

Since his birth, his soul had been closely wed to humanity, for without people and their hunger for retribution, Vengeance would not exist. But somehow, some of the peoples of the Earth began to put greater and greater belief in him. Divine Vengeance began to fill the empty voids in the souls of many, shunning Love and Peace and Wisdom and Mercy. And their numbers grew every day.

Death prospered. Hope and Joy weakened, withdrawing to the quiet confines of the heart, and there burned silently and waited. Bloodlust raged, and Vengeance cast even Honor aside, seeking only the company of Strength and Death.

Vengeance grew mighty, and his being darkened. He fell blind to everything that was not his duty. He took an eye for an eye and never counted the costs, for evening the score made everything right in the end, did it not? Sick with power, Vengeance began to tear humanity to shreds. And they loved him all the more for it. Crusades, Inquisition, Revolution, Insurrection, War, Terrorism all sprouted like weeds in his footsteps. Death reveled in his wake.

Madness nipped at his heels as Vengeance lashed out, unthinking and random. Even Strength and Death became afraid of him. Feelings of betrayal and anger fed the darkening abyss of his soul, and he took his own retribution against his siblings through the lives of the men and women who worshipped him like a god. Countless lives were lost the world over, all in the name of a prideful Vengeance. No one could understand his bloodlust, and no one knew how to stop him.

His headaches and blackouts increased as humanity carried out grand schemes of revenge born of his now-cold heart. Often, they were senseless acts, upsetting the balance instead of bringing order. When an army opened fire on a group of rebellious children throwing stones at their tanks, even Death knew that Vengeance must be stopped. The tide of blood rose higher every passing day, and they all could see the danger in it, for blood begot blood. The spiral of vengeance seemed never-ending as feuds raged across borders and through generations.

If nothing changed, humanity would annihilate themselves. And they would take the light of Divinity with them.

It was decided that Joy would go to a place she was sorely needed: New York City.

And she would take Vengeance with her.

If Joy, as constant and eternal as Death, could not return his spirit to its karmic intentions from the swamp of degradation into which it had sunk, then Hope would be the first of her siblings to die.

A year and a day pass far more quickly than one would ever think possible.

Julian slept soundly beside her, his nightmares having fled for the moment. She touched his face, his strong hard cheekbones, his firm and stubbly jaw, his velvety dark curls. She pressed her face against his back and breathed in the scent of his skin. He smelled of sleep, of warm comfort, and of spices dark and exotic.

She loved him, she knew. She had for quite some time. His darkness appealed to her, his fearlessness, his commitment to his work no matter how bloody or how difficult. He strove to make amends, to bring retribution to those who deserved it, and *only* those who deserved it. But then he had fallen. Vengeance, the dutiful and steadfast anti-hero of humanity, had fallen, and now revenge was being meted out upon the innocent and undeserving.

Joy and Faith had stood by him, even though he did not see it. Vengeance had become a creature of darkness with the shades of demons writhing in his shadow. His last chance for salvation had begun almost a year ago.

If Joy failed, he would be lost forever. She could not bear such a thought. She loved him too much.

There were only a few days remaining. November was ending.

MIRACLE

JULIAN HAD FIRST SEEN the ad for the contest sometime before Halloween. Probably on the subway, or walking by a bus stop, he couldn't remember anymore. Wherever it had been, it certainly hadn't grabbed his immediate attention. It was actually his favorite morning talk show that began to inspire him. They had been discussing the Thanksgiving Day Parade, and it was making Julian downright queasy to think about. It was only the second week of November, but yet they were already planning and cooing over it. Then the dark-haired hostess began talking about the contest.

"It's our first annual Create your own *Miracle on Thirty-Fourth Street* contest," she explained, looking at once both serious and giddy. "If you aren't familiar with the film, it's about a little girl who stops believing in Santa Claus and how the man himself comes to be the grand finale in the Macy's Thanksgiving Day Parade. A wonderful holiday classic! I like it so much better than *It's a Wonderful Life*."

"I don't know," the weatherman chastised her, smiling. "I really enjoy *It's a Wonderful Life*. How can you resist little Zuzu saying, 'Teacher says every time a bell rings, an angel gets its wings'?"

They bantered on and Julian stared, perplexed, at the screen until they scrolled the website for the *Miracle on Thirty-Fourth Street* contest. He flicked on the computer and barely waited for it to boot up before pouncing onto Internet Explorer. To enter the contest, an essay of no more than five hundred words was to be submitted. He was to write about his dearest wish and, if he won, it would be performed as a "miracle" during the Macy's Thanksgiving Day Parade, right there on Thirty-Fourth Street.

He turned off the computer as Eponine wandered in. She was still looking sleepy, but she was dressed to go out.

"Where are you headed?" Julian asked her as casually as possible.

She poured a cup of coffee into her glittery blue travel mug and sliced a bagel. "To the Met," she told him, cramming her bagel halves into the toaster that was just barely too narrow to accommodate the thick, homemade bagels she got at the Farmer's Market. "There's a gallery event up there, something to do with a new addition to the Sackler Japanese Galleries. There's a big reception afterwards, with a tea ceremony and a sushi buffet."

"Wow, sounds nice. You'll be gone all day, then?"

She nodded as she pried up the slightly singed bagel and began to coat it with cream cheese. "The reception is by invite only, but Phina got me and Naomi-Makie on the guest list. We could probably smuggle you in, too, if you were interested."

"Nah." He grinned and stretched. "I was looking forward to a mellow day at home. Catch up on some web-comics, and it's Thursday, which means there should be a new *Insomniac Nights* post up. Maybe clean the bathroom and the kitchen."

She quirked an eyebrow at him over her coffee. "Well, I'd be ecstatic if you were to clean the kitchen and bathroom."

"Would you give me a good reward?"

"Mmm, maybe." She took a flirtatious step toward him, then looked at the microwave clock. "Ack! I'm late! Okay, sexy talk will have to wait for later. I have got to go! See you tonight!"

She blew him a kiss and dashed out the door with her breakfast in hand.

Julian waited quietly until she left the apartment. He heard the fire door to the stairwell slam loudly and her footfalls beginning to make the descent. She didn't return. He smiled broadly and turned the computer back on.

At first the small square of entry space looked daunting. Julian had never written anything like this before. He sat back and took a deep breath. He knew what he wanted for Eponine, and he knew why she should have it. The trick was getting the concepts, the pictures, and the ideas in his head to settle down into comprehensible words. He began simply.

"I have come to New York City as a student. It has been almost a year since my arrival. Like so many students, I thought I knew so much that I thought there was nothing here for me to learn. I thought I was too old to start again. And like so many students, my greatest teacher has been no professor, no intellectual, but the girl sent here on assignment with me. A girl whom I have learned to listen to, to admire, to respect, and to love," he paused, his heart racing. In his mind, the essay spun out like ribbons in the breeze, so many colors and textures dancing and waving. He typed quickly, trying to get the ideas down before they fled.

"In her eyes is a love unimaginable, a love I knew I was not worthy to receive. But in her smile is the forgiveness of every wrong I have ever committed, and in her hand holding mine is the blessing that chases away any shadow of doubt. With her kiss she bestows upon me the sanctity that makes me worthy.

"But all things must—invariably—end, and our time together grows short. We will return to the lives we led once upon a time before coming to New York City. And although we will be in close contact, it won't ever be the same as it has been here and now. In the light of her love, I have truly become the person I have always dreamed I could be, since time immemorial. I want, more than anything, to show her what this past year has meant to me, how it has changed me for the better. And I want to take my chance, to find out if there may be more for the two of us ahead."

Julian then laid out his plan for what his Thanksgiving miracle would consist of in painstaking detail. Finally, after reading over his work and correcting a few errors in spelling and punctuation, he whispered a heartfelt prayer and clicked *Submit*.

IT WAS MONDAY, TWO and a half weeks after Julian had written the essay. He was sitting in one of the executive meeting rooms far upstairs in the main Macy's building on Thirty-Fourth Street, just off Herald Square. He could look into the park from there.

He'd read the discreet e-mail they'd sent. He had come to the store. He'd been shown up to the secret places by a charming young man in a business suit. He was sitting in the small conference room with a bunch of stodgy older men drinking coffee and eating Krispy Kreme doughnuts. But he still did not believe it. He'd told Eponine he was going out walking, that he needed a few hours alone. It was a lousy excuse but the best he could come up with, and it had the added benefit of being entirely true.

The executive and marketing managers chuckled amiably and pushed catalogs his way.

"Now, we'd *like* you to pick from Macy's merchandise, of

course," said a balding man with a crescent of sandy-reddish hair around the back of his head. "But we understand that it's your choice, and however you want it to be, we'll do it. Just like in the movie, if we haven't got it here, we will get it for you from wherever we can. At Macy's, our number one goal is customer satisfaction."

Julian smiled, weakly. He didn't think he'd ever been inside of Macy's. He knew Eponine had, but there was no way he could have brought her along and not ruined the surprise.

"You're overwhelming him." Julian turned to see a slim woman enter the room. She was dressed in a sharp dove-gray suit with her hair pulled back into a high bun. It was graying, but still mostly brown. She smiled at Julian and leaned on the chair next to him. She gave it a quick shake, and the marketing guy in it hopped up and offered it to her.

"My name is Sylvia," she told him, still smiling. "I am the vice president of public relations. This is *your* day, Julian, and I want you to have it *your* way."

He nodded, still feeling numb but slowly warming to this kind stranger. He realized she was the type of person who became whatever she felt necessary to become in any given situation. She saw that a motherly tone would work best with him at that moment, and so she was maternal and sweet and unendingly calm. Ordinarily, he'd be seething and riding the end of the tether on his temper, but today, he could see that it would get him nowhere. She did genuinely want to help him, for making him happy would make her company look very good. And if he snapped or snarled at her, he would lose this chance. So he smiled and pointed to one of the catalogs. Sylvia gave him the top book from her stack and settled down beside him.

"What do you want to say with it?"

"That I love her," he whispered, feeling suddenly shy about saying the words. "I want her to know she is the single most important thing in my life."

"Does she like antiques? Modern styles?"

"Well, I think she'd like anything I was to give her." *Hadn't she said that on Christmas Eve? That I could give her a rock and she'd be happy?* "But I want to give her something that really has a lot of light and life to it. I'll know it when I see it."

It was going to be a long morning, he knew. And although Macy's was providing him with every last thing he needed to make his plan work, he knew the favor he was doing them was just as big. He smiled and began to narrow down his selections.

"Neiman Marcus page forty-six goes into the 'maybe' pile. Oh, I *definitely* like the one on the bottom of page twelve of the Macy's Holiday Specials circular; put that one in the 'yes' pile. And could someone bring me a doughnut? Chocolate-covered, please."

BY WEDNESDAY, ALL THE necessary papers had been signed and all the decisions made. The plan was set. There was naught to do but wait. Julian shivered and felt as if the adrenaline would never ebb from his blood. Time was rushing past him so quickly, yet it seemed as if Thanksgiving Day could not come soon enough.

His big chance to show Eponine his love and gratitude was seven days away. After that, not much more than forty-eight hours remained before the end of their lives.

GIVE THANKS

THE ALARM RANG TINNILY and shrilly, sending Julian shaking and sprawling across Eponine to silence it. It was so loud in the deep pre-dawn darkness. Eponine was sitting bolt upright in bed, her brown eyes wide and her face drained of color. Julian could see the pulse beating fierce and rapid in her throat. He stuck his finger between the hammer and the bells of the little brass clock and managed to push the switch to the off position.

Eponine sighed and rested her hands on his back, trailing little swirls across his shoulders as he lay across her lap.

"Julian, it's four in the morning. Why was the alarm clock set?"

"It's Thanksgiving," he said, smiling and turning over onto his back. "We're going to the parade."

Eponine sucked the corner of her mouth and looked at the sheen of ice on the outside of the bedroom window. She snuggled down beneath him and the blankets.

"Maybe we should just watch it on TV."

Panic flared momentarily, but Julian managed to laugh it off. "Oh, no, you told me you wanted to go, so get up, throw on a couple of coats, and let's go!"

She grumbled good-naturedly. "If you insist."

"'Nine, you'll regret it if you don't go. You've been talking about it since last Thanksgiving when we just missed it. You can't have lived here in Manhattan the whole year and ditch out on the *one* Macy's Thanksgiving Day Parade that you're ever going to see."

"I wouldn't say 'ever.' I may come back some day."

"The only one you'll see with me, then." He covered the sting of hurt with a convincing pout.

Eponine giggled, "I just can't say no to you, mister." She clambered out of bed and shivered.

"That's just what I'm betting on," he whispered, then hopped out from the warm blankets beside her, his feet stinging as they hit the cold wood floor. "I'll go get some coffee for us!"

THEY WERE WAITING EXACTLY when and where Julian had been told they'd be.

Eponine was confused. "Julian, we shouldn't be back here. . . ."

"Oh? Shouldn't we?" He couldn't hide that infectious, wicked grin of his, the one that warmed Eponine to the tips of her toes.

"And just what have you got planned, mister, hmmm?" She put her hands on her hips, somewhat buried beneath the layers of winter clothes she wore. It was currently nineteen degrees up on Eighty-Fourth Street beside the park.

Julian took her arm and pointed to the float that was parked nearby. It was mostly red and gold, and it shimmered in the icy street light. It depicted a miniature Thanksgiving Day Parade complete with scale model floats and balloons that were only "miniature" in comparison to the size of the genuine articles. Each piece was nearly the size of an economy car. Above the mini-parade was a raised balcony that sat above the overscaled and glittered words: "Macy's Miracle on Thirty-Fourth Street."

"I don't understand," she said, feeling more than a little dazed. She turned to find Julian and saw him in a loose knot of Macy's executives who were shaking his hand and clapping him on the shoulder. A woman who was entirely too stately and composed for such an obnoxious hour stood smiling knowingly at her.

"Julian, what's going on?"

He came toward her and took her gloved hands in his own. "We're going to be the guests of honor of the parade."

"*What?*"

"We're riding this float!" He grinned wider than she'd ever seen him smile before. "I won a contest."

She glanced away from his jubilant, dancing eyes and found

the smiling face of the woman. She was holding a red shopping bag.

"I'm Sylvia," she told Eponine, holding the bag open. "And we need to get you dressed and ready."

She took Eponine's little fleece hat and replaced it with a chenille cap that was lined in rich dark fur and came down far over her ears. She then gave her a matching wrap and a muff, both constructed of thick, velvety chenille and silky rabbit fur. She handed Julian a winter cap of black shearling leather with its layer of heavy fleece and a pair of matching gloves. She did not bother to offer him a scarf to replace the burgundy cashmere one he wore with pride.

A squat security guard and a black-clad parade technician helped them onto the float. Once situated, two more techs buckled them into safety harnesses and switched on the small space heater at their feet. It was still beastly cold, and Eponine shivered visibly beneath her jet-black furs.

"Do you want to go back home?" Julian whispered.

She shot a look toward him, eyes wide in shock. "Oh, no! No, not at all! No, Julian, this . . . this is *phenomenal!*" Tears welled up in her eyes, feeling hot on her lashes but becoming icy as soon as they touched her cold-reddened cheeks. "This is the most exciting thing ever!"

And you haven't even seen the half of it! "Good," he smiled and pulled her close to him for more than warmth.

THE RISING OF THE sun did little to warm the frigid day, but the cold did not dampen the spirits of the throngs of people who gathered all along the parade route. Clowns and performers kept them occupied and entertained while TV crews checked and rechecked their equipment and feeds as the clock ticked closer to eight-thirty.

Eponine was excited and nervous. She waved to the people nearby and blew kisses to the clowns, who in turn fell to the streets with their hands over their hearts, pretending to swoon.

"She's mine!" Julian hollered down to them in a mock jealous rage. "Back! Back, you! All of you! You can't have her! She's mine! She's all mine, mwa-ha-ha-ha!"

"I'll never forget this, Julian," she whispered.

"You'd better not." He kissed her softly at first, then with more passion as the crowd and clowns cheered him on. The float lurched forward and jostled them apart. "Here we go," he said breathlessly.

The sun's rays were prismatic and pure in the crisp, cold air. The trees still held onto many of their autumn-jeweled leaves, throwing them high against the deep and clear blue sky. Eponine could see her breath in shimmering puffs and feel it prickling her lungs with its frigid force. Julian's nose and cheeks were red and he sniffled, but he wouldn't cover his face with the scarf. He simply pulled it up to his ears so he could smile at the people who cheered for them and laugh with Eponine.

Tears threatened again as she watched him, so full of jubilation and high spirits. He waved and smiled to everyone. Flashes flickered from cameras all along the road, from commercial quick-snaps to professional pieces with telephoto lenses. But Julian did not need that light for him to sparkle. He might never realize it, but he was probably taking the greatest revenge of all at that moment. He was living it up, drinking in the best that life had to offer, not caring that he was on national television. He waved and smiled and blew kisses and put his arms around Eponine and pressed icy kisses to her cold cheeks and whispered in her ear how lovely, how fun, how magical it all was. He was ablaze with life, with love, with that fine, passionate, fiery spirit of his that so many thought had been lost for all time.

He is healed. He has to be. Eponine shook the tears from her eyelashes; they were making her see stars. It took a long moment before she realized that it was not a trick of the light, but the glittering of his wings she saw as they curved protectively and lovingly around them both.

She glimmered in his eyes, the aura surrounding her a shifting spectrum of color and light. Her wings, iridescent and kaleidoscopic, were folded close along her back, echoing the curve of his own.

Like the moon pulling the tides of the Earth, her radiance caught the attention of the sea of people around her. They stared grinning and awestruck, moving slightly along her path as if to follow her.

She was beautiful. He reached out and clasped her hand, squeezing it tightly to feel her beneath the padding and leather.

"'NINI," HE BREATHED, BUT she didn't hear him over the din of the crowd and the rising and falling of the soundtrack of their float.

The parade turned the corner alongside Macy's, then headed into Herald Square and fortresses of TV camera set-ups and commentators. Julian fumbled with something in his pocket. It looked as if he was jiggling change. It was something he did when he was nervous. Eponine raised an eyebrow, suddenly wondering if there was something more to his surprise.

"Julian?"

He glanced over at her as the float slowed to a stop behind a high school marching band playing a medley of holiday and patriotic tunes.

He grinned. "What is it?"

The smile on her face was sly. "What is it you're not telling me?"

He paled momentarily then gave up a careless chuckle. "Well, it's a little daunting, facing all those cameras, you know."

She glanced up ahead and nodded. "Well, it seems we sort of broke that little guideline about staying out of the public eye back on New Year's Eve. I don't think anyone will mind that we're doing it again. I mean, we're not doing any harm, and we're having so much fun!"

"So as long as we enjoy it, being the stars of the day is all right?"

"Well, *I* think so, but I am a hedonist, and no one really listens to me."

Julian took her hands. "I listen to you."

"I know you do." She smiled and would not quite meet his gaze. "It means the world to me, actually."

Impulsively, Julian pulled off first his gloves, then hers. He folded her fingers into his palms to keep too much heat from escaping.

"Are you crazy? We'll get frostbite!"

"I want to touch your hands, 'Nine. Just trust me, okay?"

Eponine sighed. "Okay, but if my fingers turn blue and fall off, I'll be quite put out, you realize." She wrinkled her nose at him, and he laughed aloud. It was a clear, joyous laugh, the kind that rises like a sacred spring from the depths of a purely happy soul.

The float lurched a little as it rolled onto the festively painted square, coming into range of the hundreds of cameras, both of the TV crews and of the people seated on the grandstands.

"And here come our contest winners now, Julian d'Sanguise and the extremely lovely Eponine Allegresse!"

Somewhere on the Upper East Side, Jeremy cuddled Ursula and pointed at the television.

"Aww, what a cute couple," he told her with a smile.

On the parade route, the crowd cheered for a long moment, then fell silent as the float eased to a stop. Eponine waved gaily and blew kisses with her red and rather numb fingers. Everyone simply stared. There was no music, no applause, no sound whatsoever.

"Julian, what's. . . ." The words died in her throat. He was chillingly pale and trembling, with his hands cupped together.

"Eponine," he whispered, but his words carried up and down the road by the small microphones on the railing before them. He cleared his throat and began to shake even harder. "Eponine, I know in a few days we are going to leave New York and go back to our own lives, go our own separate ways. But if there is any way to change that, any way at all, I want you to know that I would wish that above anything else."

Blood rushed to her cheeks and thundered in her ears. "I don't understand."

"'Nine, if I could . . . I. . . . You see, I asked for a miracle and this is what I got: you and me, on a float in the Macy's Thanksgiving Day Parade, in front of millions of people. But that's not all I asked for. I asked for a chance to show you what you mean to me, to truly thank you for everything you've done, every huge thing and every tiny thing. You have made me the person I have always wanted to be. I am not whole without you; I am not real."

"Of course you are. You didn't need me for that, you big silly." She was beginning to get self-conscious in front of the crowd that was beginning to edge forward, as if they knew something she did not.

"I did. I did need you. I love the person I am when I am with you. And I love you."

Pure joy illuminated her face, her eyes, her smile. She turned to throw her arms around him, to kiss the lips that had finally given her the golden words she had longed to hear.

Julian was crouched down on one knee, she realized. Eponine's heart shivered and seemed to stop. The people all around them gasped with one great collective breath.

He held in his outstretched hand a shimmering ring. It was platinum with a large round central diamond that caught the chilly, wintery light and sparkled like a tiny star. The ring itself was covered in a delicate filigree pattern that could have been twining vines or knotwork or just nothing at all but the artist's fancy. Two smaller diamonds seemed to hold the larger one aloft, glittering in a small supporting way that made the brilliance of the central stone all the brighter. It was a masterful piece, elegantly modern yet charmingly antique.

Eponine pulled her gaze away from that tiny blaze of white fire and looked down at Julian.

Please, say yes. Let's pretend we can get married and live out our lives with a house full of friends and children until we are old and gray. Please, do this for me, my love. I want to be your husband, and I want you to be my wife.

She nodded, feeling numb and distant. The tears flowing, feeling as if they were freezing to her skin, brought her back to the present as she found her voice.

"Yes! Yes, of course! Yes! Oh, Julian, I love you! Yes, yes, yes!" she cried.

He pressed the ring over her cold-chapped knuckle. It stung and felt even colder than the chilly tears on her face, but she didn't care. She gazed at it only a moment before throwing her arms around him and showering him with a thousand kisses. The roar of cheers shocked her, and she realized she was sitting on the grand float out front of Macy's being showering with sparkling confetti.

"And there you have it, our own *Miracle on Thirty-Fourth Street*," some announcer said, his voice booming over the accolades of the crowd.

"That was beautiful," said his teary-eyed co-host. "Congratulations!"

Eponine waved, the ring leaving a sparkling wake in the series of flashbulbs that exploded like fireworks all around them. Julian put his arm around her and held her tight to his side, imagining that he was being escorted to a wonderful new life with the woman he loved.

"I don't care that the dream will be over in two days," he whispered close to her ear once he felt certain the microphone was no longer on. "I wanted to live it. I wanted it for you, and for me. I wanted you to know how I felt. I wanted to say thank you. And I meant every word I said. If I had but one wish, it would be a lifetime here with you."

"We have forever together, Vengeance," she replied, her voice so quiet he wasn't sure if she were even speaking at all.

"It's not the same and you know it. Joy and Vengeance belong to the world, to eternity, but I want to be Julian here with you, Eponine."

She rested her head against his chest. He could feel her smile. It dawned on him that he could feel a warmth flowing through him each time she smiled, whether he saw it or not.

"I'd like that, too," she mused. "But we can't dwell on it, or else everything here will just be. . . ."

"A regret?"

She nodded.

"No. I thought so too, once, but not any more. There is Joy in my heart, and she won't ever leave." He kissed the top of her head and waved to the reporters waiting for them at the end of the parade route. The techs came to unhook their tethers, and Julian helped Eponine to the ground himself. As he lifted her from the last step he swung her in a wide arc, then hugged her close. "I thought I was lost, but I think I have found the path again. As they say, I am not out of the woods yet, but I know where I have to go. And I know that no matter what happens, you will be there to help me. No matter what happens, you are going to love me, isn't that so?"

Eponine smiled through her tears. "Yes, it is so."

With the utmost gentleness he wiped the glistening drops from her cheeks and eyelashes, then gave her a soft, warm kiss.

His whisper stirred her soul. "No regrets."

FULL CIRCLE

THE SKY WAS BRILLIANT winter blue, crisp and high and flat as if someone had taken an azure-glazed china bowl and placed it over the city. The buildings and lacy-branched trees stood out starkly and sharp-edged against the sky's hard contrast. Even the edges of scarves and plush winter coats seemed to have an almost brittle quality to them. Only the swirling puffs of warm breath that caressed everyone's lips provided any sort of softness to the day.

Julian loved it, almost forgetting that it was his last whole day there in the city, and on the Earth. He strolled beside Eponine in the bright wintry light and enjoyed the pleasant sting of cold air in his lungs.

She'd woken him with a playful flurry of kisses: the kind that came from her lips and the kind made of chocolate.

"I wanted to lure you out and surprise you, but I just can't keep the secret any longer!" Eponine held out two tickets to the Chocolatiers Convention.

Julian beamed, "You remembered!"

"How could I forget the *one* thing you were excited to see when we first came here?"

THEY WALKED NOW, UP to the vintage Metropolitan Pavilion on West Eighteenth, knowing the city so much better than they had a year ago. Their steps were intimately timed with the changing of the streetlights, so that they arrived at each corner during the walk signal. Julian remembered when he had tried to work out the timing, but he had soon learned that there was no forcing it, that if he relaxed and let it sink in, it would just come to him. And it had. It was one of the hundreds of strange, small lessons continuously being taught in the city. A minute sliver of Zen where one would least expect it.

"I wanted to go Day-After-Thanksgiving shopping," Eponine said, quietly, "but I knew you'd like this much better. Besides, what would I have bought?"

Her question hung in the cold air between them as they crossed Broadway, not even looking at the street signs or signals, just walking along in tune with the city and with one another.

Julian put his arm around her waist. "You don't need to buy anything. You have everything you need."

"Well, there is something I need."

"Oh?"

"A nice steamy, frothy cup of Italian hot chocolate!"

"Ah, yes, my lady has excellent taste!"

IT WAS QUITE COOL inside the building, which elicited complaints from some. But Julian understood the purpose behind it.

What will it be this year? A chocolate Empire State Building? He nearly drooled to remember last year's milk chocolate Brooklyn Bridge. Letting his curiosity simmer and slowly build, he wandered the small side hall crammed full of tables showcasing vendors from around the world. They sampled tidbits of chocolate from tongue-curling sweet to black-coffee bitter. He loved it all. Luckily, Eponine had a sweet tooth to match his and kept up with him bite for bite.

They stopped off for the Italian hot chocolate they both so loved before proceeding into the main pavilion. Eponine bought another box of the stuff to replace their spent supply back home. Julian beamed for a moment before realization set in and his smile crumbled.

She silenced him with a touch of her silky and chocolate-smudged fingertip to his lips. "We should have some for tonight, and tomorrow morning."

He nodded and heaved a heavy sigh. "Let's see what magic they have created this year."

The words had hardly left his mouth when he beheld the first creation. It was over seven feet tall and was carved from a block of dark chocolate. Eponine whistled and bowed her head in respect.

"Can you imagine the immigrants being greeted with *this*?"

"I have never thought of Lady Liberty as *delicious* before. This has got to be the greatest place on Earth, 'Nine. I am in awe, just plain awe."

"'Center of Divinity of New York City' I think is what you called it last year. And with good cause: look."

The centerpiece was an enormous structure of white chocolate. A model of Notre Dame in Paris was resplendent with colored-sugar windowpanes depicting the famous leaded-glass masterpieces, milk chocolate bells in the belltowers, and even little carved white chocolate gargoyles. At its highest point it was just over six feet tall and extended almost eight feet across the dais, which was covered in fondant lawns and marzipan stepping-stone walkways.

"I'm ... I'm ... just speechless." He gripped Eponine's hand and trembled slightly.

She tried not to giggle. "Oh Vengeance, my darling," she whispered against his ear with velvety cocoa breath, "to see you undone at the sight of confections. That is, as Phina says, 'worth the price of admission.'"

He tickled her waist and laughed out loud. "This has been ... an adventure. This has been 'worth the price of admission.'"

She kissed him, not passionately, not gingerly, but with a purity of emotion that nearly brought tears to his eyes.

IT WAS LATE AFTERNOON when they wandered back out into the city, giddy with a sugar-high and wishing for some real food.

"What would you like for dinner?" Eponine glanced in the window of one crowded restaurant after another. "Yeesh, the city's a madhouse this time of year."

"Looks like we'll be battling crowds no matter where we go," Julian grumbled. "Maybe I'm not really that hungry after all."

"Aw, come on, its going to be our last dinner in the city. Let's go someplace nice!"

"Actually, I'd just like to go to Veselka's, if that's okay with you."

"I couldn't think of anything nicer."

He smiled, "It's a good way to end things, going back to the beginning. The Chocolatiers Convention and Veselka's. Makes me think of the first few days here."

"Only if we go to Dojo's for breakfast tomorrow."

"Will we have time?"

"I think we can manage."

THE CROWDS WERE THINNER in the east village, and the wait for a table was surprisingly negligible. They were seated right away.

Julian watched the light fall into heavy shadows between the steel-colored buildings.

"Once upon a time in New York City," he whispered.

"Once upon a time?"

Julian shrugged. "It seems like a hundred years have passed, but no time at all."

"How do you feel?"

He shrugged again, his dark eyes fixed on the passing figures of the people on the other side of the window. Dozens of people: happy and unhappy, rushed and leisurely, alone, in pairs, and even in groups now and again. People who would continue to go on with their lives when next the sun set.

"Julian?"

He shook himself free of the reverie. The smiling, slim waitress wanted to know if he wanted his pierogi boiled or fried and would he like a refill on his coffee?

He asked for fried sauerkraut and mushroom pierogi. The waitress nodded with some indescribable glint of understanding in her eyes and dashed away, clipping out their orders to the cook in hasty Ukrainian.

I wonder what she thinks she knows about me. . . .

"Do you think much has changed at home?" Eponine asked over her cup of coffee.

Julian sighed and absently nodded his thanks to the waitress as she returned to fill his mug. He was going to miss coffee, and this coffee in particular. Before they had changed the menu, the quote about it had said it was "black as a moonless midnight." He took a scorching sip. *So true.* "No, nothing ever changes there."

"Nothing?"

He shivered, knowing she meant the strange turns of events that had led him to this assignment, how he had changed into something entirely different from what he had been. But there was still much he could not remember. "Do you think it will be the same?"

"No, it will be entirely different." Her words chilled Julian, although she was smiling.

He managed a feeble smile back at her. "Different isn't always bad, I guess."

The food came quickly, and Julian tried to savor the tastes, the textures. He really rather liked sauerkraut and mushroom pierogi, even though Eponine always wrinkled her nose at him when he ordered it. But he found his mind wandering as he chewed, his eyes going glazed and blank. Eponine nudged him countless times saying, "Are you listening to me?" or "You're drifting again, mister." He'd shiver and come back only to fade away again.

The clank of his fork on the plate brought him abruptly to reality as he realized all his food was gone. *So much for savoring it.*

The pretty blonde waitress came back and took their plates. She returned with the check and a dish of vanilla ice cream topped with strawberry preserves and rainbow sprinkles. A single candle stood proudly in a dollop of whipped cream.

"Happy anniversary," she told them softly, and retreated with a grin.

"'Nine, did you. . . ?"

She gave him a sheepish smile. "Maybe I tipped her off a little. But come on, it really is. Our birthdays and anniversary in one. One year ago today. . . ."

"The strangest and most wonderful year I have ever known."

She lifted her mug, "Here's to doing this again sometime."

"With you? Just name the time and place; I'll be there." He

tapped the rim of her mug with his own. And picked up a spoon. "I'm actually glad they didn't bring us chocolate."

Eponine reached across the table and took his hand. "Don't take a bite 'til we blow out the candle! And we can't blow out the candle until we make a wish!"

"But there's only one candle."

"Then I guess we'd better wish the same thing, then?"

"But what if we don't?"

"Then only one of us gets their wish, I suppose." She squeezed his fingers. Pale blue wax was beginning to dot the whipped cream. "Hurry now, the candle's melting. Don't think so hard, just wish. One ... two ... three!"

For a moment the flame just hovered still as equal gusts of air from opposite sides hit it. It flickered a moment, then the base of the flame went out but the tip remained frozen for an instant in time before it too disappeared in a slender plume of gray smoke that made one lazy curl off the wick and dissipated.

Eponine cheered and plucked out the candle. She licked the bottom and set it aside, spoon at the ready.

"Happy anniversary, Julian. We made it; we've come full circle!"

And tomorrow we leave, and it will be like this never happened. But he smiled. Because it *did* happen, and it was still happening. For a few more hours, anyway. He was definitely going to savor those hours to come.

EVANESCENCE

SHE SLEPT PEACEFULLY IN the room next door, the childlike slumber that comes to those truly clear of conscience and pure of heart. Eponine was both of those things and more.

Julian paced the dark living room, sipping hot chocolate. The TV was on, the sound turned low. He was watching CNN and had been for hours. Was the world any different than it had been a year ago? Had he changed enough to alter the course of the bloody, grim future toward which humanity was hurling itself?

He sat for a time, stared at the computer for a while, tried to read, but ended up gazing vapidly at the television showing images of wars.

Did I cause all of this? Or is this the result of my not being me, not being what I needed to be? How am I supposed to fix it, either way?

He waited, but no answer came.

All he wanted was to spend his last hours on Earth beside Eponine, but he continued to pace the living room floor, agitated and restless. He'd left her in bed, dozing contentedly with her long hair trailing over the edge of the mattress. He knew she'd wake eventually. The lack of his presence often woke her. He slumped back into the couch.

Then how will she sleep now? When I'll never share her bed again?

THE EARLY MORNING SUN startled Julian. He grumbled and rubbed his eyes. The TV was off. Confused, he made to rise and realized that Eponine was sleeping in his lap. She had one of her woven lap blankets wrapped tightly around her, with her head pillowed against his leg. His left hand was caught beneath her cheek, and his right arm hung around her shoulder. Eponine's eyes flickered open and she stretched.

"Mornin'," she said, like she had nearly every day before.

Julian bowed his head over hers and kissed her cheek, inhaling her scent, trying to memorize the sensation of his lips against her skin.

"Don't start. We've time yet; we've time."

"But, 'Nine—"

"I am not ready to think about goodbye yet. It's still so early. We have time."

"It'll be gone before we know it."

She shrugged and nodded. "It's always so." She reached her arms out to embrace him.

It was awkward, so he pulled himself out from under her and lay out beside her on the deep seat of the couch. "This is better. How long 'til we need to leave?"

"Hours, yet." She snuggled against him, pressing him between the back cushions and the length of her body. She kissed his nose. "What would you like to do?"

"You need to ask?" He kissed her mouth, drawing her closer. He could feel her heart beating rapid and fierce. Or was that his?

EPONINE CONSIDERED IT LUCKY once again that Dojo's served breakfast all day. After making love on the couch and then in the bed, then taking a shower, and getting distracted again, it was past noon when they finally got out of the house. She was giggly and rosy-cheeked, and teased Julian about the great silly grin on his face.

She begged for a seat on the patio, even though it was quite frigid outside. But the obliging staff came and lit the tall space heaters and set one on either end of their table and never let up on the flow of fresh, hot coffee.

It was a bright, crisp Saturday, and all manner of folk were out and about. Eponine just smiled and watched them.

"It's a happy world, you know. Regardless of what the news says."

A few people pointed and waved, shouting "We saw you on TV. Congratulations!"

"Thank you!" Eponine waved back, and Julian nearly jumped across the table to plant a kiss on her lips. They fell back into their chairs, giggling. "This has been fun; it really has. And if we were real people, I think I would have a wonderful time being married to you."

Julian's face grew solemn. "Yeah, I know what you mean. I meant it when I gave you that ring. Given the chance, I would marry you." He pulled the glove from her left hand and touched the brilliant ring. It was as warm as she was. "Are you going to wear it when we leave?"

"Yes, I couldn't possibly take it off."

"What will happen to it?"

"I don't know, honestly. Perhaps it will come with me ... or lie in the silt at the bottom of the spring for years to come. But I won't willingly part myself from it."

"Thank you," he whispered, fighting tears. "It means a lot to me. That you treasure it so."

"I do." She cupped her bare hand around his cheek. A shiver ran down her spine, and she looked up at the sky. "It's time to go."

Julian had both hands pressed to the tabletop. "Damn...."

"Shush. Pay the bill."

ALTHOUGH THERE WAS NOTHING to take from the apartment, Eponine wanted to go back. She changed into her blue flannel skirt and suede hiking boots, trying to remember what sweater she'd worn on that first day. Julian had no problem remembering. His wardrobe was limited, and for some reason he'd placed that set of clothes into the farthest corner of his closet and had never worn them again.

Eponine found him dressed with his shoes in his hand staring up at the picture of their kiss on New Year's Eve. He absently put his arm around her.

"Just think, if we'd begun this then, instead of being so cautious and waiting so long...."

"Shhh, don't start thinking that way. Everything happens in its own time."

"I just feel like I could have had so much more time with you."

"Silly, we have *forever*."

"Not like this." He pulled her tight to him and let out a shuddering sigh.

"Come on, Julian, we have to go. It's a long way to Central Park yet, and we shouldn't keep things waiting on us."

He nodded and followed her to the door. He put their keys on the kitchen counter with a sweet thank you note to Hannah. With one last glance around the apartment, he stepped out into the hall and shut the door behind him.

IT WAS COLD IN the shade. A few pools of dappled sun cascaded down through the bare branches, making the surface of the brook glitter. They stood together and watched as one broad beam of early afternoon sun washed down through the branches and struck the head of the brook, where the spring bubbled up and into the world.

"It's time," Eponine released his hand. "I'll go first."

He wanted to speak, but he could only stand still and silent as he watched her scramble up the rocks and inch toward the spring's pool. She took off her shoes and waded toward the sunbeam.

"Wait," he bolted forward, following Eponine up the small slope. Forgetting his shoes, he splashed in after her, catching her up in his arms.

She gave him a quizzical raise of her eyebrow. "Yes?"

The water was icy cold, numbing his feet, his toes. He didn't care; he pressed his face against her shoulder.

The sunlight brightened around them. He felt the soft chenille sweater beneath his stubbled cheek begin to disappear.

"No," he clutched tightly to her. "Not yet!"

"Vengeance, we must...." Her voice was fading. Eponine's

voice was fading, sounding like the ethereal, eternally jovial Joy. "It's time to go."

"No," he rasped. "Not yet, not ever, please."

Her skin glimmered like opals, and she regarded him with those violet eyes. "Vengeance...."

He touched her mouth softly, running his fingers across her lips. "Julian. Call me Julian."

"I can't," she said, her words touched by sadness despite the warm smile on her face. "Let's go home."

The light was brighter now, and Julian could hardly see the trees around them. He could feel his clothes evaporating as well.

"Home? My home is with you. My home is a small apartment in the East Village."

"You can't hide forever."

"Eponine, I love you. Tell me you don't love me!"

"You know I can't."

He took her hand, shimmering and surreal, but still bearing the engagement ring. He pressed it to his lips even as he felt the world dissipate around him like the fog, like a dream. The cold faded, the sensation of his body, his clothing, everything. He held tight to her hand.

"Don't let me go, 'Nini. Don't let me go."

He felt her sigh as the light changed and time stood still. "Everything will be fine. I promise. I promise."

"I don't want to lose you."

"I'm right here. I'll always be right here."

"Don't let go."

"I won't...." Her voice echoed from far away.

The sensation of Julian was only a lingering memory. He was falling and spinning through the sunlight, through the water, through the black lace of the winter branches and the last few golden leaves.

"'Nine," he called, but there was no answer. The light faded into shadow, and shadow into darkness. The darkness smelled like blood.

Have I really learned nothing? Have I just staved off the inevitable? He stood in familiar territory, that realm of tears and blackness reeking of fear and pain and blood. *Ah, home. Where live the nightmares and brutal thoughts of revenge.*

He sat down and crammed his hands into the pockets of his coat, his favorite winter coat so dark a blue as to almost be black.

His brow creased. How did he get his coat? In the pocket, he felt something cool and round. It slid onto his finger almost effortlessly. He knew he had left it on the dresser in Eponine's room, left it sitting there with her locket.

He pulled out his hand, glaring at the ring.

What does it mean? Who am I? To what must I be true?

There he saw her face, her long coil of a braid and the sprinkling of tiny freckles across her cheeks and nose, the rosebud of her mouth always smiling, smiling at him. He took a deep breath and looked around. A laugh escaped him, and he kicked at a shard of rock on the ground.

She knew, the little minx. I tried to shield her from this, but she knew. Who was I kidding? I tried to keep all this from her, the nightmares, the darkness, but she saw it. She saw it all. And she loved me anyway.

He laughed again. It was a rough sound, choked with tears, but it carried through the dim expanse around him. He closed his fist around the silver band and absently stroked the lettering.

I wish you could see me now, 'Nine. I get it. I finally get it. He sighed and swiped fiercely at his tears, shaking them to the ground. For a moment, it seemed a tiny blade of grass or minuscule flower bud sprang up from the patch of moisture before evaporating. He rummaged around in his pocket and pulled out a handful of papers, most of them folded into tight little squares the way Eponine used to do. Two were shopping lists; one was a note saying she'd gone to the Met and would be back after lunch. The third had Jeremy's address on it, which he threw away without a second thought. But the fourth was a love note. Something she'd written that said, "Good morning, I love you!" to which he'd added, "My lady's love is warmer than the sun in the morning and makes my days so much brighter."

"You are a big silly," followed his words, "but that's why I love you. XOXOXO"

He carefully folded the papers back up and put them deep in his pocket. He smiled, although tears threatened again. He'd see her soon. Not soon enough, and not the way he'd like, but he'd see her again soon. He smiled to think of that. Even the imbalance of the world around him didn't phase him.

Guess I had better get to work. He began to hum "On My Own" from *Les Misérables*, the "Dream Cast" version, of course. *No rest for the wicked.*

EPILOGUE

God Rest You Merry, Gentlemen

SUNLIGHT STRUCK HIS CLOSED eyelids, and he shifted uneasily in his sleep. He was disturbingly aware of the cold, hard ground beneath him. He groaned and rolled over, trying to drown out the racket around him. It sounded like *birds* and *squirrels*.

What the. . . ?

One eye slowly opened, and he blearily saw dirt and grass. There was sod in his mouth, and something crawling down the back of his neck. He sat up abruptly, spitting and gagging and slapping at his collar.

He was sore and bitterly cold. He hugged his coat around his body and took a look around. Strangely enough, he was in a copse of trees beside a small stream.

I know this place. He stood, slowly, stretching his protesting muscles. *I'm in Central Park. How many damned times have I woken up in this place?*

He walked toward the spring at the head of the brook and bent over it, looking for his reflection. He saw himself a disheveled young man with a bit of scruff on his cheeks and with twigs and bits of earth caught in his long hair, which had nearly worked entirely free of its elastic. And if he squinted he could see the angular planes of his face set perfectly atop his broad shoulders just in front of two great black wings that glimmered like a starry night.

How did I manage this, I wonder?

"You could say 'Thank you,' you know."

"Who'd have thought *he'd* go all vain on us?"

He looked up to see the two women who'd spoken. They sat side by side on a large stone outcropping and looked hauntingly familiar.

"I know you," he said to them. The blonde stood, a smile on her face. "Faith," he said, recognition dawning.

"Very good."

He looked to her left, at the beautiful woman there. He knew her as well, her blue-black hair and her vast and deep blue eyes. "Love? What are you two doing here?"

They exchanged a conspiring glance.

"We've gone into the business of granting wishes," Faith told him, hopping down off the rock. She strolled down toward him in her cute khakis and plush winter coat. Love followed close behind, looking far more stylish and seductive in velvet leggings and a matching wrap.

"Look at you. You look like you just spent the night in a park," Love teased, picking the bits out of his hair. She caressed his ears as she did so, letting a sultry smile curve her ruby lips.

"Listen," he said, backing off, "just tell me what the hell is going on!"

Love followed him, step for step. "You love her; I know you do. I can see it, smell it, hear it. It's the most obvious thing about you." Her smile was far more matronly now.

"So? Like that's news? You've brought me back here just to taunt me about it?"

Faith smiled and handed him an envelope. "You believe in her, in her love."

"Yeah, what about it? I mean, she's Joy. Who doesn't love her?"

Faith laughed, "Your sister doesn't. But she sends you her regards anyway, and wishes you luck."

"What are the two of you talking about?"

"Open the envelope," Love said quietly, hardly able to contain her wide smile.

It was blank on the outside. Within was a slip of paper. He knew the handwriting.

Julian~ Come home.

"What does this mean?" He felt the heat rising into his cheeks, anger coursing through him suddenly. If they were joking somehow. . . . "This is impossible. The assignment is over! There is no more Julian! And no more Eponine. . . ."

Faith rolled her eyes. "Don't ruin it for yourself." She put her hands on his shoulders. "What have you wished for? What is it that you have wanted?"

"More time," he whispered. "The chance at a life with her, more than an angel's love, a real human life. But how?"

"Believe," she whispered. "Have faith."

"What about my job? What about the world?"

"Eh, the world survived just fine for the year you were here. It got better, actually. Or hadn't you noticed?"

He nodded, and echoed Eponine's words from that last morning at Dojo's. "It's a happy world, regardless of what the news says."

"Go on," Love said. "You have earned this chance."

He felt numb. "You are serious. You are entirely serious."

"Get going, Julian! Or you'll miss the Christmas tree lighting ceremony at Rockefeller Square!" Faith made a shooing motion with her hands.

Julian looked in the envelope again and saw his apartment key lying there. It was attached to a heart-shaped charm with Eponine's picture inside.

"That's from me," Love told him proudly. "Oh, and here," she tossed him a plain brown paper bag. "Since you'll be *really* human from now on, you might want these."

He caught the bag and peeked inside. There were three boxes of condoms.

Julian blushed furiously. "Thanks."

"That should be enough to get you through the first week," Love grinned with a mixture of holiness and wantonness in her smile. She looked like Aphrodite. "Now scoot!"

He found tears in his eyes. *Damn, I'm such a big crybaby these days.* He wiped them hastily and went to thank them again, but he was alone in the clearing. "Thank you," he whispered anyway, and turned away from the spring, jogging toward the subway station at the bottom of the park.

HE STOOD IN THE hallway for a long time, his pulse beating rapidly in his ears. The doorman had given him an ordinary hello, like no time had passed, like nothing was different. He'd ridden up in the elevator with Hannah and she'd badgered him into promising to come by for cookies after the ceremony later that night.

He now stared at the brass numbers on his door: 3-D. On *their* door. The key slid into the lock, sticking a little about halfway, like always. But it turned easily, and the door swung open with its usual brief squeak.

He swallowed the lump in his throat and walked in.

It smelled like tea and incense and peanut butter cookies. He shut the door as quietly as he could behind him and listened. The silence drew out long and chilling.

Finally, "Hello? Julian, is that you?"

He stepped into the kitchen. She was sitting at the table beside Phina. They had Phina's blue teapot and a heaping plate of cookies between them. Obviously, Hannah had already paid them a visit. They were looking at stacks of bridal magazines and catalogs.

"Yeah, it's me."

"I was starting to get worried." She stood and came toward him. "I was afraid you weren't going to come home after all."

Phina hopped up and grabbed her coat and her bag. "I'll see you guys tonight, won't I?"

"Yes, I think so."

"Well, if you're late, I'll understand. I have my cell phone, so give me a call when you get there." She gave them both a swift kiss on the cheek, her eyes lingering on Julian for a moment. There was a knowing smile on her lips. "It's good to see you, Julian. I'll see you both later."

She shut the door behind her, and time slowed.

He could feel every breath, every heartbeat. She was just the same, even the impossibly long braid of hair that nearly touched the floor. With a smile that could light a nation she took his hand, interlacing her fingers with his.

"I didn't let go," she whispered.

He threw his arms around her and kissed her neck, her cheeks, her lips. "Oh, God, Eponine, I love you."

She laughed. "I certainly hope so. I was hoping to be married in May."

"Then what?"

She shrugged, "Anything you'd like. We live; we die; we do it again, maybe."

"And how long until the wedding?"

"Well, I haven't officially announced a date yet or anything. Phina brought the magazines by this morning. She was in the area and came to sit with me while I waited for you. Hannah brought cookies. Do you want some?"

"How long have you been waiting?"

"Not long."

"What did I do to deserve this?"

"You were yourself. Your *real* self." She smiled. "You let Joy into your heart."

"Joy will be mine all the days of my life."

Eponine's smile broadened. "And after." She kissed him, and he saw light and color and kaleidoscope wings. "What's in the bag?"

"What? Oh, a *gift* from Love. She thought we'd need them."

Eponine peered into the bag and giggled. "I see."

"We don't *have* to need them, not right away, if you don't want. . . ."

She cocked an eyebrow and laughed softly. "I have missed you. Don't tell me you haven't missed me, too?"

He laughed. It was an unfettered, unhindered sound. He glanced over at the table. "You don't want to decide on the color of the table linen right now?"

"No!"

"Good, neither do I."

He swept her close, kissing her, every memory clear and solid of the past year and beyond. Even into his darkness, he could see. He saw the bleakness around him, the pit of desolation where the walls ran with blood. He felt his anger, his betrayal slide aside. The ache of madness left him, and the taste for blood slipped from his tongue. He embraced his isolation there in the eye of the tempest of humanity, because he knew he was not alone. Blood, hate, and war still ravaged the world, but it always had. And to some extent, it always would. Even *he* could not change human nature. But he could help put things to rights and he could already feel the skewed balance slowly begin to shift back into place. It would take time, but things would get better; he knew they would. She would see to it that it would.

He felt no fear, no hesitation. How bright the future looked with Joy in his arms.

Yes, his wish was granted. A wish made so long ago when he had first kissed her.

She had her candles lit even though it was still broad daylight; he could smell the beeswax. Through the partially opened door, he could see them glimmering there, warm and welcoming. She knew he would come, she had never doubted that. She had been waiting, expectantly.

He left the darkness behind and followed Eponine into the bedroom, into life, into the light.